HARD TIMES ON WEAVER STREET

CHRISSIE WALSH

Boldwood

First published in Great Britain in 2023 by Boldwood Books Ltd.

Copyright © Chrissie Walsh, 2023

Cover Design by Colin Thomas

Cover Photography: Colin Thomas

A CIP catalogue record for this book is available from the British Library.

Paperback ISBN 978-1-80280-950-3

Large Print ISBN 978-1-80280-951-0

Hardback ISBN 978-1-80280-949-7

Ebook ISBN 978-1-80280-953-4

Kindle ISBN 978-1-80280-952-7

Audio CD ISBN 978-1-80280-944-2

MP3 CD ISBN 978-1-80280-945-9

Digital audio download ISBN 978-1-80280-948-0

Boldwood Books Ltd
23 Bowerdean Street
London SW6 3TN
www.boldwoodbooks.com

To my family, as always.
In memory of my dear friend Kay Jones (1942–2023)
'We could have talked and talked all night.'

PART I

1

WEAVER STREET, LIVERPOOL, 1924

Weaver Street was slowly coming to life, the pale morning light swallowing the remains of the night as it spilled over the grey rooftops of the redbrick houses. In the big double bed in the front bedroom of number eleven, Kitty Conlon lay dreaming. She was standing on the towpath by the glassy river that flowed between banks of drooping willow and riots of colourful wildflowers. Behind her was the café she had struggled to buy and turn into a successful business, its blue and white painted boards sparkling in the bright sunshine. The man she loved was coming towards her, and as he drew nearer, she could see the love in his eyes and in the curve of his lips. Her heart swelled, and she held out her hands to greet him.

A hot, sticky little hand with pudgy fingers grasped hers and tugged on it. The dream disintegrated. Startled, Kitty's eyes flew open, and in the dim light filtering through the bedroom curtains she saw her daughter, Molly.

'Mammy, Mammy, I feel poorly. I'm hot and itchy.' Molly gulped back a sob.

Kitty shot upright, and scooping Molly up onto the bed, she

looked at her closely before running practised hands over her fore-head and then into the neck of her nightdress to her chest. The heat rushed into her palms. *Holy Mother, the child was burnin' up!*

'Lay down, darlin', Mammy's going to light the mantle.' She lowered her daughter onto the pillows then leapt out of bed, the soles of her feet cold as she crossed the floor. A gusty March wind rattled the windowpanes. The gaslight popped and flared, eerie shadows dancing over the walls as she hurried back to the bedside.

'I'm too hot,' Molly whined, her flushed face wet with tears.

Gently, Kitty stripped her daughter of her nightdress, gasping when she saw the mottled red rash. 'Oh, sweet Jaysus!' If this was scarlet fever, it was a killer. Her chest tight, she struggled to keep calm.

'Tis all me own fault, she silently berated herself. *I've been so wrapped up in me new house an' me wedding that I've neglected her.*

The wedding! Kitty thrust the thought aside. This was no time to be thinking about getting married. Only yesterday morning as they'd got ready to walk to school in the pouring rain, six-year-old Molly had complained of a sore throat. *An' what did I do?* Kitty fumed. *I gave her a jallop of honey an' lemon an' told her that 'ud cure it.*

Crippled with guilt, she held Molly against her breast, murmuring soothing words and stroking her hot little back. Her skin felt like sandpaper. Then she laid her in the bed and pulled up the covers. Molly pushed them aside, her wails getting louder and louder. 'I itch all over, and my throat hurts,' she croaked, big fat tears rolling down her cheeks.

'Lay still, darlin'. Mammy's going for something to make you feel better.'

Kitty rushed to the bathroom and was back in seconds with cool, damp flannels. She bathed Molly's flushed face and then her chest and back, and with each simple action she could feel panic building in her chest.

Molly's cries abated. She gazed helplessly at her mother, her bright blue eyes awash like delphiniums after a shower of rain. Kitty gazed back, her jangled thoughts alerted by the patter of feet on the landing. She darted to the door.

'No, Patrick!' she ordered, barring his way into the room. 'Be a big, brave boy for Mammy. Go ye back to bed an' I'll be along in a minute.'

Patrick stuck out his lip then began to bawl. Kitty didn't know which way to turn. 'Help Mammy, darlin',' she cried as she shooed her four-year-old son back to the bedroom he shared with his sister. 'Molly's sick, an' I don't want ye catchin' it, so stay here like a good boy. I'm going to fetch Auntie Maggie an' the doctor.'

Shocked by the urgency of her words, Patrick climbed onto his bed. He looked like a gnome in striped pyjamas. 'Me be a good boy. Stay here. Molly sick,' he said.

'That's right, darlin',' Kitty said, relief washing over her as she hared from the room and down the stairs, hurtling across the kitchen and out of the back door.

Rain had fallen during the night and the mad March wind tugged frantically at Kitty's nightdress as, skidding and slipping, she ran to the house next door. It was bitterly cold and her flesh froze, her chilled knuckles stinging as she hammered on the peeling green panels.

'Maggie! Maggie! For God's sake, answer the door.'

'What the...?' Maggie Stubbs stared through bleary eyes. She was also still in her nightclothes, her face puffy with sleep and her bleached blonde hair hanging like rats' tails. 'What's up?'

'Go an' mind the kids while I go for the doctor. Molly's got scarlet fever.'

'Are you sure?' Maggie asked, grabbing her coat from behind the door.

'I think so,' Kitty panted, already halfway back to her own house.

The two women hurried inside. 'Don't let our Patrick near her,' Kitty warned as she pulled on her coat. 'I'll go an' see if I can rouse Dr Metcalfe.' She looked frantically at Maggie. 'Of all the times for this to happen,' she wailed.

'Go on,' Maggie urged. 'I'll see to 'em. It might not be as bad as you think.'

* * *

'Open wide, young lady.' Dr Metcalfe peered into Molly's mouth. 'Hmm! You were right to be alarmed. Tongue's swollen and coated,' he mumbled, running his bony fingers under Molly's chin, 'and the neck's slightly swollen. And, of course, there's the rash.' He straightened and turned to Kitty. 'She's not the worst case I've seen, Mrs Conlon, but I'll have to send her to Oxford Street – can't risk the spread of infection.' He picked up his bag. 'I'll arrange for the ambulance.'

At the mention of the isolation hospital in the city and the ambulance, Kitty burst into tears. 'How long will we have to wait?' she sobbed.

'Who can tell?' Dr Metcalfe replied laconically. 'Keep her cool and comfortable.' He shambled from the room, a tall spare man bent with age. Kitty stared at his back, wild-eyed. Then she clattered down the stairs after him. The doctor paused at the front door. 'Keep the boy away from her. I'll let Oxford Street know you're coming. I'll be back shortly.'

Kitty's knees sagged as the door closed behind him.

The next hour seemed interminable. As she sat by the bed, she recalled the time George Metcalfe had attended her aged neighbour, Margery Boothroyd. He'd taken one look at Margery, saying, 'Bad heart, nothing I can do. Let her die in her own bed.' And she had, two hours later. A shiver ran down Kitty's spine.

Molly tossed and whimpered, and almost choking with panic, Kitty applied yet more cool cloths to her skin. 'Sweet Jaysus, what's keeping him?' she cried hysterically. 'Where's that blasted ambulance?'

'It'll be on its way, Queen. Don't get yourself in a state,' Maggie soothed, 'you'll only set her off again.' She nodded at Molly, who was now lying quite still, her eyes tightly shut. Maggie was standing outside the bedroom door on guard duty. Patrick wheeled his cars up and down the landing, asking every two minutes, 'When will Molly be better?'

'Take him down an' give him some breakfast,' Kitty said, her voice ragged. 'The porridge is in the cupboard by the sink.'

'Yeah, I know,' Maggie said, making for the stairs, and Patrick skipped after her, brightening visibly at the idea of the house getting back to normal.

When Kitty heard the front door open again, she ran to the head of the stairs.

Dr Metcalfe's grey head bobbed up to meet her. She hurried back to the bedroom, the doctor plodding behind her. He set down his bag then slowly pulled off his thick woollen gloves. 'Bitterly cold morning, Mrs Conlon,' he remarked.

Kitty felt like screaming. She opened her mouth, and when the words came out she was surprised how calm she sounded. 'Where's the ambulance?'

'Ah, well, there's the thing,' Dr Metcalfe said heavily. 'The Oxford doesn't have a place for her. Overcrowded, you know, what with all this diphtheria and fever going about.' He harrumphed. 'Not enough beds – not enough nurses.'

Kitty paled. 'So what do we do? Where will she go?' Her voice had almost risen to a shriek.

'I've given it careful thought,' he said ponderously, 'and I say we keep her here. Far less infection in this house than at the Oxford.'

'But... but... how will she get better if she's not in hospital?'

'Hopefully with your good care and mine, Mrs Conlon,' he said, taking a small packet of yellow powder from his bag and giving Kitty an enigmatic smile. 'You see, Mrs Conlon, I've long believed that infection spreads infection. Where is there more infection than in an isolation ward, I ask you?'

Kitty suppressed a groan.

'When I learned that they didn't have a bed for her in the Oxford, or anywhere else in the city for that matter, I thought where can the child receive the best care she can get,' he continued, 'and the answer was obvious – at home with her mother.' He moved to the side of the bed. 'Fortunately, you're a sensible woman, Mrs Conlon, unlike some who call me out at the first sneeze or clutter up my waiting room with nothing more than a cut finger that simply requires a plaster.'

Kitty supposed she should have felt flattered, but his prevarications were sorely trying her patience. 'So what do we do now?' she asked curtly.

'We start by easing the throat,' he said, opening the packet of yellow powder.

Kitty watched him take a sheet of white paper from his bag and form it into a cone. He next produced a teaspoon and inserted it in the packet of powder. 'Watch carefully, Mrs Conlon,' he ordered, withdrawing the spoon. 'Flowers of sulphur, one level teaspoonful.' He shook the powder from the spoon into the cone and set it on the bedside table. Then, smiling gently at Molly and tweaking her nose, he said, 'Now, young lady, I'm going to work some magic to make you feel better. Raise her up on the pillows, Mother.'

Kitty propped Molly up. The doctor lifted the cone. 'Open wide, Molly,' he said then demonstrated with his own mouth. Molly's eyes were bright with fever and fear as she formed a big O. 'Time for a bit of magic,' he continued, inserting the end of the cone in her mouth. Mesmerised, Molly could do little else other than make a soft moaning noise. Kitty's mouth had gone dry as she watched him blow gently into the cone. Molly gasped then spluttered and spluttered again, violently. She fell back on the pillows, breathless. Kitty bit her lip: *what had he done?* Molly gasped and swallowed a few more times then gave a little smile. 'My throat's not scratching any more,' she said.

Until now, Kitty had considered Dr George Metcalfe to be an old dodderer. It was rumoured that he was a bit too fond of the whisky bottle, and she'd caught the whiff of something sharp on his breath. *He seems sober enough, but then it's not yet nine in the morning. But does he know what he's doing?* She really didn't know what to think. Apart from the time she'd had an abscess in her ear and Patrick had croup, she'd had little to do with him.

Now, as she looked into her daughter's flushed, smiling face and thought of the comforting manner he was using with Molly, she found her opinion changing.

'Now, Mother, you can work the magic twice a day for three days, but I suggest you mix the sulphur with a spoonful of treacle. It's easier that way. You do have treacle?'

Kitty nodded. 'A big tin, I use it in me baking.'

Dr Metcalfe gave a satisfied nod then turned his attention to Molly, who was lying peacefully on the pillows. Kitty could have kissed him.

'There, Molly,' he burred, 'the magic's getting to work.' He glanced up into Kitty's fraught face. 'We caught it early. Carry on with the bathing to keep down the fever, and this will stop the itching.' He delved in his bag then handed Kitty a brown bottle.

'Calamine, an ancient but marvellous remedy.' He patted Molly's arm. 'She's young and strong, so keep your chin up and she'll be as right as rain within a month or so.'

Kitty sagged. 'A month or so,' she echoed. The wedding was less than six weeks away.

Dr Metcalfe stepped away from the bed, his ageing limbs creaking as he packed his bag and gave further instructions. 'Keep to this one room, just you and Molly. Hang a sheet soaked in carbolic over the door to stop the spread of infection, and make sure you wash her cups and dishes thoroughly.' He turned to check on his patient, and assured he had done what he could for now, he said, 'I'll call back after midday.' Molly was dozing, worn out by the fever and the unusual events of the morning. Kitty followed him out to the landing and down the stairs. As they stood in the hall-way, they could hear Patrick and Maggie hooting and laughing in the kitchen.

'If you take my advice, you'll send the lad to a relative for a few weeks, keep him out of harm's way,' the doctor said, and as Kitty opened the front door to let him out, he added, 'and you might put a sign on the doors warning of infection in the house.'

Kitty felt a flash of panic. *Send Patrick away! A sign on the door! Oh, my God!*

'I will, I will, doctor. I'll do everything you say. An' thank ye, thank ye for all ye have done for Molly,' she gabbled, grabbing his hand and shaking it vigorously. It felt like a bundle of twigs.

Dr Metcalfe smiled wearily. 'It's my job, Mrs Conlon.'

Kitty watched him go, thinking what a wonderful old gentleman he was. Then she hurried back upstairs and daubed the lotion on Molly's angry rash. That seemed to do the trick, and when Molly began to doze again, Kitty ran down into the kitchen, just in time to see Patrick flinging a cushion at Maggie. She tossed it back. Patrick whooped as he caught it.

'Whoo!' yelled Maggie just as loudly. 'Dead on, kid.'

Kitty's nerves already frayed, she yelled, 'Hey, them's me good cushions. Ye'll knock something over.' She glared at Maggie. 'Catch yourself on, woman.'

'I'm keeping him occupied,' Maggie said to Kitty, and to Patrick, 'We're having fun, aren't we?'

'Trust you to create havoc,' Kitty said, picking up a cushion and at the same time giving Maggie a contrite grin. Pull yourself together, she chastised herself, annoyed at sounding so ungrateful. Maggie was her dearest friend, always there for her. Over the years, they had stuck by one another through thick and thin.

'S'all right,' said Maggie, unperturbed. 'What did the doc say?'

Before Kitty could embark on the detail, the back door opened and Mavis Robson walked in, looking anxious. She lived two doors up at number fifteen. 'I saw the doctor's car at your door, Kitty, and I wondered who was ill.'

'It's Molly. She has scarlet fever.' Kitty felt as if she might crumble into tiny pieces at any minute. She was itching to get back upstairs and check on her daughter, but arrangements had to be made for Patrick. As she told Mavis and Maggie what Dr Metcalfe had said, her troubles were immediately lessened.

'I'll take him,' Mavis offered, her little currant bun eyes twinkling and her smile beseeching. 'I'm due some leave from the hotel, and I'd love to have him. It'll be easier for me to look after him than you, Maggie,' she continued, glancing in Maggie's direction. 'It'll be company for me, and you have enough on with Lily and Vi.' Lily was Maggie's seven-year-old daughter and Vi Bottomly her mother. Maggie grimaced then lit a cigarette.

Kitty's heart warmed at Mavis's eagerness. She knew exactly how Mavis felt.

Mavis's fiancé had been killed in the war and she had never married, but she still had yearnings to be a mother. She smiled at the small, birdy woman who was the pastry chef in the Adelphi Hotel. Then she thought of her café on the towpath. She owned and ran it single-handed. She'd have to close down for now.

'That's very kind of ye, Mavis.' She turned to Patrick, who was wheeling cars across the table. 'What do ye say to going for a wee holiday to sleep in Auntie Mavis's house, Patrick?'

Amazed, Patrick's eyes boggled. Then his brow furrowed. 'Sleep there?' he said in a wobbly voice, looking anxiously at his mother then at Mavis. 'Will you make them buns with pink icing on? And will Jack let me dig in the allotments?' He was still in his pyjamas.

Mavis glowed. 'As many as you like, Patrick, and Jack'll let you dig with him,' she said enthusiastically, sure that Jack would do that just to please her.

She and Jack Naughton, who lived at number seventeen, were the closest of friends, and although the little spinster and the lame, one-eyed bachelor still kept to their own houses at bedtime, they spent so much time together that it didn't prevent Maggie from speculating that they were more than just good friends.

'After all, they're still only in their thirties, and they must have needs,' she'd say lewdly and, sighing, 'I know I bloody do.' When she went on about it, Kitty told her it was nobody's business but Mavis and Jack's.

'What will you do about the café?' asked Mavis, ever the practical one.

'Close it for now – an' just when it's coming' up to Easter,' Kitty said despondently. 'I'll miss the trade, but I'm sure me customers will understand.'

Mavis gave an emphatic nod. 'Of course they will, and they'll come flocking back once the weather turns.'

Kitty smiled gratefully. Mavis always managed to say the right thing.

'I'll get Patrick dressed,' she said before turning to Maggie. 'Thanks, love, for being such a pal. Ye really helped me out this morning.' She didn't for one moment want Maggie to think she was ungrateful, or that she was favouring Mavis over her. Maggie prided herself on being Kitty's greatest ally, and Kitty was the first to acknowledge that she'd seen her through some of the roughest times in her life.

'Think nothing of it, Queen,' said Maggie, airily blowing out a cloud of smoke. 'Do you want a hand putting up that carbolic sheet?'

2

Later that same afternoon, long after Patrick had toddled off with Mavis, and Maggie had helped her hang the carbolic sheet over the door, Kitty was sitting with Molly in the darkened bedroom. She'd been there for most of the day. As promised, Dr Metcalfe had called again to check that Molly was not deteriorating, but it had done little to calm her anxiety. When he'd said he would visit that evening, she had begun to doubt his words: he was being awfully vigilant. Did he really believe Molly would get better?

Outside, the sky was black and rain spattered against the window. Wearily, Kitty lit the gas mantles. Two bright yellow orbs sputtered and popped, lighting up the darkest corners.

'Don't, Mammy,' Molly wailed. 'They hurt my eyes.'

'Sorry, darlin', but I have to if ye're wanting another story. Mammy can't see to read in the dark.'

'No more stories, Mammy,' Molly said drowsily. 'Just sit and hold my hand.'

Kitty lowered the mantles, the pale, sickly light adding to her despondency as she sat holding Molly's hot little hand. Molly said she itched all over. Her mother dabbed on more lotion, aching to change places with her little girl and spare her the discomfort. She breathed a sigh of relief when eventually Molly fell asleep.

Kitty let her gaze roam the gloomy room, her eyes coming to rest on the edge of the carbolic sheet visible through a narrow gap in the door. They'd soaked the sheet in the bath then smeared carbolic soap all over it, Maggie getting wet right up to her armpits in order to prove her usefulness. Then Kitty had climbed on a chair to fix it to the top of the doorframe. Maggie had stood below, passing up the drawing pins. As Kitty climbed down, the weight of the water and soap tugged the pins out of the wood.

Like a sopping wet wraith, the sheet enveloped Maggie in its sticky folds. She flailed her arms and kicked out her feet but the more she struggled, the more she became entangled. Kitty laughed for the first time that day. She was still laughing when Maggie had burst from the sheet, spitting out carbolic and her hair plastered to her scalp. But she didn't feel like laughing now.

Stealthily, so as not to disturb Molly, she got to her feet and went to the window. She gazed at the rosy redbrick houses on the opposite side of the street, houses just like her own: two windows above and a bay window below at the side of the front door. The wet pavements glistened in the light from the gas lamps and the sparsely branched plane trees that never seemed to grow – one outside every third house – swayed in the wind.

Eight years. Was it really eight years since she had come to live in Weaver Street?

She marvelled at the thought. Eight years that had seen her change from a feisty young girl with her head in the clouds to an adoring mother, then a disillusioned wife, and finally an independent businesswoman. Suddenly, she was assailed by memories. Resting her hands on the windowsill and her forehead against a cold glass pane, Kitty recollected her joys and her sorrows.

Molly and Patrick were the children of the devastatingly handsome Tom Conlon, the man she had fallen head over heels in love with and married in Dublin: a man she barely knew. He was the reason she had come to live in Liverpool in the summer of 1916. His great-uncle Tom had left them the house, and its contents, in Weaver Street. Although the war was raging, they had packed their bags and crossed the Irish Sea to take up residence, hardly able to believe their good fortune. Then, Kitty had thought the world was her oyster.

She had fallen in love with the house in Weaver Street with its back door and garden looking out onto a lane and the allotments beyond, and its front door opening onto the street that at the bottom had a public house, the Weaver's Arms, and at the top St Joseph's Catholic church.

After a shaky start with one or two of her neighbours – they didn't like the Irish – she had made the truest friends she would ever have, and any yearnings she might have had for her home in Ireland had long since faded. Kitty had believed that Tom loved her as much as she had loved him. Oh, how they had loved. It had been magical, too good to be true, and it had proved to be so.

Coming to Weaver Street had been hers and Tom's undoing.

Tom had been a bookmaker. Shortly after they arrived, he had opened a betting shop in the back room of the Weaver's Arms pub. The business had been improving steadily when, much to his dismay, Tom was called up to fight in the war. After a stint in the navy in which he had been slightly injured, Tom returned a changed man.

Whatever way she looked at it, Kitty now reflected as her eyes rested on the roof of the Weaver's Arms, he had changed from being a loving husband into an avaricious, unfaithful playboy with delusions of grandeur. He had reopened the betting shop and as the money had rolled in, love had flown out of the window.

Kitty stepped back and drew the curtains, then crossed to the dressing table, her mind still playing with memories as she gazed at her reflection in the mirror. A tired-looking young woman with golden-flecked hazel eyes in a finely shaped face framed by lustrous tawny curls gazed back at her. *I was nineteen when I first stood in this bedroom and looked in this mirror, just a girl, newly married with no children, and all me life before me.* She remembered how she and Tom had laughed at the big, ornate double bed with its high carved ends, and how they'd tumbled into it on that first night. *I never thought then that three years on we'd not even be sleeping in the same room.*

As Tom's prowess on the gambling circuit at the racetracks had thrived, so had his lust for the high society life that he craved. In the last year of their marriage, when Kitty discovered that he was involved in an adulterous relationship with the daughter of a wealthy horse owner and trainer and was preparing to leave her, she had refused to share his bed and had grown used to their being apart but not apart. Like ships that pass in the night, she'd thought then.

Now, as she began to tidy her brushes and combs, hairpins and pots of make-up, she thought, not for the first time, that maybe Tom had been that sort of man from the start and she too much in love to notice his flaws. When she became aware that the only person of any significance in Tom's life was himself, and that he was prepared to sacrifice his family to achieve his ambitions, she had made plans to ensure her own and her children's futures. To realise that she and Molly and Patrick meant so little to Tom had devastated Kitty, and had it not been for the support of her good friends, she doubted she would have coped during those dark days. But somehow she had.

Smiling wryly, she went and sat beside the bed, gazing fondly at her sleeping daughter. Molly's glossy black curls scribbled the pillow and although her eyes were closed, Kitty knew they were the brightest blue: just like her father's. *He might have betrayed ye, Kitty, but ye won through in the end*, she thought, recalling how she had struggled to buy the café where once she had waited on tables. She'd worked her fingers to the bone to make that happen.

She'd taken in sewing, altering garments for her customers when new clothes were in short supply. She'd also learned to bake. Mavis had taught her how to bake professionally in readiness for when she bought the café. Then she had worked in munitions making shells, the memory of which still made her shudder, for it was whilst she was working in the factory that she almost lost her life in a massive explosion, and surely would have done had it not been for the wonderful man who was soon to become her second husband.

John Sykes to the rescue, she mused. *He's always on hand when I need him most. Sure, wasn't it him who got me safe home on that awful winter's day when I got caught in a blizzard an' me ready to give birth to Patrick.* Reaching out and stroking Molly's brow – she was still sleeping – Kitty recalled how John had fetched the midwife then stayed and looked after Molly, and later as she'd cradled her son, he'd brought her tea and made sure she had all she needed. *I don't know how I missed the love in his eyes then. I must have been blind.*

The memory of Patrick's birth made her think how lucky she had been to have John's staunch friendship, because in those days, she had looked on him only as a good friend. However, when he confessed his love for her, she realised she had always been in love with him, and now she was free she returned that love with every breath in her body. Her heart lurched as she thought of John. Their wedding was so soon, but if anything worse happened to Molly, would she still be able to go through with it? She buried her face in her hands. What if Molly were to die? Surely, a wedding would be out of the question, no matter how much she loved John. Was this God's way of punishing her for not attending mass every

Sunday? Or was it His way of letting her know that He didn't approve of widows marrying?

To those whom God has joined in holy matrimony let no man put asunder. *But Tom's dead, and he didn't love me anyway*, she protested, as one crazy thought after another filled her head. *Oh, Blessed Mother, Mary most holy, help me.*

She closed her eyes and folded her hands in prayer. She begged forgiveness for all her sins and pleaded with the Blessed Virgin to spare her beautiful daughter and let her marry John. *I love this man with all my heart*, she told her, *and he loves and respects me. I was a good wife, and will be again if you intercede for me, my Blessed Mother. You are a woman like me. Ask God to grant me that favour.*

Lifting her head from her hands, Kitty opened her eyes. She sat perfectly still, feeling calm and serene. It was as if some unseen hand had poured a soothing balm into her frenzied mind and troubled heart. She took a deep breath, convinced that the Holy Mother had listened. *I should have pointed out that it had to be before the third of May.*

She got to her feet and went downstairs to heat a drop of soup. Maybe she could tempt Molly when she wakened. As she waited for the soup to heat, she wondered if other women who were marrying for a second time dwelt on their first marriage. She shook her head. *'Tis a great day for the memories*, she told herself ruefully.

More often than not, whenever Kitty thought of Tom, she chose to remember him as the man who had swept her off her feet and not the avaricious adulterer he had been at the time of his death. Now, Tom was in the graveyard at the top of Weaver Street, and whilst she had grieved his passing, she reasoned that they would not have spent the rest of their lives together.

John had restored Kitty's happiness and her faith in human

nature, and although she might never forget the hurt that he had caused her, there would always be a tiny corner of her heart that belonged to Tom Conlon.

Life hadn't turned out quite like she had expected, mused Kitty, as she poured soup into a cup, and at times she found it hard to believe how, in the space of eight years, her life had been filled with so much grief and yet so much happiness. Bewildered, she shook her head to dispel such thoughts, and placing the cup on a saucer, she hurried upstairs.

Molly wouldn't take any soup. Disappointed, Kitty sat and held her hand while Molly dozed. Kitty's eyes drooped and her chin sank to her chest. She felt utterly drained, but when she heard John's car purr to halt at her front door, she hurried to the bedroom door, walking slap bang into the wet, sticky sheet now held in place by a few nails. Cursing softly, she blundered round it and ran downstairs. John met her in the hallway.

Kitty put up a staying hand. John's eyes widened.

'Don't come any further,' she panted.

'Wha... whatever do you mean?' he cried, taking a step towards her. He saw the strain on her face and the frightened look in her eyes. His heart missed a beat.

'Molly's got scarlet fever,' she said brokenly. Her reserves crumbling, she pitched into John's arms, pressing her face into his chest. He wrapped her in his embrace, stroked her hair and felt her tears dampen his shirt. Kitty clung to him, feeling his warmth and strength seep into her cold, tired body. Already she felt stronger and braver. She pulled away from him.

'I don't know that I should be even touching ye,' she said, her voice wobbling. 'I might give it to ye.'

'I'll take my chances.' John kissed her. 'Now, take me up to see her.'

'Ye can't go in the room,' Kitty warned as they mounted the stairs.

She held aside the damp sheet as John peered across the distance at Molly. She lay flat on her back, her flushed, pretty face framed by a halo of black curls fanning the pillow. Her eyes were closed, but he knew they were the brightest blue. Whilst Patrick favoured Kitty with his tawny hair and hazel eyes, there was no mistaking that Molly was Tom Conlon's daughter, but John had grown to love both children as though they were his own.

They stood in the doorway watching Molly as Kitty softly told John all that had happened that day. 'What if she doesn't get better?' she concluded with a sob.

'She will,' John insisted. 'She has you and the doctor taking care of her, and as he said, you've caught it early.'

'Scarlet fever's a killer, it can lead to meningitis or pneumonia, so I've heard,' Kitty said hollowly. 'The postman lost his little lad to it last year. They thought he'd pull through, then he got meningitis an' died.'

'But he wasn't Molly, Kitty. Don't fall into the trap of imagining the worst. Molly's strong and healthy.'

'She's not now,' Kitty said forlornly. 'An' just when we thought everything was going to plan, the house near finished, an' the wedding all organised.' She turned and plodded wearily along the landing and down the stairs.

'And it will go to plan,' John persisted as he followed her. 'Did you get in touch with the Adelphi about the food for the reception?'

Kitty, now at the foot of the stairs, whirled round to face him, angry red spots burning her cheeks. 'I can't be bothered with things like that now,' she said harshly, amazed that he could think about something so trivial. 'There won't be a wedding if she doesn't get better.'

She strutted into the kitchen, her back rigid.

Kitty's pronouncement was so bleak that John's stomach plummeted. He hurried after her.

'You're overwrought and need some rest. Go and lie down in Patrick's room. I'll keep an eye on Molly. I'll call out if I need you.' He pulled Kitty into his arms, kissed her tenderly then ushered her back into the hallway. 'Off you go, get some sleep. I'll waken you before I go home.'

Kitty didn't argue.

3

One day blurred into another. All of Kitty's waking hours were spent nursing Molly, and her friends and neighbours pitched in to lend a hand wherever they could. Maggie did the shopping, Beth and Mavis made tasty meals, and May Walker washed and ironed for her. Kitty was overwhelmed but not surprised by their kindness, but as one week drifted into two, she began to wonder if this imposed state of affairs was the shape of things to come. Although Molly didn't appear to be getting any worse – no signs of meningitis or pneumonia – neither did she appear to be getting better. She was fretful and listless, her pleas of, 'Don't leave me, Mammy,' tearing at Kitty's heart, and tears streaming down her cheeks as, in the second week, she cried, 'Mammy, my skin's coming off.'

Whenever something catastrophic happened in her life, Kitty didn't look for sympathy or seek pity. She simply wanted her old life back – everything just as it had been before Molly caught scarlet fever. She felt as though her life had been stolen from her, and it was soul crushing. Day after day, she peered into Molly's throat and at night she listened to her breathing, her ears alert for signs of pneumonia as she watched Molly's chest rise and fall. At other times, she'd gaze into her dull blue eyes, trying to detect the dreaded meningitis: Kitty had heard that it had something to do with the brain.

Dr Metcalfe called often. He seemed pleased with Molly's progress. 'See, we caught it in time,' he said cheerily, and, 'Yes, peeling skin is only to be expected. Give it time, Mrs Conlon, give it time.'

But time was something Kitty didn't have. She couldn't and wouldn't dream of neglecting her daughter, she loved her too much for that thought to even enter her head. However, she was extremely aware of all the other things she needed to be doing. Molly and Lily's bridesmaids' dresses needed sewing and the things they were taking with them to the new house needed packing. It seemed ages since she had walked across the lane to what was going to be her home, and she felt cheated at not being there to see the progress that John assured her was being made. The more she thought about it, the more there seemed to need doing. Time was running out.

'I can't help panicking when I think of what's to be done before the wedding,' she told Maggie one day at the end of the third week of Molly's illness. She was standing at her back door, still too afraid of letting anyone other than John into the house in case of infection. Maggie had scorned the idea, and when Kitty had reminded her she needed to protect Lily, she'd replied, 'Our Lily's as tough as old boots.'

Now, Maggie dumped the groceries she had fetched for Kitty on the doorstep then lit a cigarette. 'Don't go thinking you can use your Molly as an excuse to back out now,' she said, jabbing the cigarette in Kitty's direction.

'I wasn't thinking anything of the sort,' Kitty snapped. 'I'm just saying I don't know how I'm going to manage it. I don't want to call it off but...'

'In that case, you'd best make a list of what needs doing, and me, Beth and Mavis'll do what we can. Don't we always help one another out?'

Kitty nodded, but she didn't look convinced. 'I can't see Beth doing much,' she sighed. 'She'll not come near as long as she thinks there's any chance of her catching anything. You know how she is about her health since she lost the baby.'

Beth, who lived at number thirteen, was also a very close friend of Kitty's. She had miscarried her first pregnancy due to a bout of flu and being of a nervous disposition and desperate to conceive again she was too afraid to do anything other than leave food on the doorstep.

'Not that I should be complainin',' Kitty continued. 'She sent another tasty shepherd's pie an' a casserole round this week, an' although I wash the dishes in scalding water an' leave them on the wall for her to collect, I bet she washes them all over again,' she remarked.

'Knowing her, she more likely smashes 'em and chucks 'em in the bin.'

Maggie could never resist getting a dig in at prim and proper Beth, partly because her timidity and sense of propriety irritated the hell out of Maggie, and furthermore she was jealous. She didn't like sharing Kitty.

'Well, like I said, tell us what you want doing and we'll get stuck in,' Maggie said in a businesslike manner. Kitty raised her eyebrows. It wasn't like Maggie to be so organised. It was usually the other way round, Kitty sorting out Maggie's chaotic life.

'I can't expect ye to pack my house up and cart stuff across the lane.' Kitty didn't like feeling beholden to anyone.

'And why not? You'd do the same for us. Beth Forsythe wouldn't be married to Blair if you hadn't given her the gumption to stand up to her rotten dad, and I'd still be Fred's punch bag if you hadn't helped me throw him out. Packing a few boxes and moving bits of furniture's the least we can do.'

'Oh, Maggie, what would I do without you?' Kitty sounded close to tears.

'What would any of us do without *you* is more to the point.' Maggie's voice was thick with emotion. 'Go on then, make a list of jobs and Saint Margaret Stubbs, the saviour of Weaver Street, will do the rest.'

Maggie went off to ask the grocer for some empty cardboard boxes before she went back to her mending frame. Before she got pregnant, Maggie had been a weaver at Holroyd's, the cloth mill in Mill Lane. Faced with having to give up her job, she had trained as a mender. Then she'd given up working in the mill shortly before she gave birth to Lily, and still needing an income, she now worked on a mending frame in her own front room, fixing the flaws that marred the fine worsted cloth's parallel perfection. Fred, her estranged husband, had been a wife batterer.

Kitty hurried back upstairs. Keeping an eye on her daughter's health and finding things to amuse her was a full-time occupation. She was helping Molly make a jigsaw when she heard the knock on the back door. At least twice every day, Mavis brought Patrick to see his mother. 'That'll be Patrick and Mavis,' Kitty said. 'I'll just pop down an' have a word.'

Molly nodded solemnly. 'Mammy, I'm sorry Patrick can't come home.' She looked so penitent, Kitty's heart went out to her.

'You've nothing to be sorry for, darlin',' she cried, hugging her daughter and thinking how cruel it was that she should blame herself for her illness. 'I won't be long. See if ye can find the pieces to finish the rabbit before I get back.'

Molly smiled, and Kitty hurried downstairs.

Patrick was on the other side of the wall that separated Kitty's garden from Beth's. At a safe enough distance, so his mother deemed. She was still terrified of spreading the infection. His face lit up when he saw her.

Kitty perched on the wall, her heart swelling at the sight of her son. Oh, how she missed him. 'Well, darlin', what have ye been up to?' she asked cheerily.

'Me and Auntie Mavis went to the park, and we made buns and I put icing on them, and me and Jack made a fort out of boxes. Jack's going to get soldiers for it,' he blithely gabbled. Mavis smiled at his use of the courtesy title. She wasn't related to either Kitty or Maggie, but it pleased her when their children called her 'auntie'.

Kitty felt a twinge of envy. It should be her he was doing these things with. But then he came nearer, his smile slipping. He looked up at her, his hazel eyes teary and his voice cracking as he said, 'When can I come home, Mammy?' Kitty's jealousy rapidly dissipated. She ached to lift him into her arms and kiss him.

'Soon, love,' she said. Dr Metcalfe had told her that the chances of spreading the infection lessened with each passing day.

'Can I go and play with the kittens?' Patrick glanced hopefully at the allotment, his homesickness forgotten. Jack had found a nest of abandoned kittens and put them in a box in his shed.

'If Jack says you can, darlin',' she said, marvelling at how children rarely dwelt on grief when there was something more appealing to be getting on with. *An' perhaps it's as well*, she thought, *'cos who knows what sorrows they'll have to deal with as they grow older*. Sadly, she watched her son go back to Mavis's house.

When John came round that evening, she told him of Maggie's offer to start packing up the house. 'That's a grand idea,' he said. 'I've already moved the furniture from my place. The painters have finished and all Frank has to do is varnish the floorboards, and his mate to put some tiles up.'

Once again, Kitty couldn't help feeling as though she was missing out on things. 'What does it look like?' she asked eagerly.

'Just perfect, like you,' said John, cupping her face in both hands then tenderly running his thumbs under the dark shadows under her eyes. 'You look worn out, love. But guess what?' He gave a wicked chuckle. 'Our new bed arrives tomorrow and after we're married, you can catch up on all the sleep you've missed.' He pulled her into his arms and kissed her.

'Is that what we'll be doin'? Sleeping?' she asked coquettishly.

John laughed out loud, and Kitty felt the weight of the past three weeks leaving her shoulders and her heart. Regardless of how bad things had seemed, John's love, and the kindness and compassion of Maggie, Mavis, May and Beth, had sustained her. She flung her arms round her intended husband and planted a smacking kiss on his waiting lips.

The next morning, Maggie lumbered in with a pile of flattened cardboard boxes and a fat roll of sticky tape. 'I'll make 'em back up and start filling 'em with stuff from your front room,' she announced importantly.

'That'll be grand,' Kitty said. 'Leave the sewing machine in case I need it again. I've finished the bridesmaids' dresses an' me own, but ye never know what'll crop up. John's been sittin' with Molly to let me get on with 'em, bless him.'

'He's a lovely fella, Kitty. You don't know how lucky you are.' Maggie sounded wistful.

'Oh, but I do,' Kitty replied.

4

'I think it's safe to say that this young lady's out of the woods, Mrs Conlon.'

Dr Metcalfe gently placed his hand on Molly's brow and smiled down at her. She gave him a smile, all teeth. Four weeks had passed since Kitty first sent for him and now her heart soared to hear his words. She turned to him, her face alight with gratitude.

'An' it's all thanks to ye,' she said fulsomely. 'If ye hadn't watched over her like the good shepherd, I dread to think what might have happened. I'll never be able to thank ye enough.' Her eyes moistened as relief swept over her.

'Think nothing of it, Mrs Conlon. I did my job and you played your part,' he said gruffly, but Kitty could tell he appreciated her thanks.

'Does that mean Patrick can come back home, Mammy?' Molly gleefully asked.

Kitty chuckled. 'I never thought I'd hear her say that. She's usually telling him to leave her be.'

'Yes, Molly,' said the doctor, laughing along with Kitty. 'Your brother can return to the bosom of his family.' He picked up his worn leather bag, his jovial smile suddenly making him look ten years younger.

Molly's eyes flew to Kitty's pert breasts beneath her flowered apron. 'I don't have bosoms,' she chirped, 'but I will when I'm as old as Mammy.' She picked at a flake of peeling skin off the end of her nose and flicked it onto the bedcover.

Laughing even louder, George Metcalfe pronounced, 'A complete recovery, wouldn't you agree, Mrs Conlon?'

Kitty positively danced down the stairs as she showed him to the front door.

* * *

A week had passed since the doctor had given Molly the all-clear, and she had begged her mother to let her go back to school. She'd had a joyous reunion with her friend, Lily, and was now keen to let her schoolfriends know about her narrow escape from scarlet fever. It made her feel quite important. Kitty had had some misgivings about letting her go back to school so soon, but when she saw how happy Molly was to be back in Lily's company, she'd relented.

The late April morning was dry and sunny as they walked up Weaver Street then down Mill Lane, Molly and Lily holding hands and chattering nineteen to the dozen, and Kitty and Patrick bringing up the rear. They left Molly and Lily at the school gates. Kitty had called the previous day to tell the teacher that Dr Metcalfe no longer considered Molly infectious, and the teacher had welcomed the news.

'I'm so pleased she made a good recovery, Mrs Conlon. I'll be glad to have her back,' the teacher had said. 'She's a lovely girl, so well-mannered and clever too.' Kitty had never doubted Molly's attributes, but it was nice to hear someone else sing her praises.

Now, as Kitty and Patrick headed for home, a sudden April shower had them quickening their paces.

'Come on, love, let's make a dash for it.' Kitty grasped Patrick's pudgy hand as raindrops big as pennies began pelting the pavements.

Patrick pumped his short, sturdy legs, glad that he would soon be in the warm, dry haven of his mammy's kitchen and not inside the grim school building close by the mill. It was all right for big girls like his sister Molly and Lily Stubbs, who at six and seven respectively had to go every weekday, but he preferred to be at home. And boy, was he glad to be back living with his mammy and Molly again. Auntie Mavis and Jack were nice but they weren't as nice as his mammy and his sister.

'Here we are,' Kitty panted, opening the front door and ducking into the shelter of the hallway with Patrick at her heels. 'Take off ye, darlin',' she said stooping to unbutton his tweed over-coat then pulling it off and shaking the rain out of it. 'Get ye in by the fire an' dry off.' Patrick needed no second bidding.

Kitty took off her coat and hung it on the hallstand. As she did so, her image was reflected in its little mirror. She gazed at her reflection: *not bad for twenty-seven, and soon to be a bride again*, she thought, patting her damp curls.

Her mood still thoughtful, she went into the kitchen. Patrick was on his knees on the hearthrug in front of the fire. 'Brrrrr,' he rumbled as he whirled one of his favourite toy cars round in circles. Kitty smiled: *him an' his beloved cars, an' football*. He was a lovely child and she felt blessed to have brought two such beautiful children into the world, and furthermore she knew without a doubt that she'd fight tooth and nail to make their futures bright. They were her number one priority.

'Are your socks dry?' She bent down to feel Patrick's toes,

squeezing none too gently. He wiggled his feet, laughing as he rolled free. He held a car in each hand.

'Which do you want to be, red or blue?' he chirped, setting the cars on the lino.

Kitty had played this game a hundred times. 'Blue,' she said as Patrick whizzed one car after the other across the floor. Kitty's collided with the table leg but the red car carried on under it.

'I win. Mine went furthest,' Patrick cheered.

'Well done! Always be a winner, son,' his mother cheered, and leaving him to play, she began washing the breakfast dishes. Her movements were deft but her thoughts were a jumble of memories that her reflection in the mirror had evoked.

Where had all the years gone?

Come May the third, I'll be Mrs John Sykes, she told herself as she rinsed the last cup. *Not every woman's as fortunate as ye are, Kitty Conlon. This time round, ye'll have a marriage built on love and respect – and a hefty dose of passion.*

'Yoo-hoo! Anyone at home?' Maggie's raucous shout broke Kitty's reverie.

'Where else?' Kitty called back as she stacked the cleaned plates and dishes into the cupboards in the alcove beside the black iron range.

Maggie strolled in, as familiar with Kitty's kitchen as she was with her own. Although, Maggie being Maggie, her kitchen was cluttered and none too clean. 'Rotten weather, in't it?' she moaned. 'Have you time for a cuppa?' She sat down at the table and lit a cigarette.

'Always,' said Kitty, filling the kettle at the sink. 'An' yes, the weather is lousy. Me an' Patrick got soaked on our way back. I hope it's not like this on me wedding day.' She grimaced as she put the kettle on the hob. 'Lily an' Molly were in school before the heavens opened, thank goodness.'

'Did our Lily give you any bother? She didn't want to go this morning. Carried on something shocking, so she did, the little mare.' Maggie loved her daughter with a passion, but she didn't have much patience with Lily's tantrums.

'She was as good as gold, went in like a lamb,' said Kitty who, in the early years of Lily's life, had helped Maggie rear her: mothering didn't come naturally to Maggie.

Lily was the result of an affair that Maggie had had during the war whilst her husband, Fred, was in Egypt. He'd doubted her paternity from the start. When his suspicions were confirmed, he'd beaten Maggie cruelly, and with Kitty's help, Maggie had thrown him out. Seeing as how he was a workshy, vicious drunk who regularly used his fists on Maggie, she had been glad to see the back of him.

'She never acts up with you,' Maggie groused, failing to realise that it was Kitty's natural love for children and her patience that kept Lily in check.

The kettle whistled and Kitty brewed the tea.

'What were you up to before I came in?' Maggie asked.

Kitty smiled. 'Remembering,' she said, filling two cups. 'We were only nineteen when we first met. Can ye believe that, Maggie? I'd just arrived from Ireland, an' ye came out an' let me know ye didn't think much of the Irish.' She laughed. 'Some welcome that was.'

'Yeah, an' look at us now. We stick together like shit to a blanket,' said Maggie, raising her cup to toast her words.

'Language, Maggie.' Kitty glanced in Patrick's direction before readily agreeing. 'Aye, we do, an' in these past eight years we've surely had some hard knocks but we've always risen above 'em.' She sipped her tea, a faraway look in her eyes as, unexpected, her thoughts drifted back to Tom and his betrayal.

'What are you daydreaming about?' Maggie demanded. 'You were miles away.'

Kitty smiled gently. 'I keep thinking about Tom, Maggie. Even memories that hurt have a habit of sneakin' up and catching ye unawares.'

'You're dead daft remembering stuff like that. You've put it all behind you. You've got a bloody smashing fella in John Sykes, and your Molly an' Patrick are a credit to you.'

'I know. I couldn't want for more,' Kitty said wholeheartedly. 'It just feels a bit strange, me planning to get wed again.'

'Strange!' Maggie squawked. 'You've kept the poor bugger waiting long enough. I'm sure John's fed up to the back teeth,' and mimicking Kitty's Irish accent, she added, 'Ye an' your carpin' on about it's only dacent to wait two or three years. I don't know what you were thinking. Everybody knew Tom was cheating on you so it's not as though they expected you to be the grieving widow for the rest of your life.'

'Shush, Maggie!' Kitty put her finger to her lips, glancing anxiously again in Patrick's direction, but he was paying them no heed. In his opinion, his mother and Maggie talked too much about all sorts of boring things.

'And for your information, Maggie, I was grieving,' Kitty said in a low voice. 'Tom and I might have lived separate lives but he was still my husband.' Gold flecks flashed dangerously in Kitty's hazel eyes.

'All right, keep your hair on.' Maggie gestured carelessly with her cigarette. 'I was only saying that John's been patient long enough, so don't go thinking you can put it off any longer.'

'I've no intentions,' Kitty said tartly. 'On the third of May, ye'll see me striding down the aisle, come hell or high water.'

Maggie had spoken the truth. Kitty had delayed marrying John for more than two years after Tom's death, although by then she knew she loved him dearly. It was only right and proper, she had pleaded. She didn't want people thinking she was jumping out of one man's bed into another. John had failed to suppress a snigger but being the kind and thoughtful man he was, he had reluctantly agreed. However, he had made it quite clear he would not live in Weaver Street after they were married.

'You can't expect me to live in Tom Conlon's house, Kitty,' he'd said. 'It wouldn't seem right.' Then Kitty had made it plain she didn't want to move to his house in Old Swan. The thought of leaving Weaver Street and all her friends was unthinkable.

They had discussed several options, none that appealed to her until John provided a perfect solution that Kitty still found hard to believe.

One morning, some nine months ago, she'd been tidying the children's bedroom, the room that looked out onto the back lane and the allotments, when she heard the noise of heavy machinery. She'd rushed to the window. A monstrous digger was churning up the soil on the piece of wasteland next to the allotments. Curious, she'd dashed next door to Maggie, then down the lane to May Walker at number five and back up to Beth's. Her neighbours had been just as much in the dark as she was.

When she saw Jack Naughton coming out of his allotment, she'd called out to him; Jack must know what was going on. Jack had worked the allotment ever since he had been pensioned out of the army in 1915, the injuries he had received during the war leaving him with a crippled leg and only one eye. He was the one who had kept his neighbours supplied with fresh fruit, eggs and vegetables when times were lean, and he still did to this day. Jack had been very cagey when Kitty had blurted her urgent question. He'd winked his one good eye and told her to ask John.

It was common knowledge that after Tom's death, John spent every evening after he finished work in the engineering factory he owned in Wavertree with her and her children. It was almost as though they were already married. He stayed for dinner, played with Molly and Patrick, helped her to put them to bed. Then they sat talking and sharing kisses, both of them finding it hard to suppress their desires but doing so at Kitty's insistence. 'I want our wedding night to be right and proper, to come to you like a young bride,' she had said, and John, respecting her wishes, returned to his own home at the end of the night.

So, as John walked through the door that same evening, Kitty had immediately taken Jack's advice. 'Why do I need to ask ye what's going on across the way?' she'd asked, her gold-flecked hazel eyes alight with curiosity.

'We have to live somewhere, so I'm building us a house on that spare ground. It's as close as damn it to Weaver Street.'

Kitty had clapped her hand to her mouth, lost for words. John had then taken her in his arms asking, 'Happy?'

'Happy! I'm over the moon.' She'd flung her arms round him, thanking him with a smacking kiss.

Now, Kitty said, 'It's stopped raining. Let's go over to the house an' see how they're getting on.'

Maggie stubbed her cigarette and sprang to her feet. She loved being involved in Kitty's affairs. 'Yeah, let's,' she chirped, 'I've not much work on today, worse luck.'

'Aye, I heard the mill was on short time,' Kitty replied as she rattled coal from the scuttle to bank up the fire. 'Still, I'm sure it'll pick up in a week or two.'

'It 'ud bloody better,' Maggie moaned. 'I'll be lucky to meet this week's rent.' She shrugged carelessly then flicked her bleached blonde hair and grinned impishly. 'Come on, then. I don't half fancy that big, beefy brickie with the moustache. If I'm lucky, he might ask me out.' She headed for the door.

Kitty raised her eyebrows and shook her head. Maggie was always hard up. And she was always on the lookout for a new man.

'Hang on a minute,' Kitty said, going into the hallway and lifting the still damp coats off the hallstand. 'These got soaked on our way back from school but they'll have to do,' she complained, shivering at its clammy feel as she put on her coat then buttoned Patrick into his tweed overcoat.

Stepping round the puddles, they walked across the lane to the new house. Kitty's heart swelled each time she looked at it. Redbrick walls reached up to a grey slate roof and two squat redbrick chimneys. Two windows either side of a stout front door and two above looked out into the lane, one for the kitchen, the other the dining room, and over them two bedroom windows. Kitty smiled at the reflection of the watery sun gleaming on the dusty panes. *They'd need a good wash and polish when all the work was done.*

They walked down the side of the house to the rear and entered by the back door. From the outside, the house appeared to be finished, the team of bricklayers, joiners and roofers having departed to another site, but as soon as Kitty stepped into the small lobby, the sharp rap of a hammer let her know there were still things to do.

'Well, they sound to be getting on with it,' Kitty said as they left the lobby and entered a long hallway with a flight of stairs at the end that led up to four bedrooms and a bathroom. She opened the door into a large airy kitchen. The beefy brickie glanced round and Maggie primped her hair and gave a flirtatious smile.

He was fixing tiles behind the sink. The foreman was screwing knobs into the doors of the cupboards on one of the walls. It was Kitty who had suggested the recessed cupboards above the counter tops and the cupboards below. She'd seen a picture of a kitchen in her *Woman's Journal* and fallen in love with it. Granted, it was in a house in America, *but what's good enough for the Yanks is good enough for me*, she'd told John. Laughing, he had agreed.

'They're looking fine,' Kitty said, scanning the cream and green fitted cupboards. 'Set back like that, I'll not be banging me head when I'm working at the counter.'

Frank, the foreman, removed a screw from between his lips. 'Glad you think so, Mrs Conlon. We're getting on rightly in here. As soon as Bert's got them tiles up, we're more or less finished.' He gestured at the patch of wall behind the gleaming white pot sink. 'Do you want to have a look round, see what we've done since you were last in?'

Kitty certainly did. So, taking Patrick by the hand, she made to follow Frank out of the kitchen, but Maggie lingered. Kitty gave her a naughty wink. 'Mind where you're putting your feet, Patrick,' she advised as they stepped over scattered tools. Maggie pulled a face. She knew that her friend meant *mind what you're doing, Maggie. Don't be making a fool of yourself.*

'Will I live here?' Patrick asked the same question on every visit, his tone a mixture of awe and confusion.

'Yes, darlin',' Kitty said as they entered the large parlour at the rear of the house. It had been her idea to locate it at the back of the house so that they had a view of the allotments and the sycamore trees from the windows either side of the tiled fireplace.

'Ooh, this is lovely!' Kitty's gaze roamed the cream walls and the brown moquette three-piece suite: furniture from John's house in Old Swan. She crossed to the fireplace. 'An' this is a step up from having to black-lead a stove every week,' she continued, running the palm of her hand over the smooth tiles surrounding the grate. She stood back to admire the small, square cream tiles and the border of narrow green ones embossed with ivy leaves. 'He's made a lovely job of it.'

'Aye, you can't beat these modern tiled hearths,' Frank agreed. 'He's a good lad, is Bert. He can turn his hand to owt.'

Kitty wondered if Maggie had persuaded him to turn his hands on her.

Next, they surveyed the dining room. The long table and six tall-backed chairs had come from John's house, and she now pictured it set for dinner with a crisp white cloth and gleaming crockery and cutlery.

'The decorators did a good job,' Frank said, giving a nod to the pale green walls then turning back into the hallway and mounting the stairs to the bedrooms.

'Which is my room? Where will I sleep?' Patrick anxiously tugged her hand.

'I showed ye last time,' Kitty said, leading him across the landing to a bedroom at the back of the house, understanding his anxiety about moving from the only home he'd ever known, and sleeping in a room he didn't share with Molly. Kitty had chosen a warm, bright blue in here. 'This is your room, an' look, ye can see the trees an' Jack's allotment.'

Patrick liked Jack. He went over to the window and peered out. 'He's not there,' he said, crestfallen.

'I should think he isn't in this weather, love,' his mother replied, 'but when he is you'll be able to wave to him.'

Next, they looked in the bathroom with its gleaming white tub, basin and lavatory, their footsteps echoing as they stepped across the new floorboards to the two bedrooms overlooking the lane. The pale pink walls in Molly's room had Kitty thinking of angels. In what would be hers and John's bedroom, the new bed sat in solitary splendour against the wall facing the window. Kitty admired the walnut head and footboards and was filled with lust as she imagined what would soon take place on its thick pink mattress.

They trooped back downstairs, Kitty thinking about curtains

and bedspreads, and satisfied with everything she had seen. She popped her head round the kitchen door. 'I'm off now, Maggie.'

'Wait for me,' Maggie said. 'I won't be a mo.'

'Thanks, Frank,' Kitty said as she waited for Maggie. 'I'm ever so pleased.'

'Glad to be of service, Mrs Conlon.' Frank grinned. 'But not for much longer, eh? And never you worry, we'll have it all done in time for you to get the rest of your furniture in afore the big day. Next Saturday, isn't it?'

Kitty smiled. 'That's right, Saturday the third of May.'

'Well, if you think of anything you want doing in the meantime, just let me know and I'll see to it. I never leave a job until me customer's satisfied.'

'I'll do that, Frank,' she said, and to Maggie as she danced into the hallway, 'you took your time.'

'I hope you haven't been keeping that lad back from his work,' Frank mocked with a twinkle in his eye.

'I couldn't if I tried,' Maggie chirped.

'Ta-ra then, Frank,' said Kitty as she hustled Maggie through into the lobby.

Outside, Maggie positively bounced up the path at the side of the house. 'He's thirty, he's not married, he hasn't got a girlfriend, and he drinks in that pub at the bottom of Mill Lane,' she gabbled as they crossed the lane.

'An' has he asked ye to join him for a sweet sherry?' Kitty said, sarcasm dripping from her tongue.

Maggie's face fell. 'Not yet, but I'll keep working on him. I might call back later.'

'Aye, well, don't let it interfere with him putting the tiles behind my sink. I don't want him getting shoddy 'cos he's droolin' with mad passion over what he thinks ye're goin' to give him.'

'Aw, Kitty, don't spoil it,' Maggie wailed. 'I'm entitled to a bit of fun.'

'Well, make sure that's all it is. Ye didn't find your last encounter wi' that fella who collects the insurance funny when he dropped ye like a potato. Ye moaned till I was sick of listening to ye.'

'It's all right for you,' Maggie groused as they walked across the lane. 'You've got yourself a lovely man, *and* you're getting married again. All I've got is our Lily and me mam – and the pair of 'em can be a bloody nightmare.'

'All I'm sayin' is just mind what you're doin',' said Kitty as Maggie prepared to go into her own house. 'An' if you've nothin' on this avvy, ye can come an' do a bit more packin'.'

'Right you are. It'll give me a chance to have another go at him when we drop it off.' Maggie bounded up the steps like a spring chicken.

Kitty raised her eyes in desperation. Patrick, who all this time had been listening, his eyes big and his head turning from his mother to Maggie, now required answers.

'Who dropped hot potatoes?' he piped. 'And what's droolin' and mad passion?'

Sometimes Kitty wished that her little son wasn't so perspicacious. She had no intention of stifling his curiosity or his vocabulary, but in future she and Maggie needed to curb their tongues whenever he was within hearing distance. 'Never you mind,' she said as they went into their own house.

A shiver of excitement tingled up her spine as she stooped to poke the fire. Flames shot through the coals and up the chimney. Her spirits rose with them; it was all coming together nicely.

Over at the sink washing her hands, she gazed across at her new home. A home she would share with the most loving man she had ever met, where they would make new, happy, and wonderful memories. *Sometimes, Kitty Conlon soon to be Kitty Sykes, I think ye are well an' truly blessed.*

Maggie had taken her role as chief organiser seriously and number eleven was looking almost empty, only the furniture they were leaving behind and the bare necessities for everyday use still in situ. Today they were packing the children's toys.

'You don't realise how much stuff you have until it comes to moving,' Maggie said as she squashed a teddy bear into a clothes basket. Patrick, Molly and Lily looked at the toys that were about to find a new home. Molly picked at her chin; her skin was still peeling.

'Mammy, will I be pretty again in time to be a bridesmaid?' Molly asked.

'Sure ye will, darlin', ye an' Lily will be the loveliest brides-maids ever,' her mother said as she folded a blanket and set in on the basket.

'You'll be proper pictures, Queen,' Maggie agreed, lifting the basket ready to trek it across the lane to where Beth and Mavis were unpacking boxes.

'I don't want to wear my clothes,' Patrick grumbled, pulling a face at the idea of wearing a blue satin shirt and trousers.

'Ye'll look like a prince,' Kitty told him.

'Princes have swords,' he said. 'Can I have a sword?'

'I'll think about it,' she replied, rolling her eyes at Maggie as between them they carried the basket downstairs and outside.

Kitty had cried when John had taken her across one evening after Molly was better and Mavis was minding the children.

'Oh, it's beautiful,' she'd wept as they stood in the parlour, the setting sun streaming through the windows that looked out over the allotments to the sycamore trees. She'd turned to embrace John. 'Thank you,' she'd said fervently, 'it's more than I ever wished for. We'll fill it with love and happiness.'

'More than you've ever known,' he'd said, his kiss taking her breath away.

Now, as she entered the house with Maggie, she felt the same thrill as she had then. It happened every time she went through the door. She gazed down the long hallway to the stairs. Soon, she'd be sleeping up there with the man she loved.

'Yoo-hoo,' she called out in response to the rattle of crockery from the kitchen.

Mavis and Beth smiled as she walked in.

'I've put your best tea set in the top cupboard out of harm's way,' Beth said, pleased to be helping without taking the risk of going into Kitty's old house. It had been Maggie's idea to take care of the packing at one end, leaving Mavis and Beth to do the unpacking at the other end.

'See, it's all working out great,' Maggie crowed. 'I'm a bloody genius when it comes to organising.' The others exchanged amused glances as they each considered Maggie's chaotic home and the way she handled her love life.

With that in mind, Kitty asked, 'By the way, what about the beefy brickie? I never got round to asking you about him.'

Maggie's smile slipped. 'He didn't bite. I popped in once or twice to see him but then Frank sent him off to another house.' She gave a careless shrug. 'I must be losing me touch.' She paused, scowling. 'Do *you* think I am?' She glanced from Kitty to Mavis and then to Beth.

'No,' they chorused, hearing the wobble in her voice. Kitty gave her a nudge and a cheeky wink. 'He just didn't know what he was missing,'

'You'll find someone when the time's right,' Mavis consoled.

Beth kept silent. She didn't wholly approve of Maggie's casual love life.

There were still several boxes to unpack, and as Kitty advised and helped to distribute the contents, they chatted about the weather and the forthcoming wedding day. 'I hope the sun shines,' she said with feeling.

'It'll not dare do owt else if it knows it has you to answer to,' Maggie chirped.

Kitty grinned and threw a handful of tea towels at her. Maggie caught them, and extracting one from the pile, she draped it over her head. 'Here comes the bride,' she warbled tunelessly. The others fell about laughing.

'I'll just take these upstairs,' Kitty said, lifting the basket of toys, 'then I'll go back across an' see how John's getting on with taking the kids' beds down.'

After depositing the toys in the children's bedroom, she peeped into the one she would share with John. Feeling like a young bride, she gazed at the new bed.

5

Kitty spent the night before her wedding snuggled between Molly and Patrick in the bed she had once shared with Tom. She was leaving it behind in number eleven for when she rented out the house.

'This is cosy,' she remarked as she placed an arm round each of her children and pulled them close.

'Will I be sleeping in my own bed in my new pink room tomorrow night?' Molly asked, her voice high with excitement.

'Yes, darlin', an' Patrick will be in his room. Ye'll be able to spread your wee cars out, son, now ye have lots of space.' She worried that he might not settle sleeping on his own in a strange house.

'I'll put them in the fort till Jack's finished making me a garage,' he said solemnly. Then he leaned across his mother's bosom and gave his sister a stern look. 'And you and Lily will only be able to come in if I say so.'

'Same here,' Molly loftily replied.

'We've a big day tomorrow,' Kitty said, releasing them from her embrace, 'so the pair of ye close your eyes and get to sleep.'

The children turned onto their sides obediently. They both understood the importance of the next day. Their mammy was getting a new husband and they were getting a new daddy, one that they already adored. Of the two of them, only Molly remembered Tom Conlon, and even those memories were vague.

Kitty rested her eyes on Patrick's tawny head, gazing fondly at the wispy curls fanning the nape of his neck and curling round his shell-like ears. She could just see the rise and fall of one plump cheek as his breathing deepened and she felt her heart melting for her serious-minded little boy with his love for new words and all things mechanical. She had a feeling he would go far.

She shifted her gaze to her bold little daughter. Even in sleep, Molly's determination and her zest for living shone through. There was no denying she was a beauty. Her lustrous black curls and long dark lashes kissed her rosy cheek. *She'll break some hearts, just like her da*, mused Kitty as she slid further under the covers, relishing the feel of the warm little bodies pressed against her own.

Outside, a bright moon lanced a gap in the curtains, lighting the open wardrobe doors draped with two blue bridesmaids' dresses, a blue satin suit and Kitty's mint-green dress and coat. She could just about see them, and sleep evading her, she mentally checked off the list of accessories scattered about the room: three pairs of white socks and new white shoes – *goodness knows when they'd wear them again* – her own cream shoes, her stockings and fascinator, and two pretty floral headbands that Mavis had concocted out of silk lilies of the valley for Molly and Lily. Assured everything was in order, Kitty closed her eyes, willing sleep to take her. *I don't want bags under me eyes tomorrow.*

This is the last time I'll sleep in this bed, she thought as, unbidden, the memory of sharing it with Tom on her first night in Weaver Street crept into her mind. Since then, both her children had been born in it.

We enjoyed this bed, she mused dreamily, *until I found he was cheating on me and put him out of it.* It all seemed a long, long time ago and she fell asleep with the certainty that the man she was about to marry would always share her bed: theirs would be a marriage built on love – and respect.

* * *

Saturday, 3 May dawned dry and sunny. Upstairs and down, Kitty's house was bustling with excitement and some fraught nerves. Kitty and Maggie and their daughters were in Kitty's bedroom, dressing for what the women and the girls considered to be the day for looking their absolute best. Patrick sat on the bed pulling at the cuffs of his satin shirt, a disgruntled scowl on his face.

Down in the kitchen, Mavis and Beth were busy making posies for the bridesmaids and buttonholes for everyone else. Mavis had gone to the florists on the market first thing that morning. Now, a bouquet of red and white roses interspersed with gypsophila and ferns sat in the centre of the table, and white carnations and cornflowers were being cut down to size.

'You do the buttonholes, Beth, while I finish the posies,' Mavis said, lifting a single carnation and a bit of fern, then taking a bit of silver paper from the bag she'd brought with her. Mavis was an avid collector of useful things. 'Wrap a bit of this round the stems,' she demonstrated, 'it'll hold them together.'

'How many do we need?' Beth asked as she deftly formed a little corsage.

Mavis paused, her head tilted to one side. 'Well, there's Jack for a start, then Maggie and Vi and the three Walkers, that man Frank who built the house, and your dad and Blair.' She giggled. 'I've lost count already.'

'Nine,' said Beth, twisting silver paper round a carnation and a sprig of fern then gasping, 'No, it's eleven. You forgot to count us.' They burst out laughing.

'It's a good job John and his best man and his guests are seeing to their own,' Mavis said. 'But that's John all over. He's very organised.'

Beth carried on making buttonholes. Mavis interlaced blue and white flowers through the holes in a white paper doily then gathered them together with a narrow ribbon to make the second posy.

'I must say, you've made a lovely job of Kitty's bouquet,' said Beth. 'It's clever the way you've draped the fern and some of the roses into a long tail.'

Mavis flushed prettily. 'Nothing but the best for our Kitty.'

An impatient cry from up above had them both raising their eyes to the ceiling. They exchanged amused, knowing smiles.

Upstairs, Maggie had a face on her. 'Stand still while I fasten these hooks and eyes, you fidgeting mare,' she scolded as Lily twirled in front of the mirror. She knew she looked a picture in the blue taffeta frock with its heart-shaped neck and puff sleeves, and couldn't resist whirling round so that the full skirt flared out.

'Calm down, Maggie, it's me should be a bag of nerves, not ye,' said Kitty as she pinned a coronet of flowers on top of Molly's glossy head, her daughter standing obediently as her mother fixed it into place. 'There,' Kitty said appraising Molly. *She looks like a cherub in one of them religious paintings*, she thought, and felt her heart swell. 'Come here, Lily and let me do yours.' Lily danced over, her glorious red hair bouncing. 'Right, that's you two done, an' ye both look beautiful. Now, sit at peace, it's my turn to do meself up.' She took her own outfit off the hanger.

'Don't be getting any mucky marks on them white socks,' Maggie warned.

'Oh, for goodness' sake, Maggie, stop carping,' Kitty said as she slipped the dress over her head. 'It's a day for being happy. The sun's shining an' in less than an hour, I'll be Mrs John Sykes.'

'Yoo-hoo, Kitty,' Mavis called from the hallway. 'We've finished the flowers. Your bouquet and the posies are on the table. We're taking the buttonholes with us to the church. We'll dole them out as the guests arrive. I've taken some pins from your sewing box. We'll not come upstairs. It'll spoil the surprise.'

'Thanks, you're an angel,' Kitty called back as she fiddled with her fascinator.

'See you in church,' Beth and Mavis chorused.

'I'm off down to see what they've done,' said Kitty, satisfied that the fascinator was sitting at the right angle. They all trooped downstairs.

'Oh, it's beautiful,' Kitty gasped when she saw the bouquet. Tears sprang to her eyes. 'An' just look at the posies.' She handed one to Molly and the other to Lily.

Molly held hers in front of her midriff and adopted an angelic pose. Lily jigged up and down flourishing hers. Maggie let out a shriek that made Patrick jump.

'For goodness' sake, Maggie! Ye sound like the banshee,' Kitty cried.

'I don't know why I'm getting all het up,' Maggie grunted. But she did. She yearned for a proper wedding of her own. When she'd tied the knot with Fred, it had been a registry office do, him in his army uniform and her in a dress she'd worn a dozen times before. The registrar had been a grumpy old man, the witnesses Fred's mate and a registry office employee, and only her mam, Vi, and Fred's mother there to wish them well. *No bridesmaids, no bouquet, and to cap it all, as soon as it was over Fred went off on a pub crawl with his mate and I went back home with me mam. Is it any wonder it didn't work out?*

'It's her what has me nerves wrecked,' Maggie said out loud, pointing a finger at Lily. 'I don't want her spoiling your day.'

'She won't,' Kitty said. 'Nothing will.'

At a quarter to midday, one of John's friends arrived in his car to take Maggie, the girls and Patrick up the street to St Joseph's Church.

'They can walk up,' Kitty had told John, 'an' so can I.'

'Indeed you will not, and neither will they,' he had protested. 'I want nothing but the best on our wedding day. You will all arrive in style.' Then he'd kissed her tenderly. 'I'll be waiting for you. I'd wait forever,' he whispered against her hair.

Now, she stood at the front door as Maggie and the children climbed into the shiny grey car. John's friend saluted her. She waved back.

The car glided up Weaver Street, and watching it go, Kitty's mind wandered to the first time she had met John. She'd held a going away party for Tom before he went to join the navy. John had arrived with Sam and Cora Bradshaw, the landlord and landlady of the Weaver's Arms. Kitty had danced with him, and he had fallen in love with her that very evening – or so he said. After that, whenever they chanced to meet, Kitty had always felt happy in his company, but she had looked on him only as a charming man and a good friend until the day she realised she was in love with him.

She waved across the street to a few well-wishers standing at their doors to watch the wedding party leave. 'You look lovely,' Betty Haigh called out, 'that green suits you to a T.'

Then the grey car glided back up the street and halted at Kitty's gate. She lifted her bouquet from the hallstand. As she closed the door behind her, she whispered, 'Goodbye, number eleven.' She walked serenely to the car. This was it: the start of a new life.

When she alighted from the car, there was a chorus of 'oohs' and 'aahs' from the women who seemed to always gather outside the church whenever there was a wedding. 'Doesn't she look a picture,' someone called out.

'Are you ready for this?' Maggie asked as she and Kitty and the girls assembled in the porch.

'Ready as I'll ever be,' Kitty said, then took a deep breath.

'Do I look all right?' Maggie asked doubtfully as she began fiddling with the hat she'd bought at the flea market, a stiff cartwheel affair in lemon silk. When she'd tried it on, Kitty had remarked that it looked like a dustbin lid.

Now, Kitty smiled. 'You look perfect, Maggie; that hat's a real showstopper.' She spoke sincerely, for her dearest friend really did look glamorous in the lemon dress and jacket that Kitty had made for her the previous Christmas.

Molly and Lily jigged impatiently, eager to perform their duty in front of the crowded church. Patrick, uncomfortable in his hateful blue satin suit, stood solemnly, waiting to walk his mammy down the aisle.

'Are we all ready?' Joey Walker asked. He was acting as usher along with a lad from John's factory. May, Joey's mother, had been thrilled to bits when Kitty had asked him to perform the duty.

'Sure, an' didn't he run errands for me when he was a wee boy, an' help paint the café when I did it up?' Kitty had told her.

The organ pealed. Maggie darted into the church and hurried to a pew at the front. Kitty took Patrick's hand, and Molly and Lily fell in behind. Heads turned to greet their arrival, all eyes on the bride. Her mane of red-golden curls caressed her shoulders, contrasting beautifully with the dark green velvet fascinator, and her pale green calf-length linen dress and loose coat showed off her slender figure and trim ankles. The congregation exchanged nods of approval.

Kitty, her heart drumming a steady tattoo, fixed her eyes on John's broad back. She thought how solid and dependable he looked in his dark grey worsted suit. He stood tall and straight, waiting for her, as she knew he always would. She felt as though she was walking on a cloud.

When she reached the altar and John's side, she gave him a triumphant smile, the golden flecks in her hazel eyes dancing. His warm brown eyes met hers and they exchanged a look that said *at last, we're here.*

Father Connolly welcomed them and the congregation. Then, in his thick west of Ireland brogue, he intoned the words of the mass. Kitty barely heard a word.

Behind them, Molly and Lily were having a whispered argument over who should hold the bouquet. Eventually they agreed to hold it between them.

Patrick, feeling silly in his fancy suit and only half-listening to the priest's rumbling voice, almost jumped out of his skin when Fr Connolly asked, 'Who giveth this woman to this man?' and his mammy gave him a sharp nudge and a wide smile. 'I do,' he shouted. The congregation tittered.

Maggie sat with tears in her eyes, wishing she could change places with Kitty.

Mavis and Jack sat alongside her, each of them wondering if they should take the plunge and marry. *But it might spoil a beautiful friendship*, Mavis thought, and Jack convinced himself that *what we have is fine.*

May Walker was sitting with her husband, Bill, glad that he was almost sober, and proud as punch of Joey in his merchant navy uniform. At twenty-five, he was still single, as was Steven, her youngest. He was also in the navy, and Ronnie was married and living in Toxteth. *Joey and Steven will get wed one day, but my poor Sammy's lying in a field somewhere in France. He'll never get married*, she thought, dabbing her handkerchief to her eyes at the memory of her firstborn son who had lost his life in the war.

Beth sat with her thigh pressed against Blair's and thanked God that she had heeded Kitty's advice and stood firm in the face of her domineering father. She reached for Blair's hand and squeezed it. *I'd never have become a wife and known such joy if it hadn't been for Kitty's friendship. And maybe one day I'll be a mother like her.*

John slipped the plain gold band on Kitty's finger then clasped both her hands in his as they made their solemn vows to love and honour, John speaking with such devotion that for an instant, Kitty felt as though she was floating above the altar. She tilted her head, waiting for his lips to meet hers. It was the tenderest of kisses, fleeting as a butterfly's wings. 'I love you, Mrs Sykes,' he whispered.

'And I love you with all my heart, Mr Sykes.'

After that, she heard nothing but the beating of her heart.

'The Lord be with you,' Fr Connelly announced in a strident voice.

'And also with you,' the congregation echoed.

'Go in peace to love and serve the Lord.'

Oh, she would, Kitty promised as the congregation's response and the priest's command brought her back to the moment.

The organist burst into a rousing rendition of the wedding march. Kitty linked her arm through John's and they walked proudly down the aisle, Patrick hanging on to his mammy's free hand and Molly and Lily giggling and skittering behind. The wedding guests tumbled out of the pews, and shrugging off the solemnity of their surroundings, they all trooped out into the sunshine. One of John's friends clicked away with his Box Brownie camera, everyone wanting a photograph with the bride and groom.

'Take one of me on me own,' Maggie shouted, striking a pose like Gloria Swanson. She was mad that her latest squeeze hadn't turned up for the wedding, and the chap with the camera was rather attractive. Hoping he thought she was, she smiled lasciviously into his lens.

Then it was time to go to the reception in the Adelphi. Cars filled up with as many people as they could carry, while the stragglers went to catch a tram.

Kitty's eyes filled up as she gazed round the large room: at the crisp white tablecloths, gleaming cutlery and glasses glittering under the large chandeliers. John led her to the top table, where Mavis's wedding cake took centre stage: three tiers of Madeira coated in white icing decorated with red and white rosebuds.

'Now this is what I call a wedding,' Kitty said as they sat down, her cheeks glowing and her eyes moist as she watched her guests take their places.

'I told you I wanted nothing but the best for you,' John said, 'but if we were sitting in your café eating a spam sandwich, I'd still be the happiest man in the world. I want us to remember this day, Kitty.'

They ate and drank with relish, and after the speeches, they danced until they were exhausted. When the five-piece band slowed the pace, they sang along to 'If I Had My Way Dear' and other romantic songs. Molly, Lily and Patrick skidded up and down the highly polished dancefloor and ate far too many sweet treats. Maggie made a play for the man with the camera, a pleasant-looking chap with a shock of fair curly hair. She was heartily disappointed when she discovered he was married to a rather plain girl nursing a baby and looking daggers at her each time she danced with him.

The afternoon light faded and the celebrations trickled to an end. After much shaking of hands, hugging and pecking of cheeks and best wishes for the future, the guests departed. As John and Kitty made their way to the car, John carrying a sleepy Patrick but

Molly still lively enough to skip along holding Kitty's hand, John said, 'Time for our first night in our new home, Mrs Sykes.'

Kitty thrilled at his words and the look of promise in his eyes.

Later that same evening, Kitty descended the stairs of her new home in an almost dreamlike state. She had just been to check on her children who, without a word of protest, had been put to bed an hour or so earlier, both of them worn out with excitement, and thrilled to be sleeping in their new bedrooms.

'This has been the best day of my life,' said Kitty, flopping down beside John on the couch in her new parlour.

John placed his arm round Kitty's shoulders and pulled her close. 'I promise you there'll be others even better,' he said, his lips finding hers in a passionate kiss. She tasted the wine on his tongue and smelled the spicy scent of his cologne. She felt like pinching herself to make sure that the wonderful day hadn't just been a dream. The wedding had been beautiful, the reception in the Adelphi Hotel a huge success, and the homecoming to the new house the icing on the cake. Nestled in John's arms, she couldn't ask for anything more. *Well, not quite*, she thought, pulling away from him and looking deep into his eyes. John's lips curved roguishly. He got to his feet, pulling Kitty with him. As they mounted the stairs, she felt her heart racing.

Later, listening to her husband's steady breathing, Kitty relived the magic of the last hour. It had all been worth the wait.

PART II

6

LIVERPOOL, AUGUST 1929

Rain was lashing out of the heavens as Mavis Robson ducked into the foyer of the Adelphi Hotel in Ranelagh Street, her folded umbrella held like a jousting lance dripping water on the red and gold carpet. In a flurry of jerky movements, she dropped the umbrella in the brass receptacle by the door and then flapped droplets from her brown mackintosh. Victor Green, the under-manager, smiled fondly. She looked like a half-drowned sparrow, and he was about to make a cheeky comment as Mavis returned his smile. Instead, his smile slipping, he stepped smartly from behind the reception desk, his stern expression causing Mavis to widen her eyes.

'A moment, madam, if you please,' Mavis heard him say, as he extended a restraining arm to bar the passage of a young woman hurrying across the foyer towards Mavis and the door into the street. He spoke again, his voice low, and Rosamund Brown-Allsop's suitcase landed with a thud at her feet as the colour leached from her face. A few more words had her hands flying to her face to cover the embarrassment reddening her cheeks.

Curious, Mavis fussed with the buttons on her mackintosh as Victor and the young woman exchanged yet more words. She couldn't hear what they were saying but it was quite obvious the young woman was pleading with Victor. As he listened, his expression changed to one of sympathy, and nodding his head, he stepped back. The young woman swept past him, her suitcase abandoned as she dashed for the door. Mavis dodged out of the way to let her pass. The door swished closed behind her. Mavis hung up her mackintosh.

Victor gave a resigned shrug. 'That's probably the last we'll see of her,' he said, lifting the suitcase and putting it behind the desk.

'What's the problem, Vic? She looked pretty upset.'

'I asked her to settle the bill. She's gone off to get the money – so she says.' He shrugged again. 'I should have known something was up when she and the gentleman she arrived with a couple of nights ago signed in as Mr and Mrs Smith.' Victor rolled his eyes. 'You'd think they could be a little more inventive, wouldn't you?'

'When you're planning a dirty weekend, your imagination doesn't run to conjuring up fancy surnames, Vic. It's full of entirely different matters.'

Victor chuckled. 'You'd think I'd be wise to 'em by now. Mind you, I was suspicious from the start. They looked no more like a married couple than me and that coat stand.' He flicked his thumb to where Mavis's mackintosh hung.

'And where is her so-called husband?'

'You tell me,' Victor snorted. 'She says she doesn't know, that when she woke up he'd left and taken all her money with him. So, there you have it. The blighter's gone, and the bill is unpaid.' Victor ran his fingers through his thinning grey hair. 'It's the last day of the month and if the books don't balance, there'll be hell to pay. You know how Mr Henry double checks every booking.'

Grimacing, Mavis nodded She was well aware of the owner's vigilance. She'd worked at the Adelphi as the cakes and pastries chef for over twenty years.

'Anyway,' Victor puffed, exasperated but trying to sound cheerful, 'what brings you here today? You don't usually work on Friday.'

'I've been to the dentist and now I'm just dropping off some cake decorations before I go back home.' Mavis wished Victor the best of luck with his problem then made her way through to the kitchens. Over a cup of tea with the staff, she related what she'd witnessed in the foyer.

'I knew they weren't a married couple even though they were sharing a bed,' Peggy the chamber maid exclaimed knowingly, 'you can always tell. She was a bag of nerves, but he was the flashy type. Very good looking, mind you. A man of the world, you might say, and quite a bit older than her.'

'I knew there was summat dodgy about 'em too,' said Arthur, the waiter. 'He didn't know she never drank coffee.'

'And it seems like she knew even less about him,' Mavis said, gathering her gloves and her handbag and telling them she'd see them all on Tuesday.

'Well, did she come back?' Mavis asked when she went back into the foyer to retrieve her umbrella and mackintosh.

'Yes, surprisingly she did, but minus the diamond ear studs she'd been wearing. I felt sorry for her. The poor lass must have sold them to raise the cash.'

Victor shook his head despairingly.

'More than likely to Archie Wiseman.' Mavis was referring to the pawnbroker further down the street. 'She really was in an awful state.'

'She was, and she couldn't apologise enough. She seemed like an awfully well-bred little thing. I'll bet it's the first time she's faced a predicament like that, but I couldn't let her off even though it made me feel rotten.' Victor smiled ruefully.

'Never mind, Vic, mark it down to experience. You never know who you'll come across next in this place.' Mavis put on her mackintosh, still damp from the downpour.

'Don't forget your brolly,' Victor reminded her as she did up her buttons. 'It's still tipping down.'

Mavis retrieved her umbrella, and pushed open the door. 'See you Tuesday, Vic.' She stepped outside, heaving a sigh of disgust as she opened her umbrella. These days you never knew what the weather was going to do. It had been the same throughout the year, dry, sunny days changing overnight to torrential rain; there had been serious flooding in May in some parts of England. So far, August had been a scorcher, but now on the very last day it was wet and miserable.

Wind and rain gusted in her face threatening to blow her umbrella inside out. As she battled with it, she saw the same young woman she had seen earlier in the hotel foyer. Her suitcase at her feet, she was sheltering in the doorway of the adjacent offices, rain dripping and trickling from its narrow lintel, soaking the shoulders of her coat and flattening her hat. Expensive garments, Mavis judged, having noted her soft leather shoes and matching handbag as she'd watched her pleading with Vic. Taking pity on her, Mavis approached.

'Have you been standing here all this time?' A good twenty-five minutes had passed since she'd first seen her.

Rosamund Brown-Allsop nodded, drops of rain bouncing from the brim of her hat and dribbling down her cheeks. She brushed them away impatiently.

'May I ask why?' Mavis gently enquired, stepping closer so that her umbrella protected both of them.

'I... I have nowhere to go.' Rosamund's tears mingled with the rain on her cheeks.

She looked so dejected that Mavis's kind heart went out to her. 'Then you'd better come with me,' she said firmly.

Inside a nearby teashop, they sat facing one another, steam rising from their wet coats. Mavis ordered tea and hot crumpets, and when they arrived, she deliberately ate hers in silence, allowing time for the young woman to do the same. Rosamund's hand shook and her cup rattled in the saucer each time she set it down. Gradually she gained some composure.

'Now, tell me how you come to be in this unfortunate position. Maybe I can help.' Mavis drained her cup. 'I saw you earlier in the Adelphi. I work there. I'm Mavis Robson.' She smiled encouragingly.

'Yes, I recognised you.' Rosamund's pale cheeks reddened.

Mavis studied her elfin face, pale grey eyes, and straight, mousy hair that had been plastered to her face but was now drying. *She's a plain little thing, and not at all the type that I imagine men like the one Peggy described would go after, but clearly he had an ulterior motive.* Mavis had recently turned thirty-eight and she reckoned that her companion was only half her age. She gave another encouraging smile. 'So, what's your name?'

'Ros...' the girl hesitated. Stumbling over her words, she said, 'Rose... Rose Brown.' She gave a wan but satisfied smile.

Mavis suspected that it was nothing of the sort, but more concerned with what she could do to help the girl, she let it pass. 'Do you want to talk, Rose, or will I mind my own business?'

Rosamund, or Rose as she must now think of herself, looked into Mavis's kind face and saw a genuine desire to be of some use. Mavis was her only hope: who else could she turn to? She took a deep breath.

'I'm ashamed to say I've been very foolish.' Her voice almost a whisper, she blinked away threatening tears.

'We're all guilty of that at times,' Mavis said, her tone rich with sympathy.

Rosamund couldn't imagine the neat little woman in her sensible mackintosh and stout shoes ever being foolish enough to make the mistakes she had made. She looked into the bright, beady eyes and at the pointed chin and nose under the vivid red beret that covered feathery brown hair. Thinking that she looked like a friendly little bird, Rosamund decided to put her trust in her.

'I came here with a man I thought I was in love with,' she said flatly. 'I thought he loved me, but in the end it proved otherwise.' She sighed heavily. Then, sounding like a child deprived of her favourite toys, she whined, 'He sneaked out on me, taking my money and my jewellery – and my pride.' She swallowed hard.

'I have never been so mortified as I was when that nice man in the hotel thought I was trying to leave without paying the bill. I thought Lewis had settled it.'

'Yes, so Victor told me.' Mavis leaned across the table and placed her hand on Rosamund's. 'Tell me, did you sell your ear studs to pay the bill? Victor said you weren't wearing them when you returned.'

Rosamund nodded glumly. 'I had no choice. They were all I had left. Had I not slept in them last night, I suspect Lewis would have taken them too.' Tears spilling over, she covered her face with her hands. Mavis sat deep in thought then, feeling rather hot and bothered, she pushed back her chair and said, 'Excuse me a moment. I need the lavatory.'

Rosamund uncovered her face, panic flitting across it at the thought of being abandoned yet again, but when she saw that Mavis had left her gloves on the table and her scarf over the back of her chair, Rosamund's breath gushed out of her. She had never felt so helpless.

Oblivious to the bustling waitresses and chattering customers, she mulled over her predicament. *Here I am in a strange city with no money and nobody to turn to other than this kind little woman*, she thought miserably. *It was foolish of me to run away with Lewis. I'm sure I've broken Daddy's heart.* Wistfully, she pictured her father and the comfort and safety of the grand mansion that she had called home until two days ago. *But I can never go back*, she told herself bitterly. *My mother will condemn me – soiled goods, she'll say – and torture me for the rest of my life. So what am I to do?* Feeling utterly hopeless, Rosamund drained the last drops of tea from the teapot into her cup.

In the coolness of the little cubicle, Mavis leaned with her hands on the washbasin and her face puckered in consternation. Should she give the girl the few shillings she had in her purse and leave her to her fate, or would it be kinder to take her to her own home, give her a warm meal, dry out her wet coat and take it from there? Deciding on the latter, she dabbed cold water on her cheeks, patted them dry with her handkerchief then marched back to the table.

Mavis stayed on her feet, and picked up her gloves and scarf. 'Come on,' she said, very businesslike, 'I can't leave you like this. You'd better come home with me until we sort something out.'

Rosamund sagged with relief.

On the tram to Edge Hill where Mavis had lived all her life, she deliberately avoided the subject of why Rosamund was travelling with her. Instead, she chatted about her job and resisted asking too many questions other than where Rosamund had lived before arriving in Liverpool. She assumed from her accent that it was somewhere in the south of England.

Rosamund, now more at ease, replied, 'A village in Buck...' and then just as quickly changed it to, 'London.'

Mavis took that to be another lie, and as the bus jounced along the road, she talked about Liverpool whilst silently drumming up place names beginning with 'Buck...' She settled on Buckinghamshire as the most likely place.

'Here we are,' she said, as the tram clanked to a halt in Broad Green, a busy thoroughfare with shops and offices on either side of the road.

Rosamund retrieved her suitcase from the luggage compartment under the stairs and they alighted on to the wide pavement. 'This way,' Mavis said, walking briskly to the end of the row of shops and arriving at the entrance to a lane that ran behind a row of Victorian redbrick terrace houses. 'Up here,' she said, turning the corner, 'this is the back way into Weaver Street. My front door's there, but my back one's in this lane. I usually go in that way.'

They began walking up the lane, Rosamund thinking that the soot-stained row of houses on her right looked rather small and drab, and even though they each had a small garden, they were nothing like her own home. A detached house on the left next to what must be a market garden looked much newer and smarter. In one of the gardens on the right, a woman was taking shirts from a clothesline. 'Hello, Mavis,' she called out as they drew level with her. 'Are you bringing the rain with you?' The woman glanced up at the black clouds.

Mavis stopped, and so did Rosamund. 'Hello, May, it looks like it, doesn't it? It's lashing in the city. You'll have your work cut out trying to dry that lot.'

'Aye, I'll have to put 'em on the clotheshorse round the fire,' May said cheerily before sarcastically adding, 'I don't want Bill going without clean shirts.' She glanced at Rosamund. 'Who's this you've got with you, then?'

'This is Rose Brown,' Mavis said. 'She's staying with me for a day or so.'

'Welcome to Weaver Street, love,' May said warmly. 'You'll be well looked after. Mavis does some lovely baking. Ta-ra, then. I'll be seein' you.' Lifting her clothes basket up to her hip, she went indoors.

'That's May Walker; a good hard-working woman is May. She has three lovely sons, one married and living in Toxteth and the other two in the merchant navy. Her husband's a workshy boozer.'

'Mmmh,' said Rosamund, rather taken aback by this wealth of information.

A few more paces and they met with a woman and a girl of about twelve.

'Hiya, Mavis,' the brittle-haired blonde said, waving the hand that held a cigarette and patting her hair with the other when she clocked Rosamund.

'Hiya, Auntie Mavis,' the girl said, her bright red curls bouncing as she stepped nearer. Mavis chucked her under her chin. 'Hello, Lily of the Valley,' she said impishly. 'Where are you off to?' Lily giggled.

'We're just going across to Kitty's.' The blonde woman gestured with her cigarette at the new house with its bright paintwork and neat flowerbeds.

'This is Maggie Stubbs and her daughter Lily,' Mavis said, addressing Rosamund. To Maggie and Lily, she said, 'Meet Rose Brown. She's staying with me for a day or so. Maggie and Lily are my neighbours.' She pointed to the shabbiest house in the row. Its garden resembled a rubbish tip.

Maggie looked Rosamund up and down then gave Mavis a quizzical look before saying, 'See you later, Mavis – an' you an' all, Rose,' her words weighted with curiosity.

'No doubt you will,' Mavis replied, moving on, and Rosamund

trailed behind her, feeling rather overwhelmed by her introduction to Weaver Street.

'This is us,' Mavis said, as they arrived at a gate further along the terrace. Rosamund followed Mavis up the path to the door, but before Mavis had chance to open it, the door of the next house above flew open. A thin man limped down the steps and across the garden to the dividing wall.

'So you're back, then.' He smiled fondly at Mavis. 'I've got the kettle on.' Then, as if he'd only just noticed her, his one good eye strayed from Mavis to Rosamund. His other eye was closed over, the lid puckered at the corners. 'Oh, I didn't see you'd got company.' He sounded surprised. His eye lit on the suitcase.

'Rose Brown,' Mavis said by way of introduction and Jack Naughton looked even more surprised when she told him Rose might be staying for a day or two. 'You'll not be coming in for a cuppa, then,' he said, disappointed.

'Not just now, love, but thanks for the offer. It was lashing in the city and we need to get out of these damp coats. We'll pop round later for a cup.' She leaned over the wall and pecked his cheek.

A warm smile creased Jack's damaged face. 'Right you are, love. Now you get inside. We don't want you catching a chill,' and as Mavis unlocked the door, 'I've kept your fire banked up, it'll be nice an' warm in there.'

'Thanks Jack, you're a pet. See you in a bit.'

Mavis led the way into a warm, cosy kitchen. Rosamund followed, feeling even more bemused. She had been trying to imagine her own mother walking along a street in the village where they lived and being greeted like this; a polite nod, yes, or more likely a mere glance, but certainly not the smiles and friendly words that Mavis had received.

'Take your coat off and make yourself at home.' Mavis propped her umbrella behind the door and then hung up her mackintosh.

Rosamund set down her suitcase and slipped off her coat, glad to be rid of both of them. Her fingers ached from gripping her suitcase and the shoulder pads of her coat were so wet that the rain had soaked right through to her silk blouse.

'Give it here.' Mavis reached for the coat, darted out of the room then returned seconds later with the coat draped on a hanger. She suspended it from the drying rack above the fire. 'There, it'll dry out soon enough. I'll make a hot drink. We'll have something to eat later.'

At Mavis's instruction, Rosamund sat by the blazing fire, luxuriating in its warmth and feeling strangely comfortable. Mavis was busy in the alcove next to the fireplace that held a gas cooker, a sink and a counter with cupboards below it. Rosamund's eyes roamed the neat, tidy room that contained a table and four kitchen chairs, a sideboard, and by the hearth, two plush armchairs with gaily patterned cushions. Pegged rugs covered the floorboards and landscape prints hung on the walls that were papered in a delicate flower print. Rooms within a room, mused Rosamund, picturing the austere dining room and formal drawing room and the cavernous below stairs kitchen in her own home. This room was so much more inviting. She wondered where she would now be had she not met Mavis. The thought made her shiver.

'You'd better take off those shoes and dry them by the fire too,' Mavis said, handing her a steaming cup of cocoa.

Rosamund did as she was told. Mavis stuffed the flimsy shoes with screwed-up newspaper then set them on the hearth on their sides, Rosamund marvelling at how natural it felt to be sitting in a complete stranger's kitchen sipping delicious hot chocolate. 'Your neighbours are very friendly,' she ventured, feeling the need to say something and yet not wanting to talk at all.

'They're the salt of the earth,' Mavis said, sitting down in the opposite chair and taking some knitting from a bag beside the chair. 'There's nothing they wouldn't do for you, though they don't all have it easy. As I said, May's a hard-working, kindly soul but her husband's a rotten drunk.' She rolled her eyes. 'And Maggie's a single parent to Lily. Her husband was in the army and while he was away, she had Lily to another chap. When Fred found out, he gave her a beating and she chucked him out. Maggie says she's better off without him.'

'And Jack?' Rosamund asked shyly. Mavis's cheeks turned pink.

'Jack is my very special friend,' she said warmly. 'We have an understanding that suits us both perfectly.' Rosamund wondered what that meant.

'How did he lose his eye?' she asked, curiosity outweighing her reticence.

Mavis gave a little sigh. 'The war, love, it did terrible things to a lot of people.' Her thoughts flew back to 1915 and the man she had been going to marry that Easter. He had been killed in France on Valentine's Day.

'I don't really know much about that,' Rosamund said, as though the war had taken place hundreds of years ago instead of not much more than a decade.

Mavis thought how innocent and unworldly the girl seemed. 'You were only a youngster, so I don't suppose you do, but some of us still bear the scars and remember the suffering.' She wiped under each eye with her index finger. Rosamund appeared not to notice her distress. Everyone she'd met so far appeared to be warm and friendly, unlike the cold, impersonal people she had left behind at home. 'Yet you all seem so happy now,' she said.

Mavis smiled. 'I suppose we are, more often than not. We all have our ups and downs, but we always stick together and help one another through the bad patches. That way, nobody has to struggle on their own.'

Rosamund understood exactly what she meant. 'Is that why you're helping me now that I'm in a bad patch?' she asked solemnly.

'Something like that,' Mavis said with a smile. 'Now, if you've finished your cocoa, we'll talk about what we're going to do about you.'

Rosamund looked alarmed.

'Now let me get this straight,' Mavis continued rather briskly. 'You said you ran away from London and came to Liverpool with a man you were in love with, but he turned out to be a liar and a thief. Is that right?'

Rosamund nodded.

'So, where did you meet him, and why did you have to run away? That's the bit I don't understand.'

'I... I met him in the... office where I worked, and... my parents didn't approve of him.' Rosamund floundered for words. 'They... they forbade me to see him...'

'And he persuaded you to run off with him,' Mavis interjected tartly.

'Yes,' Rosamund whispered, her tears brimming. 'And I can't go home because my mother wouldn't allow it, and now I've no money and nowhere else to go,' she gabbled, fear loosening her tongue and tears streaming down her cheeks.

'You are in a pickle, aren't you?' said Mavis, sounding thoroughly exasperated as she got to her feet and went and gazed out of the window. Storm clouds had gathered overhead and the afternoon light had faded. She made another impulsive decision.

'The day's nearly over,' she said, turning to look at Rosamund. 'You can stay here for tonight, and we'll decide what you're going to do in the morning.'

Rosamund blinked with surprise. 'Oh, thank you, thank you,' she gushed.

'Come on then, I'll show where the bedroom and the bathroom is. You might like to get out of that damp blouse and skirt.'

Mavis led the way into a hallway and up a flight of stairs, Rosamund following in her stocking feet. On the turn of the stairs, Mavis paused. 'That's my room,' she pointed to a door at the other end of the landing, 'and next to it's the bathroom. You can sleep in here.' She pushed open the nearest door and walked into the small bedroom. Its window looked out to the back lane.

'I'll leave you clean towels in the bathroom. There'll be plenty of hot water seeing as Jack kept the fire tended.' She turned to leave. 'Come down when you're ready.'

After Mavis had gone downstairs, Rosamund gazed out of the window. Across the lane was the detached modern house, much grander than its neighbours, and to the side of it the land was divided into small plots with sheds and greenhouses on them. The flourishing plots reminded her of the neat rows of vegetables old Harry, the gardener, grew in abundance in the large, walled kitchen garden behind the mansion that was her home. Turning to assess the tidy room, she noted that it was no bigger than the dressing room where she had so foolishly packed her belongings three days ago. *What romantic, high hopes I had then.*

She flopped onto the pretty patchwork quilt that covered the bed and curled her toes into the pegged rug beside it. *What am I doing here?* Bewildered by the confusion of the past few hours, she stood and opened her suitcase, and shaking the creases from a dress that she had hastily packed along with a few other garments, she thought wistfully of the lovely clothes she had left behind.

After taking out her wash bag, dressing gown and slippers, she went along to the bathroom, thankful that the house had indoor facilities. She had wondered if they did when she first saw them.

Some of the tenants on her father's estate still had to make do with tin baths and outdoor lavatories.

In the bath, she soaped and scrubbed her body from chin to toe, feeling as though she was cleansing it of Lewis Aston and every other mistake she had made in the past few days, and as she languished in the hot, soothing water, she chastised herself. How could she have been so naive? Why would a handsome, worldly man like Lewis be truly interested in an insipid creature like herself? He had sworn that she was the love of his life, and she had believed him. Knowing that he had come into her life when she was feeling particularly bereft was no consolation. She had fallen for his charms and had been only too pleased to run away with him. Slowly sinking lower in the water, she let it run into her ears in an attempt to drown out the thoughts racing through her mind, but try as she might, she couldn't erase the awful memories of the past few days.

Scowling, Rosamund climbed out of the bath, feeling cleaner but no happier. If her mother had been kinder, she wouldn't now be here in this strange northern city watching the scum from Lewis Aston's touch gurgle down the plughole in a bath belonging to a woman about whom she knew nothing. But here she was, a penniless fool relying on charity. It made her feel cold and shrunken.

Downstairs, preparing a shepherd's pie for the evening meal, Mavis was questioning her impulsive nature. She knew little or nothing about the girl except that she was sparing with the truth. *She seems harmless enough, but appearances can be deceptive*, Mavis mused as she heated a pan of mince. *Will she knock me over the head and steal my valuables?* Giggling at her overactive imagination, she gave the mince a frivolous stir. *I needn't worry. Jack always keeps an eye and an ear out for my well-being*, she told herself, tipping the meat into a casserole dish.

The lavender-scented towels that Mavis had put out were thick and fluffy and Rosamund rubbed her skin until it glowed. Back in the bedroom, she put on clean underwear and one of the four dresses she had packed on the night Lewis had persuaded her to run away with him. He'd stressed the importance of travelling light. 'Just bring your jewellery, darling, and the precious bits and bobs you wouldn't want to leave behind,' he'd urged, holding her close, kissing her and making her head swim as he'd whispered, 'You're all I need. Our love will take us to places beyond your wildest dreams.'

Now, standing in a small bedroom in the dirty city of Liverpool, a place she'd heard of but never dreamed of visiting, Rosamund lifted the battered little rabbit that she had slept with for all of her nineteen years and hugged him to her chest. 'Lewis didn't consider you worth stealing, Mister Snuffy Snuggles,' she murmured into the rabbit's floppy ear, 'and you will always be Snuffy Snuggles whereas I, Rosamund Brown-Allsop, will have to remember that now I'm plain Rose Brown.'

* * *

Across the lane in Kitty's house, Maggie and Lily couldn't wait to tell her what they had just witnessed. 'She looked proper posh even though her fancy coat was dead soggy,' Lily said, rolling her eyes at Molly.

'Yeah, and her suitcase was one of them real leather ones with brass buckles and straps. You know, the sort that cost a fortune in Cripps – not that I ever shop there.' Maggie grumpily stubbed her cigarette in an ashtray.

Kitty put the kettle on the stove ready for a jangle, at the same time asking Molly and Lily if they'd go to the shop. She needed a fresh loaf.

'What did ye say they called her?' Kitty asked as the door

closed behind the girls, Lily almost bursting to give Molly her version of Mavis's visitor.

'Rose Brown.' Maggie lit another cigarette.

'I can't say I've ever heard Mavis mention a friend of that name.'

'She's years younger than Mavis, I'd say she's about seventeen.'

Kitty brewed the tea, and the two women speculated on the new arrival to Weaver Street.

7

'Just one more day after this and I'll start my new school,' Molly Conlon said as her mother, Kitty, twisted three hanks of long black hair into a thick, glossy plait.

It was a Saturday, the last day in August, and the school year would start on Monday. Molly sounded both apprehensive and excited at the prospect of attending the girls' grammar school in Hope Street. Kitty's heart went out to her firstborn child and only daughter. She knew how it felt to make new beginnings.

'Aye, an' our wee Robert's for the Convent nursery. I don't know what the nuns'll make of him. They'll have a job stopping him talking.'

'They'll slap him. The nuns are horrible if you misbehave, but Mary Carney says they don't do that at the grammar. I just hope I like it.'

'Sure an' ye'll take to it like a duck to water,' Kitty told her confidently. 'Ye'll soon get used to travellin' into the city every day along with the other girls in your class that won the scholarship.'

'I'd feel happier if Lily was going with me.' Molly and Lily had barely spent a day apart in all of Molly's eleven years.

Kitty started on the second plait. 'Aye, it's sad that Lily didn't pass the exam but ye did, my girl, so make the most of it. I'm proud as punch for ye.' She tied a bright green ribbon into a bow at the end of the braid then tugged at the ends of both plaits. 'Now, off ye go, an' while you're out there, keep an eye out for that rapscallion of a wee brother of yours.' Molly jumped off the stool ready to run, but before she reached the door, her mother delivered further instructions.

'If you see our Patrick, tell him he's not to go wandering off on his bike, an' see that our Robert doesn't go out of the lane.' Robert was John's son and John had been over the moon when Kitty had given birth to him a year after their wedding.

Molly pulled her face and jittered by the door. She was well aware that Patrick paid her no heed even if he was a year younger than her, and as for little Robert, she'd need eyes in the back of her head to keep him out of mischief. Four-year-olds could be a proper pain at times.

'Can I go now?' she said, and before Kitty had time to answer, she was off.

Kitty crossed to the sink under the window in the bright, airy kitchen and watched her daughter dart across the lane, her plaits swinging and her legs pumping under the skirt of her blue checked summer frock as she bounced up to the Stubbses' back door then disappeared inside.

Kitty turned the tap and as water gushed into the sink, she smiled wistfully. It seemed no time at all since Molly was a babe in arms and they were living in number eleven. Now, here she was in her not so new home, looking out onto her past. She shook her head then began clearing the breakfast dishes from the table.

Back over at the sink, Kitty saw the Stubbses' back door open. Molly and Lily came out and stood on the steps. Deep in conversation, they had their heads together, Molly's as black as a raven's wings and Lily's a tangle of fiery red curls. Kitty compared her daughter's pretty, tanned face and flashing blue eyes to Lily's pale complexion and rather flat features. That her mother thought Molly was the lovelier of the two girls was not merely maternal bias. Molly was a beauty by anybody's reckoning. She was also blessed with a lively mind. As Molly talked, Lily's face lit up. She nodded in agreement and then they were off, haring down the garden path, up the lane and out of sight.

Kitty washed and wiped the dishes and was putting them into the cupboards when she heard the lobby door open.

'Is there anybody here to give a dying woman a cuppa?' Maggie called out, slouching into the kitchen looking decidedly frazzled. Her hair was in curlers, and the crossover pinny that she wore when she was mending lengths of worsted was dotted with bits of fluff.

'Always,' said Kitty, lighting the gas under the kettle.

'What's up with ye this morning?' she asked as she spooned leaves into the teapot. 'Ye look like ye've been dragged through a hedge backwards.'

'I've been up since six doing one of me pieces,' Maggie groaned. 'I'm behind with me rent so I've taken on extra, and Holroyd's are collecting it today.' She flopped into a chair at the table and lit a cigarette.

Kitty had heard it all before. Maggie was always chasing her tail. She brought the teapot and two cups to the table and sat down, ready to listen to her friend's latest woes.

Maggie's moans were interrupted as the door burst open. Molly and Lily tumbled in, closely followed by Patrick and Robert. Kitty got up to dole out four glasses of Tizer and some custard creams.

'We saw that girl who's come to live at Mavis's,' Molly said.

'She was looking out of my bedroom window,' Patrick piped,

meaning the room he'd slept in when Molly had scarlet fever.

'Yeah, I waved but she didn't wave back,' Lily scorned.

'That's 'cos she's a stuck-up, snotty mare,' Maggie sneered.

'Now, Maggie, you don't know that,' Kitty chided.

'Is she going to live with Auntie Mavis forever?' Robert asked. He was Mavis's favourite and he didn't like the idea of being usurped by a drippy girl.

'We'll have to wait and see,' said Kitty, ruffling his hair and smiling into his big brown eyes that were so like his father's.

The glasses empty and the biscuits demolished, Molly suggested that they go out and play hopscotch. Patrick gave her a disdainful look and announced he was going to play football with Mickey O'Malley.

Lily tossed her bright red hair. 'I'd rather play football,' she said, looking challengingly at Molly.

'Is that 'cos you fancy Mickey O'Malley?'

'Eh! Don't you be sayin' that,' Lily snapped, giving Molly a push. The girls were the best of friends most of the time but whereas quick-witted Molly was kind and amiable, Lily had her mother's rough, tough temperament and was inclined to be feckless and quarrelsome.

'Only sayin' what's true,' Molly teased, her flashing blue eyes and charming, placatory smile so like Tom's that Kitty's heart flipped.

'Bugger off, the lot of you,' Maggie said waving her hand dismissively through a cloud of cigarette smoke. 'Leave me an' your mam in peace.'

Patrick darted off, Robert at his heels. Molly made to follow but Lily paused and glared at her mother. 'There's no need to swear an' shout,' she retorted cheekily before strutting out of the kitchen.

Maggie glowered. 'The cheeky mare.'

'I wonder who she takes after?'

'I hope you don't mean me!' Maggie's mock horror turned to raucous laughter.

'It never crossed my mind,' said Kitty, innocently fluttering her eyelashes as she refreshed their cups. Left in peace, the two old friends continued gossiping.

The late August sun streamed through the large window, lighting the heads of the two women, Kitty's red-gold curls a rosy halo and Maggie's bleached blonde locks wound tightly round her curlers. They were very different in appearance and temperament, Kitty being the shorter of the two, with a shapely figure, very pretty features and a wise head on her shoulders. Maggie, on the other hand, was taller and heavier and carelessly put together in both body and mind. Yet the hearts of these thirty-two-year-old mothers beat to the same drum.

During the past thirteen years, they had stuck together through thick and thin, commiserating their misfortunes and rejoicing when times were good. And now, in the late summer of 1929, as they chatted, things couldn't have been better. Kitty was happily married to John and settled in the home that was her pride and joy, with her three beautiful children, and Maggie, who had suffered terribly at the hands of her drunken husband, Fred, had a new man in her life.

'Tell me, how are things going with you an' Pete?' Kitty sat back to listen. Her kitchen, just like the one in number eleven had been before she moved, was the place they shared all their hopes, dreams, troubles and secrets.

Maggie related what she knew about Peter Harper. Kitty thought it didn't sound much but every now and then she made suitable comments.

'I'd given up hope of getting a regular chap – well, I say regular – he still goes off for days on end on that driving job of his, like,' Maggie remarked dolefully.

'But he always comes back,' Kitty said encouragingly. 'He must want to.'

'Yeah, I suppose you're right,' said Maggie, somewhat cheered. 'It's just that I've got to the stage when I can't believe in anything any more.'

'How about believing that this year I'll be thirty-two! I feel positively ancient,' Kitty said, pulling a face but still managing to look much younger than her years.

'You've changed your tune. It's not two years ago you were telling me life begins at thirty.'

Kitty grinned. 'Aye, I did, but I was just trying to cheer you up.'

'Well, you didn't,' Maggie groused, getting up to leave.

* * *

'Done yer gossiping then?' Vi Bottomley's caustic remark had no effect on her daughter as Maggie strolled into her own kitchen. Vi was a tawdry-looking woman not yet fifty, and without the make-up she slapped on to go to her job in the Wagon and Horses public house, she looked even older. Maggie gave her a disparaging glance and crossed the kitchen, ready to go into the front room where her mending frame awaited her attention.

Vi looked pained and irritably flicked ash from her cigarette into a saucer on the table. 'Where's our Lily? I'm on me last fag,' she whined. 'I need her to go to the shop for me.' Intent on ignoring her mother, Maggie opened the door into the hallway. 'Is he coming back here tonight or has he somewhere better to be?' Vi continued, her sneering remark bringing Maggie up sharp. Her mother neither liked nor trusted Pete Harper.

Maggie flushed uncomfortably and mumbled, 'He has a long-distance trip and won't be back till Monday.'

'So he says,' Vi scoffed. 'He's playin' you for a mug, you silly mare. You're just somebody to hop into bed with when there's nuthin' else on offer.' She gave a nasty cackle that ended in a choking cough, phlegm rattling in her throat.

'You're just jealous 'cos nobody wants to get into bed with you,' Maggie spat, flouncing through the door and slamming it behind her.

Stamping into the front room, she glowered at her mending frame and the taut length of cloth with its yellow chalk marks indicating the flaws waiting to be mended. Tears sprang to her eyes. Pete did come and go as he pleased, his job as a chauffeur giving him an excuse for his frequent absences, and he'd yet to offer her any money towards the rent or the food he consumed. Deep inside, she couldn't help thinking that there might be some truth in her mam's words. But Maggie wasn't ready to believe that.

* * *

Three doors up, in Mavis Robson's back bedroom Rosamund moved her aching head restlessly, trying to find some ease on her damp pillow. Last night, she had cried herself empty, and she now regretted the lies she had told Mavis. She was a good, kind woman and deserved better, but instead of being honest, Rosamund had embroidered the untruths she had already told her.

Lying on her bed staring at the ceiling, her head full of tangled thoughts, she wished she could retract her words. Down below, she heard the back door open and close and the sound of muffled voices: a man and a woman. It must be Mavis and Jack, she thought. Were they talking about her?

She thumped the pillow in vexation, chastising herself for not simply owning up to coming from Buckinghamshire, and that her father was a wealthy landowner and home a mansion with a fleet of servants to take care of every need. Instead, she'd pretended to be an ordinary working girl living in London and working in an office where she had met the scurrilous Lewis Aston.

Behind closed eyes, she saw his charming smile, and imagined she heard his soft, persuasive voice. She sat bolt upright, sickened by the feelings coursing through her veins. He'd tricked her, made a fool of her, and in the rosy bubble he'd created from the very first time she had met him in the stables where he had been employed by her father, she'd happily believed every word he had spoken.

They had ridden out together, Rosamund on her beloved Flicker and Lewis on one of the string of horses her father owned, finding secluded places to linger and for Lewis to work his magic. It was their secret, and so exciting that Rosamund lived in anticipation of each outing. Being an only child, her one brother dying of diphtheria when he was ten and she eight, her father had cosseted her all the more, and her cold, stony-faced mother had blamed her for still being alive. Rosamund had been home-schooled by a spinster tutor with no more experience of life than her, her world so narrow that the life Lewis had offered was beyond her wildest dreams. On the day he told her he was leaving, they had been lying in a leafy hollow, his lips making her crazy with desire, and she had begged him to take her with him.

Lewis had neglected to tell her his reason for going was that her father had sacked him for thieving. They hatched a plan and the next day, on the pretext of wanting to buy her mother a birthday gift, she had withdrawn a tidy sum of money from her bank account. That night, she had sneaked out, taking the money, her jewellery and a few clothes – travel light, Lewis had said – thrilled to be embarking on a whole new life. She hadn't given a thought to where they would go or how they would live. She'd never before had to consider such things.

It was only when they arrived at the Adelphi Hotel in Liverpool that she realised the enormity of what she was doing. She'd stood shame-faced and nervous as Lewis booked them in as man and wife, feeling sure that the desk clerk saw them for what they were. And whilst she had willingly submitted to his fondling in their secret places in the woods and fields, sharing a bed with him somehow seemed wrong.

In their hotel room, Lewis had slowly undressed her, kissing parts of her body that had never been kissed before. Wretched with desire, she'd watched as he stripped off his own clothes. She had never seen a naked man, or been naked herself in the presence of one, and when he pushed her roughly onto the bed, she had known that she couldn't say no to the step he was about to take. But it had been painful and disgusting. He had plunged into her, telling her he loved her over and again, but instead of experiencing something intensely beautiful, it had been ugly and painful, and in her mind's eye all she could see was her father's loving face, aghast with shock and disappointment. It was soon over and she had tried to convince herself things would get better. Lewis loved her and she loved him, and nothing else mattered.

But things hadn't got better. She couldn't prevent herself from flinching when he tried to make love to her again, and he had grown tetchy, then downright angry, accusing her of being a silly little girl. On the second night of their stay, she had woken to find him and her money and jewellery gone, along with all her foolish hopes and dreams.

Now, on Mavis's spare bed, she hugged her knees to her chest, and resting her chin on them, she struggled to think of a way out of the whole sorry mess. She heard the back door slam. Jack must have gone home. Rosamund slid off the bed.

Mavis was filling the kettle when Rosamund arrived in the kitchen. She turned and smiled. 'Feeling better, are you?' Rosamund managed a smile. 'I'm making tea, would you like a cup?' Mavis placed the kettle on the hob. Rosamund sat down at the table. When the tea was made, Mavis sat across from her, and as they nursed their cups, Mavis asked, 'Have you thought about what you're going to do, Rose?'

Rosamund nodded. Then, her voice wobbling pathetically, she said, 'With your permission... I'd like to stay a few days longer.' Raising her limpid eyes to meet Mavis's, she added, almost in a whisper, 'I promise not to be a burden.'

She reminded Mavis of a beaten puppy.

'Right,' said Mavis, unsure that this was what she had wanted to hear.

* * *

'She's stopping another night, then.' Jack sounded distinctly opposed to the news when Mavis popped in to see him that evening.

'Yes, there doesn't seem much else for it for the time being.'

'You're makin' a rod for your own back,' Jack grumbled. 'You've said yourself she's not being honest with you, that you think there's something fishy about her. That doesn't sit well with me. I can't pretend to know what her game is, but I don't like it. She could be taking you for a mug. You're too soft by half, Mavis Robson.' He saw the glint of protest in Mavis's eyes and shrugged. 'Aye, well, don't be pandering to her every whim because before you know it, she'll be walking all over you.'

'I'm not that foolish,' Mavis said tersely. 'I'll give her no more than room and board, and maybe I'll lend a friendly ear and throw in some sound advice, but that's about the height of it.'

'Aye, well, make sure you find time for yourself – an' for me,' he said with a rueful smile.

'I'll always find time for you, Jack,' Mavis assured him fondly.

8

'There's an egg for breakfast,' Mavis said the next morning when Rosamund came downstairs into the kitchen. She was cleaning out the ashes from the fireplace. Sitting back on her heels, she added, 'You can have it either boiled, scrambled or fried, the pans are on the shelf and there's lard and milk in the cupboard.' She tipped a shovelful of ashes into the bucket, dust motes swirling and dancing in the pale sunlight shining through the window.

'Thank you very much, that will be lovely.'

Mavis got to her feet and lifted the bucket of ashes before glancing at Rosamund sitting at the table, patiently waiting to be served. Mavis raised her eyes to the heavens. *She's clearly not used to doing things for herself*, she thought, recalling the wet towels in the bathroom; one draped over the bath and the other in a heap behind the door.

Leaving the bucket by the door, she washed her hands and repeated the offer.

'Scrambled, please,' Rosamund replied.

Maybe I'm misjudging her. Perhaps she's doesn't want to appear too familiar in a stranger's house, Mavis thought, breaking an egg into a bowl and adding a blob of margarine and a drop of milk. 'You can toast the bread if you like,' she said, whisking the mixture and pouring it into a pan on the gas ring.

'Can I?' Rosamund said, sounding very unsure, and Mavis thinking *it's bread you're toasting, not flying to the moon.*

Mavis handed her the toasting fork. Rosamund took hold tentatively, looking at it as though she had never before seen one. 'Sit close to the fire,' Mavis instructed, and when Rosamund complied, she handed her a slice of bread. 'Hold it near the red part, not in the flames, otherwise it'll get sooty.'

Rosamund crouched forward, the hand holding the fork shaking, and in between stirring the egg and making a pot of tea, Mavis kept a close on eye on the proceedings. When the bread was browned on one side, she said, 'Turn it round and do the other side.'

Rosamund fumbled with the bread, and when it was toasted, she brought it to the table. 'I've never done that before,' she said, looking and sounding amazed by her success. 'It's rather clever, isn't it?'

'Very,' Mavis said dryly. 'You see, you learn something new every day.'

'I hope I'm not being too much trouble,' Rosamund said, contrite.

'Not at all,' said Mavis, her kind heart going out to the girl.

Breakfast over, Rosamund left the table, murmuring her thanks but making no attempt to clear her cup and plates or wash them. She dithered uncertainly as Mavis attended to them and a few other necessary chores, including emptying the ashes in the bin outside and then washing the dusty hearth.

'Don't you have someone to do that for you?' Rosamund asked innocently, and sounding rather concerned.

Mavis's eyebrows shot up into her hairline. What kind of a life had this girl been used to? Not one in a working-class household, that's for sure. She decided that they needed to have a good talk. If the girl was being honest about having no money to go elsewhere, then she wouldn't expect her to leave immediately, but if she were to stay then some ground rules would have to be laid out and serious words about long-term prospects exchanged.

Mavis had had her breakfast a good two hours before Rosamund, and feeling in need of a boost for what she was about to do, she made a fresh pot of tea. Rosamund was sitting in the armchair hugging the fire, and after handing her a cup, Mavis sat down in the other. Rosamund was gazing intently into the flames, and Mavis was just about to ask some pertinent questions when the back door opened.

'Morning to ye both, an' God bless all in the house,' Kitty chirped as she entered the kitchen.

Mavis turned. 'Good morning to you, Kitty,' she said, smiling, yet feeling annoyed at the interruption. The questions she'd been about to ask melted on her tongue and she felt somewhat cheated.

'I just popped in to get the biscuits. I'm on my way to the café to give Bridie a hand,' said Kitty. 'It being Saturday, it might be busy.'

'Would you like a cup to help you on your way?' Mavis fetched another cup.

'Don't mind if I do.'

'This is Kitty Sykes from the house across the lane,' Mavis said, addressing Rosamund, 'and this is Rose Brown, Kitty. She's staying with me for a day or two.'

Kitty smiled at Rosamund and received a shy response. Mavis filled Kitty's cup and after handing it over, she went to the sideboard and took out two large, square tins. 'Ginger snaps and oatmeal puffs,' she said, placing them on the table.

'Lovely,' said Kitty, chuckling as she added, 'they sell like hot cakes.' She took her purse from her coat pocket and laid out some coins.

'Kitty owns a café on the riverbank behind the church at the top of the street,' Mavis explained. 'I do a bit of baking for her each week.'

'An' I don't know what I'd do if she didn't,' Kitty said, addressing Rosamund. 'It's Mavis's delicious buns and biscuits brings the customers in.'

Kitty turned to Mavis. 'Business's been rotten this week what with the weather being so up an' down. Too many wet days. What is it they say? It never rains but it pours.'

'I know what you mean, Kitty,' said Mavis, reminded that a pouring wet day was the reason for Rosamund being here. Not that she really regretted it, but Jack's warning had struck a chord and she did wonder if she'd bitten off more than she could chew.

Kitty got to her feet. 'I'd best be on me way. Ta for the tea, Mavis. Enjoy your stay in Edge Hill, Rose.'

'We'll call at the café after we've been for a walk,' Mavis said, thinking that a walk on the towpath would be a good way of passing the time with her strangely quiet visitor. The poor girl didn't seem to know how to behave in company. In fact, she'd looked at everyone she'd met so far as though they were from a different planet. Mavis's curiosity was burning on her tongue.

'She's a wonderful woman is Kitty,' she said after Kitty had left. 'She's had some terrible disappointments in life, but she always comes back fighting. And there's nothing she wouldn't do for you.' Mavis sat down again. 'It's funny, really. She helped make Weaver Street the friendly place it is.' She paused. 'I've lived here all my life, and whilst I was on friendly terms with everybody, I didn't really know them and they didn't know me. Then along came Kitty – that was in 1916 – and she threw a Christmas party that brought all the neighbours together.' She smiled fondly. 'That's when Jack and I became the good friends we are, and ever since then, everyone at this end of the street has stuck together.'

'You said she'd suffered terrible disappointments,' Rosamund said, wondering if they were as horrible as her own. 'She looks happy enough now.'

'Oh, she is, and that's because she's strong. She didn't allow herself to wallow in grief and let it ruin her life.' She gave Rosamund a meaningful look.

'What happened to her?'

Mavis cheered inwardly. She'd managed to capture Rosamund's interest.

'She was married to the most handsome, charming man I've ever come across. Sadly, he wasted his charms on people he thought would elevate his position in life. He was a bookmaker and spent a great deal of his time at the racetracks. He got involved with what you might call the racing elite. He wanted to be one of them, so Kitty told me. He had an affair with the daughter of a wealthy man who owned a racing stable near York. Kitty was heartbroken. She truly loved Tom Conlon.' Mavis got to her feet to mend the fire.

'Then what happened?' To hear that she wasn't the only woman to be hurt by an unfaithful man lit a spark in Rosamund's troubled mind.

'He was beaten to death in the alley behind the Weaver's Arms,' Mavis said, clanking the scuttle back on the hearth and shaking her head despairingly.

Rosamund gasped. 'Murdered! That's shocking.'

'Yes, it is,' Mavis agreed, leaning on the mantelpiece as if she required some support. 'And even though Kitty's sure he was planning on leaving her that night and she'd have had to do without him anyway, it didn't make it easier to bear. To lose him in that fashion was absolutely devastating. They never did find his assailants,' she continued, plumping back into her chair. 'The police thought it was either a robbery gone wrong or that he had fallen foul of some of the shady characters he mixed with at the racetracks. Whatever!' she said on her breath, pressing her palms together and her hands to her lips. 'It was terrible, but Kitty rebuilt her life, and now she's married to a lovely man, and between them they have three beautiful children. Molly and Patrick are Tom's and young Robert is John's.' Mavis sat back in her chair. 'Now what about you, Rose?'

Rosamund pursed her lips together and frowned. 'I don't know what to say.'

'You could start by telling me the truth, love.' Mavis sounded like a schoolmarm. 'If you're going to stay with me until you get back on your feet, I think I have a right to know more about you.' She sat back, ready to listen. Rosamund blushed and nodded. Then she took a deep breath.

'I'm deeply ashamed to admit I've been sparing with the truth,' she began. 'My name is Rosamund Brown-Allsop. My father's the squire of Heathcote Manor in Buckinghamshire but...' her voice quickened, 'I didn't tell you that in case you thought me a silly rich girl – which I am – and withdrew your offer to help me.'

Rosamund flushed uncomfortably.

Mavis snorted. 'That was rather snobbish of you. I may be working class but that doesn't mean I limit my compassion.' Two angry spots stained her cheeks.

Rosamund hung her head. 'I know, and I'm sorry. You have been more than kind. But I was so afraid that I didn't know what to do,' she cried hysterically, her shoulders heaving as she sobbed into her hands.

Taking pity on her, Mavis said, 'Look, love, we'll leave it for now. Pull yourself together and dry your eyes. Crying never solved anything.' She got to her feet and began clattering dishes into the sink.

In the afternoon, Mavis suggested that they go for a walk. Rosamund's fashionable little hat was beyond repair after getting soaked, but her coat had dried out. Mavis handed her a head-square. 'Here, put this on. It can get breezy down by the river.' Rosamund looked with misgiving at the flowered piece of cloth then shoved it in her pocket: only common women wore head-scarves – or so her mother said. Mavis glanced doubtfully at Rosamund's soft leather shoes. Wrinkled and mottled with rain spots, their little pointed heels were totally unsuitable for walking any distance. 'What size shoe do you take?' Mavis asked.

Startled, Rosamund glanced down at her feet. 'A five,' she said.

'Then you'll have to make do with them. Mine are size three,' Mavis replied.

They walked up Weaver Street past spindly plane trees growing in little plots cut out of the pavements on either side of the street: Rosamund thought of the giant oaks and towering poplars in the grounds surrounding her own rambling home. Here, even the houses and the trees seemed drab and diminished.

'This is my church, St Joseph's,' Mavis said as they drew level with a pair of wrought-iron gates at the end of a driveway leading up to a fine gothic building with a squat tower. Rhododendrons bordered the driveway, and beech and ash trees grew here and there in the graveyard.

'This end of the street is much nicer than where you live,' Rosamund said, her eyes scanning the larger detached dwellings facings the church.

'It may well look it, but appearances aren't everything,' said Mavis, her curt retort implying that she preferred her end of the street. Rosamund flushed, aware that she had sounded snobbish. 'Down there's Mill Street,' Mavis continued, pointing to the left, 'and that huge monstrosity with the chimney is Holroyd's Mill. They manufacture woollen cloth. We're going this way.' She moved to the right and then a down a shallow flight of ancient stone steps. 'This is the towpath.'

'It's lovely,' Rosamund exclaimed as they walked by the river, its banks bright with wildflowers. Willow wands dangled in the shallows, and moorhens careened over the surface of the misty, green water. 'Who'd have thought there was somewhere like this so near to those drab little houses at the other end of the street.'

'Those drab little houses are home,' Mavis retorted through clenched teeth.

Rosamund flushed. 'I... I'm sorry. I... I didn't mean to offend you. I just wasn't expecting anything as picturesque as this is.'

'We have some beautiful scenery in Lancashire,' Mavis said, and probing for more information than she had already been given, she added, 'Is it pretty where you come from?'

'Oh, yes, we have...' Rosamund gushed, and then clamped her lips as if to stop them running away from her. 'It's very pleasant,' she mumbled, deciding it was unwise to describe the mansion's grandeur.

They crossed the bridge to the opposite towpath and walked on, Mavis commenting on the variety of little birds that flitted from tree to tree. Coming to another bridge, they crossed it, and as they neared the steps they had used to access the towpath, they arrived at Kitty's café.

'Oh, this is delightful,' Rosamund declared, gazing at the jaunty blue and white striped wooden building with blue and white checked curtains at the windows. In the past three years, Kitty had extended it to include a veranda overlooking the river, and an extension to the side allowed a larger seating area.

'Are we going in?' Rosamund asked. Mavis led the way, the delicious aroma of hot coffee, cocoa and freshly baked rolls filling their noses.

Kitty greeted them cheerily. Only four of the twelve tables were occupied by customers tucking into sandwiches and pastries.

'You've arrived at a good time,' she said when they were seated. 'It's not busy. Now, what can I get you?'

'I'll have tea and a bun,' said Mavis. 'What about you, Rose?'

'I'll have the same, thank you.' Her cheeks reddened. Would she be expected to pay? To her relief, Mavis intervened.

'My treat,' she said with an understanding smile.

'No, these are on me,' Kitty said, whisking away and telling Bridie that she'd see to the order. She returned minutes later with three steaming mugs and a plate of ginger snaps. She sat down beside them. 'Well, Rose, are ye enjoying your visit?'

Rosamund was growing quite used to being addressed as Rose by now – after all, her father had sometimes call her that when he was feeling affectionate. She told Kitty about their walk on the riverbank, but when her cup was empty, she asked to be excused. 'May I go for a walk?'

Mavis nodded. 'Don't go too far. I don't want to have to come and find you again.' Rosamund's lips twitched into a little smile.

After she had gone, Kitty said, 'I've never heard you mention Rose before.'

'That's because I've only just met her.' Mavis grimaced then explained how she came to be staying with her.

'Poor girl.' Kitty paused to wave to two departing customers. 'So where's she from?'

Mavis sighed. 'Somewhere rather grand in Buckinghamshire. She's certainly not working class. That girl's never done a hand's turn in her life.' She told Kitty about the wet towels dumped in the bathroom and how she'd sat waiting to be served breakfast. 'She even asked me if I didn't employ someone to clean the ashes out of the fire.'

Kitty burst out laughing. 'Maggie said she looked posh and that her suitcase must have cost a fortune. That coat she has on was surely expensive, and ye can tell by the way she talks that she's been well reared.'

'She might talk fancy but she's not much good at lying,' Mavis sneered. 'She told me a pack of lies to begin with and...' she giggled, 'and as she told 'em, she looked as though she'd just solved the riddle of the sphinx. I got a bit more of the truth out of her this morning but it ended up with her sobbing her heart out, so I let it go for the time being. All round, she's a bit of a mystery.'

'Do ye believe the bit about her being penniless, or is that just another fib?' Kitty asked, her brow creasing. She didn't want her friend to be duped.

'Oh, yes, I believe that. She wouldn't have sold her diamond ear studs otherwise. I think the chap she was with is the sort that preys on vulnerable, silly girls. He's most likely done that sort of thing before. The problem is, what do I do with her?'

A group of hikers tramped into the café. 'Sorry, I'll have to go and help Bridie. We'll talk later,' said Kitty, leaving Mavis to ponder her quandary.

Not long after she had married John, Kitty had rented out number eleven to Bridie O'Malley and her family. She'd liked Bridie from the moment she and her husband, Mick, had called to enquire about it. 'You're Irish,' Bridie had said when Kitty let them in.

'Roscommon,' Kitty had divulged, 'and you?'

'Sligo. We're not long off the boat.'

Kitty had showed them the house.

Afterwards, John had laughed when Kitty told him, 'I like the O'Malleys best out of the three couples we've seen so far.'

'That's because yer ould Irish heartstrings are rulin' yer head,' he'd replied, mocking her Irish accent.

''Tis not,' Kitty had exclaimed. 'Sure, that middle-aged couple did nothin' but find fault and wanted the rent reducin', and the Methodist minister and his wife seemed awfully sanctimonious.'

'They'd be a safer bet for paying the rent.'

'Maybe, but Mick has a good job as a bricklayer, an' I want to like the people I rent it to. I have a good feelin' about 'em,' Kitty had insisted.

A few days later, the O'Malleys and their three sons aged between six and fourteen moved in.

When Bridie told her that she was looking for a job and that she had been the under cook in a grand house in Sligo, Kitty had offered to let her try out for the job of running the café. Her gut instinct had proved her right: the O'Malleys were a boon.

'Molly's for the girls' grammar on Monday morning, bless her,' Kitty said as she made ham sandwiches for the hikers.

'Aye, our Mickey's for the Christian Brothers at the Sacred Heart. He's not lookin' happy about it, him not being one for edification,' Bridie said as she loaded a tray with cups, saucers and a teapot.

'Ach, he'll soon settle to it,' Kitty assured her, at the same time hoping that her Molly would like her new school and not find the daily journey into the city too taxing. In between serving customers, the women's chat continued.

'Mind you,' said Bridie, 'neither Liam nor Donal are scholars. Liam's goin' into the building with his da and Donal when he leaves school at Christmas.' She put the sandwiches on the tray. ''Tis only our Mickey has the brains, but he just doesn't like being told what to do. He says school's boring.'

Bridie delivered the tray to the table by the window overlooking the river. When she came back to the counter, Kitty said,

'Kids grow up fast these days. Before ye know it, they're leavin' school an' going out into the big world to make their own way.' The women exchanged rueful glances at the thought of their offspring growing up and moving away.

Rosamund arrived back from her walk, her cheeks glowing.

'Sorry I didn't get much chance for us to have a longer wee chat, Rose.' Kitty smiled at Rosamund, and at that moment, Rosamund decided that from now on she would only think of herself as Rose. Everyone she'd met so far called her by that name and she liked it; Rosamund Brown-Allsop belonged in the past.

Kitty waved them off, and Mavis and Rose walked back to Weaver Street.

'Look, I've been thinking,' Mavis said, once they were back indoors and sitting by the fire. 'If you want to go back home, I'll give you the money for your fare.'

Rose blanched, her pale grey eyes widening with fear. Tears threatened. She blinked them away rapidly. 'I can't go back! It would just create more trouble for me,' she cried, her voice rising and her tears spilling over.

'Then what will you do?' Mavis asked gently.

'I don't know,' Rose whispered, looking wildly into Mavis's face, her own so desperate that it wrenched Mavis's heart. She made another impulsive decision.

'Look at it like this then,' she said kindly, 'if you don't feel that you can return home straight away you can stay with me until such times as you're ready, but...' she hardened her tone, 'you'll have to pull yourself together. I don't want you moping about the place wallowing in your mistakes.' She gave Rose a stern glare.

'For a start, you can put your troubles behind you, take them as a lesson learned.'

Rose nodded, her bottom lip quivering pitifully.

'I gather you've led a rather privileged life up till now,' Mavis continued, 'but from now on, you can begin by showing a bit more backbone. I can't be doing with waiting on you hand and foot, so make yourself useful and give me a hand with the chores, and...' she paused to give Rose another stern look, 'if you're worried about having no money, go out and earn some. That way, you won't feel as though you're accepting charity, you'll be a paying guest.' Mavis smiled encouragingly.

Rose gaped, her amazement almost comical. 'Work? What kind of work?' Her cheeks turned bright red. 'I... I've never actually...' She floundered pathetically.

'Done anything of the sort,' Mavis cut in, 'but if the situation at home is so bad that you're afraid to go back – and I can see you are – then I suggest you start by standing on your own two feet. Prove to yourself and others that you have something to offer, that you can turn your life around regardless of what's happened.' She smiled. 'Let's face it, it's not as if you've committed murder. Your only crime was being young, foolish and in love.' She got to her feet. 'Now dry your eyes and go and clean up the mess you left in the bathroom this morning, and I'll make the tea.'

Sobbing copiously, Rose trudged upstairs.

Later that evening, once Rose had taken herself up to her room complaining of a headache, Mavis decided to pop round to Kitty's. As she was leaving the house, Jack appeared on his doorstep.

'Are you coming round to see me?' he asked, smiling broadly.

'Actually, I'm on my way to Kitty's,' Mavis said, sorry to see his smile slip. 'I'll come round to yours later. Rose's lying down with a headache.'

'You're intent on letting her stay then,' Jack growled, limping towards her and leaning on the wall that separated her garden from his. As briefly as she could, Mavis told him why.

His brow furrowed, and he rubbed his jaw fretfully. 'I think you're making a big mistake,' he said. 'You're letting your kind heart rule your head.'

'Maybe I am,' Mavis said, and began walking. 'I'll see you later.'

* * *

'Ye've certainly given her something to think about,' Kitty said, after Mavis had related what she had said to Rose.

'I'd have told her to pack her bags an' bugger off,' Maggie said, blowing out a stream of smoke and jabbing her cigarette authoritatively at Mavis. 'If she can't be bothered to be honest with you, she doesn't deserve helping.'

'Jack's of the same opinion,' Mavis said wearily, 'but there's something sorely troubling that girl, and I can't just throw her to the dogs.' She sipped her tea pensively. 'We'll wait and see how thing develop.'

'She'll most likely come to her senses and go home,' Kitty said, remembering a time when she thought she might have to leave Weaver Street. She had been filled with panic as to where she would go with two small children if Tom sold the house from under them. Would she have gone back to Ireland? she wondered. Pushing the memory aside, she said, 'And if she doesn't, you might end up having to make her go.'

9

_____

'Yoo-hoo, Kitty! We're home,' Beth Forsythe called out as she let herself in through Kitty's back door. She had just returned from a brief visit to Scotland with her husband and four-year-old son, Stuart. After years of hoping and praying, Beth's desire to be a mother had been fulfilled and Stuart had been born just weeks before Kitty had given birth to Robert.

Kitty put down her rolling pin and clapped her floury hands, shaking off flakes of pastry. 'Good to see ye,' she said, beaming at her friend. 'Give us a tick to get these in the oven, then I'll put the kettle on.'

Beth sat at the table. 'What are you making?' she asked, peering into a bowl filled with a mixture of potato, carrots, onions and mince.

'A few Cornish pasties,' Kitty said, cutting the rolled-out pastry into rectangles, 'though why I'm bothering, I don't know. What with the rotten weather, it's hardly worth opening the café these days.' She spooned the filling onto the rectangles and then deftly nipped the pastry together to seal it in.

'It was pretty awful in Scotland too, lots of mist and colder than it is here. It seemed rather fitting for the occasion,' Beth said mournfully.

Kitty made the tea and set it on the table. 'Enough about the weather,' she said as she sat down, 'how did ye get on in Scotland?'

'It was dreadfully sad, but at least we arrived in time for Blair to say goodbye to his grandfather. He's terribly cut up about it,' Beth said, stirring sugar into her tea and then taking a sip. 'The funeral was a grand affair, bagpipers, men in kilts and a huge procession. Ruari Forsythe was a popular man.'

'It sounds as though you gave him a good send-off then,' Kitty said. 'He was very fond of Blair, wasn't he?' She put her head on one side and smiled at Beth. 'Wasn't it he who gave you the money to get married and buy the house?'

'It was,' Beth said, smiling wistfully at the memory, 'and if you hadn't been the good friend you are I don't suppose I'd ever have married and had a home of my own, let alone a beautiful son.' She reached across the table and squeezed Kitty's hand. For a moment, the women quietly sipped their tea. Kitty had been a big help in bringing shy, browbeaten Beth out of her shell, and Beth would always be grateful for her intervention.

'Now then,' Kitty said, setting down her cup. 'Let me tell you what you've missed while you've been away. Mavis has a lodger.'

'A lodger! Who?' Beth exclaimed, her eyes growing round as Kitty related what she knew about Rose.

'And you say Mavis thinks she's afraid to go back home. Poor girl.' Beth shuddered. She knew all about being afraid. Her father had been a bully.

'It seems like it,' Kitty said, 'but what she'll do for the rest of the time she's here, goodness knows. She can't expect Mavis to keep her, but she's been here a week an' more an' still hasn't gone out looking for work.'

'She'll be lucky to find a job in the present climate,' Beth said primly.

'It'll be a miracle if she finds one an' keeps it. Mavis says she's useless when it comes to doing housework. She even asked Mavis why she didn't employ someone to do the heavy work.'

Beth laughed. 'She must be used to better things.' She would have asked more questions about the newcomer had the door not opened and John walked in with Patrick and Robert. Kitty got to her feet.

'I picked this ruffian up from school,' said John, giving Patrick a playful punch on the shoulder. 'Saved him having to walk, and this one...' John gave a mock groan and flicked Robert's hair before winking at Beth, 'I've had him with me all afternoon.' He slipped off his jacket then pecked Kitty's cheek, Kitty explaining for Beth's sake that John had taken Robert with him to Kirby to buy wire for the factory.

'Is Stewpot... I mean Stuart home, Auntie Beth?' Robert and Beth's son were the best of friends.

'He is, love, he's with his dad. Go across and see him. He's brought you back some Edinburgh rock.' Robert whooped and hared back out again. Patrick's lips pouted and Kitty caught his hand and squeezed it, an impish twinkle in her eye. 'Don't sulk, love, there's some Black Jacks in me shopping bag. Go an' get one.' Mollified, Patrick stuffed a sweet in his mouth, and with a handful for later, he went up to his room to study. *He thinks he's all grown up, but he's still my wee serious boy at heart*, Kitty thought as she watched him go.

'How was Scotland?' John asked, going to wash his hands in the sink. Beth told him about the funeral. 'I suppose this one's been filling you in on all the latest gossip,' he said, drying his hands and then flicking Kitty's rump with the towel.

'What! Me, gossip! Wherever did ye get that idea?' Kitty cried, snatching the towel from his hand and flicking it against his broad chest. He caught her in his arms and kissed her roundly.

Beth grinned at their antics. They were still as much in love as they had been when they had married, and she thought how different John was from Tom Conlon, and how happy he made Kitty.

'What's that burning?' John said, sniffing the air.

'Oh, Jesus, Mary and Joseph,' Kitty cried, 'I forgot the pasties.'

'And you say you weren't gossiping,' scoffed John.

'I'm off,' Beth said, 'before I get the blame.'

* * *

'Have you been sitting reading all day?' Mavis asked as she came in from work. It was a week and four days since she'd taken Rose in. Rose jumped to her feet, dropping the book into the chair.

'The fire's nearly out,' Mavis said, throwing coal from the bucket onto the embers. She didn't want to feel annoyed, and yet she couldn't help it. Rose stood like a scolded child, her mouth turned down at the corners, her eyes moistening. Taking off her coat, Mavis told herself she needed to be cruel to be kind.

Coming back in from the hallway, she made a point of hardening her features, and going and standing in Rose's line of vision, she looked directly at her. 'Look, love, I'm not saying this to get rid of you. I don't want to, I like your company. But sitting on your backside reading all day isn't going to find you a job. Nobody's going to come knocking the door looking to employ you. If you want to be independent and pay your way, then you're going to have to stop hiding away in here and go out there and find something that'll not only give you a wage, it'll give you back your pride.'

She softened her tone. 'It's not just about the money. It's about you making something of yourself. I earn enough to feed us, but what do we do when it comes to you needing winter shoes or a sensible coat? You'll take twice the pleasure in buying them if you've paid for them yourself.'

'I'm sorry,' Rose mumbled. 'I'm being a nuisance, aren't I?'

'No, you're not a nuisance. You're just not helping yourself.'

The silence that followed was so deep that Mavis felt bathed in it, and feeling as though she had stabbed Rose in the heart, she went and took potatoes from under the sink and started to peel them for the evening meal; she was going to make chips for tea to go with the boiled ham and pickles. Keeping her back to Rose, she sliced rapidly through chunks of potato.

'The thing is... I don't... I don't know how to,' Rose said, her voice barely above a whisper. She paused to gather courage, afraid that she just wasn't brave enough to own up, but if she didn't speak now, she knew that she would just end up weaving yet another web that could eventually ensnare her. When Mavis turned to face her, Rose got to her feet and drew a breath so deep that her shoulders almost reached her ears.

'I'm sorry for all the lies I told you when we first met, but I was telling the truth when I told you Lewis had robbed me... he really did take my money and jewellery... but I didn't meet him at work... I've never worked. I didn't need to.'

She was trembling so much that Mavis was frightened she might fall backwards into the fire.

'Sit down, love,' she said, plopping the chips into a bowl of water to stop them from browning. Tea could wait.

Rose sank back into the chair, and Mavis leaned on the back of the opposite chair and said, 'Go on, you've made a start.'

'My parents didn't want me to go out to work, so I stayed at home. Lewis came to work for my father. That's how I knew him. So you see, I've had no training, nor do I possess any particular skills that might encourage someone to offer me a job of any sort.' She hung her head, shamed. 'I'm a disappointment, aren't I?'

'Only to yourself,' Mavis said.

But Rose wasn't listening. She was feverishly gathering her thoughts as to how much she should tell in answer to the questions she was sure Mavis was about to ask. If she told the absolute truth, Mavis might insist on her returning home. In her mind's eye, she saw the palatial mansion, servants above and below stairs, and the rolling expanse of gardens, stables, fields and woods surrounding it. Mavis interrupted her reverie.

'What does your father do?'

'He breeds horses and runs the estate,' Rose replied, now in control of her thoughts but still sounding as though she was catching answers blown in on the wind. 'Lewis Aston came to assist him.'

'So he was the stable boy,' Mavis said dryly although her eyes twinkled with suppressed amusement.

'Something like that,' Rose mumbled.

'And your parents didn't think he was good enough for you.'

Rose nodded. 'He was very charming and it was easy to fall in love with him.' She gave a little shrug. 'You see, Daddy was so busy with the estate he rarely had any time for me but I know he loved me. I don't think my mother ever did.' Her mouth twisted in a bitter line. 'She just wanted to marry me off to a rich man with a title and get rid of me.'

'And do you have any brothers or sisters?' Mavis was inwardly priding herself on her probing. The picture was becoming much clearer.

At least I can answer this truthfully, Rose thought, before saying, 'I had a brother, Oliver. He was two years older than me. He died of diphtheria when he was ten. Mummy was devastated. I don't think she ever forgave me for still being alive when Ollie was dead.' She looked so sad that Mavis believed every word. The poor girl, neglected by one parent and disliked by the other, and seen only as a chattel to be married off to whoever would take her. No wonder she didn't want to go home.

'If what you've just told me is true, then I can see why you fell for that blighter so easily and ran off with him. And if you're not yet ready to go back home, then you can stay with me, and...' Mavis hardened her tone, 'in the meantime make something of yourself, girl, show some independence. You'll never know what you can do until you try.'

'It's all perfectly true, Mavis, and I don't want to go back to being what I was.' Rose's fervent reply made Mavis smile.

'Good, and for the time being, we'll keep what you've just told me between us. Nobody else needs to know the details.'

'Thanks, Mavis. I'd prefer that they didn't. And I promise to change my ways.'

Rose pushed back her shoulders and held her head high. 'I'll look for work in one of the shops. I'm good at counting, and I am polite,' she said firmly, 'and if I don't find anything in Edge Hill, I'll go into the city.' And surprised by how confident she sounded, she gave Mavis a watery little smile.

Mavis smiled back. 'Right then, I'll get the chips on.'

Throughout the weekend, Rose kept telling herself that she could do anything if she put her mind to it. It couldn't be that difficult standing behind a counter and serving people. Or if she came across a vacancy in an office, she thought she might be useful there. She didn't know how to use a typewriter, but Miss Sprigg, her tutor, had always complimented her neat handwriting and correct spelling. The more she thought about it, the happier she felt.

'They're wanting a carder at Holroyd's, Iris Mullan's leaving to have a baby,' Maggie said, when Mavis told her that Rose was staying on and looking for work. 'An' if rumour's true, they'll be wantin' a weaver. Flo Woodhead's having to give up 'cos she's got a bad heart,' she continued.

'Carding or weaving?' Mavis grimaced. 'I can't see Rose doing anything like that. I don't think the mill would suit her.' They were sitting in Kitty's kitchen,

'It suited me for bloody years before I started out-mending,' Maggie growled, 'I didn't have a choice.'

It was common knowledge in Edge Hill that girls with little education usually ended up working in Holroyd's Mill unless they found a job in one of the shops. But shop workers earned a pittance compared to the mill workers and if, like Maggie, you had to support yourself, and later on a child, the mill was the best option. Maggie's lip curled as she confronted Mavis. Kitty knew that look.

'Is your mam's bronchitis any better?' Kitty didn't much care for Vi, but a change of subject was required. In her opinion, Maggie's mother was a hard-bitten, selfish woman with a tendency to drink too much.

'No, an' it never will be if she carries on smokin' fifty fags a day,' Maggie grumbled as she lit a cigarette. 'She's a pain in the arse, cough, cough, coughing an' keeping everybody waken.'

Kitty and Mavis exchanged amused glances.

'I'd best be getting off,' Mavis said as she got to her feet. 'I want to see Jack before I go back home. His nose is a bit out of joint.'

'Aye, go and kiss it better. Don't let your lodger stand in the way of true romance,' Maggie chortled.

Blushing and giggling, Mavis darted to the door.

'I'll keep me ear open for any jobs going that Rose could do,' Kitty called after her, 'an' if I hear of anything, I'll give ye a shout.'

* * *

On Monday morning, Rose overslept. When she awoke, the house was eerily quiet but inside her head, her thoughts were so noisy that she felt as though she couldn't face the day. She groaned and closed her eyes again, but she couldn't sleep.

Much later, after mooching about the empty house with her mind in turmoil, she put on her coat and went out of the back door. She stood shivering on the steps, not because the air was cold but at the idea of what she was about to do. Her brave decisions over the weekend had deserted her.

'Setting off somewhere, are you?' Jack Naughton was clearing fallen leaves from his flowerbeds. He hoped she was going for good.

Startled, Rose turned in his direction. 'I... I'm... I'm going to see if I can get a job,' she stuttered.

'Good for you,' he said, limping closer and giving her a warmish smile. 'You can only do your best, lass. Don't be letting Mavis do too much for you.'

'I won't,' Rose said, descending the steps and walking out into the lane.

Maggie was lolling in her doorway, smoking. 'Going job hunting?' Rose nodded. 'Best of luck then, Queen,' said Maggie flourishing her cigarette triumphantly.

'Thanks,' Rose called back.

May Walker was brushing her steps. When she saw Rose, she shouted, 'Take care, love, it's slippy underfoot what with all them fallen leaves.' Rose hadn't even noticed the soggy clumps of sycamore leaves that overnight had blown from the trees in the allotments. May waved the brush.

Rose waved back, her head spinning at the kindness of people she barely knew. Their affectionate greetings and good wishes warmed her thudding heart and she quickened her pace, courage sweeping through her as she stepped out into Broad Green.

After almost two hours of walking the length and breadth of Edge Hill, Rose had lost heart and her feet ached, but Mavis's words kept ringing in her head. *Nobody's going to come knocking the door and offer you a job, Rose. You have to go out and find one.*

She had mulled over those words all weekend and long after Mavis had left the house that morning to go to the Adelphi, and she was sorry that she'd left it to the middle of the afternoon to actually pluck up courage to do something about them. Now, the working day drawing to a close, and dreading the thought of disappointing Mavis, she plodded back up the town on the lookout for any shops or offices that she might have missed.

The grumpy grocer on Broad Green had told her he didn't need any help, his scornful expression adding *and certainly not from the likes of you.* The woman in the bakery had been pleasant. 'Aren't you the girl staying with Mavis Robson?' she'd asked. Rose's hopes had risen at this friendly exchange, only to plummet when she was told they had all the staff they needed. Shop after shop, she was told the same thing, and feeling an utter failure, she retraced her steps. For the second time, she drew level with the hardware store with its windows filled with tins of paint, tools and stepladders. She'd dismissed it first time round; that was men's work. Then she spotted the little shop tucked in at the side of the store, amazed that she hadn't noticed it before.

Rose gazed in the small window at the colourful but haphazard display of scarves, fake jewellery and pottery and glassware, all cheap and gaudy. She opened the door. The shop smelled nice, and Rose guessed it must be the perfume of the enormously fat, heavily made-up woman behind the counter. She looked to be in her thirties, and along with her vividly patterned frock, she was wearing several of the items on sale: bracelets, earrings, a huge pendant and a flimsy chiffon scarf. She gave Rose a huge smile.

'Looking for anything in perticklar?' she asked in a breathy voice.

'I'm not sure,' Rose replied, glancing round the small space bedecked with a host of things that could be suspended from wires attached to the walls.

'Take your time, love, you might see something you fancy.'

Rose hid a smile and perused the goods, imagining her mother's horror if she were to buy any of the cheap, vulgar items on offer. Mildred Brown-Allsop was an inveterate snob.

The woman gave a wheezy cough. 'See owt you like then?' she asked.

Rose blushed. 'Actually, I came to ask if you required an assistant.' She felt rather foolish, thinking that her chances were slim in such a small establishment that stocked things she couldn't imagine anyone wanting to buy.

The woman looked surprised. 'Never mind,' Rose mumbled and was leaving when Betty Broadhead cried, 'Hold on a minute, I've just had an idea.' She'd liked the look of the girl, in her expensive coat and her hair neatly fashioned into an elegant chignon, from the minute Rose had walked in. And although she'd barely said two words, Betty liked the posh way she spoke.

Rose turned back eagerly.

* * *

She ran all the way to Mavis's back door, arriving flushed and breathless as she burst into the kitchen to find Mavis, Kitty, Maggie and Beth sitting round the table over a pot of tea. Startled to find her landlady home from work already and entertaining her friends – she'd completely lost track of the time – Rose flushed to the roots of her hair. Then, before any of them had chance to speak, she gabbled her wonderful news. As one, they began chorusing their congratulations.

'Well done, Rose. I just knew you'd find something,' Mavis crowed.

'Congratulations, Rose.' Beth accompanied this with an approving nod.

'Betty's Bijou Bazaar, that's handy,' said Kitty.

'It's a dead cushy number selling nice stuff all day,' Maggie commented dryly.

They all laughed at that and Rose's laughter turned to tears of joy.

Kitty, Beth and Maggie departed, and after eating a tasty meal of corned beef and cabbage, Mavis and Rose spent the rest of the evening hugging the fire. Usually, at this time of day Mavis listened to the wireless and knitted, and Rose would bury her nose in a book from Mavis's bookshelf.

However, tonight was different. Like two excited schoolgirls, they talked about Rose's job and who would use the bathroom first on the days they both had to leave the house early. Then, before bedtime, they drank celebratory cups of cocoa, both of them still feeling rather euphoric at the day's events.

For the first time in days, Rose slept peacefully.

Sure enough, going out to work transformed Rose. Although it meant she spent less time in the house, when she was there, she made good use of it. She washed dishes, cleaned ashes from the fireplace and filled the coalscuttle, tidied the kitchen and, after a fashion, cleaned the bathroom.

'She's not very thorough, but she's learning,' Mavis remarked to Kitty, when she asked how her lodger was getting on. 'Mind you, she still has a long way to go.'

'Give her time,' Kitty said sympathetically, 'at least she's making an effort.'

10

Kitty was making an early lunch in preparation for John's homecoming. He had left with the larks that Saturday morning to attend to some business at his engineering factory. It wasn't a huge concern, but he was proud of the machine parts they produced and exported to many different countries. He'd started up from scratch making bicycle components just before war broke out, and in between serving in the forces, he had managed to keep it going and turn it into a thriving enterprise that afforded his family a comfortable living.

Now, as Kitty put the finishing touches to the soup and sandwiches, John came through the door, a smile on his face. 'Something smells good,' he declared, his eyes lingering fondly on his wife. There were times when John could hardly believe his luck in marrying Kitty.

Kitty set the ladle aside and went to peck his cheek. He pulled her into his arms and kissed her soundly on the mouth. Giggling like a schoolgirl, she kissed him back. He pushed her away playfully. 'Any more of that, Mrs Sykes, and I'll forget all about the football,' he laughed.

He was taking the boys to Anfield to watch the game between Liverpool FC and Aston Villa. John wasn't really into football, but Patrick was a keen supporter, and wanting to be on a par with his schoolmates whose dads were avid fans, he looked to John to take him to the matches whenever possible. John was a wonderful father to all the children.

The door burst open and the boys dived in, closely followed by Molly. 'Are we still going to the football?' Patrick asked, pleased to see that his stepfather was already home.

John gave Patrick a blank look. 'Football? Where? When?'

Patrick's face fell.

'He's having ye on as usual,' his mother told him.

'Aw, you!' Patrick threw a mock punch at John. John grabbed him in a bear hug, both of them laughing as they tussled in a friendly fashion. *My wee Patrick 'ud miss out on the football an' the rough an' tumble if I hadn't remarried 'cos I'd not have filled the gap like that*, she thought as she looked on, smiling at their antics before shouting, 'Hey, you two rapscallions. Quit it!'

'They're worse than a pack of hooligans,' Molly said disdainfully.

'Am I going?' Robert cried. He was too young to really appreciate the game but Patrick was his hero and he emulated everything his half-brother did.

John plucked young Robert off his feet and swung him high in the air, saying, 'Course you are.' Robert laughed and struggled to be set down.

'Is the dinner ready?' Patrick asked. 'We don't want to be late for the match.'

'All ready and waiting,' Kitty said as she ferried bowls of soup to the table

Molly doled out spoons. John and the boys took their seats and Kitty and Molly took theirs.

'Do you think we'll win today, Dad?' Patrick looked hopefully at John as he tucked into his dinner.

'If Elisha Scott's up front, I'm sure they will,' John replied.

'Do we have to talk about boring football?' Molly's arch remark caused both Patrick and Robert to look daggers at her. They both opened their mouths to retaliate, but Kitty intervened to prevent an argument.

'I'm going down to the café as soon as you go to the match. Do ye want to come with me, Molly?'

'No. Lily an' me are going to tidy her bedroom.'

'No, you're not,' said Patrick, giving her a withering look. 'You're going to hang round Mickey O'Malley looking all soppy at him.' Molly blushed.

'Now, now, Patrick,' Kitty chastised. She knew that both Molly and Lily were experiencing the first awareness of the opposite sex and finding Mickey worthy of their attention.

The meal over, the boys donned their red and white scarves and woolly hats. A rap on the outside door announced the arrival of Beth and her son, Stuart. He too was wearing the team's regalia. 'Thanks ever so much for taking him with you, John,' Beth said by way of a greeting as she entered the kitchen.

'Up the reds,' Patrick whooped, and Stuart and Robert joined in as they followed John out to the car.

'Good riddance,' Molly called after them, and to Kitty, 'I'm going to Lily's.'

'She's getting to be a right proper little madam,' Kitty said as the door closed behind her daughter. 'I think getting into the girls' grammar's gone to her head.'

'I think we were all a bit like that at her age,' said Beth. 'I couldn't stand boys when I was eleven.'

'Oh, I don't think that's our Molly's problem. I think she's just beginning to realise they're a different species.'

'I suppose I must have been a late developer,' Beth giggled. Neat and proper in a dark blue coat fitted at the waist, and her brown hair crimped in tidy waves, she was by far the most circumspect of the three friends.

'Do you want a cuppa before I go to the café?' Kitty asked.

'No, thanks, I'll wait for you to get ready then walk to the towpath with you. I'd like a breath of fresh air before I make Dad his dinner,' Beth replied in her usual prim manner. She sat down, very upright, her back inches away from that of the chair. Even though she had come a long way from being the browbeaten daughter of Walter Garside, she still took her responsibilities for him seriously.

'Blair's decorating our bedroom,' Beth told her as Kitty cleared the dinner dishes. Kitty smiled, recalling how Blair's skills as a handyman had proved vital when she had leased the closed-down café on the towpath and refurbished it.

'He's a great one for the painting an' decorating is your Blair,' she said, drying her hands and putting on her coat.

'What do ye reckon to Mavis's lodger then?' Kitty asked as they made their way down the lane.

'I can't say I have an opinion,' Beth replied. 'When I dropped in on Mavis, Rose excused herself and went upstairs. Mavis says she's inclined to mope, but it's only to be expected. The poor girl has no friends of her own age, and there's not much Mavis can do about that.'

'Good afternoon, ladies,' May Walker trilled as they came to her gate. She threw a sheet over the clothesline. 'Are you taking advantage of the dry weather?' She fished clothes pegs from the canvas bag hanging on the line and stuck two between her lips.

'I'm goin' to the café to do a spot of work an' Beth's coming along for the walk,' Kitty replied. 'What about ye, May? Busy as usual.'

'When aren't I?' May mumbled and pegged the sheet.

Leaving May to her chores, Kitty and Beth walked on, exchanging titbits of what they knew about Rose, and sharing their concerns for Mavis.

When the café came into sight, Kitty's heart gave that little flip it always did whenever she approached it, even though it had been hers for more than nine years. The bright blue and white painted boards and checked curtains of the same colour at either side of the windows lent it the same appearance one might see in a seaside resort and not an industrial place like Edge Hill, with its soot and smoky chimneys. The café was her pride and joy, and as she saw the crowded tables on the veranda, her lips stretched into a huge smile.

The autumn sunshine had brought the birdwatchers, the anglers and the walkers out and the tables were crowded as Kitty and Beth entered. Beth sat down but Kitty went behind the counter to help Bridie O'Malley. 'Busy enough,' Kitty said, taking off her coat and rolling up her blouse's sleeves.

'Been like this for most of the day,' Bridie replied, her Irish accent more pronounced than Kitty's own.

'Long may it last,' said Kitty, lifting the large teapot.

After serving Beth with a cup of tea, she was needed behind the counter and was kept busy for the rest of the afternoon. Beth didn't stay long, and later, when the customers tailed off, Kitty left Bridie to finish up and made her way home. As she walked down Weaver Street, she caught sight of Blair, paintbrush in hand, at the upstairs window of number thirteen. In number eleven's front room window, she admired Bridie's vase of flowers. At number nine, she saw the back of Maggie's head as she toiled over her mending frame. Kitty wondered if Pete Harper would give her friend the happiness she deserved. Sadly, she doubted it. So far, none of the men in Maggie's life had done that and there had been quite a few in the past five years.

The window at number seven had new curtains, the house now occupied by the snooty secretary of the man who owned it and two other houses in the street, one of them being Maggie's. Kitty had called with a bag of fresh baked scones to welcome Lorna Bell to Weaver Street. Lorna had kept her on the doorstep, explaining politely but tersely that she didn't eat scones and that she had no interest in getting to know her neighbours. *Your loss, Lorna*, thought Kitty as she came level with number five.

Had she been able to see beyond the front room window and into the kitchen, she would have heard an overwrought May Walker berating her drunken husband, Bill, for having spent too long in the Weaver's Arms; an almost daily occurrence. Poor May didn't have it easy. She'd lost Sammy, her eldest son, in the war, and though she still had three grand lads in Ronnie, Joey and Stephen, she never had much luck with Bill. *My mother used to say that God gives you only as much trouble as ye can bear, but May's had more than her fair share*, thought Kitty as she came to number three.

She gave a wry smile. She still considered Walter Garside to be the same miserable old bugger she'd given a piece of her mind to one Christmas Day some ten years ago, but at least he no longer tormented Beth.

Behind all these doors were the friends and neighbours that had shaped her life for the past thirteen years. Weaver Street was Kitty's world.

Rounding the corner at number one where the recluse, old Cissie Stokes, lived, Kitty strolled up the back lane to her own house to find Patrick and Robert sitting with long faces and John patiently explaining that you win some, you lose some. Liverpool and Aston Villa had drawn without either team scoring.

After tea, for the rest of the evening the family sat in the parlour, the children playing a lively game of Snakes and Ladders, Molly mocking the boys and their football team when she won the game. Kitty and John listened to a variety show and then some music on the wireless, a happy, contented family who, as darkness closed in on that September night in 1929, had no idea of the troubles they would face in the years that lay ahead.

11

After the war, Liverpool had made a good recovery and there was an air of prosperity about the city. An extensive tramway system made it easier for people to travel, and work on a tunnel under the Mersey had just begun. Small businesses like John's engineering works flourished. Even the General Strike in 1926 was as ineffective as it was brief, its nine-day duration not particularly disrupting the lives of Kitty and her neighbours on Weaver Street.

When all women eventually got the right to vote in 1928, and a Labour government was elected in 1929, Kitty and Maggie had cheered: women's rights were long overdue, and the working classes had at last got a voice; or so they believed. The future looked bright.

But sometimes – just sometimes and not too often – if sleep evaded her after a particularly stressful day, Kitty reflected that life had a peculiar way of turning out as she least expected.

Just as she had predicted, Molly had taken to her new school like a duck to water, and Patrick, in his final year at primary school and determined not to be outdone by his sister, was also striving for a scholarship to the boys' grammar. Little Robert was growing more inquisitive by the day, the café was thriving, and all the members of her family were in good health. Best of all, her marriage to John was such pure joy it seemed impossible that a glitch in the world's finances could spoil things.

Therefore, on a Monday night in the middle of September, the children in bed and she and John sitting by the fire in the parlour, her heart gave a little painful lurch when she heard him say, 'I'm not liking the sound of this at all.' He turned down the volume on the wireless, then looked across at Kitty.

'The sound of what?' Startled by his obvious anxiety, Kitty rested her knitting in her lap and gave him her full attention.

'The Bank of England's reporting huge debts that people can't meet and the London Stock Exchange sounds to be in turmoil.'

'What's that got to do with us? We're not in debt.' Kitty was puzzled.

'Not yet we aren't, but if my clients start losing on their investments and can't pay me for the stuff they've contracted, we might be.'

'But why are they losing on their investments?' Although Kitty knew how to manage her own business, she had scant knowledge of stocks and shares.

'It's all to do with people living beyond their means. After the war, people went mad borrowing money and the banks made it worse by giving credit too easily. Now they're facing a big black hole in their treasure chests,' John explained, the furrows in his brow deepening as he contemplated how it would affect him. 'Businesses could go bust if the banks don't get a grip on things.'

Kitty, still not convinced that whatever was going on might have adverse repercussions on her family, got to her feet. 'I'll make us some cocoa before we go to bed,' she said.

Once she was in the kitchen spooning Fry's cocoa powder into two mugs, she pondered on what John had told her. It wasn't like him to worry for no reason. He was a sensible man, good at business and a wonderful husband and father. Sincerely hoping that his worries were without substance, she poured hot milk into the mugs. She didn't want there to be any problems to mar their lives. Things were going so well.

She carried the cocoa into the parlour. John was scouring the *Liverpool Echo*, and seeing the grim expression on his face, she silently handed him his mug then sat sipping her cocoa, deep in thought.

* * *

'Why is it that just when you think everything in the garden's rosy, something crops up to spoil it?' Kitty asked Maggie the next day when they were going to the market. As they walked from stall to stall, she explained what John had told her about the banks, and his worries over his business.

'Yeah, I heard something about it on the wireless,' Maggie said disinterestedly, 'but seeing as how I haven't any money – and never have had – it means nowt to me. You can't miss what you never had.' She gave a bitter chuckle.

'No, but if businesses go belly-up, folks will lose their jobs.'

'Ooh! Do you think Holroyd's could go bust?' Maggie cried, the severity of the situation sinking in as she fiddled with a pile of cabbages. 'I need that job. It's my money that keeps a bloody roof over our heads. Me mam spends what bit she earns at the Wagon and Horses on booze and fags.' She lit a cigarette and puffed furiously before tossing a cabbage at the man tending the stall. 'And don't be charging full price for that. It's withered,' she snarled.

'Don't take it out on him. It's not his fault.' Kitty's remark made her think of Pete Harper. 'Is Pete still not paying his way?' she asked as they moved on.

'No, he bloody isn't,' Maggie snorted, her scowl crumpling as she added, 'but he gets narky if I mention it, and I don't want to lose him, Kitty.'

Her friend sounded so pitiful that Kitty resisted saying she thought he was a sponger, out for all he could get. 'We'd best be makin' tracks,' she said instead. 'It's after eleven an' the kids an' John'll be home soon lookin' for their dinner.'

* * *

'That's it then. It's as bad as I thought,' John exclaimed as he came from the parlour into the kitchen, where Kitty was dishing up plates of Irish stew. It was Thursday, 24 October and he had been listening to the midday news on the wireless before he sat down to eat his dinner. The ladle in Kitty's hand wavered, blobs of gravy dropping on the countertop.

'Is it to do with the stocks and shares?' She still didn't fully understand the problem but knowing that it deeply concerned John, she wanted to share the burden with him.

John ran his fingers through his thick brown hair. 'America's going to hell in a handcart,' he groaned. 'They're saying Wall Street's crashed.'

'Wall Street?'

'In New York,' John said. 'The heart of world finance.'

Seeing Kitty's puzzled expression deepen, John gave her a simple explanation. 'The London Stock Exchange has suspended shares, and some chap called Clarence Hatry has been charged with fraud and forgery. You just watch. There'll be a run on the banks and everything'll go skew-whiff.'

Kitty called for Patrick and Robert to come the table. Unlike Molly, who had to stay in the city at lunchtime, the boys came home from school. Leaving aside Patrick's precious Air-Fix model planes, they clattered into the kitchen, oblivious to their dad's anxiety.

'It might not be as bad as you imagine,' Kitty said comfortingly as she put the dishes on the table. 'Sit down and eat up whilst it's still hot.'

'What might not be bad?' Robert looked to his dad for an answer.

'Nothing for you to worry about, son,' said John, wanting to believe it.

In the days that followed, things went from bad to worse: bad enough to catch Maggie's attention. 'I've just been listening to the wireless while I was doing me mending,' she announced one morning as she walked into Kitty's kitchen. 'What your John said about the banks and stuff must be right. It sounds bloody awful.' She slumped into a chair at the table.

Kitty, not feeling in the best of moods and taking umbrage at the disbelief in Maggie's tone, gave her a disparaging glare. 'He wouldn't have said it if he didn't know what he was talking about,' she snapped, clunking the kettle against the tap as she filled it.

'They're calling them days Black Tuesday and Black Thursday,' Maggie continued, oblivious to Kitty's annoyance as they waited for the kettle to boil. 'As far as I'm concerned, every sodding Tuesday and Thursday are black in my book. It's work, bloody work, and never enough money at the end of each week.' She lit a cigarette then waved it airily. 'They're saying America's gone bust. I allus thought all Yanks were filthy rich but that chap on the wireless said that hundreds of poor people are being turned out of their homes 'cos they can't pay back the money they borrowed to buy 'em.' She puffed thoughtfully, her cigarette in one hand and the other fiddling with the spoon in the sugar bowl on the table.

'So I heard,' Kitty replied, spooning leaves into the teapot. She'd started listening regularly to the news so that she might discuss things with John. 'John says we'll all feel the brunt of it afore long. He's dead worried for the business.' She poured boiling water into the pot then stood gazing thoughtfully into space.

'You'll be all right,' Maggie scoffed. 'You've got a rich husband. Me, I've got nobody. The fella from the mill that collects me pieces says it'll affect Holroyd's 'cos they send a lot of their cloth to America.' She stubbed her cigarette butt angrily into the ashtray.

'Aye, John says it'll affect his export market if it gets any worse,' Kitty agreed as she brought the tea to the table, and, reluctant to dwell on John's predicament, she asked, 'What about Pete, Maggie? Is he finally tipping up for his keep?'

Maggie flushed. 'Not as yet, but he's promised that once he's settled his debts, he'll give me something.' She gulped a mouthful of tea.

'What debts are they?'

'I don't really know,' Maggie mumbled.

'Well, make sure when Pete's put himself straight that he keeps his promise. You shouldn't have to keep him, Maggie.' Sipping her tea, Kitty hoped that Pete Harper would soon sort himself out and do the right thing by Maggie. She didn't want her friend to have to wait forever.

By the end of October, billions of dollars had been lost, wiping out thousands of investors. Panic was rife. The news bulletins talked of little else, and as Kitty and her family sat down to dinner, it appeared that it was even being discussed in the classrooms.

'My teacher told us that lots of people are very sad 'cos a wall crashed down in New York,' Robert said as they sat down to eat their tea.

Patrick burst out laughing. 'A wall didn't crash down, you dummy. They're calling it the Wall Street crash because that's where all the money in America is made. My teacher said that some of the richest people in the world have lost their fortunes.'

'A girl in my class told us that her dad told her that Winston Churchill saw a man jump out of the window of one of the highest buildings in New York 'cos he'd lost his money.' Molly sat back and looked at Patrick, the expression on her face saying, *Top that if you can.*

Kitty sat in silence, marvelling at her children's knowledge and at the same time feeling sickened by what was happening in the world.

12

'There's talk of 'em building new council houses at the top end of Mill Lane.' Maggie liked being the first to relay the latest news and she delivered the information rather smugly. She was sitting in Mavis's kitchen with Kitty, Beth and Bridie, on a dismal afternoon at the beginning of November, the fog so thick that Kitty had told Bridie not to open the café.

'Aye, that's right,' Bridie cut in. 'Big Mick's boss got the contract. He says them in Jagger's Yard have all been given notice.' Maggie glared at her: she'd been about to say that. 'They start pullin' 'em down next week,' Bridie continued, unaware that she'd stolen Maggie's glory.

'And not before time,' Mavis said, 'they're fleapits.'

'Aye, the landlord should hang his head in shame for takin' the rents,' Kitty said. 'Bessie Shaw was tellin' me the lavatories have been blocked for ages, an' none of them have doors. It's bad enough having to go outside without ye have to sit over somebody else's shite in full view of your neighbours.'

'That's the good thing about the houses in Weaver Street,' said

Beth, 'nearly all of us have a bathroom, and we don't have to share it with two other families.'

'Aye, I never thought I'd live to the see the day I'd have a house with a lavatory inside,' said Bridie.

'But we still have to share it with them who sit an' read the paper,' Kitty said, chuckling, and the others smiled, knowing she was referring to John. 'An' we have to clean up the mess the kids leave behind.'

'That used to drive me mad when Rose first came here,' Mavis said. 'She'd be in there ages, even when she knew I was in a rush to get to work. She's not so bad now, though, and she does clear up after herself.' She lifted the teapot and topped up their cups. 'You know, I have to admit I thought I might have made a mistake taking her in because I'd got used to having the place to meself. Now I don't think a thing about it.'

'Sure, ye get on very well, the pair of ye,' Kitty said, 'an' now she's working an' not under your feet all day.'

'Oh, she's not a bad little thing to have about the place, don't get me wrong. Since she got a job, she's been a changed person, and I have to admit I enjoy her company.' Mavis glanced at the clock. 'She'll be in from work any minute,' she said, getting to her feet. 'I'd hate her to think we've been talking about her, so say no more.'

'I'm off anyway,' said Kitty and stood. 'John'll be back from the factory soon and I've left Molly minding the boys. I'd best get back before she kills 'em.'

'I'm going too,' Beth said. 'Stuart will have finished doing his homework. Blair gives him extra sums and writing practice to do every day. We're preparing him for the grammar school,' she added proudly.

Maggie groaned. 'He's only five! The poor little bugger should be out playin' instead of having his nose shoved into books, and his head filled with rubbish.' She pushed back her chair and stood, challenging Beth to respond.

Beth flushed, and Kitty and Mavis chorused, 'Now, now, Maggie!' It was a well-known fact that Maggie and Beth had never really hit it off, even though they had known one another all their lives. Maggie still thought that prim, quiet Beth was a snob, and Beth had always been afraid of Maggie's rough, outspoken manner.

'It's up to Blair and Beth how they bring their son up,' Kitty said sharply, shoving Maggie towards the door.

'I was only sayin',' Maggie said, sounding wounded as they stepped outside, Bridie at their heels.

Rose saw them as they made their way back to their own houses and slowed her pace. She didn't feel like talking to any of them.

'Tea will be ready in half an hour,' Mavis said as Rose entered the kitchen. 'It's boiled bacon and cabbage.'

Rose's stomach lurched. 'I'm not hungry, thank you. I have a headache. I'll go up to my room and come down for something later,' she said, and without breaking her step, she walked through the kitchen and into the hallway and then upstairs.

Mavis watched her go, a frown knitting her brow. Something was wrong.

Upstairs, Rose was lying flat on her back on her bed, running her hands over her belly, her fingers probing. She couldn't feel any difference, but she knew that her body was sending her messages she didn't want to hear.

Just before closing time, a heavily pregnant young woman buying a scarf had reeled off a litany of complaints that being pregnant entailed. A nasty sweat had moistened Rose's body. She recognised some of those signs.

Now, up in her room, her heart raced as her mind juggled with the facts. In the past two weeks, she'd felt nauseous first thing in the morning, and on at least four occasions she had actually vomited. She'd first put it down to the fish Mavis had cooked, then to having a sniffly cold. Her skirt felt tight round her waist, and it had felt the same yesterday, and her breasts felt tender when she touched them.

What with all the trauma of the past few months, she hadn't given a thought to her periods. Now, as uncontrollable tremors invaded her limbs, she realised that she hadn't had one since coming to live in Weaver Street. She gripped the quilt with clammy hands, cold terror grasping at her innards.

What on earth am I going to do, she asked herself over and again. How could she face these good, kind people who had given a whole new meaning to her life, and tell them she was pregnant? Should she leave without saying anything, find a place where nobody knew her and start again? If she did, she'd be back in the same awful situation as when Mavis had found her, only this time it would be much worse. The very idea of leaving made her tremble even more, and she sobbed into her pillow.

She knew very little about pregnancy other than the scraps she had overheard from the servant girls at home, or what she had seen in the stables when one of her father's horses was in foal. All she really did know was that once the seed was planted, it just grew and grew and, usually, there was no way of stopping it.

The more she thought about it, the harder it was to take in that it was real. Girls like her didn't get into such compromising situations. It was loose, ill-bred girls who got pregnant outside of marriage, she told herself and then grimaced. She was no better than them. Lewis had done things to her in the same way a stable hand would with a common kitchen maid. She'd heard the gossip.

Rolling off the bed and standing on legs that felt like jelly, she went over to the window and stared into the distance. The fog had lifted. She'd grown to love the view over the allotments, the sycamores blowing in the wind, the early morning mists and pale sunsets; even the sight of Jack's bent back as he tilled the soil pleased her. She *had* to stay here, she thought, she couldn't bear to be parted from Mavis and her friends and all that they had helped her to achieve. She had a job she loved, and for the first time in her life, she felt useful and valued.

She gazed up into the darkening sky then down at the light gleaming from Kitty's windows. Lily Stubbs was running up the lane, a carrier bag swinging in her hand. Down below, the rattle of pans let her know Mavis was making dinner. An icy hand clutched Rose's heart. Would any of her new friends want her now? There was only one way to find out. She'd go and face the music because if she didn't, she thought she might go mad. Slowly, she descended the stairs, her stomach churning with every step.

Mavis was stirring a pot on the stove. She glanced round with a warm smile.

'Sit you down, love. It's ready for lifting,' she said, waving the spoon at the table.

'Can it wait? There's something I *must* tell you,' said Rose, the words sticking in her throat and Mavis's kindness tugging at her heart. Instead of sitting down, she stood with her back to the sideboard. Mavis lowered the flame under the pan, a flutter of fear taking her breath. Was the girl about to tell her she was leaving? She realised she didn't want her to go.

'What is it?' she asked softly, her eyes fixed on Rose's anxious pale face.

Rose pressed her spine against the sideboard and said, 'I have reason to believe I'm going to have a baby and I...' She burst into tears, her courage deserting her.

Mavis looked shocked. 'Oh, you poor child!' Going and taking hold of Rose's hands, she led her to the chair by the hearth. 'Don't cry,' she said, pushing her gently into the seat, but Rose couldn't help it.

Mavis let her sob, her thoughts whirling as she struggled with the implications of this news. Rose's sobs shuddered into sniffles. She looked pleadingly into Mavis's face, begging her for a solution.

Mavis swallowed. 'It's possible, given the circumstances,' she said calmly, 'and if you're right, you're not the first to be caught – and you certainly won't be the last.' She smiled wryly. 'What makes you think you're pregnant?' she said, her awareness of the young girl's naivety prompting her to ask what she thought was a damned foolish question.

Rose blushed. 'I haven't had my period since I came here,' she said, her voice no more than a whisper and her insides squirming at divulging such personal information. 'In all the turmoil of... and then... the excitement of finding work, I never gave it a thought, but now...' She stopped, exhausted.

'That 'ud make you about three months gone,' Mavis said practically. 'Then again, it could just be that you're stressed and not pregnant at all.' She saw the hope flaring in Rose's eyes.

'I tell you what,' Mavis continued, 'don't say or do anything for the time being. Just wait and see. There's no point in broadcasting it if it all comes to nothing.'

She smiled a smile that looked far more confident than she felt.

Rose burst into tears again. 'But what if there is a baby, won't you mind?'

Mavis looked pensive. 'I would have loved to have Robbie's baby, but fate decreed otherwise,' she said wistfully. 'And if you have one, we'll give it all the love we can. That's all we can do.'

'But I don't want Lewis Aston's baby,' Rose wailed. 'I don't want to be reminded of him every time I look at it. I can't do that.'

'You can, and you will,' Mavis said emphatically. 'The baby didn't ask to be conceived. It's the innocent party, and it will be far more yours than it ever will Lewis Aston's, so – find the courage – be brave enough to accept it.' She got to her feet. 'Now will you have some of dinner? It'll do you good.'

Even though Mavis had advised Rose to tell no one about her pregnancy, Mavis did decide to confide in Kitty, who was dismayed. 'Poor girl, as if she didn't have enough to contend with, being separated from her family, an' all,' she said, her sympathy plain to see. 'An' what about you? How do you feel about having a baby in the house?'

'I think I'd like it very much,' Mavis said softly. She gave Kitty a rueful little smile that summed up all her yearnings.

'Well, if there is to be one, I'm sure it 'ud want for nothing,' Kitty said gently.

'Don't mention it to Maggie. She can't keep her trap shut,' Mavis urged, 'and best not tell Beth. You know how pernickety she is about such things.'

A couple of days later when Maggie dropped by, Kitty was at sitting at her sewing machine in the dining room. Maggie peered over her shoulder.

'What are you doing?' Nosy as ever, she thought she recognised the garment.

'Letting out Rose's skirt. Mavis brought it over this morning.'

'Yeah, now you mention it, she's put quite a bit of weight on lately.'

'Do ye think so?' Kitty carried on pinning the waistband in place. She wasn't about to betray Mavis's confidence.

'Mind you, she can stand it,' Maggie said, jealously aware of her own spreading hips. 'She wa' as thin as a pickin' rod when she came here.'

'Aye, she was that,' Kitty replied, thinking that wouldn't be the case for much longer.

Rose did as Mavis advised. She went to work each day, trying hard to pretend that everything was as it had been, but deep inside, she felt weighed down by sheer dread. There were moments when she almost forgot that she was pregnant, but it only took a customer to come in smelling of stale cigarette smoke or what they'd eaten for dinner to bring it crashing back, leaving her feeling queasy and panicky, and not sure what to do next. The worry wore her out, and at the end of each day, she returned home exhausted.

Mavis was goodness itself. She'd made it her business to see that her friend ate nourishing food, even when she pleaded she had no appetite. And in the evenings, sitting by the fire, Rose gazed into the flames and as Mavis knitted, the older woman encouraged Rose to talk about her pregnancy. 'Better get used to the idea and be prepared for it,' she said when Rose shied away from the matter.

One night, she asked, 'Will you notify your parents? After all, the baby is their grandchild.'

Rose looked horrified before giving a bitter chuckle. 'My mother would have me stripped naked and whipped through the streets then most likely commit me to a nunnery for the rest of my days,' she said, half in jest.

'She sounds very harsh,' Mavis said, 'tell me more about her.'

Rose thought for a moment. 'I don't ever remember her being loving and kind. Nanny Compton took care of that,' she said, before wistfully adding, 'Mother dismissed her when I was fourteen. Even before Oliver died, she was cold and distant. I don't think she knew how to love. She was horrible to... to my father, and the servants. Daddy was lovely when he wasn't too busy running the estate.'

Oh, so she'd had a nanny. Very posh, and something else I didn't know. Mavis pursed her lips, and wanting to draw her out even further, she said, 'You got on well with your father, then?'

'That's the reason I can't go back home. I couldn't bear his disappointment,' Rose said miserably. 'He'd warned me to keep away from Lewis. I didn't listen.'

'It's never too late to admit you were wrong and to say sorry,' Mavis said, and left it at that.

Despite Mavis's solicitous care, there were days when Rose felt so low that she wanted to weep. During the day, she felt as though her life had been taken over and wasn't hers any more, and if the days were a struggle, the night-times were far worse. In bed, with nothing to distract her, she imagined she still felt the pain of Lewis plunging inside her, his face ugly and sweaty as he gasped and spilled his sticky slime between her thighs. Then, bile rising and threatening to choke her, she'd run for the bathroom to be violently sick. Back in bed, her head throbbing and her fingers constantly straying to the little bump below her midriff, she attempted to see into the future.

* * *

Rose wrapped a pretty scarf in brown paper and handed it to the young girl who said she was buying it for her mother. It was almost closing time and the shop had been busy with customers buying early Christmas gifts.

They have something to celebrate, but not me, Rose thought dismally, as she closed up for the day. Her feet ached, and she was painfully conscious of her thickening waistline. Soon there would be no way of hiding her pregnancy. The thought suddenly made her feel punch-drunk and as she stepped outside, locking the door behind her, she felt as though her feet belonged to someone else.

She stood for a moment to swallow the threatening tears and regain her balance. Across the road, a woman exited the cobbler's shop and Rose was reminded that she had promised to collect Jack's boots. Just then, a heavily pregnant young girl waddled along the pavement, her unbuttoned coat flapping either side of her distended belly.

Two youths coming towards her nudged each other and grinned, the taller of the two shouting, 'Hey, look! Tilly's got a bun in the oven. She's bakin' a bastard.'

His mate, not to be outdone, jeered, 'An' she hasn't got a husband. Dirty girl.' The girl's steps faltered. She glanced round wildly. The youths drew level with her. 'Yer shoulda kept yer legs together, love,' the tall one sneered. Doubled up with laughter, and making lewd gestures, they jigged round her while the girl hung her head and dodged past them, her cheeks blazing.

Rose felt cold and sick. Would that be her in another few weeks? Would she be the butt of such taunts? The people she'd got to know respected her, but once they found out, would they see her as being just another a girl with loose morals? The injustice of it all rooted her to the spot. Here she was, raw and aching and frightened, and Lewis Aston was no doubt plying his charms elsewhere whilst she was left carrying his bastard child. Galvanised by fear and loathing, her thoughts in turmoil, she hurried towards the kerb and stepped off the pavement into the road.

The lorry driver braced and slammed his foot on the brake. His head bounced of the windscreen as the vehicle's nearside swiped Rose back onto the pavement. Broad Green rang with screams and shouts as the driver shakily climbed from his cab, pushing his way through the crowd that had gathered round Rose, but she was oblivious to everything.

* * *

Mavis returned from the hospital late that Thursday night. Seeing a light on in Kitty's kitchen, she tapped the door and John let her in.

'Come on, lass, you must be weary,' he said, taking her arm and leading her to a chair by the fire. 'Put the kettle on, Kitty.'

Kitty was already on her feet, and before Mavis could sit down, she hugged her. 'Ye look done in, love,' she said. 'How is she?'

Mavis flopped into the chair, her face drawn and grey. 'She lost the baby,' she whispered. Her disappointment was so raw that Kitty immediately understood that Mavis had been desperately looking forward to welcoming the baby into her home.

'What about the lass?' John urged. He didn't know about the baby. 'Is she going to be all right?'

'Cuts and bruises. She was lucky.'

'Thank God for that.'

Mavis grasped the cup of tea Kitty handed her. 'They're keeping her in for observation.' She took a hefty swig of the hot, sweet tea. 'My God, I needed that.' She took another drink, tears welling on her eyelashes. She put down the cup and brushed her eyes with her fingers.

'Terrible though it is, it's maybe for the best,' Kitty said.

* * *

The hospital discharged Rose the next day and she made her own way back to Weaver Street on the tram. Mavis was furious.

'You should have rung Kitty. I'd have come and got you. It's raining cats and dogs out there,' she cried, jumping to her feet as Rose walked in, her coat dripping and her headscarf clinging to her scalp.

'I'm all right,' Rose said, her voice wobbling pathetically. 'As they said, I'm not ill. The accident wasn't too serious, and I only had a miscarriage.' She hung her coat behind the door, and peeling her scarf from her wet hair, she draped it over the back of a chair. She managed a little smile and went to sit by the fire, but

Mavis could tell by the look in her eyes that that things were far from all right.

Mavis was in a quandary. Should she fuss over her or, like Rose appeared to be doing, just accept the loss of the baby and not make a drama out of it. She shook her head despairingly and went to put on the kettle. Mavis knew from experience that to dwell on a tragedy could ruin the rest of your life. It was all too easy to sink into an abyss of misery, and whilst it was only to be expected, you had to fight back, otherwise you were lost.

She racked her brains to think of the right things to say as she waited for the kettle to boil. The wireless was playing softly in the background. She was filling the teapot when the strains of 'Yes Sir, That's My Baby' oozed into the room. Boiling water slopped onto the worktop. Banging down the kettle, she darted across to the sideboard and twisted the knob on the wireless then glanced anxiously at Rose, but the girl seemed not to have heard it. She was staring into space, her bleak expression etching lines round her mouth and eyes.

Mavis went back to making tea. When she handed Rose her cup, Rose nodded her thanks. Mavis sat down and sipped her tea: the silence was ominous. She had to say something. Setting her cup down on the hearth, she drew a deep breath.

'Look, love. This might not be the right time to say it, but you were lucky to escape with a few bruises... and the way things have turned out it could all be for the best... maybe it was meant to be.'

Rose's limpid eyes met Mavis's as her emotions see-sawed from sadness to relief. She had been crushed by the loss of her baby, for even an unborn child had the right to life, but her sadness was coupled with a feeling of guilty release. This *was* how it was meant to be.

Fate had played its part, but whilst she had survived, a tiny life had died and she would have to learn to bury her loss and her guilt in the darkest corner of her mind.

'I think perhaps you're right,' she murmured, and strengthening her tone, she added, 'I have to put it all behind me. My life will go on, and I must make the best I can of it, otherwise I'll be lost.'

Mavis jumped to her feet, and going over to Rose, she drew her into her arms, whispering, 'That's the spirit, my brave girl,' as their tears dampened one another's shoulders. They stayed like this until they could cry no more. Then Mavis went and sat back down. She lifted her knitting bag from down beside her chair and Rose's spirit crumpled. She knew that Mavis had wanted the baby even more than she had, the tiny white garments that had taken shape on Mavis's knitting needles testament to her yearning.

Mavis delved into the bag to hide the baby clothes. Needles flicking, she continued to work on a large black jumper she was knitting for Jack. 'Betty says she'll miss you in the shop but that you're not to go back until you're ready,' she said.

'I'll go back on Monday,' Rose replied and they continued talking about Betty and the shop, then Mavis's job in the Adelphi, and the weather, everything but the baby that was all each woman had on their mind; the unspoken words filling the silences in between their inconsequential chatter.

13

Nineteen twenty-nine drew to a close, the streets shrouded in thick fog or slick with icy rain that swirled the last of the autumn leaves into the gutters and clogged them into slippery mounds along the towpath. Daylight hours grew shorter and the lengthening nights colder.

'This gloomy weather's playin' havoc with my nerves,' Kitty remarked as she entered the café just before midday at the end of the third week in December. She shook the rain off her mackintosh in the doorway.

'It's not doin' much for mine either.' Bridie gave her a rueful smile. 'I haven't served a customer all mornin'.'

Kitty joined Bridie behind the counter. 'On days like this, it's only them from the mill makes it worth opening.' She glanced at the clock. 'Is there anything needs making up?'

'Not a thing,' Bridie said. 'The pies are in the oven, the soup's just off the boil an' I've made the sandwiches. I'd that much time on me hands I gave the shelves a once over, even though they didn't need doin'.'

Kitty laughed. 'You're a livin' wonder, Bridie O'Malley.'

The mill hooter wailed, its mournful blast echoing up Mill Street and into the towpath. Before long, the thud of boots and noisy chatter announced the arrival of the first customers of the day.

'It's pissin' down out there,' a young lad said as he dived to the counter.

'We know,' Kitty and Bridie chorused. The lad laughed then ordered soup and a ham sandwich.

After that, the two women served a steady stream of workers, the air in the café growing muggier by the minute as steam rose from their damp coats.

'How's things down at the mill?' Kitty asked as she delivered bowls of soup to a table by the window. John had been particularly despondent that morning as he left to go to his factory. Yesterday a contractor had reneged on a consignment of machine parts, saying he'd lost a packet on the stock exchange and couldn't afford to stay in business.

'We've plenty of work on at the moment,' an older woman replied, 'but the overseer wa' tellin' us that we could lose us export trade with the States if things don't buck up. He says ould Holroyd's in a bit of a tizz.'

'The greedy bugger's allus in a tizz if he thinks he's not mekkin enough brass,' said a younger woman scornfully.

'It'll all be summat an' nowt,' said the man sitting with them. 'The banks 'ull sort it out. It's on'y t'newspapers and the gover'ment that blow it all out o' proportion to freeten poor buggers like us.'

Hoping that he was right, Kitty left them to eat their lunch. Maybe John was being unnecessarily anxious, but she'd noticed the creases round his eyes deepening as, during the past few weeks, he chased bad debts and sought new orders, making sure his business didn't suffer.

'We might as well close after we've cleaned up,' she said in the lull that followed the midday rush. Bridie looked perturbed. 'Don't worry, I'll not dock your pay.' Kitty smiled as she stacked dishes by the sink.

Bridie flushed. 'Thanks,' she muttered, plunging her hands into the hot water then whisking plates in and out. 'It's just with it being so near Christmas, I like that bit extra. Not that Mick keeps me short,' she hastened to add, 'but Wee Mickey's wanting football boots like your Patrick's an' Liam's needin' boots with steel toecaps for when he goes to work with his dad in the New Year.'

'Aye, another child startin' out in the great big world to earn his livin',' Kitty said cheerily in order to brush aside Bridie's embarrassment. Keeping up a lively conversation about their children and Christmas, they continued washing and drying and putting the café in order. Then Kitty locked the door and they made their way along the towpath and into Weaver Street. It was still raining. As they walked and talked, Kitty tried to recapture the spirit of the coming season.

'I'll be havin' a party,' she said as they turned into the lane. 'I usually do.' Kitty's Christmas parties were something of a tradition in Weaver Street, and they were close to her heart, for it was at such a party in number eleven that she had first met John.

'I love a party. Particularly at Christmas,' said Bridie as they came level with Kitty's house. 'That's what I'll miss about home this year. All the family pilin' in for a shindig till all hours.'

'Well, when ye come to mine, I'll make sure ye miss nothin'. We'll have a right old Irish hooley this year. See you tomorrow.' Kitty went down the path leading to the back door of her house – she rarely used her front door, just as she hadn't when she lived in number eleven; old habits are hard to break.

The next day, even though it was fine and dry, Kitty didn't go to the café: Bridie could manage without her, as trade was so slack.

Instead, she called in to see Maggie and suggested they go into the city to do some shopping. Although the shops on Broad Green met their daily needs, the big stores in Liverpool offered a wider, and more often than not cheaper, variety of goods. Half an hour later, Maggie was at Kitty's door, raring to go.

'Are you ready?' she called out as she entered Kitty's porch.

'Won't be a tick. Just getting me coat,' Kitty sang out from the hallway, and before Maggie had time to join her, she stepped out, carrying a large canvas shopping bag and wearing a bottle green coat that complemented her tawny hair and creamy complexion.

'You look smart.' Maggie looked Kitty up and down enviously, at the same time brushing bits of fluff from her plain brown coat. 'If I'd known we were dressing up, I'd have made more effort – though God knows with what,' she groused.

'Ye look fine as ye are, Maggie,' Kitty responded, ushering her outside and locking the door behind them. Still, she couldn't help feeling sorry for her. Maggie hadn't had a new coat in years, and the one she was wearing now was one that Kitty had passed on to her the year before last.

'Your hair's lookin' lovely, ye have it crimped to perfection,' she said, hoping to raise her friend's spirits as they walked down the lane.

'Yeah, it's dead classy, isn't it? I wet it with sugar and water before I put the clips in – it works a treat,' said Maggie, grinning and patting the stiff waves in her bleached blonde hair. Then, tightening the belt on her coat, she swaggered to the tram stop, Kitty relieved to see her friend's mood brighten.

When the tram arrived, they climbed the spiral staircase to sit up top. Maggie lit a cigarette and they talked about what they might buy as the tram rattled along Edge Lane towards the heart of Liverpool, a city that thrived around its busy port. The transport system in and out of the city was second to none. Clanking trams and an overhead railway ferried passengers in and out of the suburbs and trains chugged out of the tunnel under the Mersey that connected the city to the Wirral Peninsula. Work was still plentiful on the docks and in the factories: Tate's sugar refinery, Barker and Dobson's sweets, Walker's Brewery and the Imperial tobacco factory, although the clouds of the economic crisis were looming. Stores like Bucklers and Cripps sold the latest fashion, and although the city centre was noisy and dirty, the buildings soot-stained from heavy industry, Kitty still loved her infrequent trips to this bustling hub.

My Molly does this every weekday, she thought as they alighted in Victoria Street. How bold the young ones of today were, she thought, as she wondered if she would have been as brave at Molly's age. The memory of the farmhouse in rural Roscommon where she had been reared came to mind. She'd walked country lanes to a school with one classroom not ten minutes from her own door.

'Right, we'll head for Woolies first,' said Maggie, hitching her bag to her shoulder and walking briskly up the street: Woolworths was always her first port of call. Kitty hurried after her.

At one end of the long cosmetics counter, the assistant was dealing with a customer, and at the other end, two girls about the same age as Molly and Lily were trying on lipsticks whilst her attention was diverted.

Maggie nudged Kitty. 'Do you remember doing that when you were their age?'

'Ballymacurly didn't have a Woolworths. In fact, it didn't even have a shop that sold lipsticks,' Kitty said, eyeing the giggling girls. 'I wonder if my Molly an' your Lily get up to such things.'

'You can bet they do. I know I did. It's part of growing up,' Maggie scoffed.

'I wouldn't like for Molly to be wantin' lipstick, she's too young.' Kitty glanced at Maggie. 'Would ye let your Lily wear it?'

'Bugger the lipstick, that's the least of your worries. I'll have her whipped up to Marie Stopes the minute she starts showing interest in boys.' Maggie gave a dirty laugh at the mention of the Family Planning Clinic in the city.

'Jesus, Mary an' Joseph, don't even joke about that,' Kitty gasped as she selected a bottle of Lily of the Valley, a gift for Mavis. The assistant hurried to serve her, the red-lipped girls scarpered and Kitty paid for the perfume.

At the counter selling fancy goods, Kitty paused to admire some small vases in pretty pastel shades. 'They're lovely,' she said but she didn't buy one. When they joined the queue at the popular broken biscuit counter, Maggie said, 'You get for both of us,' and slipped away. Kitty smiled. She had an idea what Maggie would be giving her for Christmas.

Then Maggie bought knickers for Vi, and socks and hairslides for Lily. 'I'll get slides for Molly as well,' she said, selecting a bright blue pair. 'These'll match her eyes.' At the next counter, she insisted on buying Patrick a penknife and Robert a yo-yo, even though Kitty protested.

'Ye don't have to buy my kids anything,' she said, conscious of how little money Maggie had to spare. 'They've already got plenty of presents.'

'Fair's fair,' said Maggie, 'and anyway, I want to. You made Lily that new skirt and blouse, and I know you've bought her a dressing table set like you've bought for Molly 'cos you told me.'

Kitty still had a few small gifts to buy so, after leaving Woolworths, they visited several other shops. In Cooper's, Kitty bought a whole round cheese, Maggie gasping at the price. 'It's for the party,' Kitty told her then asked the assistant for a box of crackers.

'If things are going to get as bad as John thinks they will, we might as well splurge while we can. Next Christmas, we might be livin' on crusts.'

'Where to now?' Maggie asked, lighting a cigarette as they stood on the pavement outside Cooper's. It was past midday and the pavements thronged with Christmas shoppers, and office workers out for lunch.

'The Hobby Shop in Manchester Street, then we're done. I need a starter box of Meccano for Robert. He's always pestering Patrick to let him play with his.' They dodged in and out of the crowd, before arriving breathless at the toyshop.

'A Meccano set – something simple, it's for a wee boy,' Kitty told the elderly shopkeeper and as he hobbled from behind the counter, his gait was so awkward that Kitty thought he looked as if he'd been constructed from the toy she'd asked for. Her eyes misted as she watched him peer at the boxes on the shelves before extracting one with hands so fragile and wrinkled that they looked like bundles of twigs.

'He'll be lucky to see Christmas,' Maggie remarked when they were back outside. 'He's dead ancient.'

'We'll all be like that one day,' Kitty replied, her sympathy with the old man. They were walking up the street when she said, 'Look, I've got an idea. It's not often we do this, and seeing as it's nearly Christmas, why don't I treat us to a cup of tea an' a bite to eat in T. J. Hughes?'

'Ooh! That's a bit up-market for the likes of us.'

'Sure, we're as good as anybody, Maggie.'

They walked briskly to London Road and the T. J. Hughes emporium. The massive store built from mellow York stone dominated the street, its conical roof towers sitting proudly above two rows of upper windows and the name T. J. Hughes spelled out vertically on the wall below one of the towers and emblazoned across the shop front in huge bright red letters. The large windows at street level were filled with an enticing display of goods and as Kitty and Maggie commented with longing on things they could never afford to buy, chauffeur-driven cars deposited extremely smartly dressed ladies at the main door. An elderly man in a braided uniform ushered them in.

'Do you think he'll turn us away?' Maggie asked as they approached him.

'If he does, I'll have something to say about it,' Kitty snapped. The man let them pass without a second glance.

Inside the store, they gazed with envy at the mannequins on display in the mantleware department. 'I'd look smashing in that,' whispered Maggie, pointing to an evening dress heavily embellished with sequins.

'Ye'd look like a Christmas tree,' Kitty said, leading the way to the tearooms. She'd been here before, and knowing that Maggie yearned for the finer things in life, she wanted to treat her friend.

'I don't know that I'm dressed for this,' Maggie hissed as they waited to be seated. Her eyes were as big as saucers as they roamed the sea of crisp white tablecloths, delicate china, glassware, and expensively dressed women clinking silver cutlery as they chatted in low voices.

'It's what's in ye, not on ye that matters,' Kitty said as a flunky in a black and white uniform showed them to a table in a corner. They ordered tea and hot buttered scones from a girl in a starched white apron and cap. She glared at Maggie, who was so busy gawping around the plush tearooms that she had to ask twice if she wanted raspberry or strawberry jam with the scones.

A short while later, having lost her reservations about sitting in such grand company, Maggie demolished the last of her scones. Then, with her little finger elegantly crooked, she slurped the dregs of tea from the delicate little cup and set it back on the saucer, a satisfied smile wreathing her face.

'I could get used to this,' she said expansively.

Kitty was pleased with the way the shopping trip had turned out, and when they were back in Weaver Street, Maggie went back to her mending and Kitty to wrap the gifts she had bought. Some she hid in the bottom of her wardrobe with the ones she and John had bought on a trip into the city earlier in the December, but others were to be sent to Ireland.

She was on her way back home from the post office after posting parcels to her brothers in Roscommon, socks for Paddy and Brendan, and numerous small gifts for Shaun and his wife and children, when she saw May Walker sweeping her steps. 'Getting ready for Christmas, May?' Kitty called out.

'As ready as I'll ever be,' May replied, a slow smile lifting the corners of her mouth but failing to reach her warm brown eyes. Christmas wasn't her favourite time of year. 'What about you? Have you all done?'

'More or less,' Kitty chirped, 'just some baking to do for me Boxing Day party. Ye an' Bill are comin', aren't ye?'

'I will,' said May, 'but I can't vouch for Bill.' She pulled a face. 'He'll not be sober till next year – and not even then.'

'Not to worry,' Kitty said and went on her way. There were some things in life that couldn't be helped and Bill's drunkenness was one of them.

She hadn't long been home when Maggie dropped in, her face like thunder.

'Would you bloody believe it. Pete's just told me he has to work over Christmas.'

She dragged deeply on her cigarette then noisily expelled her disgust. Smoke streamed from her nostrils.

'Ye'll set yourself on fire one of these days,' Kitty said mildly, even though her suspicions were heightened. Pete Harper was a strange one: charming to a fault when it suited, he had Maggie completely under his spell, but Kitty doubted it was work that kept him away so often. She'd even hinted at her doubts, but Maggie had pooh-poohed them.

'I'm sorry to hear that,' she said, hoping that Maggie wasn't going to mope or drink too much in his absence. 'Ye'll still enjoy yourself 'cos I'll make sure ye do.'

Maggie nodded glumly.

* * *

John Sykes parked his car and hurried indoors, a broad grin on his face. Kitty looked up from the ironing she was doing and returned his smile.

'What has you looking so pleased with yourself?' she asked fondly, her curiosity aroused.

'Come out and look,' he said heading for the door.

When they were outside, John lifted a shiny red racing bike from the back of the car, and setting it on its wheels, he held it by the drop handlebars and saddle. 'What do you think to this?' he said, beaming at his wife.

'I'd say it looks expensive,' said Kitty, knowing how tight money was, and her expression creased with anxiety at his rashness. She'd always worried about money even when they'd had plenty, which had angered her late husband, Tom, but not John; he understood her fears.

'How much did it cost?' she asked warily.

John laughed. 'That's just it. It didn't cost a penny. A chap brought it into the factory and asked me if I wanted it for parts. He'd given up cycling – too old, he said.'

'There's hardly a scratch on it. Patrick will be over the moon.' Kitty pictured her eldest son's delight at getting the kind of bicycle he'd been raving about for the past few months.

John lifted the bike back into the car. 'I'll keep it hidden at the factory. We don't want to spoil the surprise.'

'That's us more or less sorted for Christmas then,' Kitty said as they went back indoors. 'Molly's got her new clothes an' a dressing table set, an' Robert's getting a *Boy's Own* annual and crayons, an' he'll be made up when he sees the Meccano.'

'And there's three Cadbury's selection boxes that I got off that traveller I buy screws from to put in their stockings along with some nuts and oranges,' John added. 'The kids'll not go short this Christmas.' Whistling a merry tune, he went up to the bathroom.

Kitty continued ironing the clothes she had secretly made for her daughter and Lily. When Molly had enthused over a picture she and Lily had seen in the *New Penny Magazine*, Kitty had later carefully perused it and copied the idea, not once but twice, in different colours: a white blouse and navy skirt for Molly and a pink blouse and green skirt for Lily. The girls loved to dress alike and Kitty wouldn't see Lily go without at Christmas. Hearing John's feet on the stairs, she set down the iron and went to the sink to fill the kettle.

Her husband came up behind her, placed his arms round her waist and nuzzled the back of her neck. Kitty leaned back into him, savouring the touch of his lips and the strong feel of his broad chest. Washed and shaved, he smelled of coal tar soap and she breathed in the fresh, clean scent, thanking God for giving her a second chance to find such a decent, loyal man. She turned in his embrace, gazing up into his warm brown eyes.

'It's been a worrisome year, what with the banks going bust, but we'll get through this Christmas just fine and things can only get better in the New Year,' she said, her tone suggesting that she'd make damned sure they did.

John smiled at her determination. 'They will, love. As long as we've got each other and the kids are healthy and happy, we can get through anything.'

They sealed their hopes for the future with a kiss.

14

It was fair to say that in the past four months, Rose had struggled to adjust to living in Weaver Street. She'd found the casual way neighbours dropped into one another's houses uninvited or stopped her in the lane to gossip overwhelming. Initially, she'd been at a loss when she was expected to respond to the neighbours who never let her pass by without asking after her well-being; this never happened in her home village. There the people were courteous but not particularly friendly. It was all so different from the life she had been used to. Then, her days had been spent mainly in solitude – until Lewis had come along – her father too busy and her mother unwilling to share her time. At first, Rose had missed having servants, and still had to remind herself to tidy her bedroom and the bathroom and do her washing and help with the daily chores.

But in the few weeks that followed her miscarriage, she had, with Mavis's sterling support and her own steely determination, put the tragedy behind her. If she had moments of regret, they were fleeting, and she now felt so much at home in Weaver Street that come Christmas Eve, she was starting to feel happiness again.

She thoroughly enjoyed working in Betty's Bijou Bazaar, ridiculous as its name was, and had put her heart and soul into her job. She had transformed the cluttered shop into a cavern of delights, artfully creating elegant displays that lent the cheap, tasteless items glamour. Betty Broadhead thought Rose was worth her weight in gold.

'You'll be busy today so I'll stop for a bit an' give you a hand,' Betty puffed, as she squeezed her considerable bulk behind the little counter early in the afternoon on Christmas Eve.

Betty was prone to overeating and grossly overweight, she also suffered from asthma, and her already precarious health had resulted in three miscarriages during the twelve years she'd been married. Her husband, Syd, had begged her to give the shop up but it was Betty's baby, her way of easing the pain of never giving birth to a real baby. Then, in September, Dr Metcalfe had confirmed that Betty was pregnant and that she would have to be extremely careful if the pregnancy was to run full term. She had told no one but Syd, afraid that making it public might be bad luck, and being as portly as she was, nobody's suspicions had been aroused. On the day Rose had come looking for a job, Betty had seen something in her – she was slender and cultured, everything Betty would like to be – and she also saw a solution to keeping both her business and the baby safe. Now, with Rose holding the fort, and worth every penny of the twelve shillings and sixpence she was paid, Betty had the best of both worlds.

Perched behind the counter, Betty thanked customer after customer, wishing them a merry Christmas as she rattled coins into the till for, just as she had predicted, trade was brisk. Meanwhile, Rose inched her way between the shoppers, helping them choose what to buy. People were afraid for their jobs and feeling the pinch, but it didn't stop them spending a few coppers on a scarf, a pair of gloves or a trinket, Christmas gifts for family and friends.

Up until recently, Rose had never had to consider where the money came from that had bought the things she owned. Her mother had taken her into London to Harrods four times a year to replenish her wardrobe, and her father had given her expensive jewellery for birthdays and Christmas. But working in Betty's bazaar had taught her a lesson. Now, as she watched hard-working women and young girls deliberating over the purchase of a cheap scarf or pair of earrings, her heart went out to them.

A tired-looking woman lifted a rayon headsquare patterned in autumnal shades. 'It's not much of a present on its own,' she sighed. 'I want something really nice for me daughter but...' She peered into her purse and shook her head.

'I've gloves that would go beautifully with it,' Rose said, and ignoring the woman's shaking head, she lifted a pair up. 'These have a tiny flaw in them and I can let you have them for sixpence. You can put a stitch in them.' She pointed to the loose thread in the brown wool gloves, then laid them on top of the scarf. 'A perfect combination,' she said.

The woman's weary face broke into a smile. 'Oh, they're lovely. She'll like them. Ta very much, love,' she said, her voice wobbling with gratitude.

It made Rose happy, and that feeling stayed with her as she satisfied one customer after another. Seeing a woman frowning over a narrow-necked vase, she said, 'Why not go for this one with a wider neck? You could fill it with holly. You'll find some on the towpath with gorgeous red berries, and if you twined it with ivy, it will be very Christmassy.'

'What a grand idea! I'd never have thought it, and it'll cost nowt to fill it.'

'Whew!' Betty gasped as the afternoon light faded and custom dwindled. 'I don't know what I'd do without you, Rose.' She wiped her pink, wobbling cheeks with a handkerchief and beamed fondly.

'I don't know what I would do without you,' Rose replied, meaning every word of it. She was still amazed by how easily she had adapted to earning a living. Getting up every morning at seven, helping with household chores then opening the shop at nine o'clock gave her a sense of empowerment that she hadn't known she was missing. She knew she owed so much to Mavis, her neighbours and Betty. These down to earth, good-natured people had taught her that social status and wealth did not necessarily ensure happiness, and that kindness and thoughtfulness brought their own rewards. She had come to the conclusion that she hadn't much liked Rosamund Brown-Allsop, a silly, over-privileged girl who thought she was entitled to anything she desired. But she liked Rose Brown, a girl who was beginning to prove that she had what Mavis referred to as backbone, and who was making something worthwhile of herself.

'You can go home if you like,' she said to Betty. 'I can finish up here.'

Betty eased off the stool then waddled round to where Rose was tidying a display of scarves. She said, 'Here you are, love, your wages. I've added a nice little bonus. You've earned it.'

Rose surprised herself by reaching out and hugging her. Betty put her chubby arms round Rose and pecked her cheek. 'Merry Christmas, love.'

'Merry Christmas to you,' Rose said, happy tears springing to her eyes.

Ten minutes later, she hurried home to help Mavis prepare the vegetables and the small chicken they would share with Jack the next day.

Later, in St Joseph's Church at midnight, she stood between Mavis and Kitty, breathing in the sharp scents of pine and spruce, her eyes shining in the light of the many candles and the beautifully lit nativity scene. When they sang the carols, she joined in lustily, her heart swelling with joy.

A gentle flurry of snowflakes, ethereal in the light from the gas lamps, swirled around the happy worshippers who lived in Weaver Street as they made their way home. Rose exclaimed, 'Isn't this magical?' and Mavis grinned at Kitty, who raised her eyebrows and grinned back.

Little did Rose know then that her first Christmas in Weaver Street was about to bring yet more magic.

By early evening on Boxing Day the partygoers had gathered in Kitty and John's house: Mavis, Jack and Rose, the O'Malleys, Maggie and Lily, May and her son Joey, and Beth, Blair and Stuart.

'Can me an' Stewpot stay up all night?' Robert piped.

'Indeed you cannot,' Beth admonished, 'and please don't refer to him as Stewpot. His name's Stuart.'

'Then can we go up to my room and build a big bridge out of my new Meccano?' Permission granted, Robert and Stuart went upstairs and Patrick, thinking that was a good idea, asked Mickey if he wanted to join them.

Kitty dished out bowls of soup and John handed out drinks: bottles of brown ale, tots of whisky or gin. 'I'll have a glass of the hard stuff,' Maggie said, waving away the soup Molly offered her.

'You got your Christmas wish then, May,' said Kitty, handing her a bowl of soup and grinning at the tall young man standing next to her. He looked awfully smart in his black merchant navy uniform.

'I couldn't believe it when he walked through the door this afternoon,' May said, her plump cheeks wreathed in proud smiles. 'He's the best Christmas present ever.'

Joey Walker, May's son, laughed. 'I wanted to surprise her,' he said, 'and I think I did, didn't I, old girl?' He threw his arm round his mother's shoulders and gave her an affectionate hug.

'Mind me soup,' May squawked as the bowl wobbled in her hand, but Kitty could tell she wasn't one bit bothered about spilled soup. One of her sons had come home for Christmas, and that was all that mattered.

'Who's the pretty blonde?' Joey asked Kitty when she brought him his soup. Kitty followed his gaze to where Rose was offering sausage rolls to Mavis and Jack. Kitty smiled. Rose did indeed look pretty in her pastel blue raw silk dress that hugged her slender figure in all the right places. She had sought Kitty's opinion as to whether she should wear it for the party. 'Do you think it's a bit too fancy?' she had asked. Kitty had noted the Harrods label and admired the fine beadwork on the neck and hemline. She presumed it was one Rose had brought with her from home. Now, she was glad she'd persuaded her to wear it.

'She's Mavis's lodger,' she told Joey, noting the gleam in his eyes. 'She's a lovely girl.'

'That she is,' May agreed. Joey handed his soup dish to Kitty. 'That was very tasty,' he said. 'Now, if you'll excuse me...' He sauntered in Rose's direction and Kitty and May exchanged knowing smiles.

The celebrations were in full swing. Jack gave an amusing rendition of 'The Night Before Christmas' before Beth and Blair decided it was time to take Stuart home, and Kitty put Robert to bed. 'Straight to sleep, my lad, or Santa Claus might come and take your presents back,' she warned. Robert giggled. Despite his mammy's warning, he knew that his mammy and daddy wouldn't let Santa do anything of the sort.

Molly and Lily, allowed to stay up later, sweetly sang 'In the Bleak Midwinter', Maggie tipsily quipping that she wouldn't want a lamb as a pressie. 'It 'ud shit all over the place.' After everyone had stopped laughing, Maggie and Kitty gave a comical, slightly lewd performance of 'I Wanna Be Loved By You'. Kitty caught John's eye as she shimmied up and down and John responded with a naughty wink. Then Kitty and Bridie sang a couple of jaunty Irish ballads, encouraging Mick to join in as they jigged across the floor.

'See, I told ye it 'ud be a right old Irish hooley,' Kitty panted. Molly exchanged embarrassed glances with Mickey O'Malley before collapsing with laughter.

During all this jollity, Joey kept close to Rose's side. He asked her how she came to be living with Mavis, and she embroidered a tale about coming to work in Liverpool. She thought he looked extremely handsome in his uniform, and she laughed as he told her amusing stories of life aboard ship. 'Maybe you'll take pity on a poor, lonely sailor and make my leave special by going out with me,' he said eventually. Rose, buoyed by a few glasses of sweet sherry, readily agreed. She really did find him attractive and good fun.

Before the party ended, they all joined in singing carols and Rose was enraptured. She thought back to the stuffy celebrations they had at home, the local dignitaries standing stiffly, glasses in hand, making a false show of being merry, and the embarrassed faces of the servants at the pathetic little party her mother reluctantly held so that she might unctuously hand them their quarterly wages and a miserable bonus.

'I've never had a Christmas like this,' she said to Kitty, 'or this much fun.'

'It's what we do round here,' Kitty said, laughing into Rose's shining eyes. 'Make the most of it.'

Rose was going to do just that, and as they all joined hands and circled Kitty's front room, singing 'We Wish You a Merry Christmas', Rose thought her heart might burst. For all her past miseries, life had never felt so good.

PART III

15

LIVERPOOL, 1935

Sometimes Rose wondered where the years had gone; they had flown by. Each of the past five years had brought joys and sorrows to her friends and neighbours and she felt as much a part of their lives as if she had always lived in Weaver Street. It warmed her heart to see how they pulled together as they weathered the hardships the Depression had caused, neighbours helping neighbours to make sure none of them suffered unduly. Coming here had changed her life, and in many respects, it had changed it for the better.

She also found it hard to believe that she was now twenty-three, and madly in love. Her friendship with Joey Walker had blossomed into a full-blown romance and on New Year's Eve, as the church bells' chimes had welcomed in 1935, he had asked her to marry him. Of course, she had accepted. She loved him dearly.

Everyone had wished them well. May was ecstatic, and on a bleak morning at the end of February, she was already planning a wedding as she and Rose stood on the docks, waving farewell to Joey, who was about to sail for the Far East and would be away until November.

The romance had started the day after Kitty's Boxing Day party in 1929. Joey had knocked on Mavis's door and asked for her. 'There's a young man come to see you, Rose,' Mavis had called up the stairs.

Rose had just put on a pale blue wool dress and brushed her hair so that it hung in silky curtains to her shoulders, although she was going nowhere other than Mavis's kitchen. Thank goodness she'd taken care to dress up, she'd thought when she saw Joey leaning nonchalantly against the back door.

'*The Broadway Melody* is on at the Gaumont. I thought you might like to go,' he'd said, his blue eyes alight with hope. Rose's heart had leapt as she accepted. The evening turned out to be wonderful. Joey was fun as well as good looking, and that night as they emerged from the cinema, he'd waltzed her down the street, humming one of the tunes from the musical. Rose hadn't laughed so much for a very long time. After that date, they'd spent the rest of his leave together; a pantomime one night, the cinema the next, and a few evenings in the Weaver's Arms. For the first time ever, she was leading the sort of life a young woman should be enjoying, and when Joey went back to sea, he had made her promise to write to him. Since then, his ship had docked in Liverpool several times and with each meeting, their love for one another had deepened and it was only natural to expect that eventually they would get married.

However, like so many things in Rose's life, Joey's proposal brought with it a whole set of new problems; her joy marred by what had happened in the past. They hadn't as yet set a date or even a year, but this didn't make her unhappy – quite the contrary – it allowed her time to find a way to deal with the whole sorry mess. Her tutor had often quoted from Shakespeare and the words 'Oh, what a tangled web we weave when first we practice to deceive,' had never seemed truer. To that end, she pondered how on earth to tell him the truth.

Joey believed she was an ordinary working-class girl who just happened to be Mavis's lodger. She had waffled vaguely about coming to Liverpool looking for work and, of course, she'd made no mention of Lewis. She was too ashamed. But what would Joey think if she told him the truth? How would he react if he knew she wasn't a virgin, that she had once carried another man's baby in her belly? Would the fact that she was heiress to a large estate in Buckinghamshire soften the blow? She didn't think so. Joey wasn't a fortune hunter. He was a proud man who valued honesty and integrity. But could she make her vows before God, knowing that their marriage was built on lies?

A few days before, Mavis had been waxing lyrical about what a beautiful thing marriage was, concluding with, 'Of course it must be based on respect and complete honesty – no secrets, no lies.' Rose had seen the challenging glint in her eyes, and quailed inwardly. Her nerves had only been made worse when Mavis had casually dropped into the conversation that she would need to produce a birth certificate to get a marriage certificate. Not only was it a problem that hers was in her father's study in a mansion in Buckinghamshire, but of course the biggest issue was that it would give the game away. Joey hadn't proposed to Rosamund Brown-Allsop; he was in love with Rose Brown.

One Saturday in May, as Rose sat at the counter writing a letter to Joey – she wrote one every week when he was at sea – she was mulling over the consequences of her secret life. The shop had been quiet all day. With each passing year, the Depression bit deeper and deeper, people everywhere struggling to make ends meet. Many of them had been deprived of their livelihoods, and buying the sort of things on offer in Betty's Bijou Bazaar was the last thing on their minds.

Rose sat staring at the loving words she had just written, her chin resting on her fist and her eyes misty as she acknowledged that soon she would have to tell Joey the truth and risk losing him. She shuddered at the thought and hurriedly brushed away tears as two young women entered the shop. The feeling stayed with her for the rest of the day, and as daylight dimmed, she locked the shop and trudged up the lane, deep in thought. Lights shone out from Kitty's house, and Rose could see the Sykes family gathered around the dining room table, the smiles on their faces making her feel all the more miserable: would she ever sit like that with Joey and their children?

Kitty saw Rose pass by as she ladled stew into five bowls on the tray before carrying it into the dining room. Personally, she thought it a bit of a faff – it was so much easier to put the food on the kitchen table as they did for breakfast – but what was the point of having a dining room if you didn't use it? She doled out the bowls of cheap neck-of-mutton stew then sat down at the table to eat her own.

Patrick, in his last year at the boys' grammar now, had his head in a book. Kitty tapped the back of his hand with her spoon. 'Eat up whilst it's hot,' she said.

Next to him was Molly, neat and tidy in her stiff, starched nurse's uniform. She had enrolled to do her training as soon as she had left the girls' grammar and was assigned to the Oxford Street Hospital in Brownlow Place, which specialised in maternity care and children's diseases. Kitty had been surprised when Molly announced that she intended to go into nursing. She had imagined that her rather fastidious daughter might choose office work, or train to be a teacher.

'Are ye sure you'll cope with all the messy and personal things ye'll have to do for your patients?' Kitty had given Molly a bemused look.

'Of course I will. That's what nurses do,' Molly had replied archly. And thus far, it seemed as though she was managing quite nicely.

'I'm starting in the children's ward on Monday,' Molly said enthusiastically, having spent the past six months in maternity, washing mountains of bedpans and helping clear up after the mothers had given birth.

'Will you have to wipe their bottoms?' Robert pretended to retch.

'I'll do whatever needs doing to make them comfortable. I'll wash them and change their dressings and administer medication under the sister's orders, and when the doctor does his rounds, I'll listen and make notes so that I can learn,' Molly told him primly.

'And she'll probably kill a few with kindness,' Patrick said sarcastically. It amused him to think of Molly as a nurse, and in truth, he was rather envious that she was out in the working world. He couldn't wait to leave school and join his stepfather in the engineering factory.

'Now, Patrick!' John chided. 'Don't go upsetting her or it'll be you in need of hospital treatment.' He smiled as he spoke, but they all knew that when Molly and Patrick disagreed, things could turn nasty. Molly not only had Tom Conlon's black hair and flashing blue eyes, she also had his self-assured temperament. Patrick, on the other hand, had not only inherited his mother's tawny hair and gold-flecked eyes, he had the same good-natured approach to life. However, it didn't prevent him from having a go at his sister whenever the opportunity arose.

Kitty glanced at John, her heart aching to see the shadows under his eyes and the lines etched round his mouth. This Depression was taking its toll, every day a new struggle to seek out new contracts and maintain his workforce in the factory. This evening, she thought he looked particularly downcast, and when the children left the table, she voiced her concerns.

'Ye're lookin' awful worried, love. Tell me about it.'

'I'm sick of scouring the country trying to drum up business when there's none to be had,' John said, shaking his head despairingly. 'Exports are at an all-time low and my order book's never been as empty. Mind you, I'm better off than those poor buggers on the docks, fighting amongst themselves for a chance to earn a few hours' pay. And I wouldn't be Ramsay MacDonald for all the tea in China. Being Prime Minister's not all it's cracked up to be. That coalition government's more than he can handle, and Baldwin's not making it any easier. Trouble is, there's none of 'em seem to know how to stop this rising unemployment. One of my lads came back from making a delivery in Newcastle and he said that in every town he passed through, men were queued up outside the Labour Exchanges and the factories. It's not as bad here, but for how long?'

Kitty had no answer to that. 'Don't let it get ye down, love. As long as we have one another, we'll get by. We still have the café and the bookmaker's shop, even if the money from them's hardly worth counting.'

Wearily, John got to his feet. 'You're right, love. But like you say, as long as we stick together, we'll see it through.' He stooped and kissed her. 'If I hadn't got you, I'd be all at sea, my rudder gone, my oars overboard and a leak in the bottom of the boat.' Kitty stood and threw her arms round him. They clung to one another, laughing. He'd said those same words to her when he'd asked her to marry him, afraid that she might refuse. He let her go, both of them taking heart from their shared support. 'By the way,' John continued, 'I've a delivery to make to the docks tomorrow morning. Is there anything you want me to pick up while I'm in the city?'

Kitty bit on her lip as she gave it some thought. Then she

grinned. 'Tell ye what, I'll come with ye. I want some thread, an' needles for me sewing machine.'

'Then it's a date, Mrs Sykes,' said John. And somewhat cheered, he picked up his order book and went into the parlour.

The next morning, Kitty climbed into the passenger seat of John's van, quite looking forward to her trip to the city. 'I remember the day I'd have been exporting a full load,' he grunted, gesturing with his thumb to the two small packing crates in the back of the van as he climbed into the driver's seat.

'Trade's bound to pick up soon, love,' Kitty told him and, her spirits still high, she kept up a jolly line of chatter as they drove to the docks. 'I can always say I've seen the king of England even if he didn't stop to shake me hand,' she chirped as the cavernous entrance to the Mersey Tunnel came into view, and recalling the day that King George V had opened it in 1934.

'Aye, that was a grand day out,' John agreed, 'and the building of it provided plenty of men with work.'

At the entrance to the Albert Dock, John brought the van to a halt. Kitty gasped at the huge press of men crowded at the gates. 'Poor buggers,' John muttered, 'and half of 'em haven't a hope of getting set on for a few hours' work.'

Kitty's tender heart went out to the shabby, dejected-looking men with their broken boots and their greasy caps pulled low on their foreheads. Those nearest the van glared balefully at it, the glares turning to snarls as the official on the gate yelled at them to stand aside as he swung one of the large iron gates open to let John through. 'It's heartbreaking to see decent men begging for work,' said Kitty as they drove through the gates and on to where John would deposit the crates.

Whilst he was doing this, Kitty got out of the van to watch the stevedores hurrying up and down the gangways of huge ships. Above her head, massive bales swung in the air before being lowered onto the ship's decks. Kitty wondered what they contained, and where the ships were bound. She rarely came to the docks and so fascinated was she by the bustling activity that she was oblivious to the ensuing chaos at the dock gates.

A fight had broken out and the angry men, driven by hunger, poverty and unemployment, had stormed the gates. Yelling and shouting, they surged towards her. 'Jesus, Mary and Joseph,' she cried, and rooted to the spot, she looked wildly in John's direction. He was still attending to the loading of the crates a few yards in front of where she was standing, and the van was a similar distance behind her. 'Kitty, get back in the van,' she heard him roar above the cacophony.

She began running to the van but before she could reach it, she was shouldered aside by a hefty dock guard. She landed heavily on her knees, wincing as her outstretched hands scraped the concrete slabs. From that position, she watched the guards swinging their batons, lashing out indiscriminately, beating heads and legs as they tried to drive the wrathful horde back to the gate.

Terrified, and her heart in her mouth, Kitty scrabbled to her feet and set off again. When she reached the van, she dived inside and slammed the door. Shaking like a jelly, she peered through the windscreen for any sign of John, but she'd lost sight of him in the raging throng. Everywhere she looked, frantic men swarmed the dock, fists and feet thrashing at anybody and anything. One ugly-looking brute glared at her through the windscreen then thumped the van's bonnet. All at once, the van was surrounded by a baying mob shoving their weight against it. It swayed dangerously. Kitty cowered in her seat, her head clutched in her hands. *Please God, don't let them harm John, get us out of here in one piece*, she silently prayed as the van rocked from side to side.

Just as she thought her head would burst and she was about to be sick, a fleet of Black Marias screeched onto the dock. Whistles blew as the policemen leapt from their vehicles, their nightsticks at the ready. The mob battering the van peeled away, the police in full chase, and as law and order was restored, Kitty saw John limping towards her, his left eye badly swollen and his jacket ripped.

Judging it was now safe, she leapt out of the van and hobbled towards him, ignoring the pain in her bruised knees and stinging hands. 'Oh, what have they done to you, my love?' Kitty cried as he pulled her into a tight embrace.

'Some poor lad decided to take his misery out on me. He most likely mistook me for one of the bosses,' John said against her hair. 'But never mind me, what about you?' Deeply concerned, he stepped back to look her up and down.

'I'll live,' she said, giving him a brave smile, 'but me stockings are in tatters.'

Safely back in the van, they drove off the dock. A crowd of surly men, some battered and bloodstained, were still gathered at the gate, hoping to get set-on.

'Poor sods, they're desperate,' John commented. 'Their bellies and their pockets are empty, and when you can't put bread on the table to feed your family, you lose all sense of reason.'

'I knew things were bad but by all the saints, that carry-on on the dock brings it home to ye, an' no mistake.' Kitty sounded as though she was about to cry.

They drove straight back to Weaver Street, the sewing requisites forgotten, and on the way, they commiserated with each other's injuries, but their true sympathies lay with the disillusioned men waiting at the dock gate.

'I was scared out of me wits,' Kitty declared when Maggie dropped in shortly after Kitty had arrived home and John had gone to the factory, 'but I was more worried about John. He's got a right shiner an' his jacket's ruined.'

'You could have been killed,' Maggie exclaimed as she watched

Kitty peel her torn lisle stockings from her bruised and grazed knees.

'It's only a few scrapes,' said Kitty as she washed her sore hands. 'An' it's nothing compared to what them poor lads at the docks are suffering,' she continued, her voice rising. 'God, ye should have seen them, Maggie. They were like wild animals. The bloody banks an' the government have a lot to answer for, that they'd reduce men to that.'

16

On Sunday afternoon, Kitty and her friends gathered in her dining room for a make-do-and-mend session. Having a jangle while they worked made the dismal task of doing without more fun.

'Do ye think there's ever goin' to be an end to this Depression?' Kitty stilled the treadle on her sewing machine and turned to look at her friends.

'Blair says the serious repercussions it's having is bringing the country to its knees,' Beth replied. 'The speculative boom has caused an economic imbalance.'

Maggie gave an audible groan and Kitty hid a smile. Beth's husband, a studious young Scot who worked in the pattern design office at Holroyd's Mill, was fond of using long words and Beth was just as fond of repeating his opinions, even if Kitty wasn't sure she knew what they meant.

'I know John means it kindly enough,' Kitty continued, 'but if he tells me to tighten me belt once more, I'll cut meself off at the waist.' Chuckling at her own wit, she turned the thick grey blanket that she was making into a coat for May Walker under the needle and whizzed down a seam.

'What I find hard to understand is how a city as prosperous as Liverpool can just wither and die,' Mavis moaned as she ripped a length of wool from the jumper she was unravelling. 'Businesses are closing week on week, thousands unemployed and everyone just scraping by to put bread on the table.'

'Yeah, if Holroyd's are still on short time this time next week, I'll have to miss me rent again,' said Maggie, snipping buttons off an old coat and tossing them into Kitty's button tin: nothing was wasted. 'I might have to find another way of paying him, if you know what I mean,' she added lewdly.

'Do ye think he'd have the strength for it? I'd say he's gettin' all he can handle from her at number seven,' Kitty chirped. Even though she cracked a joke, Kitty worried about what lengths Maggie might go to. More than once in the past three years, she'd made sure that Maggie met her rent, and that Lily had shoes and clothes, even if they were hand-me-downs altered to fit the growing girl.

'Aye, he was there again last night,' said Bridie.

The women knew that Bridie was referring to the chap who owned numbers five, seven and nine Weaver Street. Lorna Bell, the occupant of number seven, was his secretary. A cold fish of a woman, she'd already earned the dislike of most of the neighbours with her high-handed, snooty attitude.

'I wonder what he tells his wife when he stays out all night,' Kitty said, giving a dirty laugh that tailed off into a sigh as she thought of Tom. He'd stayed out all night making the excuse that it was business when all the time he'd been dallying with Priscilla Hutchinson, the daughter of a wealthy horse trainer and owner.

'And him with a wife and three children,' Mavis sneered.

'Mick says you should blackmail him.' Bridie addressed Maggie and May. 'Get free rent to keep you from telling his wife.' The two women laughed.

'That 'ud put the cat among the pigeons.' Kitty raised her eyebrows and grinned wickedly.

'You're dead right there. He's never off her doorstep,' Maggie sneered. 'She's all fur coat and no knickers is that one.'

Beth blushed and changed the unseemly conversation to something less embarrassing by trilling, 'I finished the rug I was pegging for Stuart's bedroom. I backed it with a washed potato sack and I'm starting another for ours.' She waved the scissors she was using to cut Blair's old trousers into strips.

Rose carefully pushed her needle into the hem of the second-hand coat that Kitty had altered to a fashionable three-quarter length. She hadn't said a word all afternoon; the Depression and the sex lives of her neighbours were of no interest to her. She had something far more serious to think about. Joey's last letter was burning a hole in her skirt pocket. 'All being well I'll be home in November and I want us to get married, so start making plans,' he had written. But six months wasn't long enough to undo the mistakes she had made and the lies she had told. Not even a lifetime could do that. Even thinking about it made her break out in a cold sweat. Pinning the needle into the fabric, she pushed back her chair. 'I'm going for a walk,' she said, rushing from the room. Mavis's face clouded.

'Dear me, what's the matter with her?' Beth's tone let them know she considered the girl's abrupt departure bad manners.

'I don't really know,' Mavis replied, her beady little eyes dark with anxiety. 'For some time now, I've had the feeling something's bothering her. She should be over the moon planning to get married, but she won't even talk about it. She's clammed up, gone back to being like she was when she first came.'

'I know what ye mean, Mavis. When I mentioned the wedding, she just brushed me off,' said Kitty.

'She can be very hard to understand at times,' Beth said.

'I think all posh people are hard to understand,' Maggie said. 'They're that busy being la-di-da they can't act natural. Personally, she gets up my bloody nose with her fancy talk an' all that politeness.'

'Oh, Maggie, you are harsh. The poor girl can't help speaking the way she does.' Beth's lip curled as she glared at Maggie. 'You'd make a good friend for Karl Marx. He doesn't like the upper classes either.'

Kitty smiled behind her hand. There goes Beth, she thought, airing another bit of Blair's knowledge.

'Who the bloody hell's Karl Marx? Does he work at Holroyd's?' Maggie asked. The others laughed at that.

'I think Rose'll make a lovely bride,' Kitty said, changing the subject before Beth could lecture Maggie on the socialist revolutionary. 'She was such a little waif of a thing when she first came here but she's filled out rightly due to your good cooking, Mavis.'

'Yeah, and letting me put a bit of bleach in her hair did her a favour,' said Maggie, keen to let it be known that she'd played a part in transforming Rose.

'Oh, yes, she's nothing like that poor child I brought home with me,' Mavis agreed, 'but still she's not as happy as she should be.'

Outside, Rose glanced in the direction of noisy shouts and laughter and saw that at the top end of the lane, a lively ball game was taking place. Envious of the youngsters, she trudged down the street. They weren't burdened with a murky past that threatened their future. 'Hiya, Rose,' she heard one of them call out. She thought it sounded like Lily, but she didn't look back and hurried down the lane and out into Broad Green.

Lily shrugged then chased after the ball. Patrick booted the football over her head, narrowly missing her bright red mop of curls, and his own hair flopped onto his forehead as he doubled over with laughter. Mickey O'Malley, his teammate, caught the ball and turned tauntingly to Molly. Molly's flashing blue eyes met Mickey's and he felt a strange tightening in his chest and an even stranger one between his legs. It wasn't because he fancied Molly; she was just a friend, but he was at an age when any shapely girl had that effect on him. He threw the ball then watched Molly's pert bosom dance under her jumper as she reached out to catch it.

'Chuck it to me,' Lily yelled, bouncing on her heels ready to catch it, but Molly ignored her and tossed the ball in her half-brother's direction. Robert grinned and caught it, grateful to Molly for letting him into the game. 'Catch, Stewpot,' he yelled, tossing the ball to his partner Stuart Forsythe.

'Aw, Molly, you daft ha'porth,' Lily bawled, 'it's us against them. You're not supposed to let them have it.' Robert smirked at Stuart as he threw the ball back, but before Robert could catch it, Patrick leapt and caught it. Robert and Stuart exchanged peevish glances. The big ones always won.

Robert glowered at Patrick, but his anger was diverted when, out of the corner of his eye, he saw a commotion on the steps outside number seven. 'Look! They're fighting,' he yelled.

Five pairs of eyes followed the direction in which he pointed, the ball game forgotten as they watched two women tussling on the steps. Lorna Bell had the advantage of being on the upper step and seemed to be winning. She grabbed at the other woman's hat, flinging it down the path, then clutched at a handful of greying hair. Screaming and shouting, the older woman grabbed the front of Lorna's dress, pulling her down until they were level.

Quick as a flash, Lily raced into Kitty's to get Maggie. This was too good to keep to herself. Maggie flew out, closely followed by the others. 'Oooh, this is worth seeing,' she yelled. By now, the two women were pummelling one another on the garden path. Maggie let out a roaring laugh. 'That's the landlord's wife. She must have found out about his fancy woman – secretary be buggered.'

'Someone had better put a stop to it before they kill each other,' Kitty said, lifting her skirt and darting down to number seven as her friends ran after her. 'Stop that carry-on this instant, ye're behavin' like alley cats,' she panted as she reached number seven's gate.

'Disgraceful behaviour in front of young children,' Mavis squawked.

'Ladies! Ladies! Please...' Beth pleaded, at the same time grabbing Stuart and hiding his face in her skirt. He struggled to free himself. This was fun.

Seeing they had an audience, the women faltered. The landlord's wife gave Lorna one last thump, picked up her hat then made a break for the lane. On safe ground, she yelled, 'Make sure you're gone before I get back!' She hurried out of sight into Broad Green. Lorna Bell straightened her torn blouse and gave the spectators a withering glare before slamming back into the house.

'Snotty cow,' Maggie remarked. 'She got her bloody comeuppance all right.'

'Go back to your game,' Kitty ordered the young ones.

Tongues wagging, the youngsters sauntered up the lane and the adults went back to Kitty's to gossip. Within the hour, Lorna Bell's possessions had been loaded into a van and number seven was vacant once again: but not for long.

The Sunday afternoon make-do-and-mend session had left Kitty feeling downcast. It had been fun to giggle at Lorna Bell and her landlord's expense but the frugality of making over old clothes had wearied her. To be perfectly honest, Kitty was sick and tired of the continuing hardships she and her neighbours faced on a daily basis.

That night in bed, she lay wide awake, although she had retired almost an hour before. Outside, the night breeze was rustling the sycamore trees. Beside her, John moved restlessly. Just lately, this happened all too often, both of them afraid to rest on the darkness of the night.

'Can't ye sleep, love?' she whispered. 'Neither can I.'

'I'm thinking about tomorrow,' John mumbled. 'I'm dreading having to go in and tell four of my lads I can't keep them on any longer.' He turned so that he was facing her. 'We've overhauled all the machinery, painted the workshops and cleaned all the tools. Now there's nothing more for them to do and I can't afford to keep them on to sit about the place. It's heartbreaking. Three of them are married men with families.'

'God love them, but ye've done your best keepin' them on this long,' Kitty said, reaching up to stroke John's cheek.

'They'll not be surprised. It's been on the cards for ages. They know I work on a last in, first out basis and none of them have been with me as long as the seven men I'm keeping on. I'm almost back to where I started nearly twenty years ago.'

He sighed heavily.

'Never mind, love, this Depression can't go on forever. There's bound to be something better round the corner.'

'I only hope you're right,' John said pulling her closer and kissing her.

Kitty wasn't the only person in Weaver Street who couldn't sleep. Rose was no nearer to finding a solution to her dilemma. One scenario after the other played in her head. She could write to her father, ask for her birth and baptism certificates and risk the wrath of her parents; she thought she could bear that, and Joey might not care that he was marrying Rosamund Brown-Allsop and not plain Rose Brown: what was in a name? But could she stand at the altar and promise before God to love, honour and obey a man who believed she was a virgin? Joey had said more than once that one of the things he loved most about her was her sweet, innocent nature, that she wasn't fast and easy like so many other girls. Could a man tell whether or not his wife was a virgin? She just didn't know. Of one thing she was fairly certain. He would find it hard to forgive the lies she had told him. Joey was a man of integrity, open and up front. He never prevaricated and fabricated stories when the truth had to be told.

Rose closed her eyes. How strange it all was. Here she was lying in bed and instead of planning what should be the most wonderful day of her life, she was tossing and turning, her mind on fire and steeped in guilt. Exhausted, she came to the conclusion that when he came home, she would tell him the truth and brave the consequences. There was nothing else for it. Forcing herself to stop worrying, she fell into a restless sleep.

17

Bridie O'Malley yawned as she threw back the bedclothes in the front bedroom of number eleven Weaver Street. It was still dark, the glimmer of the gas lamp in the street below casting a faint glow through the curtains at the bedroom window. She shuffled her feet into her slippers, then stretched out her arm and gave her husband a shake.

'Time to get up, Mick, it's gone six.'

Mick groaned then broke wind noisily as he heaved to the edge of the bed. Sitting up, he clutched his head with both hands, furiously ruffling his thick black hair to shake off the last vestiges of sleep. Then, thudding his feet to the floor, he stretched his burly frame before stooping to pick up his moleskin trousers. 'What's the weather like?' he grunted.

Bridie crossed to the window and drew back the curtains. 'Dry,' she said, her voice high with relief.

'Thank God for that.' Mick had been rained off too many building sites since the start of the year: April had been a bitch of a month.

Bridie pulled on her dressing gown and out on the landing, she knocked on the attic door and then the back bedroom door. 'Time to get up, lads,' she sang out. Receiving answering groans from Liam, Mickey and Donal, she shuffled downstairs to the kitchen, Mick at her heels.

Bridie set the kettle to boil and then made spam sandwiches for Mick and the lads to take with them. They were the lucky ones; they had jobs to go to. Bricklayers and labourers were still in demand since the city council had embarked on a huge building project. They were rapidly demolishing the slum dwellings down by the docks and new homes were being built in various parts of the city. Today Mick and the lads were closer to home in Jagger's Yard at the top of Weaver Street, finishing the new development there. Unfortunately, there were too many labouring men prepared to work for a pittance and the contractors had them over a barrel. Even skilled men's wages had been cut to the minimum, much to Big Mick's disgust, and he frequently cursed them for the greedy bastards they were.

Down in the kitchen, the boys and their father stood to slurp hot tea and stuff their mouths with bread smeared with dripping, no time to sit, no time for conversation. Donal and Liam, two strapping lads as handsome as their father, pulled on their jackets and caps. Donal was twenty and Liam a year younger. Neither of them had settled in Weaver Street, and in their free time they spent much of it in the Irish Club in the city, mixing with fellows like themselves who yearned to be back in Ireland. They were both determined to return to Sligo when they'd saved enough money to set themselves up in their own business and Bridie was resigned to losing them before long.

She watched with a fond, sad smile as Wee Mickey donned a thick coat over his flannel shirt and corduroy trousers that had once been Liam's. The garment, too large, shrouded his lithe, lean body, turning him from a boy into a man; but he was still her baby.

She lifted a woolly hat and pulled it over his thatch of black curls, murmuring, 'Have a good day, love,' before planting a kiss on his cheek. A smile twitched the corners of Mickey's mouth as, without having spoken a word, he went and stood by the outside door.

Bridie patted Donal then Liam's cheek as they too made for the door. 'Ye've not far to go today,' she said. ''Tis only the top of the street.'

Their father drained his mug then nodded at his sons, ready and waiting. Big Mick blessed the day his father had apprenticed him to a bricklayer and now he was passing on that skill to his own sons. He considered himself to be a very lucky man in more ways than one.

He shrugged into his jacket then wound a muffler round his neck before pulling on his flat cap. Then he turned and put his arms round his wife, pulling her to his broad chest. She gazed up at him with pure grey eyes, almost silver, and up close her nose had a sprinkling of freckles. She was still the beautiful colleen he had married twenty and more years ago in Sligo, her waist almost as slim as it had been then, even though she had borne him three sons. He dropped a kiss on the end of her nose. 'See you this evenin',' he said, reaching for the packet of sandwiches and stuffing them into his jacket pocket.

Bridie leaned against him for a moment, revelling in the warmth of his embrace. He was her big, strong Mick who toiled in all weathers to provide for her and their sons. She brushed her lips against his then said, 'Take care, big man. Pray God be kind an' keep the rain away.' She let him go, her eyes following his muscular back and the narrow shoulders of Wee Mickey as her men slipped out of the back door into the still dark early morning. *God bless them all*, she prayed as the door closed behind them.

Back over at the small counter beside the sink, she smeared more slices of bread with dripping and brewed a fresh pot of tea.

She'd have another cuppa then do the washing. She wasn't needed at the café till eleven.

Down in the cellar, Bridie bent over the tub, possing shirts and underwear with such force that the hot, soapy water foamed and frothed, slopping suds on the stone flags. She didn't object to the chore, but she did worry about losing her job in the café. Earning that bit extra went a long way to meeting the family's financial commitments. She hadn't the heart to take money from Donal and Liam, knowing how hard they were saving to go back home, and although Big Mick's wages were adequate, Wee Mickey's were next to nothing. Bread had gone up to eightpence a loaf, meat was a luxury and there was hardly a week went by that there wasn't one bill or another to pay. Then there was the money they had to find for Mick to send home to Sligo each week to keep the wolf from his aged parents and disabled brother's door. She didn't object to that either, but it was money they couldn't really spare.

She fished out a shirt and put it through the mangle, her thoughts churning in tandem with the wooden rollers. The shirt plopped into the basket and as she reached for another, she chastised herself for feeling miserable. This Depression couldn't last forever, and she was far better off than most folks in Edge Hill.

* * *

In the cluttered front bedroom at number nine, Maggie drifted on the edges of sleep. She didn't want to get up to another day's mending, but must was her master. Snuggling under the blankets, she decided to lie on for a while longer but a sharp nudge to her ribs and then hot, pawing hands groping her thighs brought her to consciousness. She sighed heavily.

'Come on, let's be having you,' Pete grunted as he heaved his flabby body on top of hers. Maggie swallowed her objections and let him do his worst. If she was going to keep him interested, she had no alternative. He'd been at home for the past five days but she knew that come the weekend, he'd disappear for three or four days, and all without handing over a penny for his board and lodgings. As he puffed and panted, she wondered why she put up with him. He wasn't much to look at with his fleshy face, thinning hair and the beer belly hanging over the top of his trousers, but he was better than nobody, and Maggie needed a man about the place to make her feel that life still had something to offer.

Pete rolled off her, then pulled the covers over his head. Within minutes, he was snoring. He'd not move again until midday, she knew that, but now she was wide awake, so she swung her legs over the edge of the bed and got to her feet. Shuffling into the bathroom, she sat on the lavatory, pondering what it would be like to have a man who put her first, one with a good job who loved her enough to happily hand over his wages each week. She hadn't had that with Fred.

He'd been a regular in the army when she married him but he hadn't divulged his marital status to his regiment, so she hadn't even had the pleasure of a spouse's allowance. Whenever he came home on leave, he'd get drunk and then beat her black and blue. The only time he'd shown her any kindness was when she got pregnant with Lily. Fred had liked the idea of having a son. When the baby turned out to be a girl with flaming red hair, his own being mousy and Maggie's blonde, his suspicions had been aroused. Then, one afternoon in the Wagon and Horse, some sneaky gobshite had pointed out a big red-haired fellow and told Fred his wife had been messing with him whilst he was in Egypt. After a final savage beating that left Maggie utterly demoralised, Kitty had helped her throw him out and she hadn't seen him since. Not that she wanted to, but she did want to be loved. She'd had several lovers since then, some who stayed for a night and others longer, but they all left her in the end.

Still in her nightdress, she slouched out onto the landing and opened the attic door. Climbing halfway up the narrow flight of stairs, she peered through the rails into the messy room that smelled of Evening in Paris. Under the attic's sloping ceiling, Lily's bed was empty. *She takes after me*, Maggie thought, eyeing Lily's dresses and stockings draped over the chest of drawers, but glad to see that her daughter was up already to go to work in the weaving shed at Holroyd's Mill.

On leaving school nearly a year ago, Lily had announced she would no longer share the back bedroom with her grandmother, Vi, so she had moved up into the attic, declaring that this was her space and that Maggie and Vi should keep out of it. Not in the least tempted to go further up the stairs and tidy the mess, Maggie turned tail and made her way into the kitchen. It was empty. Lily had left for work.

Last night's dinner plates filled the sink. Maggie flinched as she plunged her hand into the greasy scum on the water and fished out the breadknife. Pushing aside the clutter on the countertop, she began slicing a stale loaf to make toast. She filled the kettle and put it on the gas ring, then over at the black lead range she raked the embers of the fire and threw on a shovel full of coal. What would she give for a kitchen like Kitty's with all its modern conveniences? But to get one like that, she needed a man like John Sykes.

A hacking cough on the stairs signalled that her mother was on her way down. Vi shuffled into the kitchen, her hair in curlers and a cigarette clamped between her lips. 'Do us a slice, Queen,' she croaked, seeing Maggie on her knees by the fire, toasting fork in hand. Maggie came upright, tossing the browned slice ungraciously onto the table then returning to her task with another slice.

Vi scraped margarine from its paper wrapping and smeared it

on the toast. The margarine, like the sugar bowl and brown sauce bottle, sat permanently on the table amidst a confusion of magazines, hair curlers and other detritus. Snorting, she picked a red hair off the bread and wiped it down the front of her stained dressing gown. 'Our Lily's bloody hair gets everywhere,' she spat. She bit into the toast then through a mouthful mumbled, 'Is Parasite Pete still in his pit?'

Maggie brought her head up sharp. 'What did you call him?'

'A parasite, that's what they call things that latch on an' live off other stuff.'

'You don't have to be so bloody nasty about him,' Maggie growled, coming to the table and reaching for the margarine. 'It's no wonder he stays away like he does with you picking holes in him at every turn.' The kettle whistled and she filled the teapot, banging it down on the table along with two mugs.

'Catch yourself on, girl. He's a fly-by-night. And if you think you've landed him then you're sadly mistaken, you silly mare.'

'Oh, shut up! I've enough to worry about without you moaning. If Holroyd's don't bring me another piece when they come to collect this one, I'll not make next week's rent.'

'You could allus try askin' Mister Lard-Arse to put his hand in his pocket.'

Maggie snatched up her mug and the remains of her toast and blundered into the front room where the mending frame with its chalked piece loomed malevolently.

Later that day, Robert and Stuart, just home from school, were standing talking football by Kitty's gate when a large removal van reversed up the lane and parked up outside number seven. Curious, they stopped comparing the skills of Fred Rogers, a centre forward, and Stanley Kane, the goalkeeper, and sauntered towards the van, their curiosity further aroused when a hackney cab drove into the lane behind it. The cab driver climbed out and went to speak to the removal men, who were still sitting in the van.

'That's an Austin,' Robert said, gazing enviously at the sleek black cab. He was mad about cars, and at ten years old he prided himself on recognising the make of practically every motor vehicle on the road.

The removal men climbed down and opened the rear doors of the van. They unloaded a wheelchair and the cab driver pushed it over to his cab. One of the removal men went with him. Robert groaned. 'More old codgers coming to live in our street,' he said. 'They mustn't know we've got enough of 'em already.'

'She's not that old, she's about the same age as Molly,' Stuart said as a young woman stepped out of the Austin. Then an older couple alighted.

'They look ancient, an' look at what they're wearin',' Robert scoffed.

The older woman's long black coat had a huge brown fur collar that covered her shoulders, its points reaching almost to her waist. Her hair was hidden under a round fur hat of a similar colour to the collar. The man's coat, also black, had a grey astrakhan shawl collar and his hat was a homburg perched high on his head. Robert started to giggle, and Stuart joined in. Just then, Molly came walking up the lane on her way home from work.

The cab driver and the removal man were peering into the cab, then after a few words and nods of agreement, they reached into the rear seat. As Molly drew level with them, she heard harsh protests and groans coming from inside the vehicle. Then she spotted the wheelchair. Hurrying closer, she saw what was going on.

'Don't pull him like that,' Molly cried. 'You'll do him damage.' Pushing aside the two men, she looked into the stricken face of a handsome young man with blond hair and sharp blue eyes. 'I'm a nurse,' she said, glancing over her shoulder at the cabbie and his mate. 'Let's do this properly.' With careful manoeuvring and some assistance from the men, she deposited the young man in the wheelchair. She smiled at him but his expression was a mixture of anger and embarrassment, and he did not return the smile. Fascinated, Robert and Stuart watched as Molly wheeled him up the garden path then beckoned for the cab driver to assist her in helping him mount the steps into the house. The younger of the two women folded the wheelchair and carried it in behind them. The older couple followed.

'He'll not get out much if they have to do that every time,' Robert said. 'I'll bet they didn't know the house had steps.'

'Do you think he's like Jack and got injured in the war?'

Robert gave Stuart a disparaging look. 'Course he's not. He's too young. He's just a cripple.'

'Bugger off out of the road,' the removal man told them, but the boys ignored him and instead watched him and his mate lug furniture and numerous boxes and bundles into the house. Then they ran home to tell the tale.

'Our Molly's in there with them,' Robert informed his mother.

Kitty kept an eye on the kitchen window, and when the removal men drove away, she arranged a tray with cups, saucers, milk and sugar and a fresh pot of tea then popped a few buns and biscuits into a basket.

'You carry the basket, Robert, and I'll carry the tray.'

She knocked on the door of number seven and the young woman answered. She looked startled.

'I thought you might welcome a cup of tea an' a bite to eat,' Kitty said, her smile warm and friendly.

The young woman's mouth fell open in surprise. 'That is most kind,' she said, looking slightly bemused as she invited them in, her accent revealing that she wasn't English. Molly smiled when she saw her mother.

'This is most unexpected.' The older woman looked close to tears.

'It's what we do in Weaver Street,' Kitty said, placing the tray on the draining board. 'Moving's hard enough, an' until ye've got yourselves sorted, you'll be in need of refreshment.' She turned to face the newcomers, who were watching her every move. 'I'm Kitty Sykes from the house across the lane an' this is my son, Robert. You've already met my daughter, Molly.'

'And we are the Muller family,' the older man replied. 'Gottfried,' he tapped his chest, 'Gerda,' pointing to his wife, 'and our daughter Ursula and our son Heinz. We come from Munich in Germany.' There were nods and smiles all round.

'Well, ye're more than welcome in Weaver Street,' Kitty said. 'Now we'll leave ye to enjoy your tea before it gets cold an' let ye get on with your unpacking.' As Molly moved to follow her mother, Heinz caught Molly's hand. '*Danke schön*,' he said, his family echoing his words as Kitty and Molly and Robert departed. On her way back home, Kitty stopped off at Maggie's.

'Germans,' said Maggie, pulling a face. 'First it was you Irish and then them Poles, now it's bloody Germans. It gets more like the League o' Nations every bloody year.'

'Ah, but aren't ye glad I came?' Kitty gave Maggie a cheeky wink.

'I wonder what's brought 'em here?' Maggie said, frowning.

'We'll no doubt find out in time,' Kitty replied, making for the door.

'Ta-ra then,' Maggie said. 'I'll see you later.'

'It doesn't surprise me,' John said when Kitty told him that their new neighbours came from Germany. 'That Hitler fellow's causing no end of trouble, just like Mosley's doing over here.

They probably decided to get out before it all blows up in their faces.'

'Aye, I was listening to the wireless this morning. The Germans are no better off than us what with mass unemployment an' trouble with their government,' Kitty said, pulling a face as she cut lumps of thick yellow fat off a scrag-end of mutton. She was economising, buying the cheapest cuts of meat now that each passing month saw a decline in their weekly earnings. 'It seems Hitler's whippin' the people into a frenzy against that chap Hindenburg. The newsman said Adolf surely does have a way with words, an' none of 'em bode well for peace. It left me feeling all hot and bothered.'

'I'm more bothered about having to lay off more men,' John said, closing the ledger in front of him on the table. 'I don't want to, but my order book's looking pretty lean.' He ran his fingers through his thick brown hair and screwed up his face, perplexed. 'You know, Kitty, I've been thinking quite a bit about what I'm going to ask you and it grieves me to *have* to ask it.'

Kitty laid aside her knife and gave him a quizzical stare, eyebrows raised.

Looking extremely uncomfortable, John got up and stood with his back to the cooker. 'That money that Tom left you.' He let the words hang in the air as his eyes met hers. Kitty gave him a sharp look.

'I know you've always said it was for his children's future, but it's doing nowt in the bank,' John continued, 'and if I invest it in the factory, it'll keep me afloat, and who knows...' he gave a shame-faced grin, 'you might have a steady return on it in years to come, and the children's future will be secured.'

The money he referred to was the amount the landlord of the Weaver's Arms had found in the bookmaker's shop the day after Tom had been murdered. Kitty thought of it as dirty money, much of it earned by dubious means, and she refused to use it for herself, but it was a tidy sum there for the taking. When he was alive, he'd paid scant attention to Molly and Patrick, his time and affections elsewhere, so Kitty had lodged it in the bank for the sole purpose of giving Tom's daughter and son a start in life when they came of age.

Her heart twisted as she realised how hard it must be for this proud man that she loved so dearly to ask to use it. She pursed her lips, deep in thought. John was right. Interest rates had dropped to nothing. There had even been a run on some of the banks, with people clamouring to get their money out. Did they hide it under the bed and leave it doing no good like hers was doing in the bank?

'Well, what do you say?' John asked uncertainly.

'You've had your thinking time, John Sykes. Now it's my turn.' She nudged him aside to put the casserole in the oven. 'I'll let that do slow,' she said, turning and cupping his cheeks in her hands. 'I'd put that money out of mind because I never thought of it as mine, but when I think of all you've given me, I'd be wrong to refuse ye. If ye were to ask me for the skin off me back, I'd willingly give it. I love ye more than all the money in the world,' she said, sealing her words with a kiss.

John's face crumpled, his voice thick with emotion as he said, 'Thank you.' He shook his head to dispel the humiliation. 'If I can keep the factory going, it will be there for Patrick and Robert when Patrick's got the RAF and flying out of his system and Robert's old enough to follow in my footsteps. He's already mad about engineering. And Molly will get her share.' Kitty knew John was gabbling to hide the mortification he felt at using Tom's money and she loved him all the more for it. 'I'll make it up to you,' he said.

'No need, love,' said Kitty shaking her head. 'What I never had I'll never miss.'

18

'Big Mick an' Wee Mickey are working on them new houses behind the Wagon an' Horses,' Bridie announced as she entered Kitty's kitchen one Friday morning at the beginning of July.

'That's handy,' Kitty replied as she filled a basket with the baps and pies she had baked for the café. 'They should do the weekend, what with customers being few an' far between,' she said glumly.

'Aye, it picked up over Easter but it's slacked right off again,' Bridie sighed. 'I'm just thankful my men have a job to go to even if folks like Beth's dad gives 'em stick whenever he sees 'em. Fancy him objectin' to rat holes being pulled down an' lovely clean houses put up in their place.' She pulled a face.

'Aye, he was giving off stink to me the other day. He says it'll lower the tone of the district, if they move folks out of the slums in the city centre and dump them on us. I soon put him straight, the miserable old so-and-so.'

Bridie laughed. 'I bet he didn't like that – but then, he never looks happy even though Beth's never done running, taking him meals an' doing his washing.'

'Beth's always felt responsible for him even though he led her a dog's life afore she married Blair. He's a fortunate man is Walter. I told him, times are changin' an we've got to accept it,' Kitty said. 'Then he started giving off about the Mullers.'

'They seem all right, even if they are Germans,' said Bridie, picking up the basket ready to leave. 'Big Mick says Germany's goin' to cause a lot of trouble in the world if that Adolf Hitler gets his way.'

'Aye, John thinks the same. It's just one worry after another.' Kitty sighed heavily. 'I'll be along later. Not that you'll need me, but I like to show me face to the few customers we still have.'

After Bridie had gone, Kitty stood at the sink, thinking about the Mullers. Molly was down there now, helping Ursula Muller fill in an application form for work in one of the city's hospitals, but Kitty had her suspicions that her daughter was more interested in Heinz Muller than his sister. Ah, well. Molly wasn't a child and it was only natural she should be interested in the opposite sex. She'd been on a few dates with an ambulance driver but that seemed to have fizzled out and he'd not been mentioned recently. Heinz Muller had. Kitty was aware that Molly's kind heart was drawn to someone who needed care, but did she want her daughter to fall in love with a man tied to a wheelchair? She didn't think she did. Hopeful that Heinz was just a passing fancy, she attended to her chores, at the same time mulling over an idea that she had been toying with for some time.

* * *

In the Mullers' kitchen, Molly was sitting at the table with Ursula, the completed form in front of them. Molly had done her utmost to keep her attention on the detail of the application, but she couldn't help being aware of Heinz seated by the fire reading. He had barely acknowledged her presence, but she dearly wanted the handsome young man with the sad blue eyes to notice her.

Ursula folded the form and tucked it neatly into a brown envelope. Molly looked in Heinz's direction, trying to find an excuse to prolong her visit. Ursula came to her rescue.

'I'll take you for your walk after I have helped Mama unpack more boxes,' she said to Heinz, and to Molly, 'Thank you most kindly.' She went to open the door, but Molly stayed put. She took a deep breath.

'If you have to help your mother, why don't I take Heinz for a walk – show him the sights?' Molly looked hopefully at Heinz. He turned the next page.

'Do you hear that, Heinz? Molly will walk you.' Ursula beamed at Molly. 'You would do that? It is so kind.' Then, looking at Heinz for his approval, she added, 'You will not have to listen to me complaining it is so boring and tiresome.'

His expression was inscrutable, but he nodded his consent.

Molly pushed the wheelchair along the pavement, gazing at the back of Heinz's head and wishing she were facing him. 'It's a lovely day for a walk,' she said brightly. 'I'll show you the Botanic Gardens if you like.' Heinz raised his hand in acceptance. Any further attempts at conversation were met with monosyllabic responses and eventually Molly gave up and kept on pushing.

'Is fine gardens,' Heinz commented as they passed by the neatly trimmed box hedges and colourful flowerbeds. Molly's spirits lifted, and when they came to a bench, she brought the wheelchair to a halt then sat down beside it.

'Tell me about Germany. I've never been there.'

Heinz told her about Munich and the Bavarian forests. Molly was impressed. 'It sounds beautiful. Why did you come here to dirty old Liverpool?'

'We did not want to leave,' he murmured, his sad blue eyes

meeting hers. 'It is my fault we come away. I should have been more careful, but I was thoughtless and selfish. I only think of myself.' His sadness had changed to anger.

'Why? What did you do?'

'I write for newspapers. I argued against the National Socialists – the Nazi Party – and I annoy them so much that they punish me,' he said, his words full of fire. 'That is why I am in this!' He thumped his fist on the wheelchair's armrest.

'So you haven't always been in a wheelchair? Is it just temporary until your injuries heal?' Molly sincerely hoped it was.

'It is, I think. Each day I walk a little further in the house but outside my steps are weak.' Heinz chuckled. 'Ursula says I use it as an excuse to sit around doing nothing but write articles that are dangerous whilst she will have to go out and work for a living.' For the first time since they had set out, Molly began to relax.

'Then if you are able to walk, we must work at it. I can help you. My nurse's training has taught me how to do that,' she lied enthusiastically.

'You will?' Heinz looked deep into her eyes his expression incredulous.

'Yes, it would be my pleasure.' Molly's cheeks flushed when she saw the yearning in his blue eyes.

'The pleasure will be all mine,' he cried, thumping the wheelchair again. 'It makes me so mad. Ever since I was beaten my parents fuss over me, but they do not know how to help.' He gave a bitter laugh. 'And little Ursula is jealous of their attention to me and makes unpleasantness. The sooner I get out of this damned thing, the better it will be for everyone.'

Molly pushed Heinz back to Weaver Street with a happy heart.

Later that same evening, Kitty and Maggie let themselves into Mavis's kitchen. She was sitting by the fire, knitting needles clicking to the accompaniment of the music on the wireless. She got to her feet and lowered the volume, leaving it playing softly in the background.

'Hello, you two, sit you down. I'm on me own tonight,' she said, going to the sink. Kitty and Maggie sat at the table. Water gushed into the kettle and over its rattle, Mavis continued, 'Rose's gone to bed early, and Jack's gone to the working men's club to play darts.'

'Any word about the wedding?'

'Not yet, Kitty.'

'Yeah, she's being dead cagey, isn't she?' Maggie sneered. 'If Pete asked me to marry him, I'd do it tomorrow.' Mavis and Kitty exchanged despairing glances.

There was no likelihood of that happening.

'Rose tells me she saw your Molly taking that lad of Muller's out for an airing.'

Kitty's lips pursed. 'She did. She says she's going to help him exercise so that he can walk again. I hope she's not takin' on too much.'

'She is a nurse,' Maggie scoffed. 'If anybody can help him, it's your Molly.'

'It's not just that,' Kitty said dolefully. 'I don't want her throwin' her heart at some chap out of pity. But you know our Molly. She's never happier than when she's helping somebody.'

'It's early days. Nothing might come of it,' Mavis comforted.

'Yeah. Our Lily changes her chaps as often as she changes her knickers,' Maggie commented as Mavis rattled cups and saucers onto the table. 'Still, you don't want your Molly getting into something she might regret. You never know with foreigners.'

'They seem a nice enough family,' Mavis said, pouring water into the teapot. 'Mr Muller's a chemist at British Dyes.'

Maggie sniffed. 'Aye, but they're still Germans.' Other than

Kitty, she had little sympathy for anyone who wasn't Liverpool born and bred.

'Can we talk about somethin' different?' Kitty said as Mavis brought the teapot to the table and sat down. She didn't want to talk about Molly and Heinz Muller.

'Me mam's cough gets worse an' she's an awful colour,' Maggie said, taking a Woodbine from its packet and lighting up.

'And yours will if you keep on with them things,' Mavis retorted. She objected to Maggie smoking in her kitchen but had never plucked up courage to tell her so.

'I thought she didn't look well when I called in yesterday,' Kitty said. 'An' I was surprised when she told me she's giving up working in the Wagon and Horses.'

'She has to. The landlord says they've more staff than customers. Anyway, she's not fit for it.' Maggie puffed smoke across the table and Mavis wrinkled her nose and coughed.

'How's Pete these days? I haven't seen much of him this while back,' said Kitty.

'Neither have I,' Maggie moaned. She stubbed out her cigarette and lit another one.

'Things are all right between you, though?' Mavis asked anxiously. Maggie had a poor track record for hanging on to the men in her life.

Maggie shrugged. 'I suppose so. He's not fond of me mam, and she's not too keen on him. She thinks he's hiding summat.'

'Like what?' Kitty put her head on one side and screwed up her eyes.

'How the hell would I know? She's as daft as a bloody brush. I think she's jealous 'cos I've got a chap an' she hasn't been able to get one in years.'

'Ye could be right,' said Kitty. She'd always thought Vi Bottomley acted more like a sister than a mother to Maggie, and sipping her tea, she reflected on how unlucky her friend had been when it came to being loved.

Mavis got to her feet, and over at the counter she began smearing margarine on two slices of bread.

'What are you making?' Maggie asked.

'Sandwiches for a bit of supper for when Jack gets back,' Mavis replied.

'Give us one, I'm starving,' Maggie said, cutting into Kitty's thoughts.

'Talking of starving, I met Millie Thompson in the bakery this morning. She was begging a loaf, but yon hard-faced piece behind the counter wouldn't give her one. I got one for her.'

'Millie Thompson,' Mavis echoed. 'Is she the young woman who lives in Dobb's Yard? The one with all the children?'

'Aye, she has five, an' her husband lost his job when Bell's Engineering went bust. He's not worked since, an' because she has a wee cleaning job at Medford's he's not entitled to the dole.' She curled her lip in disgust. 'She could give it up, but they'd be no better off. They had the Means Test man out an' all he said was that her husband should look for work in another part of the country.'

'What! An' leave her with five kids to look after on her own,' Maggie exclaimed.

'The government has a lot to answer for, expecting people to survive without a decent wage coming into the house,' Mavis said hotly.

'They don't care,' said Kitty. 'None of them go hungry, but when I saw her, it got me thinking. We should be looking out for them that have hit rock bottom. There are still those who have more than they need – like the toffs that go to the church – we should be askin' for their help, mebbe fill a wee basket with essentials now an' then.' Fired with enthusiasm, she continued, 'We could ask shopkeepers for damaged stuff they can't sell, like dented or rusty tins, an' bust packets an' boxes, the sort they can't put on their shelves. Tinned stuff keeps for years. I'll bet some of 'em have loads in their storerooms that they've forgotten about they've had it that long. Folks on their uppers don't care when it comes to filling their bellies an' getting through another day. We could keep an' eye out for families like Millie Thompson an' leave 'em a wee box of groceries on the doorsteps so they don't have to feel beholden.'

'That's a grand idea,' Mavis said. 'I know I can spare a bit. Especially when it comes to folk with young children.'

'Me an' all,' said Maggie rather reluctantly. 'I've not got much but I've still got me mendin' job. I could chuck in a tin of beans now and again.'

Mavis made a fresh pot of tea, and they sat planning how to help their less fortunate neighbours.

Kitty's plans to help the needy started in a small way with Millie Thompson in Dobb's Yard. When boxes of groceries started to appear on her step, Millie watched out to see who had left them, not because she was too proud to accept charity but to express her gratitude.

'I knew it was you,' she cried, flinging open the door as Mavis made her third visit. Startled, Mavis almost dropped the box. 'It's a good job I didn't let go. There's eggs in it,' she said, smiling into the careworn face of the young woman who couldn't have been any older than twenty-three. Five grubby little faces peered round her skirt, their eyes big when they saw a packet of biscuits sticking out of the box.

'Will you take a cup of tea?' Mavis declined, knowing how little Millie had to spare, but she stepped inside. 'My husband's taken the government's advice and gone south in search of work,' Millie told her. 'I still get national milk from the clinic for the youngest, and the older two get free school dinners,' she confided as she unpacked the box. 'The bit Medford's pays me covers the rent, but we've nowt to spare on owt else. You're a godsend.' She gave Mavis a grateful smile. 'Mind you, there's worse off than me. That young lass what rents a room in that house at the bottom of the yard was begging outside Holroyd's the other day. There she was in the pouring rain wi' her baby in her arms holdin' out a tin for the workers to drop coppers in. I could have cried for her.'

'The house at the bottom of the yard, you say. What side?'

'On the left, Mrs Haggerty's.'

'I'll give her a call,' said Mavis.

* * *

'What's he like then, this Heinz?' Lily's tone suggested she didn't approve of Molly devoting so much time to him. They were trying on make-up in Molly's bedroom one Saturday afternoon in July.

'He's lovely,' Molly said dreamily. 'He's so intense and serious. I've never met anyone quite like him.' She sighed dramatically then went on to tell Lily how passionate he was about fighting for the rights of oppressed people. 'He writes articles that are published in what he calls underground newspapers telling people that they shouldn't believe in Adolf Hitler.'

'He sounds dead boring, if you ask me.' Lily peered closely at Molly. 'But you fancy him, don't you?' she squealed.

Molly flushed. 'I think I'm in love with him,' she said, her voice wobbling.

'He's a German. He's not like us. Foreigners are funny.'

Molly decided she didn't want to listen to Lily's opinions and asked, 'What's Barry like?'

Barry Jones was Lily's latest fling. 'Oh, Bas's a bit of all right. He's a good laugh and he flashes the cash,' Lily boasted. 'He's taking me to the Grafton tonight.'

The Grafton was a popular dance hall on the West Kirby Road, and although Molly had never been there, she tried to picture herself and Heinz waltzing to a romantic tune. She quickly abandoned the thought and listened to Lily singing the praises of a night out at the Grafton. Just lately Lily's social life seemed to be one constant whirl. Molly contemplated how she might spend the evening.

'Heinz is walking, you know. Each day he manages to go a bit further, but he still has to use a stick. I might go and see if he wants to go for a walk later.'

'Well, he'll not be whirling you round the Grafton, that's for sure,' Lily said sarcastically as she smeared deep blue eyeshadow on her eyelids.

* * *

The 'help for the needy' project, as Mavis called it, had taken on a life of its own, with new worthy cases cropping up all over the town. As the number of homes in dire need swelled, Kitty used her persuasive charms on the butchers' shops and groceries in the town. 'Give us them scraps off the bacon slicer,' she said cheekily to Hubert the butcher. 'You can't sell 'em but there's folks round here who'd give their eyeteeth for 'em.' Hubert grimaced at her audacity. To appease him, Kitty bought a pound of stewing steak. 'You know what a good customer I am,' she said, the threat of withdrawing said custom hanging in the air.

'I'll throw in these bones and a lump of fat,' Hubert growled. Kitty had touched his moral conscience more than once. She turned to the other customers waiting to be served. 'Heart of gold has Hubert. He'd see nobody go hungry.'

She'd coerced the grocers into letting her have goods that had been sitting on their shelves too long. 'Nobody will pay good money for rusty tins or dried goods in bags brown with age, an' as for that tin of biscuits up there,' she pointed to the top shelf behind the counter, 'it's been sitting there since Christmas afore last. Give it over an' make somebody happy,' she'd said to grumpy Joe Jubb, the grocer, and to the woman behind her in the queue, she said, 'There's a man who knows his Christian duty.' Glowing under her praise, Joe handed her the biscuits.

* * *

Rose dawdled over getting dressed. She didn't have to go to work this morning as trade was so slack that the shop stayed closed on Mondays and Tuesdays. 'We don't even cover the cost of the electric,' Betty had said, and Rose had reluctantly agreed. Now she wondered how she might spend her day.

'Are you doing the boxes?' she asked as she entered the kitchen. 'Can I help?'

'You can indeed. After you've had your breakfast, you can take these boxes to...' Mavis checked a slip of paper, 'Lamb Lane, you know where I mean, that ginnel that's next to the Wagon and Horses. Numbers two and three.'

'That 'ud be a great help, Rose,' said Kitty who was finding the hours spent foraging for supplies and then doling them out time-consuming. 'It'll save me the walk if you do that end of the town. I'll drop these boxes off in Dobb's Yard,' heatedly adding, 'an' I hope that blasted dog's tied up. It near had me leg off last week.' She dropped a bag of Jelly Babies into a box: a few treats for the children.

Rose made a pot of tea and toast, then after she'd put one of the boxes into a large basket and the other into a big canvas shopping bag, she slipped on her coat and set off, eager to be of some use. With an air of anticipation, she walked briskly to the other end of the town, thankful for the sunny morning. It was her first time at delivering boxes and the first time she had ever ventured into the ginnel that was called Lamb Lane. Pausing to adjust her load, she peered down the dank, narrow passage that ran between the pub and a gent's outfitters. She stepped into the opening and began walking cautiously, picking her way over the slimy flagstones littered with filth and the carcass of a dead rat. Had she come to the right place? Was this the ginnel Kitty had described? Surely, no one could possibly live here.

The passage opened into a little enclave of shabby houses, two on either side of a dirt yard and a row of outside lavatories and ash pits facing her. A fetid smell permeated the enclosed space. The sun didn't penetrate the yard and a damp, dark hopelessness clung to the rundown little homes. A big beefy man in a grubby vest and moleskin trousers lolled in the doorway of the first house to Rose's right. He eyed her suspiciously.

'I'm looking for number two,' she said, aware that she sounded nervous.

'You've found it,' he grunted. 'What do you want?'

'To leave these gro...'

'Is that you, Mrs Sykes?' A young woman with a baby in her arms pushed past the man in the doorway, her face wreathed in smiles. The smile slipped when she saw Rose. 'Oh, I thought it wa'...'

'Mrs Sykes asked me to leave this with you.' Rose set her load on the ground then fished a box out of the canvas bag. 'I'm Rose Brown. I live with Miss Robson.'

She proffered the box.

The woman's smile returned, even wider. 'Give her a hand wi' it, you big clout,' she said nudging the man. 'She's one o' them women I told you about. Thanks ever so much, Miss Brown, you don't know what this means to us.' Rose thought how brave and pretty the woman looked, even though her smock was patched and her cardigan had holes at the elbows.

The man stopped scowling and gave an embarrassed smile. 'I'm sorry I wa' short wi' you,' he said, 'I thought the rent man had sent you. His lass looks a bit like you.' He took the box from Rose's hands. 'Thanks,' he muttered.

The woman laughed. 'She looks nowt like Willie Pearson's daughter. She's far too bonny.' Rose felt her cheeks turn pink. 'Rose Brown, you say. I've not met you before. I'm Janet Halstead, and he's Brian.' She probed the contents of the box.

'Pleased to meet you,' said Rose, her words drowned out by Janet's, 'Hey, kids, come and look! Jelly Babies!' She snatched a bag off the top of the box and waved it under the noses of the two toddlers pushing their way past her legs. Greedy fingers reached out for the sweets.

'Mrs Sykes never forgets the kids,' their mother said, blinking back tears. The delight on the children's faces twisted Rose's heart so that she too had to blink.

She swallowed painfully then croaked, 'Which house is number three?'

Janet pointed to the corner of the yard. 'Mary's home from school, she'll let you in. Her mam can't get out of bed.' She sighed and said, 'I think we're badly off what wi' Brian losing his job when Bell's Engineering closed down, but poor Sally Morgan's far worse off than we are. Her husband's gone off. Left her with four little lads an' Mary. She's on'y eleven, an' she has to look after 'em all since Sally took badly. Like I say, there's allus somebody worse off than yourself.'

Rose tucked the empty canvas bag under her arm then picked up the basket, thinking that although the Halsteads were poor Janet's cheerfulness would see them through. Two sticky little faces dribbling jelly juice gazed up at her adoringly. 'I hope to see you again,' she said, patting their heads.

'We blooming well hope to see you,' Janet chortled. 'An' tell Sally I was asking after her.' She nodded in the direction of the Morgans and Rose crossed the yard to the house in the corner. The stink from the lavatories and the ash pits was stronger here. Two missing windowpanes were stuffed with cardboard. She rapped on the door. When it opened, a pale, weary face peered round its edge.

'Who is it?' a frail, breathless voice called from within.

'A lady,' the girl at the door called back, her thin face creased with anxiety and her body so rigid her shoulders almost touched her ears.

Rose smiled. 'Are you Mary?' The girl nodded, her eyes wary. 'Oh, that's good,' Rose continued, trying to sound as friendly as was possible. 'Mrs Halstead told me you'd be at home. I've come in place of Mrs Sykes. I've brought some groceries.'

Mary's shoulders relaxed and she pulled the door wider. 'Come in,' she said.

Nothing had prepared Rose for the sight that met her eyes. From the bare floor to the stained, damp walls and the dead ashes in the grate, the sparsely furnished room reeked of poverty. The remnants of a broken chair lay by the hearth. The gaunt woman in the narrow bed against the back wall propped herself up on her elbow, wheezing and coughing.

'Ask the lady to sit down, Mary,' she gasped, forcing a gummy smile in Rose's direction. Mary dragged a chair away from a rickety table and before she sat, Rose handed her the basket. Mary set it on the table and began emptying the box: teacakes, a small block of margarine, a bag of flour, a greasy packet of bacon scraps, half a cabbage, a tin of corned beef and a tin of baked beans.

'Look, Mam!' she cried. 'There's more of that linctus Mrs Sykes gave us last week. It helped Mam's cough,' she said, addressing Rose. 'We couldn't believe it when she brought us all that stuff last week.' Mary's eyes lingered on a bag of sherbet lemons and a bag of buns she'd taken from the bottom of the box.

'Tell Mrs Sykes we're more than grateful,' Mary's mother wheezed, flopping back on her pillow, exhausted.

Rose, still shocked by the desperation of her surroundings, was struggling to find something to say. 'I will,' she said, 'and before I go, is there something I might do for you? Would you like me to light the fire?' She was feeling chilly, and the poor woman huddled under the thin blankets must be feeling it too.

'We're saving the chair for later when it gets really cold,' Mary said, poking a foot at the broken chair. 'The boys are out hunting for sticks in the Botanic. We'll light the fire when they get back.' She eyed the sweets again. 'They'll go mad when they see these.'

Mary walked over to the sink, her dress hanging like a shroud from her stick-thin frame. A woman's dress, it had been cut off at the bottom. Rose's heart ached for her. How humiliating it must be to have to wear such a shapeless garment. Mary brought a plate and a knife back to the table.

'I'll make fried corned beef an' beans for us dinner, an' they can have either a bun or a sherbet lemon to finish off,' she said, winding the key round the tin of meat to open it. Like everything else in the shabby room, the table was scrubbed clean and the plate spotless. Mary started slicing the meat.

'I think the one who does the cooking deserves a sherbet lemon to suck on whilst she's doing it,' Rose said teasingly.

Mary grinned. 'Can I, Mam?'

'Yeah, take one, love.' Sally smiled fondly at her daughter then addressed Rose. 'She's a good lass is our Mary. I don't know what I'd do without her. Their dad's beggared off, but he wa' no use when he wa' here. He's a drinker,' she panted, every word an effort.

'Will you come again?' Mary asked, her cheek bulging as she let the sherbet fizz. At that moment, she looked like a little girl of eleven should look, rather than the pale, anxious child who had opened the door.

'Try to keep me away,' Rose said, grinning. 'I'll see you next week.'

She left Lamb Lane feeling older and wiser. As she walked back through the town, the bag and basket much lighter, she reflected on what her life had been like when she was eleven: three good meals a day in a clean, heated home, a warm bed, clothes to wear and a pony to ride. Her privileged life had provided for all her basic needs and more besides, but she was left with the feeling that there was more love in those shabby little houses in Lamb Lane than there had ever been in Heathcote Manor. She felt like sobbing but she didn't want to be seen crying in the street, so she swallowed her emotions and trudged back to Weaver Street.

'Why didn't you tell me?' Rose cried, as she entered Mavis's kitchen to find her and Kitty back from making their deliveries and having a welcome cup of tea.

'You might not have gone if we had,' Kitty said. 'It opens your eyes, doesn't it?'

'That poor little girl, Mary, having to bear all that responsibility is a crime,' Rose said, her voice ragged.

'It is,' Mavis agreed, fetching another cup and filling it then handing it to Rose.

'Sit down, love, and don't get so het up. You've done what you can for today.'

'And from now on I'm going to do a lot more,' Rose replied heatedly, taking the cup and sitting down heavily at the table. 'You just tell me where to go and I'll help all I can.' She drank deeply, trying to calm her emotions. 'But first, I'm going to start with Mary. Have you any dresses Molly's outgrown?' she asked Kitty. 'You should have seen the thing she was wearing, Kitty. It tore at my heart.'

Kitty exchanged a glance with Mavis that said *I've never seen her so fired up*. 'I'm sure I have. I keep every scrap to make over into something else. We'll soon sort her out. I don't know why I didn't think of it meself.'

Rose beamed.

'Ye've learned something today then, Rose.' Kitty gave her a quizzical look. 'An' no doubt it came as a shock to ye, but it's let ye see how ill-divid the world is, for by all the saints in heaven an' Our Blessed Lady herself there's them that has an' them that has not.' She looked deeply into Rose's eyes to make sure she had understood, her own burning as, fired up with memories of past injustice, she told them about the famine in Ireland, her Irish accent more pronounced as she spoke of the horrors her people had suffered.

'The English landlords cared nothin' for our sufferin' when the potato crops turned black an' festered in their beds. We relied on the spuds for food and to sell so's we could pay the rent, an' when we couldn't, they evicted us an burned our wee homes, leavin' us to wander the roads an' eat grass. Thousands died, an' the world stood by an' let 'em.'

'That puts me in mind of that hymn "All Things Bright and Beautiful",' Mavis said. '"The rich man in his castle, the poor man at his gate, God made them high and lowly, and ordered their estate".'

'Ye never said a truer word,' Kitty growled, 'and whilst ever them in the gover'ment an' other folks that have never known hardship are content to turn a blind eye to what's happening under their noses, it's up to us to do what we can.'

'It's certainly opened my eyes,' Rose exclaimed. 'I feel ashamed by how privileged my life has been.'

'Through no fault of your own, love,' said Mavis, smiling fondly at Rose, 'and now you know what needs to be done, you can lend me and Kitty a hand to carry on the good work.'

Rose nodded solemnly and they went on to talk about what to do next.

19

'Nurse Conlon, attend to Baby Norris, and when you've done that, clean the sluice before you finish your shift,' Sister Burrowes ordered as she changed the drip attached to the arm of a young girl who had just had her appendix removed.

'Yes, Sister.' Molly gritted her teeth and hurried to lift the screaming baby from his crib, Robert's words: *Do you have to wipe their bums?* creeping into her mind. Yes, I do, she thought, for she seemed to do little else other than change nappies and wipe up sick and diarrhoea. And when she wasn't doing that, she was spooning unappetising mush into little mouths. Baby Norris ceased his screaming as she peeled off the stinking nappy and Molly's spirits lifted. She was giving comfort to a poor little mite, and she would do the same for Heinz: love and care for him. That is, of course, if he let her.

She trudged to the sluice, keeping her thoughts on Heinz. He was walking now, and had even got a part-time position with the *Northern Echo*, but he had yet to ask her to go out with him. Only if she suggested it did they spend any time together, and then all he did was talk politics, and what he was currently writing for the newspaper. Clanking a bedpan on top of another one, she had to admit it was a very one-sided love affair. But she did love him.

* * *

In Holroyd's weaving shed, Lily watched the shuttle on her loom dart to and fro as she kept a sharp eye out for loose ends or a broken warp or weft. Above her head, she could tell that the light penetrating the glass roof of the shed was gradually darkening, signalling that her shift was drawing to an end.

Across the 'weavers' alley', the walkway between the rows of looms, she spotted her friend, Sadie, raising two fingers to her lips. The constant roar and clack of the machinery made conversation impossible, but like all the women in the shed, Lily was adept at mouthing and lip reading.

'Going out tonight?' Sadie's thick lips formed the words.

'With Molly to the pictures,' Lily mouthed. '*King Kong*'s on at the Paramount.'

Sadie stuck out her jaw and swung her arms in imitation of a great ape then swiftly dropped the pose as she grabbed for a loose end in the bobbin on her loom. Laughing, Lily attended to her own loom, glad when the mill hooter marked the end of the shift. The cacophonous roar subsided as the looms stilled. Lily dashed to get her coat, pulling off the turban that covered her fiery crowning glory; the thought of getting her abundant hair caught in the thrashing loom was a terrifying prospect: she'd heard about the girls who'd been scalped.

She was walking up the back lane when Big Mick and Mickey fell into step with her. She'd long since stopped thinking about Mickey in a romantic way but they were still firm friends and often went about together. And anyway, she knew he fancied Molly. He was always asking Lily about her, and she'd seen the way he looked at her whenever they were together.

'Hiya, Mickey,' chirped Lily. 'I'm gonna ask Moll if she wants to go to the flicks tonight. Do you want to come?' Big Mick quickened his pace, leaving them to chatter. Mickey blushed, uncomfortable at Lily seeing him in his dusty, over-large work clothes for although he had no notion of fancying her, he liked to appear attractive to the opposite sex. 'What are you going to see?'

'*King Kong* at the Paramount.'

'Yeah. Okay. Give us a shout when you're ready.'

They parted company, each heading into their own houses.

'Your tea's keeping warm on the side, Queen,' Vi told Lily as she entered the cluttered, smoky kitchen. Lily slipped off her coat then went to the fireside oven, her nose wrinkling with distaste as she lifted a plate containing a soggy lump of boiled cod and mashed potato. She ate it anyway, then hurried upstairs to wash and change her overall for a grey wool skirt and stripy jumper. Seated at the makeshift dressing table in her attic bedroom, Lily daubed her naturally pale cheeks with a generous layer of tan foundation cream, then painted her lips a deep shade of raspberry. She had plucked her eyebrows in the latest fashion and now accentuated the sparse hairs with a thin brown pencil line, finishing off with a smear of bright green eyeshadow on each eyelid. Like her mother and granny, Lily loved making up her face. Pleased with the effect, she skipped down the stairs. Maggie had left her mending frame for the day and was sitting smoking a cigarette by the fire.

'I'm off to call for Molly,' Lily told her, hurrying for the door.

Molly had arrived home and had her tea by the time Lily burst into the kitchen, full of gab. 'Are we still going to see *King Kong* at the Paramount tonight? Mickey says he's coming.' Kitty and John noted Lily's warpaint and exchanged amused, disapproving glances.

After her busy day on the children's ward, Molly had thought she would just sit by the fire and read the last chapters of *Cold Comfort Farm* so that she could discuss it with Heinz, but Lily's enthusiasm was such that she changed her mind. The two girls went up to Molly's bedroom so that she could change out of her uniform. When they came back downstairs, Molly now wearing a blue flannel dress, and her glossy black hair unrolled, Kitty was pleased to see that she hadn't been tempted to emulate her friend and cover her natural, creamy complexion and sparkling blue eyes with any of the products Lily used so liberally.

'Don't stay out too late. Make sure an' catch the ten o'clock tram, ye both have work the morrow,' she advised them.

'Okay, we will,' said Molly, and the girls flounced out in a flurry of sweet-smelling cologne.

'Make sure ye do,' Kitty said firmly.

The girls hurried across the lane to number eleven. A sharp rap on the door brought Mickey out, spruced up in his good suit and white shirt, his black curls quiffed into shape with the help of sugar and water.

'Our Liam's coming an' all,' he said, stepping out, closely followed by his brother. Liam grinned shyly at Molly and Lily. A quiet, serious young man, he rarely bothered with the younger ones. On the tram into the city, he sat beside Mickey and Lily and Molly sat together.

The Paramount, Liverpool's largest cinema, was an impressive building dominating the corner of London Road and Pudsey Street. Its frontage was a towering edifice of finely worked stone with an ornate arch and rows of bevelled windows above a massive canopy that jutted over the entrance. Excitedly, Molly, Lily, Liam and Mickey joined the queue. Tickets purchased, they trooped into the dimly lit interior that was decorated in the Art Deco style with unusual metal grilles either side of the proscenium arch topped with bright red drapes; it was like stepping into a magical world of adventure and romance. To the swirling strains of the Compton organ, Lily led the way to the plush red seats at the rear: she'd decided to make a play for Liam, and she surprised Molly by sitting with him in the double seat, leaving Molly to sit with Mickey.

There was a fanfare of music and the silver screen sprang to life with a newsreel. Black and white images of real events flickered across the screen, letting the cinemagoers know what was happening in the wider world. Bored, Lily tried to smooch with Liam, but he kept his eyes fixed on the screen. A cartoon and a light-hearted short film had them all laughing and when the lights went up for the interval, Mickey treated them to an ice cream from the usherette's tray. Then it was time for the big picture.

The lights dimmed again, and in no time at all, the viewers were transported to the jungle. As the monstrous gorilla rampaged across the screen, Lily pretended to be afraid and looked to Liam for comfort, but Liam was oblivious to Lily's charms, and when Mickey slid his arm round Molly's shoulders and tried to kiss her, she shrugged him off. 'What do you think you're doing, you daft ha'porth,' she hissed. On the tram back home, they hardly exchanged a word, Lily fuming and Mickey sulking.

It wasn't until they were walking up the lane that the tensions loosened. Mickey bunched his arms and began beating his chest and roaring, 'King of the jungle.' Lily began screaming and tossing her hair, her brilliant impersonation of Fay Wray making the others fall about laughing.

'Sorry, Mickey,' Molly said when she stopped giggling. She didn't like to hurt his feelings. Mickey gazed into her contrite blue eyes and shrugged.

'It's okay. I know you fancy the German,' he said then walked on. Liam followed, silently vowing that in future he'd steer clear of the brash, mouthy Lily.

'Ta-ra then,' said Lily, and Molly went home to dream of Heinz.

* * *

Summer faded and as autumn ran its course, Kitty and her friends continued to help the needy. The recipients of the boxes looked on the women as guardian angels. One of the children had even asked Kitty, 'Are you Mother Christmas?'

On a bitterly cold Monday in November, the women were hard at it, dividing goods that came packaged in larger amounts into smaller portions to make them go further, their reasoning being that even a little of something was better than nothing.

'How many boxes are we making up?' Kitty asked, pouring flour from a large bag into two small bags. A cloud of fine dust swirled up into her face.

'Eeh, are you feeling all right, Kitty? You've gone proper pale,' Mavis chuckled as Kitty blew into the haze and wiped dust from her cheeks.

'Cheeky sod,' Kitty retorted, laughing. 'I knew I should have spooned it out. I just thought this way 'ud be quicker.' She folded the tops of the little bags of flour. 'How many boxes did you say?'

'Five,' said Mavis, slicing up a block of margarine. 'I'll deliver the Jacksons', the Porters' and that young lass, Jean's. I want to show her how to make a pot of soup out of the bones and a few carrots and spuds. She's only sixteen and she hasn't got a clue about cooking. Mind you, that baby of hers is a lovely little thing and she looks after it ever so carefully.'

'I'll wrap these bacon scraps an' bits of ham in greaseproof, just a handful in each,' said Kitty. 'They'll be tasty with cabbage, an' they'll make a bit o' drippin' an' all.' She put the small bags of flour into boxes on the table.

'I'll go to the Halsteads' and Mary's,' said Rose, pushing her feet into wellington boots and pulling on a thick woolly hat. It had snowed the day before and turned to slush overnight. Delivering the boxes wasn't the pleasantest of tasks but at least for an hour or two it took her mind off her own problems. Joey's last letter had told her he'd be back in Liverpool by the end of November: two more days then she'd bring the world crashing down round their ears and kill their romantic dream.

Rose delivered the boxes with none of her usual cheerfulness, then trudged out of Lamb Lane, her shoulders hunched and her hands deep in her pockets. She was expected for tea at Joey's mam's.

She really liked May and got on well with her, but just lately she dreaded being in her company. May talked about the wedding, saying things like, 'If you're planning to get wed afore Christmas, you'll need the banns read,' or awkward questions like, 'Are you going to have our Ronnie's little Sylvia as a bridesmaid?'

Head down, kicking her way through the slush and lost in worrying thoughts, Rose exited the ginnel and turned the corner at the same time as a man stepped out of the Wagon and Horses pub. Rose bumped right into him.

'Whoa!' he exclaimed, catching her by the arms, his beery breath wafting up her nose. Startled and embarrassed, she raised her head, ready to apologise. The man's jaw dropped. Holding her at arm's length, he took a step back and stared. *The long hair trailing from under the woolly hat was blonder, and she'd filled out since he last saw her and was now delightfully curvy, but he'd recognise that face and the timid look in those silver-grey eyes anywhere. Rosamund Brown-Allsop. She was still where he'd abandoned her, in Liverpool.*

'Well, well. Would you believe it? Look who it is.' Lewis Aston's surprised expression was now a leering smile.

The familiar Geordie accent stung Rose's ears. Her blood ran cold. Panicked, she tried to pull away, but he held her fast.

'Let me go,' she hissed, twisting in his grasp. He tightened his grip.

'Ah, now, Rosamund, that's no way to greet an old friend.'

'Friend!' she spat, her eyes blazing. 'You're no friend of mine.' She kicked him hard on his shin. Shocked, he slackened his hold. Rose tore free, and blinded by tears and burning rage, she hurtled along Broad Green, her wellingtons skidding in the slush. More than once, she was in danger of falling, but she kept on running and Lewis kept her in sight, keen to see where she was going and his brain working in overdrive. How could he best use this chance meeting to his advantage? He'd have put money on her running back to darling Daddy and the mansion in Buckinghamshire. Why was she still here?

Rose dared not look back, but she knew he was dogging her footsteps. An instinct told her it was unwise to go home, but in her panic, she couldn't think of where else to go. She just had to get away from him.

Her heart banging inside her chest, she charged up the lane into the house and up to her bedroom, thankful that Mavis wasn't at home. Cautiously, she peered out of the window. Lewis was nowhere in sight. Throwing herself onto her bed, Rose wept: her past had come back to haunt her.

When May called to enquire why she hadn't gone for tea, Mavis came up to Rose's room but she pleaded a severe headache and told her to send May away, that she'd see her tomorrow. Troubled, Mavis delivered the message then hurried back upstairs, but at Rose's hysterical refusal of tea or sympathy, she crept back to the kitchen, her thoughts in turmoil: this was no ordinary headache.

The girl was distraught, she could tell by the hunted look in her eyes. Mavis made a cup of tea and as she sipped, she asked herself over and again whatever could have happened to cause Rose so much distress.

May had glumly accepted Rose's excuse; she'd been looking forward to talking weddings. Not for the first time, she thought that Joey's fiancée was rather too refined and more delicate than some of the girls he had courted. 'I know she's our Joey's choice but I can't see her fitting into our family,' she said to Bill as they ate their tea. 'She should be on top of the world, him coming home in a day or two, not lying in her bed with nowt but a headache.'

'Aye, but she's not made from tough stuff like you, love,' Bill said tipsily.

* * *

Meanwhile, Lewis was lolling in a battered armchair in a shabby house in Mill Lane. He had arrived in Liverpool a couple of days ago, and down on his luck, he had looked up a mate he had shared a cell with in Walton Jail: Ken Jackson. He didn't much care for Ken, who he considered brash and rather stupid, but a free bed for a few nights and time to consider his options suited Lewis fine. And now, after his chance meeting with Rosamund, he had plenty to consider.

The arrogant German girl that Ken was knocking off was sitting on the couch with him, but she only had eyes for Lewis and Ken was sulking. When Lewis asked her what brought her from Munich to Edge Hill, she painted a colourful story of how she'd come to live in Weaver Street.

'So you live in Weaver Street?' That was useful. Lewis gave her a dazzling smile and Ursula fluttered her eyelashes.

'Who's the girl who lives at number fifteen? I saw her going in there earlier today. I think I've met her before, but I can't think where,' he said casually.

'That is Rose Brown,' Ursula said.

So... that's what she's calling herself these days.

'She lives with Mavis Robson and she works in Betty's Bijou Bazaar on Broad Green. Soon she will marry Joey Walker. He's in the navy, somewhere in the Far East,' Ursula gabbled, eager to hold his attention.

Lewis liked the sound of that. The fiancé was out of the way and he now knew Rosamund's place of work. 'Ah, so I was right. It is Rosam... Rose,' he hastily corrected himself. 'I knew her from way back. We were friends, *very* good friends if you know what I mean.' He winked suggestively then elaborated his story, most of which was a pack of lies. Making no mention of how he'd seduced then robbed an innocent rich girl, he gave Ursula the impression that Rose was just a girl he'd picked up and had his way with until he got tired of her.

* * *

Up in her bedroom, Molly was lonely and bored. Lily was out again with Barry, leaving Molly feeling envious at the lack of romance in her own life. She had turned down an offer to go out with the young doctor because since meeting Heinz Muller, she had been drawn to him like a moth to a flame. Lying on her bed, she thought back to the evenings in the Botanic Gardens when Molly pushed his wheelchair until they reached the paths where he would then walk slowly and steadily, each outing improving his gait. She had helped him to walk again, she thought sourly, but not once had he walked up to her door and asked to take her out. Fed up of feeling miserable, she flounced off the bed and downstairs. 'I'm going out,' she called, heading for the door.

'Wrap up well. It's cold out there,' said Kitty, glancing up from her sewing.

Her eyes met John's. She knew what was troubling her daughter and so did he.

'She'll get over him,' he said gently. 'Stop worrying.'

Molly had almost reached the gates to the Botanic Garden when she saw him. Heinz was striding steadily a few paces in front, and hearing the sound of her boots rattling the gravel, he glanced over his shoulder. His lips parted in a slow smile. 'Hello, Molly; what is it they say? Great minds think alike.'

'Hello, Heinz,' she stuttered, feeling hot and cold at the same time.

'You also wish to walk on this winter's night. It is beautiful, yes?' He gazed up at the darkening sky studded with brittle stars.

'Yes, it's beautiful,' Molly agreed breathlessly.

'Do you wish that we should walk together?' He proffered his arm. Molly nodded and linked with him, the feel of his tweed sleeve and the warmth beneath it making her fingertips tingle.

As they walked, he talked.

'But how do you know what's happening there?' she asked as they strolled around the rose garden and Heinz told her about a recent article he had written for a newspaper in Munich.

'The World Service on the wireless and communications from friends, and of course your national newspapers,' he said, his breath clouding in front of them. 'They all report on the unrest in my country and the influence Hitler and his National Socialist Party is having on the people.'

'John thinks he's a warmonger,' said Molly. 'I don't really understand much about it myself.' They came to a bench and at his suggestion they sat down. Molly no longer felt the icy nip in the air because she was warmed by the pleasure of his company as much as by the heavy winter coat and scarf she was wearing.

'Look at it this way,' Heinz said. 'The people in this country are suffering intense poverty. They are treated with contempt by a government that seems not to care. Your people are divided, one rule for the rich and another for the poor. Am I right?'

Molly nodded, her blue eyes flashing.

'But here in your country they are still one people, regardless of their wealth or lack of it,' Heinz continued. 'They do not openly discriminate against people like me, a German, and they accept the Polish, the African and the Asian peoples. They let them live amongst them without persecution.'

'I think that's stretching it a bit far,' Molly intervened. 'Some people object strongly to foreigners coming to live in Liverpool. They call them foul names and make fun of what they wear. There have been fights on the docks and the building sites, our men refusing to work with black men, and all because of the colour of their skin. At the hospital, a woman refused to let a black nurse tend to her.' Molly's cheeks had flushed, her tone clearly implying her disgust.

'You are even prettier when you are angry,' he said, giving her a smile that made Molly's heart thump and a warm glow flood her veins. She smiled back.

'It just makes me so cross,' she said.

'And you are right to be cross, but calling people ugly names is not as fearsome as that which Hitler is inciting. In Liverpool, the blacks may be made to feel unwelcome, but their lives are not in danger. In Hitler's Germany, he is leading the people to believe that those who are not of pure Aryan blood have no right to life. We were in danger because my mother's family has Jewish ancestors. Even true Aryan people who choose not to show allegiance to his Nazi party are in fear of their lives. He wants to rid the country of Jews, Communists and anyone who does not follow him to the letter. And he will drive them out, or worse.'

Molly continued listening without interrupting, the cold biting into her toes and rising up through her limbs, his words as chilling as the drop in the temperature. They had been sitting too long, and she stood. 'Let's walk, I'm frozen through to my marrow.' They started to walk back to Weaver Street, her feet tingling as her blood began to circulate again. 'But how will the articles you write prevent trouble?' she asked.

'They inform people of what is happening under their noses. Like here, in Germany there are millions unemployed because of the Depression. The people are hungry, not just for food but for change to bring back prosperity. They thought that President Hindenburg would save them. Now that he has failed, they are listening to a new voice, a very charismatic voice that is forcing people to take sides. Hitler will not rest until he has complete control,' Heinz told her as they walked from the park. 'I want my articles to warn them of the dangers if they let him have his way.'

'Do you mean so they can fight back?'

'In a way, yes,' Heinz said. 'If they have the facts, they can prepare for what is to come. I was not prepared, neither was I careful.' By now, they had arrived at the bottom of the lane. 'They found me out and beat me, confined me to that damnable chair,' he added angrily as they came to a halt at his gate. Guiltily, Molly thought that had it not been for the beating, they might never have become friends. Yet to cripple a man for writing things that they didn't agree with was inhumane.

'That was a hideous thing to do,' she said, her eyes and voice expressing her abhorrence, 'but are you still not in danger publishing your articles?'

'Yes, but it will not prevent me from writing the truth,' he said, his words as biting as cold steel. He rested his hands on her shoulders. 'They say the pen is mightier than the sword, so whenever we see gross injustice, we must write about it and bring it to the attention of the population. Or we can shout about it until the people who rule listen.'

'Do you mean that... that if I feel strongly about the things that are wrong with this country then I should do something about it?'

'Exactly!' he said. 'People do not always realise what is happening around them. They are busy with their own lives and do not see the bigger picture. But if they know, then they can act.'

There was nothing Heinz liked better than indoctrinating someone in his beliefs and having a captive audience; and Molly was certainly that. To reward her, he leaned forward and kissed the tip of Molly's nose, which was red with cold. With that, he wished her goodnight, walked to his door and immediately forgot all about their kiss.

Molly's mind was tumbling with ideas and her heart beating nineteen to the dozen as she walked to her own house on a cloud of love and dreams. She had just spent the last hour in the company of the most wonderful, interesting and handsome man she had ever known. And he had kissed her. Yes, it had been on her nose, but it was still a kiss. Maybe her love affair wasn't one-sided after all.

* * *

In a dark, narrow alley not far from the Grafton, Lily pushed her shoulders against the brick wall then grabbed the hand that was ferreting under her skirt. As she yanked and then shoved, Barry's scrawny frame bounced off the opposite wall. He let out a yell, struggling to maintain his balance, and Lily laughed nastily.

'Aw, Lily,' he moaned. 'Don't be mean.'

'I'm not letting you, and that's that,' Lily hissed.

'But we've been going out for ages. I've treated you like a queen and now I'm not getting' owt for it,' he pleaded.

'You're certainly not getting that!' Lily spat. 'You can't buy me.' She smoothed her skirt and walked out of the alley, her back rigid and her head high.

'In that case, we're finished,' Barry shouted. 'You're a stuck-up mare, Lily Stubbs, and I wouldn't touch you with a barge pole.'

'You haven't got one, you skinny little prick.'

Fuming, Lily walked on alone to the tram stop. Lads! They were all the same, thinking she'd let them have it if they bought her a drink or paid her ticket into the Grafton. They were all after one thing. Look at Pete Harper. He just used her mother for sex: he didn't love her. But she, Lily, wasn't going to be made a fool of; neither was she going to fall for a baby. Ending up like her mam was the worst thing she could imagine. She wanted someone to love her on her terms.

20

'Well, how's my best girl?' Joey lifted Rose off her feet, swinging her up in his arms. He smelled of the sea and tobacco. She nuzzled her face into his neck and clung to him, her emotions see-sawing between love and fear. His lips found hers and his kisses made her weak. She knew she would miss him beyond bearing when she told him the truth.

Joey had arrived back late in the afternoon on 30 November, and after dropping off his kitbag at his mother's and waltzing her round the kitchen, he had hared up to Mavis's. 'I'll leave you two lovebirds to get on with it,' she said and went next door to Jack.

Rose watched her go, her heart in her mouth, afraid to be alone with Joey and terrified of what she was about to tell him. But the sooner she did, the sooner it would be over. If she carried her secret much longer, she'd lose her mind.

Taking his hand, she led him into the front room. She'd make her confession there, safe from any interruption in case Mavis came back or Maggie or Kitty dropped by. She felt as though she was leading a lamb to the slaughter.

'Oh, but I've missed you, my beautiful girl,' he whispered

against her hair as they cuddled on the couch. In between passionate kisses, he told her how much he adored her and Rose responded with the same. She didn't feel as though she was deceiving Joey: she meant every loving word.

Joey loosened his hold on her and sat back, gazing into her face with such love and tenderness that Rose wanted to scream. Suppressing the urge, she drank in his tow-coloured hair, his blue eyes above high cheekbones, and the firm line of his jaw. *He was a beautiful man, but could he still be hers?*

'I find it hard to believe that a lovely girl like you wants to marry me.'

Joey's words pierced Rose's heart. 'I'm not that wonderful, Joey,' she said, the lump in her throat threatening to choke her. She sat up straight, her heartbeat quickening as she took a deep breath. 'Suppose you learned something about me, something horrible that I'd done before I met you, how would you feel then? Would you still love me?' Her bottom lip wobbled and she bit down on it.

Joey looked puzzled, then laughed. 'Don't talk daft. You're not capable of doing anything that 'ud make me stop loving you. You're the sweetest, kindest person I've ever known.' He kissed her tenderly. 'Right from the start, I knew you were different from other lasses I've been with. There's something pure and innocent about you, Rose, and I like that. I'm the luckiest man in the world to have you.'

Rose shuddered, and the words burning on her tongue turned to ashes.

'Are you cold, love? Will we go into the kitchen and sit by the fire?'

Rose shook her head. 'No, just put your arms round me and hold me tight.' Her heart felt like a lead weight. She couldn't destroy his happiness, not now. She'd let his first night at home, after being at sea for so long, be a happy one. He deserved that.

Joey wrapped her in his arms, his chin rested on the top of her head. Rose nestled against his chest, listening to the steady beat of his heart.

'I'm home for three months or more, the ship's in for a refit,' he said, oblivious to her anguish. 'We can get married before I go off again.'

'That's marvellous,' she mumbled into his shirt, and as he continued talking about getting married, she tried to make her responses sound enthusiastic, but her insides were churning.

After a few more kisses, Joey said, 'I'll go and spend a bit of time with Mam and get changed out of my uniform, then we'll go to the Weaver's to celebrate my homecoming.' Rose nodded, her smile forced and her heart crumbling as she saw him to the back door.

After he'd gone, she lingered in the doorway, her thoughts as black as the night sky. Try as she might, she couldn't dispel the awful feeling that now Lewis was in Edge Hill, she was in danger. What if Joey heard about their affair from him?

* * *

Gottfried Muller paced the floor in front of the fireplace, his expression grim. Ursula stood by the door into the hallway, the garish make-up she had applied only a few moments ago failing to conceal her petulant scowl.

'It is not right painting your face and flaunting your body,' her father barked. He ran his fingers through his thick grey hair and turned to address his wife. 'I thought once we came to England she would curb her foolish ways. It was bad that in Munich she behaved like *ein Luder*, carousing with Nazis in their nightclubs, but here I thought she would be different.'

'For goodness' sake, Papa, I am not a hussy,' Ursula cried. 'I'm going to the Weaver's Arms with a friend from work. You can hardly call that carousing.'

'Papa is right,' said her mother. 'Go wash your face.' Gerda Muller closed her eyes and folded her hands in her lap as if to put an end to the argument. She had refereed so many similar incidents that she was weary of them. Gottfried harrumphed noisily at her lack of support.

The knock on the door made them all look up, Ursula sneering as her parents hastily adopted respectful poses. Heinz, who all this time had been sitting at the table reading and taking no part in the row, glanced from one to the other, and when none of them made a move, he answered the knock.

Molly stood on the step, her cheeks flushed with embarrassment at what she was about to do. She hadn't seen him for several days, but if the mountain wouldn't come to Mohammed, then...

'Molly,' he said. She heard the surprise in Heinz's voice and her cheeks burned all the more.

'Who is it?' Gerda enquired. 'Don't keep them at the door, Heinz.'

'It is Molly,' he called back, pulling the door wider.

Molly stepped inside. 'Good evening, Mr and Mrs Muller.' They nodded and smiled, giving no hint of the aggravation they were feeling. Then she turned to Heinz. 'Would like to go to the Weaver's tonight with me?' Feeling foolish, she dropped her gaze.

'The public house?' Heinz broke the awkward silence. He gazed steadily back at her, considering. Then, sweeping back the wavy blond hair that flopped over his brow, he smiled. 'I would like that. Give me a moment to get my coat.' It would provide him with the opportunity to keep an eye on his troublesome sister, he thought, almost colliding with Ursula as she bounced back into the kitchen from the hall.

'Oh, it is you.' Molly heard the displeasure in Ursula's tone. 'Why are you here?'

'I came to ask Heinz if he would like to go with me to the Weaver's,' Molly said.

'What! Why? Is he coming?' Ursula looked extremely annoyed.

'He is,' Molly said, her tone brooking no opposition and her dislike for his sister intensifying. Then, pushing aside her antagonism, she let the butterflies that were invading her tummy take full flight in anticipation of the night ahead.

The locals in the Weaver's Arms welcomed Joey warmly. Leaving him to receive slaps on the back and field several lewd comments about girls in the Far East, Rose went and sat down. When Joey came and sat beside her, he began telling her about his Far East experiences. At a table close by, Ursula Muller was sitting with a young man Rose didn't recognise. He wasn't what she would call handsome, but she could tell by his flashy manner and his gauche attempts to ooze charm that he probably thought he was like Rudolph Valentino. He reminded her of Lewis and she immediately decided she didn't like him.

Ursula was leaning into him flirting provocatively, and speaking loudly enough for Rose to hear snatches of conversation about the nightlife in Munich, the *bierkellers*, and the high jinks she and her friends enjoyed as they prowled the city. The lad was lapping it up.

'I brought back some beautiful ornaments for when we set up home,' Joey said, taking Rose's hand and squeezing it. She dragged her attention back to him.

'That's wonderful, Joey,' she said, returning the squeeze.

'So all we need to do now is let the vicar call the banns and we can be married by Christmas.'

Rose's heart lurched. She had to tell him the truth, get it over and done with, but reasoning that the pub wasn't the right place to do it, she swallowed the words burning her tongue and cooled them with a sip of gin and lime. Joey didn't seem to sense anything amiss and finished his pint. 'Shall we have another then call it a night?' Rose nodded distractedly.

He went up to the counter. Cora, the landlady, told him she'd bring the drinks over. 'You make a lovely couple,' she said, setting the glasses on the table.

'And we'll be man and wife before the year's out,' Joey said proudly.

'Ooh! A Christmas wedding's lovely. I'll bet you're dead excited.' Cora's mawkish smile niggled Rose.

'Yes, I am. I can't wait,' she lied.

'Here's to us,' Joey said, lifting his glass and taking a sip. Rose followed suit, the taste of gin sharp on her guilty tongue. The evening was turning into a nightmare and it was all her own fault.

'Next drink's on me.' Cora went to serve more customers.

The door opened and in walked Molly and Heinz. Molly gave Rose a big smile and said, 'Mind if we join you?' Rose breathed a sigh of relief. Their company might divert Joey's attention from talking marriage.

'You're welcome.' Joey pushed a chair away from the table with his foot and Molly sat down. Heinz stood ready to fetch their drinks.

'Joey, this Heinz Muller,' said Molly. 'He's your new neighbour.'

'Pleased to meet you, Heinz. Sit down, I'll get these.' Joey got to his feet. 'What'll it be?'

'Beer, thank you,' Heinz said, and Molly asked for a lemonade.

'You must be thrilled to have him back,' Molly said as Joey went to the bar.

'I am,' Rose agreed, and filled them in on where he'd been.

'We're celebrating my homecoming and our forthcoming wedding,' said Joey, returning from the bar and handing them their drinks before sitting beside Rose and giving her a friendly nudge and a cheeky grin. Molly and Heinz raised their glass and offered their congratulations. Rose wanted the ground to open up and swallow her.

'Who is that with my sister?' Heinz nodded at Ursula and her companion. Rose could have kissed him for changing the subject.

Joey glanced over at them and, keeping his voice low, he said, 'A no-good called Ken Jackson. I'd warn her off him if I were you.'

Heinz pursed his lips and gave a serious nod then seemed to forget all about Ursula as Joey asked him what had brought him to Liverpool. His question and Heinz's answer opened up a lively conversation on the current situation in Germany and England that lasted until Cora called time.

Outside the pub, Ken said, 'I'll see you next Friday then, Ursula. Seven o'clock here on the dot,' before he sauntered off into the night.

Heinz turned to Ursula. '*Was machen Sie?*' *What are you doing?* '*Du kennst ihn nicht.*' *You do not know him.* Although Molly didn't understand a word he was saying, she could tell that he was extremely angry.

'It is no matter,' Ursula snapped. 'He gives me good time. It makes up for all that I am missing in Munich. And whose fault is that?' She hurried on ahead. Molly had had great hopes for the visit to the Weaver's Arms with Heinz, but now, Ursula's behaviour had spoiled what she had hoped would be a romantic end to the evening.

They walked on in silence, and leaving Joey and Rose to walk on to Mavis's, Molly and Heinz stopped at his gate. 'Did you enjoy tonight?' she asked.

'I did, thank you. You have been so patient giving your time to me. My gratitude is all yours.' Molly quivered in anticipation as his hand closed round hers. He raised it to his lips. 'Thank you again, and goodnight, Molly.' He walked up to his door without looking back.

Molly walked to her own door, shrouded in disappointment. First the nose, now the back of her hand – why on earth didn't he kiss her on the lips? Did he have any romantic feelings for her? She hadn't set out to fall in love with him, but he tugged at her heartstrings and tied them in knots, and she wasn't prepared to give up on him just yet.

* * *

Rose polished the glass-topped counter with methylated spirits to remove the fingerprints left by that morning's few customers. Keeping busy was her safety net in solitary moments yet it didn't prevent her from dwelling on Joey's plans. Last night, after they had left the bar, he had suggested that they should go and see the vicar this evening and arrange the wedding. Of course, she knew that couldn't happen. She had let him enjoy his first night at home but when he returned from his trip to the city to buy a new shirt, and she finished work, she would make her confession and put an end to his happiness – and hers.

Tears sprang to her eyes at the very thought of it, and the fumes from the methylated spirits made her feel woozy. She was going to destroy her future, and possibly his, but given time, he would recover; she knew that she never would. She'd never love anyone like she loved Joey Walker.

The bell above the door tinkled and she looked up expectantly, the smile pasted on her face fading when she saw Ursula. She hadn't taken to her from the start, and that dislike had deepened after Molly had told her that Ursula admired Adolf Hitler and his Nazi party. Even so, Rose politely asked, 'Can I help you?'

Ursula responded with a smile bordering on a smirk. 'Oh, no, I am not here to buy. I called to say that I met an old friend of yours. He was enquiring after you.'

'A friend of mine.' An icy shiver tingled Rose's spine. 'Who?'

'Lewis Aston.' Ursula let the name roll off her tongue, smirking openly as she watched the colour leach from Rose's cheeks. *It must be true: prim and proper, soon-to-be-married Rose and Lewis had been more than just good friends.*

'Lewis?' Rose's voice barely a whisper as she swallowed the lump in her throat. 'When? Where?'

Ursula laughed unpleasantly.

Rose clutched the edge of the counter, her knuckles white. For a second, her brain returned to the room in the Adelphi Hotel and the tangled bedcovers. She felt dirty and sick. Then she stiffened and managed to blurt out, 'Where is he now?'

'On his way to see you,' Ursula taunted, strutting out of the shop.

Trembling, Rose scrabbled feverishly for the bunch of keys in her bag. He mustn't find her here. The bell above the shop door jangled. Rose whirled round, blanching as a punch of fear and disgust hit her stomach with such force that she struggled for breath.

'Hello, Rosamund, how lovely to see you again,' Lewis drawled, and smirked when he saw the panic in her eyes.

* * *

Rose closed the shop and trudged up the lane, her thoughts tumbling. Walking up the garden path, she felt quite dizzy, as though she was treading on thin air. Her hand trembled as she twisted the doorknob and entered the warm, cosy kitchen. Mavis greeted her with a big smile.

'You're early, love, have you finished for the day? Are you

hungry? There's hard-boiled egg sandwiches, your favourite,' Mavis said, getting up from her chair and putting on the kettle.

Rose flinched. There it was, all the love and kindness she had known for the past few years offered again in a few short sentences. She felt like weeping.

'No, thanks,' she said, certain that she wouldn't be able to swallow a morsel until after she had told Mavis everything. She took off her coat.

Mavis's face creased with concern. 'Are you not feeling well, love? You look proper pale.'

'Something terrible's happened,' Rose replied, her mouth dry and her stomach tight. She flopped into the armchair they both considered hers and Mavis sat down in the other one. She leaned forward, her curiosity aroused and her beady eyes encouraging Rose to talk about whatever was troubling her.

'Tell me what's wrong and I'll see if we can't put it right.'

'I'll tell you what's wrong, Mavis. It's me.' Rose's voice was calm and even, as if she had rehearsed her words. 'I'm the wrong one and I want to put things right.' She took a deep breath. 'A few days ago, I bumped into Lewis Aston. I didn't tell you because I didn't want to worry you. Today he came into the shop. He's threatening to blackmail me.'

'Lewis Aston! Blackmail!' Mavis screeched, her hands flying to her face and cupping her cheeks. 'Whatever do you mean?'

'He's demanding two hundred pounds or he'll tell Joey about what we did,' Rose sobbed, her reserve breaking and her cries bordering on hysteria. 'He says I have till the end of the week to raise it.' She turned wild eyes on Mavis, almost screaming, 'Where am I going to find money like that?'

'Two hundred pounds,' Mavis echoed, her eyes round with amazement. 'The dirty, rotten maggot!' Two bright spots burned her cheeks as she spat out the words. 'You should go to the police.

Blackmail's a crime, and that man's a fool. Where on earth would he think *you* would get that kind of money?'

Rose's mouth turned at the corners in a bitter grimace. 'From my father.'

'Ah, yes,' Mavis said slowly, 'the filthy blaggard won't know that you haven't had owt to with your father in years. And does your father have that kind of money?'

Rose nodded. And, stumbling over her words, she said, 'But... but I couldn't ask him for it.' The thought of her father had reduced Rose to tears and caused Mavis to experience a gamut of emotions: pity for the lonely, unloved girl whose mother was a termagant and her neglectful father the aristocratic owner of a mansion on an estate in Buckinghamshire. 'You gave up a lot when you decided to stay with me,' Mavis said, slightly awed.

'I wasn't happy there,' Rose said. 'I didn't know what happiness was until I met you and the wonderful friends I've made in Weaver Street. I've even met the man I want to marry and now...' A shuddering sigh ended in a flood of tears.

'Maybe fate decreed that you had to meet someone as vile as Lewis Aston so that you could find true happiness,' she said sagely, 'and let's face it, you were an easy target. But not any more,' Mavis declared stoutly, getting to her feet and lighting the gas under the kettle: a strong cup of tea was needed. 'You're twice the person you were. I think if your mother were to meet you now, she'd be proud of you.'

'I find that difficult to believe,' Rose mustered a little smile, 'but it doesn't trouble me. I've lived most of my life under her shadow, and now that I have everything I want here, all I want to do is hang on to it. I can't risk letting Lewis tell Joey about us.'

'You've no need to,' said Mavis, spooning leaves into the teapot. 'When you first came here, you had no idea of how ordinary folks like us lived, but you've come to terms with that and I couldn't be prouder.' She walked over to Rose, pulling her upright to embrace her. 'We've both gained something from your mistake, Rose. You've found what it is you want from life, and as for me, well, you're the daughter I never had.' Rose clung to Mavis.

'But what am I going to do about Lewis, and Joey? How can I put things right?' she asked forlornly as she let Mavis go.

'Like I said, you've grown strong,' replied Mavis, her beady eyes defiantly encouraging. 'Now you're going to use that courage to beat Lewis at his own game. You're going to tell Joey the truth. That way, you have nothing to hide, and Lewis has nothing to gain.' She gave a determined little nod.

'But Joey won't want me when knows about Lewis and the baby,' Rose sobbed.

'Joey Walker loves you with every breath in his body,' Mavis said firmly, 'and if he's half the man I think he is, he'll still love you, no matter what.' She softened her tone and added, 'And if he doesn't, then maybe he's not for you.'

* * *

Later that evening, in Mavis's front room, Rose sat waiting for Joey to join her. Her head ached and her hands were clammy. Phrases she had been rehearsing ever since she had decided to take Mavis's advice tumbled inside her weary mind. Was she about to bring an end to her happiness and all her hopes for the future?

Could she bear to break Joey's kind heart? Her own was already broken.

Mavis was sitting in the kitchen, one hand wringing the other and her nerves twitching. When the knock came at the door, she stood on unsteady feet and let Joey in. 'She's in the front room, lad,' she said softly.

Rose was on the couch, her hands clenched. When he sat down

and put his arms around her, she stiffened. He drew back, surprised. 'What?' he said.

'I've something to tell you, Joey, something that might make you stop loving me,' she said, almost choking on the words.

Joey burst into laughter. 'Oh, Rose! Nothing you say or do will make me stop loving you.' He reached for her again, but she leapt to her feet.

'No, Joey! Just listen to me,' she cried hysterically, 'you have to be told.' As she struggled to compose herself, Joey made to rise from his seat to comfort her, and might have done so had she not held up her hand, crying, 'Please, Joey. You have to listen to me.' Her distress was so tangible that Joey felt as though he could touch it, but doing as she begged, he sank back onto the couch, his brow furrowed and his eyes filled with confusion. Rose pushed back her shoulders and, adopting a brave stance, she began to speak in an almost steady voice.

'I'm not Rose Brown, a girl who came to Liverpool looking for work. I'm Rosamund Brown-Allsop, the daughter of a wealthy family in Buckinghamshire.' She paused momentarily before bitterly saying, 'I'm also a fool.' She felt her confidence wavering and gulped back a sob. 'I ran away from home with a man I thought loved me. He robbed me of my money and... my virginity.' Her voice had dropped to barely a whisper. 'I let him make love to me and... and... I got pregnant.' By now, she was blinded by tears. 'I had a... a... miscarriage. There is no baby.' She shook her head despairingly and carried on brokenly, 'So you see, I'm not the virgin you think I am. I'm spoiled goods, Joey, I'm just a liar who loves you more than you'll ever know.' Collapsing into the nearest chair, she buried her face in her hands she wept.

'Thanks for telling me,' Joey said and walked from the room.

* * *

'Eeh, I'm sorry, lad,' said May, her plump cheeks wobbling. 'I'd never have thought it.' She sighed heavily as she sought the words to comfort him.

'Neither would I,' said Joey, his voice as hollow as the empty glass of rum he'd downed in one: rum he'd brought back from Japan to give to his guests on his wedding day.

May wiped her eyes. 'But you do love her, don't you?'

Joey nodded dumbly.

'Well, then, look at this way, love. She made a mistake. We all do. And all right, she dallied with a chap she thought loved her, but she was young then and didn't know better.' May cocked her head to one side and looked fondly at her son. 'I'm sure you've dallied with a few lasses that you might not want her to know about.'

He thought about the girls in Bilbao, Alexandria, Rotterdam and many other ports. He felt ashamed. He was no more innocent than his fiancée was guilty. Then he looked into his mother's care-worn face, recalling all the love she had given him and his brothers and the hardships she had suffered working all hours to provide them with the best that she could afford. She was a strong, wise woman.

He jumped to his feet, pulled his mother to him and gave her an almighty hug and a smacking kiss on her forehead. Then he ran out of the house, pounding up the lane to Mavis's door, his heart swelling with relief and overflowing with love.

* * *

Rose gazed into the mirror at her red, puffy eyes, but she was smiling. In the last hour, her world had righted itself and her hopes and dreams for the future were back on track.

'I'm not looking to you for purity and perfection or any of that old-fashioned rubbish,' Joey had said. 'I love you and want to spend the rest of my life with you. I can't live without you.'

Through her tears, Rose repeated his words back to him, and in between telling him how Mavis had rescued her, and 'sorry's and 'please forgive me's, followed by kisses and promises to always be honest with each other, they set the wedding date for Boxing Day. 'That's the day we met,' Rose had said joyfully, 'it seems just right.'

Mavis was delighted. 'You're a good man, Joey Walker. I'm so happy for you both that I could cry.'

* * *

Rose laughed in Lewis's face when, at the end of the week, he walked into the shop and demanded his money.

'You're not getting a penny, Lewis. Joey already knows about you and me. I told him everything, so whatever vile details you have to add won't make one damned bit of difference.'

Startled by her defiance, he sneered, 'That idiot might not care about your dirty past but I can still ruin your reputation in the eyes of all your friends.'

'Why would they believe you, Lewis?' Rose was white with anger. 'You're a guttersnipe that only a fool would trust – and yes, I was that fool – but not any longer. Now get out of my shop before I call the police. In fact, take my advice and get out of town.'

Lewis looked as though she had punched him. He had thought it was going to be so easy. He hadn't foreseen that the mousy, spoiled girl he had brought to Liverpool would become a woman who couldn't be intimidated, a woman whose sparkling grey eyes and sneering expression let him know that he no longer had any power over her.

'You haven't seen the last of me,' he snarled. 'I'm not finished with you yet. Get the money... or else...' He spun on his heel and barged out of the shop.

Rose hugged herself. She felt positively triumphant and the feeling stayed with her for the rest of the day. The burden she had carried deep inside for so long had been lifted. She felt as free as a bird now that she had nothing to hide.

'I can't believe I stood up to him like that,' she crowed when she told Mavis about it, 'and to know that Joey still loves me is nothing short of a miracle.'

Mavis gave a wise nod and said, 'See where telling the truth gets you. It always pays to be honest.'

'You can tell Kitty and the others if you like.'

'I'll leave that up to you,' Mavis said perkily. 'Now, you get your dinner.' She took the dish of eggs in cheese sauce from the oven and carried it over to the table as though nothing untoward had taken place. Rose loved her all the more.

* * *

Lewis was fuming. He'd be damned if he was going to let that stupid little cash cow slip through his fingers. On his way back to Ken Jackson's dump to collect his gear, he had a sudden thought. *Maybe all wasn't lost. Rose could be lying, and the mug that wanted to marry her was still in the dark.* He'd hang around for a while longer. That ugly, supercilious German bitch that Ken was hankering after could help him. Smiling wickedly, he walked on.

21

Joey was in the Weaver's Arms when Ursula Muller sidled up to him. He recognised her as the German girl from next door. She made some remarks about his forthcoming wedding and Joey nodded politely and was about to turn his attention back to his mates and the dartboard when she slyly whispered, 'Did you know that Rose had a steamy love affair with a friend of mine?'

Joey glared into the smirking face caked in make-up and his hackles rose. 'I know all about it,' he growled, 'and it wasn't a love affair. He robbed her and left her high and dry. Now, get lost! Toddle off back to the gutter you crawled out of and keep your dirty mouth shut.' Seething with rage, he pushed her aside and slammed out of the pub. Ursula followed, running up Weaver Street to Mill Lane to report back to Lewis.

Not long after Joey had burst into his own house cursing Ursula for all the gossips of the day, and May did her best to calm him, Rose was tidying the counter ready for closing up and Betty was counting the takings. She'd popped in earlier, proudly wheeling her son Henry who was going to be as weighty as his mother if she kept on feeding him the way she was doing. He sat in his pushchair, fat faced and dribbling over a Mars bar.

'How are your wedding plans coming on?'

'Just fine,' Rose replied. 'Kitty's making me a dress, and Joey and I have been to see the vicar so it's full steam ahead. He's playing football this afternoon – Joey, that is, not the vicar,' she giggled, 'and by now he'll either be celebrating or commiserating with his mates in the Weaver's Arms.'

Rose sounded positively cheery, but in the back of her mind, she was dreading what she had to do next. Tomorrow, Sunday, at Joey's insistence, she was going to telephone her father and ask him for her birth and baptism certificates.

'Well, enjoy the preparations,' said Betty, handing Rose her wage packet, 'it's your big day and you want to get it right.' She tucked the takings into her handbag. 'I'd best get off, it's already as black as pitch, them gaslights aren't working properly. I'll leave you to lock up.' She pushed Henry outside. A van was parked at the end of the lane and she wheeled the pram past it.

Rose checked that everything was in order, then put on her coat. She'd have a bath when she got home. Joey was coming round later. As she locked the shop door, a dark shape loomed up at her side. Suddenly Rose was plunged into complete darkness, the bag over her head shutting out the dim light from the street lamp and muffling her screams. Strong arms gripped her on either side. She kicked out, frantically struggling to free herself, then pitched forward as she was bundled head first into the van.

Patrick Conlon was cycling on Broad Green, on his way home when he saw the shabby van at the end of the lane, its engine running. Two men were bundling something unwieldly into the back of it. As he drew nearer, one of the men dived into the rear of the vehicle and the other slammed the doors then ran to the front and jumped in the driver's seat. Patrick cycled past. *I wouldn't be seen dead driving a scrapheap like that,* Patrick thought, noting the red paint smeared over the dents in the side of the van.

Rose heard the engine roar and felt the weight of a heavy, hot body on top of her own. As she fought to breathe, a familiar, cloying scent pervaded her nostrils. It lingered in the fabric of the bag pressed against her face. Her heart missed a beat. She knew that smell. Repugnance flooded her veins.

'Lewis,' she yelled.

* * *

'She's not here, lad. I thought she was with you,' Mavis said when Joey called for Rose later that evening.

'I was in the pub then I went home for me dinner. I told her I'd call for her at seven.' His handsome face creased in bemusement. 'I'll go and find her.'

A quick call at Kitty's and Maggie's proved fruitless, and Betty said she'd left Rose in the shop just before closing time. He ran back to Mavis's.

'Where can she be?' he cried, looking fearfully at Mavis. She saw what he was thinking. She'd been thinking the same. Had Rose done a bunk to avoid getting married?

Mavis darted upstairs and was back in a flash. 'All her things are there,' she said, 'she can't have gone far.' She looked utterly bewildered.

'I'll find her if it kills me,' Joey said as he barged out.

* * *

Rose's heart thudded painfully against her ribs, and even through the bag over her head, she smelled the nauseating stink of Lewis's sweat and cologne. She felt the urge to vomit and was afraid that if she did, she might suffocate.

'Take this bag off my head,' she pleaded, her muffled words making Lewis clamp his hand over her mouth. Frantically, Rose twisted and turned, and freeing an arm, she clawed feverishly at the bag.

'Lie still,' Lewis growled, 'I'm not going to harm you.'

What a ludicrous thing to say, Rose thought as she struggled for breath.

The van rattled to a halt. Rose reckoned that they had been travelling for no more than a few minutes. Where had they brought her to? she wondered. And what were they intending to do with her?

'Help me get her into the house, Ken,' Lewis said.

Blindly, Rose struggled as the two men trailed her from the van. She heard a door slam and the creak of hinges as another one opened. They came to a halt. Even though she sensed the heat emanating from the two nervous bodies that crowded her own, Rose felt an icy trickle flooding her veins. She flailed her arms wildly and began to scream.

'Shut up!' Lewis barked, giving her a hefty shove that sent her spinning into open space. Disoriented by her blindness and the lack of oxygen her screams had used up inside the bag, Rose floundered helplessly and sank to her knees. Rough hands bundled her upright and Lewis ripped the bag from her head. She blinked rapidly, her head swimming as she filled her lungs with air. Through blurred eyes, she saw Lewis's leering face then Ken's panic-stricken expression. They were now in a small, dingy room that might at one time have been a washhouse.

'What are you doing?' she croaked.

'Business,' Lewis snarled. 'Now you be a good girl and keep the noise down. I'll tape your mouth if you start screaming again.'

Rose swallowed the scream she had been about to emit. *Stay calm and keep your wits about you*, she told herself firmly, although hysteria was mounting by the minute. She drew a deep breath, and as coolly as she could muster, she asked, 'Why have you brought me here like this? What do you intend to do with me?'

'We'll keep you here until Daddy pays up, then we'll let you go.'

Rose couldn't believe what she was hearing. The hare-brained plan had her wanting to laugh in Lewis's face, but she could see that he was deadly serious. She knew him well enough to know that he didn't like to appear foolish and that she had to tread carefully. But he had hurt her; taken her for the innocent fool she had been and stolen her virginity. She couldn't forgive him for that. So, against her better judgement, she couldn't resist asking, 'Do you honestly think my father has enough interest in me to pay you a...' she paused sneeringly, 'a ransom... is that what they call it?'

The taunt hit its mark. Lewis's face clouded. Rose saw the anxiety her remark caused. She struck again. 'My father doesn't care two figs about me.'

'He will when he knows what we'll do to you if he doesn't hand over the money,' Lewis yelled, his steely control unravelling. 'He's your father. He's bound to care what happens to you.'

Rose felt a surge of hope at having rattled him.

'And if he does, I'll tell him and the police who it was that kidnapped me,' she continued, a glimmer of a sardonic smile teasing the corners of her mouth. 'Then the game will be up and they'll hunt you down.' She gazed steadily into Lewis's troubled eyes. 'Let me go, Lewis, and we'll forget all about it.'

'She's right. She knows who we are. Let her go, for Christ's sake.' Ken tugged at Lewis's arm. 'I knew this was a bloody bad idea. Just let her go!'

Lewis whirled round and lashed out. Ken reeled back,

clutching his jaw. 'Don't be a bloody fool,' Lewis roared, 'we've come too far to back out now.'

Rose opened her mouth wide and screamed at the top of her lungs. Lewis swung his fist. Rose's head exploded and everything went black.

* * *

Joey was distraught. He had visited every house that Rose had had contact with and drawn a blank. He vented his fury on the police, who still insisted that they didn't take action until an adult had been missing for more than three days. 'If she was a small child it 'ud be a different story,' the constable on duty told him impatiently. Joey trudged back to Weaver Street, feeling thoroughly impotent.

Mavis's kitchen was crowded, Jack, Maggie, May, Lily, Molly and Patrick all having just returned from combing the streets. They stood around dejectedly drinking tea. 'Nothing,' Joey said in response to the questioning eyes that turned to him as he entered the house. 'No one has seen or heard anything.'

Mavis began to cry. 'I can't bear it,' she sobbed, 'she could be lying dead for all we know.' Joey blanched, and a deathly hush fell over the room. Mavis had voiced what they were all thinking.

'There's nothing more we can do tonight,' John said and, nodding miserably, they returned to their own homes.

Joey couldn't sleep. Had Rose run away from him, or had something terrible befallen her? His heart felt as though it was in a thousand pieces. He gazed blindly into the dark lane, trying to quell his fears. A pale, silvery moon and a handful of stars lit the heavens but no lights shone from the house windows. Weaver Street was sleeping. But where was Rose?

* * *

Rose's head was pounding. She felt as though she was swimming through sludgy water as, gradually, she regained consciousness. Sprawled on the flagstones, the cold and damp penetrating her clothing, she fearfully reflected on her perilous situation before slowly adopting a sitting position in the gloomy washhouse. Groggily, she scanned the space: she had to get out of here. The window was boarded up and no doubt the door was locked. Her head swam as she struggled to her feet. The door had no knob on the inside. She hammered her fists against it then prised at its edges: it didn't budge. She called out, her cries reverberating against the dank walls built with stones several inches thick. Realising that there was no escape, she sank to the ground, and with her back rested against the door she closed her eyes and waited.

She wakened with a raging thirst and her bones aching, surprised that she had dozed off. She had no idea how long she had been asleep, but those minutes or hours proved restorative, her mind much clearer. She got to her feet and tottered over to an old stone sink. Turning the ancient brass tap above it, she waited for the water to flow. A gurgling in the pipes was followed by a splash of filthy brown sludge. Gradually the water cleared and Rose stuck her head under the flow, letting the water dribble into her mouth and down her parched throat. Her thirst quenched, she felt a queasy sensation in her guts. It was hours since she had emptied her bladder.

Squatted in a corner, burning with humiliation, she relieved herself. Her belly rumbled; she was hungry. It roiled and cramped and she wondered if the water had poisoned her innards. Please, God, don't let me get diarrhoea, she prayed as she leant against the wall and struggled with her emotions.

A scraping sound made her spring into action. Lewis ducked inside, locking the door behind him. 'I've brought you some food.' He tossed a bag at Rose's feet then shouted, 'Stop being a silly girl and calm down,' as Rose lunged at him. Like a skittle, he knocked her flying. Down on her knees, she looked up at him, her eyes filled with hate. She was no match for him and they both knew it.

Lewis sniggered, and spinning on his heels, he darted from the washhouse, slamming the door shut behind him.

Rose cried until she felt empty. Then, forcing herself to gain control, she lifted the bag and took out a cheese sandwich. As she chewed, a sense of utter wretchedness invaded her spirits. She looked from the boarded-up window to the stout locked door. Drained of both energy and hope, she slid to the floor. With her back against the wall and her head on her chest, she gave herself up to whatever the night might hold.

Mavis hadn't slept. She wandered into the front room and gazed out into the empty street. The room smelled stuffy, so she opened the window a couple of inches. Just then, Jack called out from the kitchen. 'I'm going to search the yards, are you coming?' Mavis hurriedly went to join him.

Joey had notified the police again, and the neighbours who didn't have to go to work were gathering in Weaver Street to form a search party. 'She could be anywhere,' Maggie said, puffing furiously on her cigarette as Kitty waited for her to put on her shoes.

'Joey's been round the town twice asking if anyone's seen her, and Jack and Mavis have searched the streets and the back yards all morning,' Kitty replied.

'Maybe she just decided to go back to where she came from,' Maggie said.

'She wouldn't leave Joey – or Mavis – just like that,' Kitty said scornfully, 'she's not that sort of girl.' Her face crumpled. 'Something bad must have happened for her to disappear like that, so hurry up and we'll join the search.'

Outside in the lane, Bill and May Walker stood talking with Joey, Mavis and Jack. 'Still no sign of her,' Mavis said brokenly as Kitty and Maggie joined them.

'The police don't seem that interested,' Jack grumbled, 'they say she's a grown woman an' she hasn't been missing long enough for them to mount a full-scale search.'

'That heartless bugger of a constable said she'll probably turn up in her own good time,' May cried.

Gerda Muller came out of her house. 'It is good that the weather is so warm and dry if she has been out all night,' she remarked, her features woebegone.

'Might Ursula know where she's gone?' Kitty was clutching at straws: Rose and Ursula were not friends. 'Did the police ask her?'

'I did,' said Joey. He looked ghastly, his eyes wild and his face leached of colour. 'She says the last time she saw her was yesterday, in the shop.' His shoulders sagged despairingly.

* * *

Ursula was in Ken's house with Ken and Lewis, and Lewis was telling them what they would do next.

'We'll send him something belonging to her that proves we have her,' Lewis said, 'that's what kidnappers do.'

Ursula snorted. 'Like what? What do we have of hers that any other woman does not have?' she sniped. 'You think if you send him a scarf or a lock of hair, he will believe you?'

Her scathing tone not only irritated Lewis, it made him aware of what a stickler for detail Ursula was; detail that he hadn't given a thought to even though he was supposed to be masterminding this kidnap. He sought to regain the upper hand.

Lewis floundered for an answer. 'Her engagement ring,' he cried.

Ursula's harsh laugh cut him to the quick. 'Fool! Her father doesn't know what it looks like.'

Lewis's cheeks reddened.

'You really do need to give this much more thought if you expect it to work.' Ursula's words dripped with sarcasm. 'We'll leave you to think about it.' She walked to the door, signalling for Ken to follow her.

'And don't take too long. I want her out of my house,' Ken growled as he got to his feet.

After they left, Lewis paced the floor. Ursula was right; his plan was in tatters. He broke out in a cold sweat, and finding the confines of the shabby little house unbearable, he put on his hat and coat and stepped out into Mill Lane. A funny little birdy woman and a man with a limp and one eye walked by without giving him a second glance. Lewis shambled in the opposite direction. He'd almost reached the bottom of Weaver Street when he saw something that made him rapidly change his mind. The window in the house where Rose lived was open, the sash pushed up and the hem of the curtains fluttering in the breeze. In her haste to search for Rose, Mavis had completely forgotten to close it.

A shifty glance in either direction told Lewis that the street was empty; raising the sash he scrambled through the window. Upstairs, he threw open the first door he came to, almost cheering out loud when he saw Mister Snuffy Snuggles propped on the bed's pillows. If that wasn't proof that he had Rosamund Brown-Allsop in his clutches, he didn't know what was. Snatching up the cuddly rabbit, he left the house the same way he had entered it.

* * *

'What now?' Ursula asked, looking at Lewis expectantly.

'I've posted the rabbit and made the phone call. Brown-Allsop's taken the bait. I panicked him rightly and he's promised not to involve the police,' Lewis said cockily.

He avoided meeting Ursula's eyes in case she caught him out in the lie. In fact, the phone call hadn't gone quite as Lewis had anticipated. James Brown-Allsop had been exceedingly sceptical. 'What makes you think it's my daughter you've... er... kidnapped?' James had said, incredulity coating his words. 'I'd need positive proof before I meet your demands.'

'Tomorrow's post will be proof enough.'

'Post? Why? What do you mean?'

Lewis heard the tremor in James's voice and knew he had struck a nerve.

'Just comply. If you don't then... next time it might be her hand.'

Smiling at the threat, he'd hung up.

22

Rose had spent the hours since she had woken up making futile attempts to break free of her prison, her hands raw and her spirits low. Now, slumped against the wall, she heard the key turning in the lock. The door opened and she gaped in utter astonishment when Ursula entered, clutching a paper bag and bottle.

Rose leapt to her feet.

'Thank God!' she cried, hurrying forward, her first thoughts being that somehow the girl had come to her rescue. But before Rose's wits were fully gathered, Ursula kicked the door shut with her heel and delivered a sharp blow to Rose's head with the bottle. Rose reeled.

'No! No!' she yelled, and regaining her balance, she stared at Ursula. 'Tell me you're not part of this madness.'

Ursula dropped the bag and set down the bottle then smirked at Rose. 'Food, poor little rich girl,' she sneered, nudging the bag with her toe. 'We don't want you to die of hunger before your father hands over the money.'

Rose felt faint. Just when there had been a glimmer of hope, she was back where she started. 'Please, Ursula, please. Stop this nonsense before things get worse,' she pleaded. 'My father isn't going to hand over any money for my release. Let me go while you still have the chance to save yourselves. I promise I won't tell anyone.' By now, tears were streaming down Rose's face, tears so hot and desperate she felt they might leave permanent tracks on her cheeks.

Ursula looked at Rose, a gloating expression on her face. She felt no sympathy for her. This was the girl whose father's money would enable her to return to Munich and support the Führer. 'Stop snivelling, and eat!' she commanded, kicking the bag towards Rose.

'What's going on in there?' Ken shouted from outside the door.

'I'm coming out now,' Ursula replied. The door opened and she backed out.

Slowly, Rose sank to her knees, then she sat down, the chill from the damp flagstones seeping into her buttocks. It would have been useless to put up a fight, and hungry and thirsty, she forced down the bread and cheese and drank lemonade, the fizzy liquid swirling uncomfortably as it hit her stomach. Sick at heart, she waited for another day and night to pass.

* * *

In Buckinghamshire, in the study at Heathcote Manor, James Brown-Allsop sat nursing a shabby fur rabbit, an anguished expression creasing his features. 'I didn't believe him for a moment when he made the first telephone call,' he said to his trusted friend and head stableman, Willie Thompson. 'I thought it was just some foolish jape. Now, I don't know what to think.' His voice cracked. 'This is definitely Rosamund's rabbit. She took it everywhere with her.' He lifted the cuddly toy and gazed at it as though willing it to speak.

'You should have called the police straight off,' Willie said.

Rose's father shook his head. 'There are a lot of things I should have done, Willie. After Oliver's death, things were never the same between Mildred and me. Her grief was unbearable, as was mine, but that's no excuse for the neglect Rosmund suffered when she was young. I was too busy with the horses and the estate to let her know how much I loved her.' He laid the rabbit back on his lap and ran his hands over his face. 'All that nonsense we put about of Rosamund having gone to a finishing school in Switzerland...' he growled. 'I should never have been party to it. And I should most certainly never have listened to Mildred when she forbade me to go find her after she ran away,' he continued bitterly. 'Mildred was afraid of what it would do to our reputation, said we would be laughing stocks, our daughter running off with the hired hand, and like a fool, I gave in to her.'

'You always did,' Willie said softly, 'and I know I might be speaking out of turn, but Mildred never cared for Rosamund like a mother should. Apart from the time Rosamund spent with that pony of hers, she was a lonely little girl. I was just as sad as you when she ran off with that blackguard, Aston.'

James reared his head. 'I think it's him that has her,' he said with asperity. 'I thought I recognised that – what do you call it – Geordie accent?' He got to his feet with renewed verve. 'Well, blast the bugger! I'll play him at his own game. When he rings again, I'll agree to hand over the money – and in the meantime, I'll contact the constabulary. They'll be waiting for him when he comes to collect it.'

'But will he tell them where he's holding Rosamund?' Willie said sagely.

'I'll beat it out of him!' James roared, marching into the hallway to telephone the local police. The antique clock on the mantel above fireplace chimed midday. 'He'll know I've received the rabbit by now,' James said, 'he'll call again today.' He hunched his shoulders and hung his head, his lithe, muscular frame looking as though it was shrivelling with each passing minute.

The telephone shrilled and both men flinched even though they had been expecting the call. James leapt to his feet. Willie followed him. Trying to still the trembling in his hand, James lifted the receiver.

'Brown-Allsop.' His voice wavered.

'I take it you found our wee cuddly friend.'

'Yes, what do we do now?'

'If you want your daughter back unharmed, you hand over the cash.'

James scowled at Lewis's brash tone of voice.

'When and how?' he growled.

The line hummed. Lewis was thinking. 'I'll be down before nightfall. Don't do anything stupid like calling the police – or else.' The threat hanging in the air, he put the phone down.

'I need a car, and fast,' he told Ken when he returned from the phone box.

Ken dithered. 'It's a bit soon to be pinching another one,' he whined, 'I was lucky with the van, but I don't know if I can get a car that quick.'

'That van won't make it to Buckinghamshire. Go and get a decent car and be bloody sharp about it,' Lewis snapped. 'I want to be on my way in the next hour.' He gave Ken a shove. 'Don't stand there gawping. Get a fucking move on!'

Ken ran for the door.

'I'm coming with you, Lewis,' Ursula announced as soon as Ken had gone. 'If you have the money, how do we know you'll come back to Liverpool?' She gave Lewis a challenging glare. He curled his lip. The bitch was so astute, he felt like throttling her.

Ursula watched him digest what she had said then coyly sidled up to him. 'Why split the money three ways?' she said huskily.

Lewis felt her hot breath on his cheek. 'Come along for the ride,' he replied coolly, although he had no intentions of taking either her or Ken. He'd intended to cut them out all along. He began pacing the floor, cursing Ken for his tardiness.

* * *

Patrick Conlon cycled slowly up Mill Lane on his way home after playing football. He saw the battered van with the dented side smeared with red paint. *Where had he seen it before?* The cogs of his brain whirred and as realisation dawned, he pressed the pedals harder, his backside in the air as he ascended the steep slope. At the top, he pedalled like fury down Weaver Street, the wind whipping through his hair. He was going to find Joey Walker.

Joey answered his frantic hammering on the back door and after hearing Patrick out, he barked, 'Go get your dad with the car. Tell him to ring the police.' Then Joey hared from the house.

'What's happening? Where are you going?' May cried from the kitchen.

'Tell you later, Mrs Walker,' Patrick yelled back before racing for home.

* * *

Rose heard the racket coming from somewhere in the house. The washhouse door burst open. When she saw John Sykes, she flung herself into his arms and burst into tears. Great gulping sobs racked her body and tore at her throat as he led her to the front room. Through streaming eyes, she saw Joey's fist connect with Lewis's jaw. Lewis's knees buckled and he sank to the floor. Ursula was cowering in a corner, protesting that it was all Lewis's idea. Patrick stood with his back to the door to prevent anyone from leaving. The wailing siren outside prompted him to open it and look out. 'They're here,' he yelled triumphantly. Two burly policemen barged into the house, batons raised.

* * *

'My dad must think I'm worth it after all,' said Rose as she nestled with Joey on the couch in Mavis's front room later that evening.

Since the aborted kidnap, Joey hadn't left Rose's side, and now they were alone, she felt more able to open her heart and reconcile all the thoughts that had flooded her mind in the past three traumatic days.

'Of course he does, you're his little girl no matter what.' Joey stroked her arm soothingly and they sat in silence, each lost in their own thoughts.

The last few hours since Rose's release had been frantic. All the neighbours, horrified by what had happened, had crowded into Mavis's to express their relief now that she was safe and unharmed. Patrick bashfully glowed as they praised him for his timely intervention, and Maggie declared that the law should string Lewis up by his balls. 'That's if he has any,' she'd cackled.

The police had been and gone. Ursula had spilled the beans to save her own skin, and as the elderly constable related the detail of Lewis's plot, Rose had wept for her father. He had been subjected to Lewis's sordid dealings all because she had been foolish enough to run away with the vile creature.

So, that evening, somewhat recovered from her ordeal, Rose walked across to Kitty's with Joey. Kitty had offered to let them ring Rose's father from her house rather than make the call from the telephone box on Broad Green. Joey's arm was round Rose's waist and she leaned into him in need of his support, her legs trembling and her mouth dry. What if her father refused to speak to her? Could she bear his rejection?

Kitty gave strict orders that nobody was to enter the hall while Rose was using the telephone. John and Robert played draughts in the parlour, and Molly and Patrick sat in his room talking about the kidnap. Kitty shut herself in the kitchen.

In the drawing room at Heathcote Manor, James Brown-Allsop was packing books into boxes when the telephone in the hall jangled. James answered it. Rose's heart lurched as he said, 'Brown-Allsop, who's calling?'

'Daddy, it's Rosamund.'

The stunned silence at the end of the line shot through her like a bullet. The telephone slipped from her hand and clunked noisily on the hall table.

'Rosamund? Rosamund, is that you? Oh, my beloved girl, where are you?'

The disembodied voice at the other end of the line echoed in Kitty's hall.

Rose knew that her father was crying and it tore at her heart. Sobbing uncontrollably, she looked wildly at Joey. He picked up the telephone.

'He's coming tomorrow on the first train,' Rose told Kitty and John over a strong cup of hot, sweet tea. 'Joey explained everything...' she smiled at him gratefully, her eyes filled with love and admiration, 'then I talked to Daddy and he was wonderful.' Her eyes filled with tears again. 'He never stopped loving me,' she hiccuped as she, then Joey, related the telephone call. Her mother had left her father for another man shortly after he had lost a great deal of money in the crash, the manor had recently been sold and her father was in the process of moving to a cottage on some land that he had kept for his two favourite horses. Rose smiled fondly. 'Daddy loves his horses.'

'And here's me thinking I was getting a rich heiress for a wife,' Joey joked. But he was relieved to know he didn't have to compete with a wealthy father-in-law.

'He can stay with Jack,' said a delighted Mavis when she heard the news. 'No need for a hotel in the city.' Her beady eyes sparkled as, like a commander marshalling his troops into battle, she darted out to organise Jack's spare bedroom. Joey took Rose in his arms and kissed her. When the kiss ended, they gazed at one another, their eyes reflecting pure joy. Their problems were over.

* * *

James arrived in the afternoon of the next day and what a joyful reunion it was. There was so much to explain, so much to catch up with, and throughout it all, not a word of recrimination passed their lips: Rose forgave him for being too busy with his horses to see how lonely and neglected she'd felt, and James forgave her for running off with Lewis.

'I've formed a very close relationship with Clarice Burridge – you remember Clarice, don't you?' he said, his cheeks reddening at sharing the confidence.

Rose nodded. Clarice, the whip-thin horsey woman who always had more time for her father than his wife ever did.

James smiled. 'When I come back for the wedding, can I bring her along?'

He went back to Buckinghamshire two days later, Rose rejoicing at being united with her father, and thrilled that he had found happiness with Clarice.

Later that evening, the friends met in Mavis's kitchen, where Rose repeated her story, though not in as much detail as she had given Mavis and Joey. Even so, her stomach felt as though a swarm of butterflies were performing arabesques and her voice wobbled with uncertainty.

'I bloody knew it!' cried Maggie, turning in her chair for Kitty's confirmation. 'Didn't I say right at the start that her suitcase cost a fortune, that no ordinary working girl could afford one like that, or that fancy coat she was wearing?' Maggie smirked triumphantly. 'I was right all along.'

'So ye were, Maggie,' replied Kitty, and in that sweet spontaneous way of hers she reached out and squeezed Rose's hand, 'but it makes no difference to us where you come from, love. You're one of us now an' it doesn't change a thing.'

'You've been very brave to put all that behind you,' Beth said admiringly.

'I'm sorry I didn't own up to the truth from the start,' Rose said, relief flooding her veins, 'but I was afraid you might reject me and send me packing.' She giggled. 'I wouldn't have blamed you if you had.'

'Why would we do that?' Kitty cocked her head, giving Rose a quizzical look. 'You were lost and alone. You needed somebody to...'

'Rescue me!' Rose whooped. They all burst out laughing, and she caught hold of Mavis's hand and then Kitty's. Kitty grasped Maggie's, who grabbed Beth's, and pushing back their chairs, they stood round the table, arms raised and hands clasped in a riotous celebration of friendship.

* * *

The prospect of Christmas lightened everyone's spirits, but in Weaver Street, things were bordering on fever pitch. They had a wedding to celebrate.

One night, five days before she was due to marry, Rose perched on a stool in Maggie's grimy bathroom, her hands clutching the washbasin's edge so tightly that her knuckles were white. A swarm of butterflies flittered in her stomach and she felt the urge to get up and run. Maggie rattled a spoon round the bowl she was holding, the noxious stink coming from it making Rose's eyes water.

'Are you sure it's safe? It smells awful.'

'Course it is. I've used it. So has Jean Harlow. I read it in a magazine.'

Rose's mind's eye pictured the star's luxurious hair in the film *Platinum Blonde*. 'I don't want it to look like that,' she cried. 'I don't want to be a blonde bombshell.'

'You won't be,' Maggie said confidently. 'I'm just going to lighten the ends and put in a few streaks like I did before but this time they'll be a bit more noticeable. It's your wedding day, for Christ's sake. You want to look like a bride.' She set the bowl down in the basin. 'Now, lean your head forward an' I'll comb it in.' Trembling, Rose closed her eyes and did as she was ordered.

Across the way, Kitty sewed the last button to a blue two-piece she had made for May Walker. Draping the suit over her arm, she lifted a pretty pink taffeta dress and went to the parlour where Robert and Patrick were untangling an intricate muddle of Christmas tree lights. Kitty popped her head round the door.

'No, Robert, go that way.' She heard the exasperation in Patrick's voice, and smiled as John calmly said, 'Now, lads, work as a team.'

Robert jigged backwards, trailing a length of flex dotted with tiny bulbs.

'Let's see if they still work,' said John, flicking the switch on the wall. A trail of red and white twinkled across the floor. 'Wow!' Robert and Patrick yelled.

'Well done! Now all you have to do is put them on the tree,' said Kitty, grinning at John, knowing it would be easier said than done. 'I'm just going to leave these with May. I won't be long.'

'Yoo-hoo,' she called as she let herself in through May's back door. May's gentle brown eyes lit up as she got to her feet.

'Ooh, you have it finished then.' She looked at the two-piece Kitty handed her. 'It's lovely,' she gushed. 'What do you think, Bill?' Holding it against her, she sashayed towards her husband.

Bill swivelled in his chair by the fire. 'You'll look a picture in that, love. You always look nice in blue.' To Kitty's surprise, he seemed perfectly sober. Her expression must have given her away for May took her by the elbow and shepherded her into the front room.

When they were alone, May said, 'He hasn't touched a drop since he met Rose's dad. They had a long chat before Mr Brown-Allsop went away.' She sounded amazed and nervous at the same time. 'He says he'll not have a drink till the wedding day, and even then, he'll not take too much and spoil Joey's big day.'

'That's marvellous,' Kitty said as May stripped off. 'Ye'll not have the worry of it on the day.' She helped May into the two-piece. 'There, it fits ye like a glove. Ye'll do your Joey proud.'

May gazed at her reflection in the mirror over the mantelpiece. Her eyes filled with happy tears. 'I'll go and show Bill,' she said.

'I'll see meself out,' Kitty said, her heart aching to think that May still loved Bill after all he'd put her through. On her way back to her own house, she prayed that Bill would keep his word.

In Jack's spare bedroom, Mavis clapped her hands in delight as Jack hung the last sheet of new wallpaper in honour of James's lady friend. 'It's fit for a queen, never mind Clarice Burridge,' she chirped, handing Jack a soft cloth to smooth out the creases.

Rose had been touched to learn that Jack was letting James have the use of his bedroom and was redecorating the spare room for Clarice. 'Maybe they share a bed already,' she'd said impishly, 'and you won't have to sleep on the couch, Jack.'

'Mebbe they do and mebbe they don't, and that's their business,' Jack had replied, and not for the first time, Rose had wondered if Jack and Mavis ever did.

* * *

Late in the afternoon on Christmas Day, a convivial crowd gathered in Kitty's house for drinks and a bite to eat. Kitty looked particularly radiant in a green dress that enhanced the lights in her tawny hair, and as she presided over the buffet, she felt a sudden rush of love for her neighbours. They had all contributed whatever they could spare: Mavis's mince tarts, May's pot of soup, Beth's and Maggie's potted meat and salmon paste sandwiches and Kitty's own Christmas cake. It was moments like this that made life so worthwhile.

Joey's younger brother, Steven, had arrived home from sea the day before to be his best man. May glowed with pride as her neighbours welcomed him, at the same time keeping an anxious eye on Bill who, glass of lemonade in hand, was talking to James.

Rose was busy introducing Clarice to all her friends. Joey stood talking to John, and when Rose came near, he caught her arm and whispered in her ear. 'I liked your hair the way it was but now you look like a fairy tale princess.'

Rose thrilled at his words and silently praised Maggie for the transformation. Contrary to her fears, Maggie's home-made remedy had lightened her mousey hair with streaks of pale gold that made it gleam, and the curlers that Maggie had wound it round earlier that day had given it body and bounce. Rose felt every bit as glamorous as Jean Harlow, and as she thanked Joey with a swift kiss, she felt as though she might explode with happiness. Tomorrow her beloved father would give her away to this wonderful man, and all these lovely people would be there to share her joy. People who had lovingly helped her discover and appreciate the true meaning of life. Pausing for a moment, she drank in the happy scene.

Jack had one arm draped across Mavis's narrow shoulders. They looked happy and Rose felt a rush of affection for them. What would life have been like if Mavis hadn't rescued her? Her eyes radiating joy and excitement, she took Joey's hand and led him over to join his father, overwhelmed by a sense of rightness and completion.

Maggie was in her element, her raucous laughter bursting out every few minutes. Lily's gaze wandered round the parlour. Her eyes landed on Steven Walker; he wasn't half bad looking since he'd joined the navy. Lily swaggered over to him just as Molly came back in from the kitchen. For one fleeting moment, Mickey O'Malley thought she was coming over to him and his spirits rose but Molly didn't even give him a second glance and went straight to Heinz. He was the only member of the Muller family at the party. After the police had released Ursula from custody for her involvement in Rose's kidnapping, with a strict caution, they had taken her to relatives in London.

Molly had cosily tucked her arm through Heinz's. Whatever did she see in that boring foreign drip, Mickey wondered, abandoning all hope as Molly gazed up at the German as though he was God, and Lily was cuddling up to the chap in a uniform. It was all right for some, Mickey thought grumpily.

Molly was only half-listening to Heinz as he talked about failed hunger marches, protest rallies and Oswald Mosley. Did he have to be so intense even on an evening like this? She wanted them to chat and laugh like Lily was doing with Steven, or for him to put his arms round her and gaze into her eyes as Joey was now doing with Rose.

Maggie burst into a tuneless rendition of 'Santa Claus is Coming to Town', Kitty and Mavis helping her out when she forgot the words. Then, as the evening drew to a close, the merry neighbours prepared to take their leave. There was a lot of hugging and Mickey made his way over to Molly, intent on stealing a Christmas kiss, but Molly was gazing up into Heinz's blue eyes, her heart thudding as she waited for him to kiss her. Instead, he turned away and began helping his mother on with her coat. Mickey saw his chance and pulled Molly into his arms. When the kiss ended, Molly gasped then grinned.

'Wow! Mickey. I've never been kissed like that before,' she said, surprised by the pleasure she had felt as his soft warm lips had covered hers. She glanced over her shoulder at Heinz, but he wasn't there. He had left the party without even wishing her good-night. She turned to Mickey. He was smiling triumphantly, his blue eyes warm with admiration. Molly smiled back.

* * *

Boxing Day dawned crisp and dry. By eleven o'clock, the friends and neighbours were all assembled in St Mary's Anglican Church on Broad Green. 'Not as nice as our church,' Mavis commented to Kitty.

'No, an' it'll not be as grand as a full nuptial mass.'

The groom and his best man, resplendent in their dress uniforms, stood shoulder to shoulder at the altar. May and a stone-cold sober Bill smiled proudly at one another. The organ peeled and the bride, radiant in a cream muslin dress, walked down the aisle on her father's arm. Joey's niece trotted behind, looking adorable in pink taffeta. Rose and Joey exchanged such loving smiles as they made their vows that Kitty's eyes moistened and she squeezed John's hand. His eyes met hers. 'I love you, Mrs Sykes,' he mouthed. Mavis's tears spilled over and Jack gave her his handkerchief. Molly glanced in Heinz's direction. He looked bored and aloof. Maggie and Lily looked at one another: when would it be their turn?

23

SPRING 1936

Rose wakened early. After twelve glorious weeks as a wife and lover, she still hadn't got used to finding the bed in May's back bedroom half-empty.

In early April, she had stood on the docks saying goodbye to Joey on his way to Rotterdam then further afield on what would be his last long-distance voyage: he was leaving the merchant navy and getting a job ashore.

Now, each morning she awoke with the same hungry yearning to feel his lean, hard body next to hers and the delicious moments when they made love, for not once had their lovemaking raised the spectre of Lewis Aston, as she had feared it might. Marriage was more beautiful than she had ever imagined and she now missed Joey more than ever.

When she went down to the kitchen, May was making toast at the fire. She smiled at her daughter-in-law. 'One or two slices?' she asked.

'Two, please,' said Rose as she set cups and plates on the table. They had fallen into an easy pattern of sharing the chores, and

Rose felt blessed at having such a kind, welcoming mother-in-law. 'Has Bill gone to work?'

'Yes, he went off first thing,' May said, her pleasure written large on her face.

The week after the wedding, Bill Walker had acquired an old pushcart and started collecting scrap iron. 'The way things are going in Europe with Hitler's occupation of the Rhineland, I have a nasty feeling we might soon be facing another war. If so, metal will be in great demand. It could be a profitable business,' James Brown-Allsop had said. Bill had taken his advice.

'I'm off to open the shop,' Rose said, putting on her cardigan then pecking May's cheek. May beamed. *She might not have been brought up to it but now she's a good hard-working girl and she makes a lovely wife for our Joey*, May thought as she watched her go. Then, raising her gaze to the clear blue sky, she gave thanks for all the good things 1936 had brought: Bill was working, Joey was leaving the merchant navy in June to take the good job that his naval experience had secured for him on the docks, and in the house, Rose was like a breath of fresh air. Of course, it was sad that King George V had died in January, but now they'd got a new, younger king – a handsome, dashing sort of chap who'd promised to improve the lives of the working class – so who knew what the year had in store.

In Joey's absence, Rose continued to visit her needy families. It did her heart good to see Mary Morgan tidily dressed in Molly's hand-me-downs and to know that she was regularly attending school now that her mother was in better health: no doubt due to the nourishing food Rose provided on each visit. And she had another reason to feel pleased. She had suggested to Bill Walker that he could use some help collecting scrap, and he now employed Brian Halstead a few days a week. Janet was over the moon, and Rose felt as though she was really making a difference to their lives, and her own.

* * *

'Joey Walker's home, this time for good,' Mavis said as she settled into a chair at Kitty's kitchen table on a Saturday afternoon in June. 'Rose's dead chuffed. She says they're looking for a place of their own as soon as he's settled into his new job.'

'He was lucky to get one,' Maggie sniped, 'but it's a case of who you know, not what you know.' She had arrived shortly before Mavis looking for a jangle with Kitty as she did most days after a long day at her mending frame. The sun streaming through the window harshened the lines round her eyes and made her bleached hair look brittle.

'I imagine it was all those years at sea got him the job,' Kitty rebuked. 'Give credit where credit's due, Maggie.'

Maggie's reply was interrupted as loud voices in the porch made the three women look towards the kitchen door. It opened and Kitty's son and daughter entered, accompanied by Lily. They had met up on their way home, Molly from the hospital, Lily from the mill and Patrick from the Technical School that he attended part-time in between working in his stepfather's factory.

'I could,' Patrick was protesting as Lily laughed tauntingly.

'What? Are you gonna grow wings?' Lily sneered, flicking her red hair and pushing her face into Patrick's.

'Hey, hey!' Kitty yelled. 'What's all the fuss?'

'He says he's gonna fly to Australia as soon as he's old enough,' Lily scoffed.

'And he could if he wanted,' Molly cut in, always the peace-maker and keen to defend her brother.

'I could, Mam, I could,' Patrick yelled. 'Amy Johnson's done it so

I don't see why I couldn't.' He glowered at Lily. 'She's daft, she is. She said I'd have to grow wings.' His face was red with aggravation. At sixteen, tall and handsome, he was desperate not to appear foolish in front of the girls.

'Calm down, love. And ye, Lily, stop going on about summat ye know nothing about. The world's changing fast, an' our Patrick's right. When me an' your mam were your age, there were hardly any cars, let alone aeroplanes. Now, the roads are full of 'em, an' John says that chap who owns Cartwright's flies to America.'

'See,' said Patrick, giving Lily a superior smile. Lily stuck out her tongue. The argument settled, Kitty went back to sit with Mavis and Maggie.

'You see, Lily, if you'd paid more bloody attention at school, you'd know what Patrick's on about,' her mother snapped. She was always annoyed when Kitty's offspring seemed more knowledgeable.

'It's true what you say, Kitty,' said Mavis. 'Why, only last week, the chef was telling me he'd been talking on the telephone to his sister in Australia. Such a thing would have been unheard of not that long ago.'

'I'd like a telephone,' Maggie said enviously.

'Who would you ring?' Kitty sounded amused. 'Ye haven't even used the phone box at the end of the street in all the years I've known you.'

'Not you,' Maggie groused, grinding her cigarette into the ashtray. She stood, and Mavis followed suit.

Shortly after they had gone, and Molly and Lily had gone up to Molly's bedroom and Patrick to his, John arrived home. Kitty was scooping flour from the crock. 'Where is everybody?' he asked before dropping a kiss on Kitty's cheek.

'Our Robert's over in Beth's playing with Stuart and the others are upstairs.'

Only when she put down the spoon to return the kiss did she see that he was smiling broadly, and the worry lines that so often creased his face these days when he came home from the factory were noticeably diminished.

'You look pleased with yourself,' she said, scooping up a spoonful of flour.

'I have every right to,' he replied, startling her by giving her an almighty hug. Flour flew in all directions.

'Oh, look at that now,' she cried, but her eyes were alight with curiosity. She dropped the spoon and gave him her full attention.

'Today, Mrs Sykes, your husband secured a contract with Cartwright Motors.' His brown eyes danced as he told her that he had risked bidding for it on the strength of using the money she had loaned him – Tom's money – to buy the materials. 'And it paid off, love,' he cried, 'it's a big one, Kitty.'

'Well done, love, I'm glad it helped.' She hugged him, but whilst she was pleased for him, she didn't want to dwell on where the money had come from. 'These Yorkshire puddings are not going to make themselves,' she said, letting him go.

She cracked two eggs into the flour and began beating the mixture. 'So, we'll be all right for a bit,' she said, her thoughts straying to those less fortunate.

'It'll keep us going for the rest of the year,' said John, his voice high with relief.

'Aye, we're lucky, but the shipyards in Newcastle and Sunderland are doing badly,' Kitty said, pouring the batter into a tin and sliding it in the oven. 'They've laid that many men off, unemployment's never been as high.'

John glumly agreed. 'Yeah, I might have saved the jobs of the lads who work for me, but it's a drop in the ocean. We're still paying for what the war cost, and even though they've raised taxes and cut public spending, the economy's still shot to hell.' He shrugged helplessly. 'Still, we're okay for the time being.'

'We'll always be okay, love.' Kitty washed her hands then began setting the table. 'Shift your stuff,' she said, setting down plates.

John lifted his ledger and a pile of invoices. 'You should get Molly to give you a hand.' He'd no sooner spoken than Molly clattered downstairs. They heard her say, 'Ta-ra,' to Lily before she entered the kitchen.

'When's dinner going to be ready? I'm going to a meeting with Heinz at seven. We're making placards for the big march through the city.'

'Twenty minutes,' Kitty said, casting anxious eyes at John for his support before adding, 'but I don't like the sound of you getting involved in that, Molly.'

'Heinz says it's what we have to do.' Molly flounced out.

John heard the anxiety in Kitty's voice, and knowing how she worried over her daughter's friendship with Heinz, he put down the ledger and invoices and came back to the table and put his arms round her. 'I don't like it any more than you do but she'll come to her senses in time,' he said, holding her to his broad chest and stroking her hair.

Kitty leaned into his embrace. As always, his calm common sense and warm affection gave her comfort. 'Don't mind me, ye know what I'm like. I'm just being a mother hen. But I don't have any faith in that relationship and I don't want Molly getting hurt.'

'I do understand, love, and when it fizzles out as it will, she'll still have us and we'll still have each other.' John found her lips and kissed her comfortingly. Kitty kissed him back. Of course they'd all be all right.

* * *

Later that same afternoon, in a house in Liverpool's docklands, Molly daubed slogans on placards and Heinz discussed strategies with the group of likeminded individuals preparing to march through the city.

'We want jobs'; 'Work for the workers'; '2 million unemployed'; 'Say no to the Means Test', the placards read, and as they worked, they talked about the crises facing the country. Molly felt out of her depth as she listened to their views, and reflected on her own lack of knowledge.

'Do you think there's going to be a war?' one of them ventured.

'Winston Churchill's speech warned that there might be,' said a serious-looking girl wearing thick black horn-rimmed glasses as Heinz appeared at Molly's side. 'What do you think, Heinz?' she fawned. Molly decided she didn't like her.

'I have seen what is happening in my country,' Heinz replied. 'Now that Hitler is chancellor, he will stop at nothing until he is the supreme ruler. That will be bad for Europe and the rest of the world. He is manipulating the people and they are allowing it because, like you, they have no work and want better things.'

'And we're not prepared to be manipulated,' a young man with a scraggy beard interjected. 'We have to make the government listen to us,' he cried.

'You are right,' Heinz replied with fire in his eyes. He continued talking at length, his audience enamoured by the strongly held opinions of someone who had witnessed Hitler's domination at first hand. Molly felt proud and fearful at the same time. The debate raged on, suggestions flying like a swarm of gnats, and she was soon caught up in the fervour. Adrenaline running high, she came away from the meeting with her heart and mind in tune with the man at her side.

Heinz often had that effect on her but he was never as romantic as she would have liked. He'd never even kissed her and whenever she thought about that, Mickey's Christmas kiss came to mind. But Mickey was just Mickey, and Heinz was different. Now, as they walked arm-in-arm down the street Molly felt sure that she wouldn't have to wait much longer for Heinz prove that he loved her.

'Will you attend the march?' he asked as they waited for the tram to Weaver Street. He had already been on similar marches in Newcastle and Sunderland.

'I'd love to,' she said, her cheeks flushed with excitement at the thought of being included in something so close to Heinz's heart. As the tram trundled onwards, she reflected on how dull life had seemed before Heinz came along. She felt the warmth of his body touching hers and was filled with joy that bubbled up from somewhere deep within her.

* * *

'I've finished with Barry Jones,' Lily said the next evening as she and Molly were in Molly's bedroom, Lily sprawled on the bed and Molly filing her nails.

Molly almost said, *Oh, is that why you're here spending time with me,* but on second thoughts it seemed spiteful, so instead she said, 'I'm going on a protest march with Heinz on Saturday.'

Lily seemed not to hear her. 'The silly sod thought I'd let him have it just 'cos he'd paid me ticket into the Grafton and bought me a few drinks. They're all the same, are fellas, wantin' to get their end away then bugger off when there's a baby nobody wants.' She sat up, thumping her fist on the bedspread.

'No, they're not.' Molly tried to imagine Heinz doing anything like that, and failed. He'd kissed her nose and her hand, and that was it.

'I don't mind kissin' and lettin' 'em have a feel up here,' Lily grumbled, patting her breasts, 'but I'm not lettin' 'em go any further.'

Molly wondered what she would do if Heinz groped her breasts and felt a hot tingling inside her blouse. The nailfile stabbed into the underside of her thumb and she dropped it into her lap. 'It's not right leading fellas on. You need to be careful,' she said, wondering just who she was advising.

* * *

May Walker gave her husband a warm smile as he entered the house. 'Dinner won't be five minutes. Did you have a good day?'

'Can't complain,' Bill replied, taking off his jacket. 'I got a load of copper from them houses they're demolishing on Stanford Street.'

Nobody in Weaver Street, including May, had imagined that Bill would keep on collecting scrap. Instead, they'd waited with bated breath for him to hit the bottle, but he had done no such thing. To everyone's amazement, he was making a success of his burgeoning business, and none of her friends begrudged May her pleasure.

One night, not long after the work had taken off, May had asked Bill why he'd given up drinking now that he had more money than he'd ever had to spend on it. 'I don't need to,' he'd replied. 'I on'y drank to blot out what a bloody failure I was. Now, I'm a man with his own business and a lovely wife and home. I've no need to drown me sorrows. I haven't got any.' Then he'd kissed her. May had cried, remembering all the wasted years and money when she'd railed at him night and day to stay sober.

Now, as she set a plate of sausage and mash on the table in front of him, she dropped a kiss on the top of his balding head. 'Enjoy that, love, you've earned it.'

* * *

Kitty plopped a lump of margarine into a bowl of flour then mixed the two together with deft fingers. Although she left the running of the café to Bridie, she still did all the baking. Counting her blessings, Kitty added dried fruit and then milk to the bowl, and blending the ingredients into a stiff paste, she told herself that fruit scones were a bit like her and John: a really sweet mix with a lot of heart.

The scones still warm, she put them into tins then set off for the café. It was a sunny Friday morning and on the towpath tall foxgloves towered over yellow rattle, red campion and blue scabious. Kitty loved the riot of colour and the sunshine glimmering on the water. There were customers on the veranda and more inside and her heart swelled as she stepped inside.

'Not too bad today,' she said to Bridie as she handed her the tins. Bridie took off the lids and sniffed. 'These'll sell like hot cakes.' Kitty chuckled at the remark, and after exchanging a few words with her customers, she left Bridie to it.

On her way home, Kitty popped into Mavis's. Rose and Maggie were there. Rose was just back from delivering a box of groceries to a needy family, for like Mavis and Kitty, she still kept up the good work. 'She's married to a penniless artist,' Rose said about the woman she'd just visited. 'They have two children to care for and she takes any cleaning job she can get, leaving him free to paint all day,' she said, her voice rich with admiration as she poured a cup of tea.

Mavis sniffed. 'It must be true love.'

'She sounds a right bloody fool to me,' Maggie said, puffing out a cloud of smoke from the cigarette she'd just lit.

'Talking of love,' Rose said to Kitty. 'What about your Molly and Heinz?'

Kitty frowned. 'She sees him now an' again, but I wouldn't call it a romance. To be honest, he's not my cup of tea, he's full of ideas that don't sit easy with me.' Her frown deepened. 'He's got our Molly all worked up about fighting for rights, hunger marches an' all that. He's taking her on one of them demonstrations.' She paused to sip her tea. 'Don't get me wrong. I'm all for folks standing up against the gover'ment to do something about unemployment and suffering, but them demonstrations are dangerous. They turn into riots, an' I'm afeared for her.'

'Oh, dear me, yes,' Mavis twittered. 'Do you remember what happened in Birkenhead when they held that rally? The police used their batons and the crowds threw bottles, rocks and even hammers. A chap I work with had his head bust open.'

Not to be outdone, Maggie compounded Mavis's remark with scary stories of her own, none of which left Kitty feeling any happier.

* * *

Molly woke bright and early on Saturday morning, glad she had the day off, and pleased to see it wasn't raining. Today she was going with Heinz on her first protest rally. Nervous and excited, she went down for breakfast.

'What time are ye setting off?' Kitty's face was creased with anxiety as she put a plate of scrambled egg on the table in front of Molly.

'About eleven. The march starts at midday. I'm quite looking forward to it.' Molly tucked into the egg and a slice of toast.

'Aye, well, ye be careful,' warned Kitty. 'It could turn out nasty.' She gave Molly an imploring look. 'Ye do know that me an' your dad don't want ye to go,' she continued, raising a staying hand when Molly opened her mouth to object. 'An' it's not because we disagree but...' she placed a hand on Molly's shoulder and squeezed, 'you're our little girl an'...' She got no further.

The forkful of egg halfway to Molly's mouth hovered in mid-air then fell onto the plate. 'Oh, Mam! I'll always be your little girl,' she cried, 'and I love that you and John care so much for me, but you've got to let me grow up. Heinz says we need all the support we can get.'

'Heinz says a lot of things,' Kitty said bitterly, 'an' ye can't blame us for not wantin' ye to get hurt.'

'Hurt? Everybody knows it's for a good cause. Who's going to hurt us?'

'The police, for starters,' said Kitty grimly. 'They're under orders to break up them gatherings, an' for another there's allus them that want to cause a riot just for the sake of it. Heinz had better take good care of ye.'

Molly finished eating but the food didn't go down as easily as it had before her mother's intervention. The nearer it got to the time to go and meet Heinz, the more apprehensive she became. However, when she arrived at the Mullers' house, Heinz was raring to go and Molly's spirits were raised when he held her hand on the tram taking them into the city.

As they approached the city centre, the streets were crammed with people, many of them carrying placards and banners. 'They must be joining the protest,' Molly said, sounding somewhat taken aback.

'Looks like it,' Heinz replied, his sharp blue eyes dancing. 'The Union has obviously spread the word.' By that, he meant the National Union for Unemployed Workers, which had organised the marches he'd already attended. This also took Molly by surprise. She had expected to join with a small group of protesters, not half of Liverpool, or so it seemed.

Alighting from the tram, they joined the hordes of people

surging up William Brown Street, placards held high and banners unfurled. Molly stared in amazement at the enormous crush of men, women and children already assembled on every inch of pavement and road outside St George's Hall. Overwhelmed by the furious activity all round her, she clung to Heinz's arm as he led her through the seething mass to where their group had gathered.

A man gave Heinz a yellow armband, and he sped off, leaving Molly feeling suddenly alone. Someone thrust a placard in her hand. It wasn't one she had made. This one had 'We're fighting for bread and beans' daubed on it.

Jostled by the crowd, Molly found herself herded along next to a woman wearing a big turban. She was pushing a pram, the toddler in it sucking a dummy and waving a small black flag. Molly was tempted to ask the woman if she thought it wise to bring him, but one look at the woman's hard-bitten, grim expression made her change her mind. She broke out in a sweat as the yelling crowd behind her surged forward. Where was Heinz?

Boom! Boom! Boom! The strident beat rang out as a man staggering under the weight of a huge bass drum struggled to the front of the crowd. Molly looked round at the sea of faces, which stretched as far as she could see. Two mounted policemen appeared in the end of a side street close by where she was standing. Molly shivered.

'Mounted police,' she gasped.

'Aye, the black-hearted buggers,' the woman in the turban growled. 'Watch out for their riot sticks.' She pointed to her own head. 'I've got a pan lid under this,' she added with a smirk. 'One o' the buggers gave me a right clout at the last do. This time, I've come prepared.' She puffed defiantly on her cigarette.

Molly paled. She wasn't even wearing a hat.

Another mounted policeman trotted so near to her that she could feel the heat from the horse's flanks and smell its musty breath. The clanging of a bell pealed out over the booming of the drum and the marchers surged forward. Molly's feet barely touched the ground as, hemmed in on all sides, she was propelled nearer the Hall. To her surprise, the crowd was unusually quiet, no shouting or yelling, just the buzz and hum of conversations.

Still keeping her eyes peeled for Heinz, she saw the bobbing helmets of foot policemen marching alongside the column. They were swinging their truncheons threateningly. Were they there to protect or attack the crowd, she wondered, anxiously recalling her mother's words.

Up ahead, a lone voice rang out before other voices immediately joined in and like a wave washing to the shore, the sound rippled and swelled through the crowd until all the demonstrators were chanting as one. To the rhythm of the various cries: 'Working men need work' and 'Struggle or starve' and 'Down with the Means Test,' Molly's blood pulsed in her veins, and finding her courage, she joined in. Never before had she felt so powerful. This is why she was here: to make the government sit up and listen. She held her placard high. There was still no sign of Heinz.

Then, suddenly there was bellowing and screaming coming from those nearest the Hall. The mob behind Molly pressed forward and she found herself carried along in a surging mass of seething humanity. Mounted police charged at the crowd, swinging their riot sticks. Screaming, bewildered men and women ran for cover. Some fell under the horses' hooves and heads were split as policemen slashed their batons. The crowds found themselves corralled and Molly cast wild glances around her at the bleeding bodies strewn on the ground. A woman was sitting with her head in her hands, weeping and wailing. An overturned pram lay close by, empty. Molly felt sick, and as she wondered where its occupant now was, she lifted an elderly woman to her feet and dusted down her shabby coat. No words were exchanged. What could anyone say?

Then a man with a megaphone demanded the right for a peaceful assembly. Hoisted up on the shoulders of his comrades, he began to make a speech. Instead of bringing order to the chaos, it had the opposite effect. The crowds outside the corral swarmed forward, fighting their way through the barrier, and once again the police slashed with their riot sticks, the screams and shouts drowning out the man's words. Molly shrieked as a riot stick thwacked her shoulder. She staggered to her knees and the policeman raised his baton again.

Suddenly, Molly was swept up by a pair of strong arms, her rescuer yelling abuse at her assailant as he carried her to safety. Gathering her wits, she raised her head and looked into the anxious face of Mickey O'Malley.

'Mickey!'

'Are you hurt?' His concern was so apparent that Molly's heart went out to him. The pain in her shoulder flared.

'I'll live,' she said stoutly and forced a smile. Mickey gently lowered her to the ground then brushed the dirt from her skirt, the simple gesture bringing tears to her eyes. 'My shoulder's a bit bruised.' In fact, it was throbbing painfully.

'Let's get you back home,' Mickey said. 'What in God's name were you doing here on your own?' His blue eyes flashed angrily. He already knew the answer.

'I came with Heinz Muller.'

'And where is he now?' Mickey looked absolutely disgusted.

'I've no idea.' She was surprised to realise that she didn't much care.

By now, the huge mass had dispersed, the police hanging back but still alert. Men with megaphones on the steps of the Hall continued to blast out speeches. *Talk all you like*, Molly thought, *but you've achieved nothing today. And all I've earned is a badly bruised shoulder and aching feet.* She felt terribly deflated.

One thing she had learned was that the government and those in their employ cared nothing for the ordinary working-class men and women who formed the backbone of the country. She looked round her at the dismal faces, some bloodstained, and she wanted to weep. All they were asking for was respect and dignity and the right to work. Another thing she had learned was that she didn't mean a thing to Heinz Muller. He had forgotten all about her. When she saw him making his way towards them, she clenched her fists and stiffened her spine.

'Thanks for bringing me with you,' she said tartly. Heinz appeared not to notice her sarcasm, the manic glint in his eye letting her know that he cared nothing for her safety. He started to rant about police brutality, but Mickey cut him off.

'You could have got her killed,' he barked, taking Molly by the arm and leading her away. On the tram back to Weaver Street, he put his arm round her and Molly rested her throbbing head on his broad shoulder.

'That'll make more news than if it had gone peaceably,' Mickey said grimly. 'It's another black mark against the government and the police. Enough of those and they'll have to capitulate.'

Molly honestly wanted to believe him but instead she was reminded of the Irish famine and the poor cottagers her mother had told her about. They had pleaded with the landlords to let them keep their jobs and their homes but instead they had burned down their homes, leaving them to trail the roads and eat grass. It pained her to think about it.

'I thought I was doing some good,' Molly said, 'but now I'm not so sure.'

'That bloody idiot should never have left you on your own,' Mickey growled.

CHRISSIE WALSH

'I dread to think what might have happened if you hadn't rescued me.'

Mickey pulled her closer. 'I'd never let anybody hurt you, Molly.'

Molly believed him. Feeling safe again, she chatted with Mickey about ordinary everyday things, neither of them wanting to dwell on the awfulness of might have happened to her had he not come along. They were still talking when the tram pulled into Broad Green. They walked up the lane arm in arm. At her gate, she thanked Mickey again.

'Do I deserve a kiss?' he asked lightly. Molly kissed him on the lips, thinking how much easier things were in Mickey's company: Heinz would have been spouting every detail of the protest by now. She kissed him again and it felt good.

'Ta-ra, Mickey, see you tomorrow.'

'I could kill that Heinz Muller,' Kitty exclaimed after Molly had related her narrow escape to Kitty and John. 'And just look at the state of ye,' she added, shocked by Molly's dishevelled appearance. 'Thank God Mickey O'Malley was on hand to rescue ye.'

'Aye, and thanks to that bloody fanatical German, you could have been killed or dragged off into custody,' John declared, horrified to learn that Heinz had left his beloved stepdaughter unprotected. 'He'll feel more than the edge of my tongue when I see him,' he said, thumping his fist into his palm.

Molly was suddenly aware of the danger she had been exposed to and burst into tears.

'I always thought the police were here to protect us,' she said, sounding thoroughly disillusioned. Kitty and John exchanged exasperated glances at her naivety. When Molly went up to her bedroom, her mother gave a deep sigh of satisfaction.

'Thank goodness she's safe. And if today has achieved

anything, at least I think Molly's finally seen the light as far as Heinz Muller's concerned.'

* * *

The summer of 1936 ran its course, and in the autumn the gossip centred on the Jarrow Crusade and the new king, Edward VIII. In October, three hundred people walked from the north of England to London to beg the government to address the critical situation of unemployment and poverty.

'I thought such a valiant effort might bring about some change,' Molly moaned, still anxious for the country to be put to rights, but no longer interested in Heinz.

'The government are useless when it comes to ending this Depression,' Kitty consoled, 'an' as for the Jarrow marchers, my heart goes out to 'em. They came away with nothing but empty promises.'

Spicier news was King Edward's affair with an American divorcee, Wallis Simpson.

'She looks a right hard-faced mare. She's only marrying him for his brass,' Maggie sniped.

'He's nothing but a playboy. I'll stop being a royalist if she becomes queen,' Mavis declared. But she didn't have to. In December, Edward abdicated and his brother, George, was to be the new monarch: a married man with children – Mavis heartily approved.

And so, Christmas was celebrated in much the same way as in the previous year and as the friends welcomed in 1937, life in Weaver Street went on apace. The neighbours, as usual, pulled together and saw to it that no one was left feeling desperate. The needy families were cared for, and sometimes Kitty helped settle unpaid rent or a doctor's bill, her fortunes back to being more stable now that John's factory was thriving again.

Molly had surprised her mother by quickly recovering from her lost love affair with Heinz Muller. 'I was daft, Mam,' she'd confided not long after the protest rally. 'It was all one-sided. I thought because I loved him, he was bound to love me. I know now that all he wanted was for someone to listen to him banging on about the economy, politics and Hitler.' She'd giggled. 'And boy, did I listen. Not that I don't agree with his beliefs, because I do. But that's all he cares about, and I can't blame him after what the Nazis did to him. I'll still be his friend, but I've got over my infatuation, 'cos that's what it was, and I've realised I don't want a boyfriend who makes me feel like I'm a nobody. I want somebody more like me, someone to have fun with and share what I like.'

Kitty had smiled sagely, impressed by how grown up her daughter sounded. Secretly, she put it down to the fun Molly was having on her frequent outings with Mickey O'Malley, for there had been plenty of them in the past few months.

As for Molly, she was really enjoying being Mickey's girlfriend. He was kind and funny, and romantic enough to make her feel like a girl of nearly nineteen should feel. Lily was jealous. She still hadn't found 'the one' and flipped from one fellow to another month by month.

Rather than attend protest rallies, Molly discovered that she could still make a difference to people's lives by helping the needy. On her free evenings, she often delivered boxes of groceries that Kitty and Mavis had scrounged from the local shopkeepers, and sometimes Mickey would go with her.

Tonight, as they walked back home, hand in hand, she felt thoroughly content. 'We're lucky, you and me, Mickey. We both have jobs, not like them poor beggars, and if what we do brings them the smallest comfort, we're serving a purpose.'

'I think we're lucky just having one another,' Mickey replied with feeling.

They turned into the lane just in time to see Heinz Muller going indoors. 'Do... do you still...?' Mickey stuttered, nodding in Heinz's direction.

'No, not at all.' Molly sounded surprised that her boyfriend even had to ask. Mickey breathed an audible sigh. When they reached Molly's house, they stood in the shadow of the gable end. Mickey leaned with his back against the wall.

'I think I might be in love with you, Molly Conlon,' he said, pulling her into his arms, knowing there was no might about it. He made to kiss her, but she began to speak.

'I don't think I'm in love with you, Mickey,' she said, smiling inwardly at the disappointment in his navy-blue eyes and the furrows in his brow. 'I know I am.'

He tightened his hold on her, his relief palpable as his lips sought hers. When the kiss ended, he said, 'You're not supposed to talk when a fella's trying to kiss you.' But he was oh so glad that she had.

Molly laughed. That's what she loved about Mickey. He was so straightforward and uncomplicated. She thought how handsome he was as he ran his fingers through the long black curls that fanned his forehead and curled round his ears. 'So that's us then?' he asked seeking confirmation.

'That's us, Mr O'Malley,' Molly said firmly.

After a few more kisses and fond words, they said goodnight; they both had to get up early for work the next day. Mickey whooped as he jigged across the lane to his own house, and Molly walked slowly round to the back door of hers. She was sure that this time it was the real thing and not just infatuation. In one way or another, she'd always loved Mickey. She paused before going inside, gazing up at the purple sky speckled with stars. *What a great big world it is, and how small we are*, she thought, *yet there's so much love and hope and a wonderful life waiting to be lived.*

24

On an evening in early spring, Rose and Betty left the shop together, remarking on the balmy weather as they walked up Broad Green.

'Don't be doing too much in your condition, that baby's your priority now,' Betty said as they prepared to go their separate ways. 'I'll mind the shop tomorrow morning and you come in after dinner.'

'I'll see you then,' said Rose, turning into the back lane.

Outside Walter Garside's house, she met his daughter, Beth. She was carrying a casserole dish inside a tea towel. Rose nodded at the dish. 'Something smells good.'

'It's brown stew for dad's dinner,' Beth replied. 'I'd best get in with it before it goes cold.' She hurried up the path to Walter's door.

Rose continued on her way, musing at how forgiving Beth was. Mavis had told her how cruel and domineering Beth's father had been when Beth was young. Only when Kitty had intervened did Beth find the courage to defy him. *How lucky we are to have such good friends. I wouldn't be where I am today and married to a wonderful man and having his baby*, she thought, and was about to open the Walkers' back door when she heard the shout.

'Rose! I think my dad's had a stroke. He's lying on the floor and he can't speak.'

Beth darted back into Walter's house. Rose opened the Walkers' door. 'May,' she yelled, 'come quick.'

'Eeh! What's to do?' May bustled out and as she followed Rose, John drove into the lane with Patrick beside him. May flagged him down. 'Walter's had a stroke,' she gasped.

'Go get your mam,' John said to Patrick, and as soon as he had alighted, John swung the car round and drove off. Patrick ran and fetched his mother, and John came back with the doctor. A short while later, an ambulance took Walter to hospital and Beth went with him.

Patrick wasn't sure what a stroke was, and he didn't much care. Walter Garside was a cranky old bugger. Still, whatever a stroke was, it must be pretty serious to have them all running to help him. His mam was minding Stuart whilst Blair went to be with Beth at the hospital, and Mavis was making a meal for when they came back. He should be used to it by now, he told himself. That's what they did in Weaver Street. Whenever somebody needed something, they all pitched in.

'Is he going to die?' Patrick asked bluntly.

'I don't know,' his mother replied, lifting John's half-eaten dinner. Her thoughts on life and death, she turned to meet her son's troubled gaze. *My, but he's a beautiful boy.* 'Don't dwell on it, love,' she said gently. 'Death comes to us all and Walter's had a good innings.' Her fingers flicked her forehead then her chest and either shoulder as she spoke. 'In some ways, it'll be a blessed relief for Beth. She's been running round after him all her life.'

'He isn't a nice man, is he?' Patrick dragged his words as if he was loath to speak ill of a man who might be dying. 'He was always shouting at us when we played in the lane. And he never gave me back my football.'

Kitty couldn't help smiling at her son's childish assessment of a man who had made her friend's life a misery.

'No, he wasn't always,' she said, 'but he is Beth's dad and she loves him no matter what, so don't you let her catch ye saying anything bad about him. She's had enough sorrows to bear. Now, off ye go to Jack's with the shirt I've mended.'

Patrick didn't like to think of anybody dying. It frightened him. He walked across the lane, wondering what he would do if either his mam or John were to die whilst he was still young. It was a sobering thought. He loved both of them dearly. He knew John wasn't his real dad, and he could barely remember Tom Conlon. The things he did remember were how tall his dad had been and how nice he smelled. He'd heard gossip about his dad and was sad to learn that his father hadn't been kind to his mam. He loved his mam with a passion, admiring her strong will and the way she always saw the best in everybody. He wanted to be like that. So, shrugging off any bad thoughts about Walter Garside – and death – he went on his errand, returning a short while later with a bag of freshly dug early potatoes.

'Where's our Moll?' Patrick asked, flopping his long, lean body onto a chair.

'Over at Mickey's,' his mother replied, smiling fondly.

'You like him, don't you? But you didn't like Heinz.'

Patrick's remark took Kitty aback. 'It's... it's not that I don't think he's a decent enough lad... I just didn't think he was right for our Molly,' Kitty stammered.

'I think he's dead weird.' Patrick pulled a face. 'He says that Hitler's going to take over the world if we don't put a stop to him. I don't know what our Molly saw in him. I reckon he's barmy,' Patrick jibed. 'I'm just as interested and concerned about what's going on in the world, but I don't think for one minute that Germany would dare attack us. Everybody knows we have the best army and the greatest navy and air force in the world. And if they do, I hope I'll have finished my training as a fighter pilot. I'll show 'em what they're up against.'

'It'll be a year or so before ye can even join the RAF. You might have changed your mind by then,' Kitty said, hoping for it to be true as she washed the dishes. She didn't fancy her darling son flying up in the clouds with nothing to catch him should something go wrong, and she certainly didn't like to think of him as a killing machine if the country went to war.

She clattered plates into the sink, telling herself that she was worrying needlessly, that Patrick's immediate desires were the rites of passage all teenagers experienced as they grew into adults.

She was drying the dishes and counting her blessings when the door burst open and Molly came in, her blue eyes flashing. *Just like Tom's*, Kitty thought as she welcomed her.

'Guess what!' Molly said breathlessly. 'Donal and Liam are going back to Sligo.'

Kitty looked shocked. 'I always knew the lads intended to go back one day, but not so soon.'

'Donal says England's going to war and he'll not fight and die for them.'

The word 'die' reminded Patrick of Beth's emergency. 'Mr Garside might be dying.'

Molly flung her coat over the back of a chair, more concerned with her own news than she was by the state of Walter Garside's health. 'Bridie says she'd like to go as well, but I've told Mickey...'

At one and the same time, Kitty's heart sank and her hackles rose. 'Did ye not hear what Patrick told ye?' she interjected, her tone so sharp that Molly flinched.

Her daughter had the grace to blush. 'Yes, and I'm truly sorry.'

'I hope so,' said Kitty, and spying the coat, she snapped, 'an' hang that up.' She gave her daughter a frustrated glare. 'I know Mickey's family are important to you, but you shouldn't disregard everybody else.'

Molly hung her head. 'I know, Mam. It's just that I don't want Mickey to go as well if his mam and dad do.'

Kitty nerves jangled. She felt miserable for Beth, and anxious that Bridie might soon be leaving. Even so, she gently reassured Molly.

'If I know Mickey, he'll not go anywhere without you, love.'

* * *

'This'll hit Beth hard,' Kitty said as she handed Maggie a cup of tea. 'Still, Walter's in the right place. They're very good at the Infirmary.'

'He'll be a bloody awful patient,' Maggie said, taking out a Woodbine and lighting it. 'The nurses won't know what's hit 'em.'

'I told Beth an' Blair we'll mind Stuart for 'em while they sit with Walter. We'll just have to wait and see how things go.'

They didn't have long to wait. Walter died that night.

* * *

On the day of Walter Garside's funeral, after the ceremony all the mourners congregated in Beth and Blair's house.

'I feel a right bloody hypocrite,' Maggie said as she deliberated over ham and cheese and egg and cress sandwiches. 'I didn't even like the mardy old bugger.' She settled on egg and cress, demolishing it in two bites as she glanced round the crowded room. 'Still, he must have been more popular than you'd think. There's half of Holroyd's Mill here.'

'I suppose it's only to be expected. He worked there all his life,' said Kitty.

'Have you got everything you need, ladies?' Blair flourished the large teapot the landlady at the Weaver's Arms had lent them especially for the occasion.

'That teapot's been to more funerals than I've had hot dinners,' Kitty quipped, holding out her cup.

'You're looking pleased with yourself,' Maggie said, giving Blair a snide grin.

Blair chuckled. 'I can't say I'm heartbroken, but for Beth's sake I'll pretend to be,' he whispered, not bothering to hide his dislike of his father-in-law. He sallied off with the teapot to refill more cups.

'Is there anybody here other than Beth sorry to see the back of Walter?' Maggie asked, wrapping four sandwiches in a paper napkin and shoving them into her handbag.

Beth joined them, pale and red eyed. 'It's a very good turn-out,' she said, gesturing at the groups of mourners. They were chattering loudly or stuffing their mouths with sandwiches, Walter already forgotten as they talked about the weather or anything that didn't concern his demise, but luckily Beth seemed not to notice. 'He'd have been proud to see so many,' she said, turning aside to thank Joseph Holroyd, the mill owner, for coming, and agreeing with him that her father had been a wonderful man.

'It's funny how she forgets how rotten he was to her before you put him wise,' Maggie whispered through a mouthful of iced bun.

'It's perhaps as well we can forget those people who are cruel to us,' Kitty said, thinking of Tom. 'If we didn't, we'd be miserable for the rest of us lives.'

They certainly weren't miserable on 12 May when, like all the other streets in England, they celebrated the coronation of George VI with a street party. Tables were placed down the middle of the lane and loaded with cakes, jellies, and whatever could be knocked together for a treat.

'He'll make a lovely king,' Mavis gushed as she doled out sandwiches.

'Maybe he'll do something to put this country to rights,' Kitty said. 'It's rumoured that Baldwin's for the chop and that fella Neville Chamberlain's in line to be the next PM. Perhaps the king will have a word in his ear.'

'We can only live in hope,' Mavis said brightly.

* * *

Things moved fast in Weaver Street during the last few weeks of summer. Rose and Joey moved into Walter's house, and she gave birth to a healthy boy. They named him James William after his grandfathers. Rose was thrilled to be a mother, and to have her own home amongst the people she loved. There were fleeting moments when she remembered the baby she had miscarried. After all, it was a little life lost, and Rose thanked God for giving her a second chance.

On Harvest Bank Holiday, John organised a trip to New Brighton to celebrate the day off and the fact that his factory was back on an even keel: the dark days of the Depression seemed to be waning at last. There was still great hardship for many but everyone had grown used to making do and life carried on.

'Well at least it's not raining,' Kitty said as she packed a basket with sandwiches, buns and biscuits to take on their trip.

'I'm looking forward to this,' Maggie said, lifting the baskets Kitty had filled. 'Pete's doing a wedding, an' it's better than having to listen to me mam coughing her guts up. She gets worse by the hour.'

Shortly after ten, they all piled into the car, Kitty and Robert up front with John and Maggie and Lily squashed in the back with Molly and Patrick. They drove out of Edge Hill, excitement mounting with every mile. The nearer they got to New Brighton, the heavier the traffic became, as other holidaymakers made their way to the seaside resort too. Molly was disappointed that Mickey wasn't with them, but he had taken on an extra job building a wall at a house by the church. Secretly, he was saving up to buy an engagement ring.

'I wish they'd get a move on,' Maggie groaned, 'I'm dying for a fag an' a pee.'

'Well, you'll have to wait till we get there,' John said, rolling his eyes at Kitty.

* * *

Pete Harper stood in front of the mirror above the sideboard to fasten his black tie. In the chair by the hearth, Vi coughed and coughed. Living with Maggie had its benefits, but her mother was a pain in the arse. Vi tore a strip of paper from the magazine on her knee then stuck it into the fire, and as it flared, she lit a cigarette with it. Two deep drags and she was barking and spluttering, her haggard face turning puce.

'For Christ's sake, Vi! Have you no bloody wit? You'll cough your bloody lungs up one o' these days.' He rammed his chauffeur's cap hard down over his forehead and glared at her before adding, 'An' when you do, don't expect me to clean up the bloody mess.'

He made for the door into the hallway, Vi croaking at his back, 'I wouldn't expect anything from you, you heartless bugger. You're a bloody parasite.'

Vi would have liked to prolong the row but this blasted bronchitis was getting her down and she felt as though every breath she took might be her last.

Pete barged into the hallway, slamming the door behind him. Vi threw the stub of her cigarette into the fire then reached for another one.

* * *

The trip to New Brighton exceeded everybody's expectations, and they returned home tired but happy. Molly scooted off to find Mickey, Lily went to the Grafton and the boys went up to their rooms. John went into the sitting room to catch up with the news on the wireless and Kitty and Maggie sat at the table, drinking welcome cups of tea. 'I'm making the most of today,' Maggie said, taking another biscuit. 'I don't fancy going home to sit with me ma.'

She'd no sooner spoken than John came into the kitchen, saying, 'What do you say to a drink in the Weaver's to round the day off?' The women readily agreed. Letting Patrick and Robert know their plan, off they went.

The Weaver's Arms was packed, but they managed to find a table at the back of the room. Molly and Mickey were already there sitting near the bar and although she waved when Kitty, John and Maggie arrived, she was relieved when they didn't join them. Mickey had just asked her to marry him. Her insides were fluttering and fizzing, and she realised she had never before felt anything like it. Now, as he looked deep into her eyes, her heart drummed a tattoo.

It was almost eleven o'clock when they all left the pub. Kitty and Maggie linked arms with John as they strolled ahead of Mickey and Molly. Outside his own house, John stopped sharply. An eerie red glow lit Maggie's kitchen window.

'My God, Maggie! I think your house is on fire.'

They all dashed across the lane. With Mickey at his heels, John raced up the path and pushed open the back door. Too late, he realised his mistake. A whoosh of flames lit up the kitchen. 'Get back! Get back!' he yelled at the women. 'Kitty, ring the fire brigade.'

The two men entered Maggie's kitchen, stamping out the flames licking their way across the worn linoleum. The big, deep armchair by the hearth was a smouldering black mass of moquette and horsehair belching out acrid smoke. 'Get water, Mickey, I'll go and find Vi,' John yelled, dashing out of the kitchen into the hallway then into the front room before charging upstairs.

'She's not here. She must be down in the Wagon and Horses,' he panted, clattering back into the kitchen. Mickey had found a bucket under the sink and was pouring water over the back of the armchair. John filled the washing up bowl and between them they doused the burning chair until the fire sputtered and fizzled.

'Thank God Vi's not here,' John said, his eyes stinging as the dense smoke began to clear. Rounding the chair, he stared, horrified to see a pair of feet in chequered slippers. Vi's mouth hung open and her unseeing eyes stared back at him. Mickey stood gaping. 'I thought she'd gone to the pub,' John cried.

The clanging of the fire engine's bell woke Patrick and Robert, and the ensuing commotion roused Mavis. She hurried out in her dressing gown, Jack limping beside her. By this time, half the street were standing on their doorsteps to ascertain what was going on, and asking if they could be of any help. As the firemen went in, John and Mickey came out and Molly ran and kissed Mickey's soot-stained face.

John went and put his arms round Maggie, who was sobbing and would have run into the house had not he restrained her. She was still shrieking and wailing as the firemen hosed the kitchen floor. May Walker, having run up the lane to offer her assistance, hurried back home and returned a short while later with a large steaming jug of cocoa and a tray full of cups.

Wakened by the hubbub, Blair Forsythe, wearing only his pyjamas, ran for Dr Metcalfe whilst Kitty and Beth tried to calm Maggie. Once the blaze was out, the firemen left with strict warnings that nobody should sleep in the house that night. John and Blair stood outside the house awaiting the arrival of the doctor, and inside Kitty, Beth and Maggie huddled together, staring hopelessly at Vi. Dr Metcalfe arrived, his blue and white pyjama bottoms flapping underneath the hem of his overcoat.

'She wouldn't have known a thing,' he said, closing Vi's eyes then stepping away from her body. 'She's been dead several hours, a brain haemorrhage, by the looks of it, no doubt activated by a severe bout of coughing. She wouldn't have known about the fire.' John and Mickey heaved huge sighs of relief. They couldn't have saved her.

'Your mother's lungs were in tatters, as I'm sure you know, Maggie,' said the doctor. 'I did advise her to give up smoking when you sent for me last week.'

'The firemen said it was most likely a cigarette that started the fire,' John said. 'They think it was dropped down the side of the chair. They said the horsehair must have been smouldering for hours. It was me opening the door that caused it to flare up – oxygen, you see,' he added guiltily for the women's benefit.

'You'll need an undertaker to remove the body,' Dr Metcalfe said. 'A post-mortem won't be necessary.' He lifted his bag, preparing to leave.

'We'll keep her here,' Maggie said, suddenly coming to life. 'She'll want to be in her own bed.'

'Then I'll leave the arrangements to you. I'll see myself out.'

John and Blair carefully lifted Vi from the chair and carried her upstairs just as Lily arrived back from the Grafton. The smell of burning filled her nose and she hurried inside. She gaped at the burned chair then, hearing noises overhead, she ran upstairs.

Molly was helping Kitty and Beth cover Vi's charred body with a clean white sheet. Maggie was slumped in a chair by the bedside. 'I'm staying here with her tonight. She shouldn't be on her own,' she said hollowly.

'Dead? Like really dead?' Lily said, when Molly and Kitty gently broke the awful news. 'Like she's not coming back.' She was slightly tipsy.

'I'm afraid so, darlin'. But the doctor said she didn't feel a thing. She didn't suffer, and she didn't know about the fire. The angels had taken her long before that.' Kitty blessed herself as she spoke.

Lily bit down on her bottom lip. 'She was an old mare most of the time,' she said solemnly, 'always shoutin' at me and complaining, but she was me granny. I'll miss her. What about me mam?' Maggie was quietly sobbing.

'She's staying with your granny tonight. You're staying with us.'

'Okay,' Lily said and went back downstairs.

Later, when the boys were in bed and the two girls were in Molly's room, Kitty and John sat by the fire in the parlour. Kitty was musing on Lily's reaction to Vi's death. Given time, Lily would no doubt grieve in her own way.

'Young ones have a funny way of dealing with death,' she said, half to herself.

'It's perhaps as well they have,' John replied, giving her a meaningful look.

* * *

'An' where were you last night?' Maggie asked Pete when he arrived home the next morning shortly after eleven. She was still sitting beside Vi's bed, her face blotched and her hair sticking out where she'd tugged at it as a punishment for being at the seaside enjoying herself while her mother sat dying. An overflowing ashtray spewed its contents onto the bedside cabinet.

The back of Pete's neck reddened and he shuffled his feet. He'd stayed the night with another woman, something he regularly did in order to have the best of both worlds.

'In Kirby with one o' the other drivers,' he lied. 'I wa' too knack-ered to drive back here.'

Grimly, Maggie accepted his excuse. 'I suppose I'd better think about organising her funeral,' she said, looking hopefully at Pete through puffy red eyes that begged for him to offer to help.

'Yeah, I suppose you will,' he said, making for the door. 'I'm off for a shave.'

* * *

Vi's funeral was in danger of turning into a wingding. After a short service in St Peter's Anglican Church – Vi's first time to darken its doors – then interment in the bleak graveyard attended by family and friends, and a larger contingent of clients from the pub where Vi had worked, the mourners scarpered to the Wagon and Horses to celebrate her life.

'I still feel bad about not being there when she died,' Maggie wailed above the singing and shouting of the revellers. She downed the dregs of her umpteenth port and lemon, then looked round for somebody to refill her glass.

'There was nothing you could have done. Dr Metcalfe told you that,' Kitty said through gritted teeth. She'd lost count of the number of times she'd said it.

'She's gone to a better place, love,' Dora Hawkins slurred, the thick moustache of foam from her stout sputtering on her upper lip. A Wagon and Horses regular, she was best known for her ability to drink eight pints a night. The decibels became deafening as the crowd at the bar burst into Vi's favourite song. 'All of me, why not take all of me,' bawled twenty or so raucous voices as they raised their glasses in tribute to Vi.

'Me mother loved that song, she'd have loved a do like this,' Maggie croaked, her eyes moistening again. 'She should have been here to enjoy it.'

'She's gone to a better place, love,' Dora slurred again. Lily and Molly exchanged frustrated glances, each wondering how soon they could make an escape without offending Maggie.

25

Maggie heard the knock and hurried down the hallway, her face creased with anxiety. Callers at her front door usually meant trouble: the rent man or the man from the Providence Cheques company looking for money that she didn't have.

She opened the door, and a girl of about twenty with a pale, peaky face and a distended belly glared at her.

'I'm looking for Pete Harper.' The girl spat out the words.

Utterly taken aback, Maggie stared at her, then mumbled, 'He's not here.'

Pete had left about an hour ago, saying he was going to work. Maggie gathered her wits. 'What do you want with him?' She thought she already knew the answer and her insides seethed with mixed emotions.

'When he gets back, tell him Sarah's looking for him. The baby's due and I need him,' the girl said flatly.

Maggie's face crumpled. 'Is that his baby?' Her voice sounded hollow.

'Yeah. Why else do you think I'm here?' Sarah gave an ugly laugh.

Maggie looked into the girl's pinched, pathetic face. Jealousy competed with a sense of shame and sympathy. 'I didn't know about you and... er, the baby,' she said to explain her surprise.

'Seems he's made fools of both of us, then.' The girl shrugged. 'I don't really want him, I'm just here 'cos of this baby. I thought he'd cleared off for good.'

By now, Maggie had shrugged off her guilt and was burning with rage. 'Oh, he'll be clearing off all right,' she roared. 'Clearing off out of my bloody house. I want nothing more to do with the rotten, bloody liar.' Looking askance, she sneered, 'I'm surprised you want the bugger.'

'I have to,' Sarah said, patting her bump.

Her remark made Maggie feel dirty. 'I'll tell him to pack his bags,' she said softly and made to close the door.

'Yeah, make sure you do.'

* * *

Maggie rested her elbows on her mending frame and propped her chin on her clenched fists. The acid yellow chalk marks that highlighted the flaws in the worsted stretched over the frame blurred as she gazed at them through her tears. Up above her head, she could hear the sound of Pete moving about. The drawers in the tallboy creaked and scraped and then the wardrobe door slammed. A few minutes later, his feet thudded on the stairs. She tensed, waiting and wondering if he would say goodbye, or would he just sneak out like the cheat he'd turned out to be?

Pete dumped his suitcase on the floor in the hallway and slowly pushed open the door of the front room. It squeaked on its hinges as it had done for years but Maggie didn't turn round. She stayed as she was, gazing at her mending frame and thinking how some of her neighbours would snigger behind her back when they learned that he'd gone.

'I'm off then,' Pete said. Maggie ignored him and he repeated his words.

'I heard you the first time,' she said, her voice thick with emotion. She swivelled round to face him. 'Go if you're going, don't let me keep you.'

Pete flinched at her scornful tone. 'You know how it is, Maggie,' he pleaded.

Maggie jumped to her feet. 'I'd have known a damned sight better if you'd been bloody honest from the start,' she yelled, the venomous look on her face making him quail.

'Sarah needs me,' he said pathetically.

'I bloody need you,' she cried, her shoulders heaving as she began sobbing.

Pete moved to put his arms round her but she pushed him off roughly. 'Don't bloody touch me,' she hiccupped, 'I've done with you an' your lies.'

'I can still come round sometimes if you want. We can still...' He reeled back under the full force of Maggie's hand as she swiped him across his face.

'Get out! Get out! And don't bloody come back – ever.'

* * *

'Pete's gone for good,' Lily said later that day as she entered Molly's bedroom. Molly was paring her fingernails, her tongue sticking out of the corner of her mouth: nursing demanded that she kept her hands in good order. She pulled her tongue back in and let her mouth hang open as she looked at Lily, surprised.

Pete had been around for so long that she thought Maggie had at last found what she was looking for.

Lily tossed her mane of red hair carelessly. 'He's got another girl – and she's in the club. Me granny always said he was a lying, cheating bastard.'

She lifted a pink lipstick off Molly's dressing table and began twisting it in and out of its case. 'Me mam's been crying,' she said, her voice wobbling. 'She says if he comes back, I've to tell him to bugger off.' She looked deeply into her best friend's face. 'It's been the same all my life, Molly. Men come an' they go an' cause nothing but misery.' She extended the lipstick to its full length then peered into the mirror. 'I've allus wanted a dad like yours,' she said, great gulping sobs escaping her throat as she slashed thick pink stripes of lipstick across both cheeks.

'Oh, Lily, don't cry,' said Molly, dropping her nailfile and hugging her. 'You can share John. He's always nice to you just like he is to me and Patrick.' She gazed into her friend's sad face, searching for more words of comfort. Instead, she began to giggle. 'Your cheeks look like two slices of streaky bacon,' she spluttered from behind her hands.

Lily looked at her reflection, and laughing raucously, she jumped to her feet, her copper curls bouncing as she jigged up and down, chanting, 'Bugger off, Pete. Me an' me mam don't need you. Bugger off, Pete, and all the other rotten fellas in the world. Bugger off, everybody. I don't need anybody.'

A rollercoaster of memories of all Lily's 'pretend dads', her numerous boyfriends and relentless social life hurtled through Molly's mind as she leapt to her feet, her heart aching for the girl she looked on as a sister. Lily was telling lies. 'Don't, Lily! Don't,' she cried, throwing her arms round her and bringing Lily's hysterical dancing to a stop. 'You've still got us. You've got to care.'

Downstairs in the kitchen, Kitty was saying much the same thing. 'It's not the end of the world, Maggie. Ye've bounced back before an' ye will again,' she said, shoving the plate of biscuits nearer Maggie's elbow.

Maggie lifted her head from her arms then brushed away her tears with the back of her hand. 'Do you really think so?' she said pitifully. 'I'm getting too old for this game. Look at me, Kitty. Who'd want me?'

Kitty smiled gently into Maggie's face. Her eyes were red and the bags beneath them like purple prunes, her blonde hair unbrushed and black at the roots. Kitty took a deep breath: sometimes you had to be cruel to be kind.

'Aye, look at ye, wallowing in self-pity, an' all because of that cheating bastard. He did ye more harm than good with his comings an' goings. Now, dry your eyes an' count your blessings.' She clasped Maggie's hands. 'Ye have a lovely daughter, an' you've allus got me, so what's to cry about, ye snivellin', lovable bag o' bones?'

Maggie's eyes popped. 'Some bloody comfort you are,' she crowed. 'An' as for a bag of bones, I weigh two stone more than I did in me twenties.'

'Aye, an' everyone of 'em worth ten times Pete Harper.'

After Pete's departure, Maggie declared she was finished with men, and so did Lily. They were closer now than they had ever been, going out and about like sisters. Kitty thought of Maggie and Vi's relationship and wondered if history was repeating itself, but she was glad that Maggie was once again wearing her rough, tough shell and cocking a snook at whatever life threw her way.

Molly saw little of Lily as she accompanied Maggie on jaunts to the pub and elsewhere. Molly didn't mind. Her free time was spent with Mickey, planning their future together. They had so much in common, and both of them were prepared to wait and save so that they could start married life on a stable footing. They were both concerned about what was going on in the wider world so, in October, when Mickey suggested they attend a British Union of Fascists rally in Walton, Molly readily agreed. 'It's only right to protest against 'em,' said Mickey. 'That bugger Mosley is stirring things up something rotten.'

On the tram, Molly told Mickey what Heinz had told her about Oswald Mosley, the founder of the BUF. 'Heinz says he's an ambitious and ruthless politician exploiting the situation for his own personal power. His admiration for Adolf Hitler and his call for Corporate Law will result in a dictatorship and the poor will suffer as they always do when aristocrats like him gain control,' she repeated prosaically.

Mickey looked pained as jealousy flared. 'Seems like you paid a lot of attention to that barmy German,' he snarled.

'Oh, don't be daft, Mickey. I couldn't care less about him. I'm just letting you know about Mosley. It's you I love, not Heinz, and...' she sniggered, 'I know you won't beggar off and leave me like he did if things get nasty.'

Somewhat appeased, Mickey squeezed her hand and said, 'Go on then, tell us.'

'Well, he talks about jobs for everyone and decent wages,' Molly continued, 'but Heinz says he's using the political platform to achieve his own ends. If he succeeds, he'll manipulate the masses by force, like Hitler, that's the way he works,' Molly concluded acidly.

Queen's Drive was a seething mass of people, the noise deafening. Union Jacks and fascist flags flapped and slapped in the gusty October breeze. Molly and Mickey took up a position on the edge of the crowd. Gangs of men wearing black shirts were patrolling the throng in a militaristic manner.

'They're Mosley's men,' Molly said, Heinz's words proving tragically true as she watched them shouldering their way through the crowds, brutally attacking and hauling away those who were holding anti-fascist banners or placards. A huge black-shirted thug kicked mercilessly at a woman he had thrown to the ground.

'No! No!' Molly cried, her distress causing her to leap forward and Mickey yanking her back and crying, 'Keep out of it.' She stared helplessly as the woman's body absorbed the toe of the thug's boot. Molly felt sick.

Oswald Mosley climbed on top of a van with a loudspeaker. The roars of the crowd abated as, pacing the van roof like a panther intimidating his prey before pouncing, he prepared to make his speech. Molly was mesmerised by the flash of Mosley's gleaming white smile – he was a handsome man – but she scowled when he raised his arm in a Nazi salute. Then, before he could utter a word, someone in the crowd hurled a large stone. It hit Mosley fair and square, and a second stone knocked him unconscious. Chaos broke out. Molly and Mickey ran for their lives, laughing at Mosley's humiliating dispatch.

'That showed him we scousers won't listen to his vile speeches,' Molly said as they waited for a tram.

'It won't shut him up, though,' Mickey said grimly. 'Me da says he has friends in high places, and if he gets their support, he could start a war.'

Molly shuddered. 'Winston Churchill's also saying there could be a war. My mam says the last one was awful,' said Molly as she stumbled aboard the tram.

'They'll not start another,' Mickey said, 'they're not that crazy.'

* * *

As the year 1938 progressed, things seemed to be a little easier for the friends in Weaver Street. John's Sykes's factory had weathered the worst of the Depression and Kitty was relieved and happy to see his worries diminish by the day. She was pleased that Robert was doing well at school and Patrick working happily alongside his stepfather in the factory, and more than pleased that Molly had found true love with Mickey O'Malley and was now wearing his engagement ring. After all the hardships of the past few years, she was looking forward to the future with renewed hope.

There had been no more mention of Bridie leaving, even though her two sons had returned to Sligo a few months ago. 'I miss 'em terribly, so I do,' Bridie complained frequently, but she gave no indication of following them and Kitty stopped worrying.

Rose and Joey were eagerly awaiting the first birthday of their son, James, and May had treated herself to a stair carpet. She'd have given her eyeteeth for one in the old days and now she had a sober husband whose scrap business had gone from strength to strength, she was thrilled to be able to afford one: James Brown-Allsop's advice had proved wise, and Bill's hard work was paying off. He'd found a dealer who was buying scrap metal for a government contract; things were looking up.

Beth was finding life much easier since Walter's death even though, every now and then, that made her feel guilty. Blair told her she had no reason to reproach herself; she had done her duty. She had also paid an embarrassing visit to the family planning clinic to make sure she had no more children: Stuart would be their one and only priority.

Things were looking up for Maggie too. On a night out with her friends from the mill, Maggie met Stanley Pickersgill. 'He's a widower, and a right proper gentleman,' she'd told her friends, and as the months went by, it was proving true. He was courting Maggie in such a gentlemanly fashion that it had gradually softened her rough, careless manners and she had never been happier. As for Lily, she was delighted for her mam, and on the lookout for a younger version of Stanley.

Patrick Conlon was restless. He had completed his course at

the Technical College and although he enjoyed working with John in the factory, he was waiting for the day he could join the Air Defence Cadet Corp: he was determined to be a flyer. Although Hitler was threatening war in Europe, Patrick was more interested in Howard Hughes, the American tycoon who had flown round the world in four days. As far as he was concerned, 1938 couldn't pass quickly enough.

The prospect of Christmas made everyone's hearts a little lighter. Even in the poorest of houses, there was an air of expectation and a determined effort to celebrate the festival. Hitler might be doing his damnedest to wreak death and destruction, but it wasn't stopping the friends in Weaver Street from celebrating.

By mid-afternoon on Christmas Day, most of them were sitting down, bellies stuffed, listening to the king's speech. He talked of Britain's continuing friendship with foreign powers to promote understanding in the spirit of the Anglo-German declaration that had been made that September, but those who were paying close attention couldn't help feeling uneasy when he told them that the Defence Forces were making rapid progress to secure the safety of their country. The threat of war had not gone away.

'This has been the best year of my life,' Maggie enthused as she sat with Kitty and Mavis and Rose and Beth in Kitty's kitchen one afternoon just after Christmas. 'Stan's so thoughtful and caring, I don't know I'm born.'

'I know just how you feel,' Beth said. 'Blair's the same, and having a good man by your side makes all the difference.'

'I agree,' said Kitty. 'If it wasn't for John, I'd never have got through these last few years. We've tightened our belts that much it's a wonder we haven't been cut off at the middle, but things are definitely getting easier, even though there's all that trouble with Hitler.' She sighed and shrugged. 'Still, if Chamberlain's as good as his word, that treaty he's signed'll keep us out of the war.' She got to her feet. 'Does anybody want another cuppa?'

'It's the poor Jews I feel sorry for. The news of what Hitler's doing to them is shocking, and there's nothing we can do about that,' Rose said dismally then brightened as she added, 'but we are helping the needy families we visit. It's heart-warming to know that all the children got something this year from the used toys we managed to collect. I'm so glad you had that idea, Kitty.'

'Aye, Millie Thomson's lads loved them old cars that used to be our Robert's,' said Kitty, chuckling at her duplicity as she added, 'He doesn't know I've given 'em away yet he's still got that many.'

'And her girls were thrilled with the doll's house Jack knocked up for them out of an old crate.' Mavis's beady eyes lit up. 'What with the jacket and a bonnet I knitted for Jean's baby and the cardigan for Mrs Morgan, I really feel as though I'm doing something worthwhile.'

'Aye, and the presents hopefully made up for less groceries,' said Kitty, 'seein' as the novelty of being charitable has worn thin with the shopkeepers and the better-off contributors. Still, we'll keep at 'em in the New Year.'

Over a fresh pot of tea, the women let their enthusiasm run away with them as they planned what to do next for the needy families.

Mavis raised her cup. 'Here's to a happy 1939, girls,' she chortled.

'Oh, it will be,' Maggie crowed. 'This year, I had me very own Father Christmas to kiss me under the mistletoe, and who knows what he'll do next.'

'Stan's the man,' Kitty cried, and they all laughed.

26

Ice and snow held Weaver Street in its deathly grip for the first two months of 1939 and the news in Europe was just as chilling. Germany's occupation of Sudetenland and its oppression in Czechoslovakia less than a year ago were extremely worrying, and although the British Prime Minister, Neville Chamberlain, and Adolf Hitler had promised that 'Britain and Germany will never go to war with one another again', the promise now had a hollow ring to it, the clouds of war gathering and growing more ominous with each passing week.

'Chamberlain says that if Hitler invades Poland, we'll defend them,' John told Kitty and Maggie one evening in February, the rain lashing the windows and a chill draught blowing under the parlour door adding misery to the news.

'I don't like to think of the Polish people suffering but I don't want us to be dragged into another war. The last one was too terrible. When ye think of all the lives that were lost an' men like Jack damaged beyond repair, it makes me shudder to think what it'll mean for young lads like our Patrick, an' Mickey an' Joey, an' every mother's sons,' Kitty said, her voice rising an octave.

'Don't go imagining the worst,' John comforted her, 'if they keep talking, they might sort it out peacefully.'

'Not if they're talking about putting up bloody air-raid shelters,' Maggie intervened. 'Lily Moss's mam lives down by the docks and she said they're building one at the top of her street.'

'It's just a precautionary measure,' said John, but he didn't sound convinced. He glanced at the window, frowning. 'Maybe I should put one in our back garden. Better to be safe than sorry.'

Kitty looked horrified.

Spring crept in but it did little to lighten the mood of the older inhabitants in Weaver Street for, as it became apparent that Hitler was determined to plant his jackboots all over Europe, they talked of little else.

However, Molly Conlon had no time to dwell on the turmoil that was taking place in countries that, to her, seemed so far away that she thought their affairs couldn't possibly impact on her life. She was thinking of marriage.

At first, when she knew that Mickey was her one and only true love, she had agreed to getting engaged but had said they were still too young to get married. Mickey had agreed, saying they would save up for a couple of years, get a place of their own and start married life with money in the bank. Molly had thought that was a grand idea, and when Maggie had asked in that forthright manner of hers, 'Any word on when you an' Mickey are gonna tie the knot?' Molly had said, 'Oh, not for ages. We're saving up for a house of our own and we'd like to go to Paris on our honeymoon.'

'Paris!' Lily's jaw had dropped. 'That's in France,' she'd said as though it was the far side of the moon. Other newly married couples in Weaver Street made do with a weekend in Scarborough or a trip to London.

'We want to see the Eiffel Tower and visit the Louvre,' Molly then told them excitedly. Lily had looked blank. She'd never paid much attention to her geography teacher. She'd pulled a face and decided she'd heard enough. Molly had seen the look and was sorry for showing off. Lily had yet to find a boy who made her as happy as Mickey did Molly.

Now she was having second thoughts. It seemed silly to wait when they were so much in love that they were having difficulty keeping their hands off one another whenever they were alone in Bridie's or Kitty's parlours.

'We don't have to wait for years if we don't want,' she said rather breathlessly one night in April as she struggled up for air from Mickey's ardent kisses.

Mickey misread the meaning of her remark. He looked slightly shocked, but he couldn't prevent the hope that flared in his blue eyes. 'You mean you'd let me...?'

'No-o-o!' Molly exclaimed, pushing him away. 'I meant we could just get married sooner, and if your mam agrees to us living here, we can still save up for our own place without always having to stop what we both want to do.' She gave him a cheeky smile.

'You're right, it's killing me,' he groaned, tugging at his trouser crotch.

They giggled at his discomfort then began talking seriously.

Over at the Sykes house, 1939 was turning out to be kinder than its predecessors. John was sure they had seen the worst of the economic downturn, and in some ways, he was proved right.

'Orders are looking good, love,' he told Kitty on the evening of the day he'd secured a government contract for small machine parts in anti-aircraft guns.

Kitty heard the relief in his voice and, drying her hands on the tea towel, she went to give him a hug. 'I'm glad for you, love,' she said, placing her arms round his neck and kissing him, and at the same time feeling sad to think that the upturn in business was due to the threat of war; but if manufacturing weapons that killed – or defended – was the order of the day, then so be it.

The door scraped open and Maggie came in, cigarette in hand. She too looked pleased with her lot. She and Stan had spent the weekend in New Brighton, and Kitty wondered how long it would be before Stan proposed. He was the old-fashioned type and his wife had been dead less than two years. Lily liked him, and she and Maggie had never been closer. 'We're like sisters,' was one of her mother's favourite sayings.

Kitty had been tempted to say: *Well, I hope you turn out to be a better sister than a mother because you were useless at that.* But she held her tongue, not wanting to take the pleasure out of Maggie's newfound interest in her daughter.

'Last night me and Stan were down at the Wagon an' Horses for a drink and they've started clearing that land behind the pub,' she announced as though she had a vested interest in the building of the new council houses that had been proposed months before. She was wearing a bright red dress with a white lacy collar and she'd crimped her hair into tiny waves that swooped over her ears and caressed her cheeks. Her appearance had improved no end since Stan came into her life.

'That'll give work to a few chaps that haven't had a job in years,' John said, taking a mug of the tea Kitty had just made. 'Mind you, unemployment's dropping what with all the re-armament that the government's insisting on.'

'Do you want a cup?' Kitty said, gesturing with a mug and thinking it was a daft question. Maggie never refused something for nothing.

'Aye, go on then,' Maggie replied as though she'd been forced. 'Do you think me an' Stan should put us name down for one of them new houses?' she continued, looking to John for his advice.

John grinned. 'If you left Weaver Street, things 'ud never be the same. She'd have nobody to gossip with,' he quipped, jerking his thumb at Kitty.

'Cheeky sod,' his wife retorted, 'I'll have ye know we never gossip, we discuss.' She went back to peeling potatoes, a smile curving her lips. 'Still an' all, I'd miss ye if ye did move,' she said, giving Maggie a mock tragic look.

'My arse,' Maggie cried, 'you'd be glad to see the back of me.'

They both knew this wasn't true.

After Maggie had gone back home, Kitty wondered if she was serious about moving and starting somewhere new with Stan. And then there was Bridie. Each time they met, Bridie moaned about how much she missed her sons and that if there was going to be a war, she'd be better off in Sligo. All this talk of leaving made Kitty feel uneasy.

A few evenings later, when John had gone to the pub for a pint and the boys were upstairs, Kitty was in the parlour reading when Molly walked in and sat down.

'Mam,' she began tentatively, 'I want to talk to you.'

Kitty closed her book and gave her daughter a quizzical look at the same time feeling her heart give an unpleasant lurch. Was Molly about to tell her she was pregnant? 'Go on then,' she croaked as she tried to quell her fears.

Molly took a deep breath. 'You know me and Mickey agreed to wait a couple of years before getting married,' she said nervously. 'Well, things have changed and...' She screwed up her face, searching for the right words.

Oh, no. Here it comes, Kitty thought, her heart sinking.

'I know you think we're too young, Mam, and at first I thought you were right but...' Molly's emotions got the better of her. 'Oh, Mam! I want to be Mickey's wife more than anything, and he feels the same. We can't wait any longer, if you know what I mean.'

'Are you expecting?' Kitty's voice sounded hollow.

'No! No!' Molly's hands flew to her cheeks and her eyes boggled. 'It's just... it's just we want to be together so much that it hurts to...' Her cheeks had turned bright red.

Kitty suppressed a smile. She knew all about longing and lusting. Hadn't it been the same for her and John? 'So you want to get married sooner than later,' she said, then added, 'and ye're sure ye don't have to.'

'I'm sure, Mam. We haven't done anything like that but...'

'I know, love,' Kitty said gently. 'I was young meself once.'

Molly visibly relaxed. She gave an impish smile. 'And if I said we wanted to get married at the end of this summer, you wouldn't mind?'

'Not if you're sure, and Mickey is, of course.'

'Oh, we are, Mam,' Molly gushed, her blue eyes flashing and a smile wreathing her face as relief washed over her. She jumped up. 'I'll go and tell him,' she said.

* * *

'September? What happened to saving for a house and flying to Paris?' Lily asked, trying hard not to sound envious. She began fiddling with the things on Molly's dressing table to hide her dismay. *Why couldn't it have been the other way round, her telling Molly she was getting married?*

'Yeah, we decided it wasn't worth the wait,' Molly replied, her cheeks glowing and her eyes alight with excitement.

'Where will you live?'

'With Bridie and Big Mick,' Molly chirped. 'It makes sense, there's only the two of them in their house whereas here there's our Patrick and Robert as well as my mam and dad.'

'Your Patrick's hardly ever at home these days, he's always off on that air cadet training thingy, and when he is, all he talks about is learning how to fly aeroplanes.' Lily raised her pencilled eyebrows, thin brown lines above eyelids coated in dark green eyeshadow. 'Mind you, he looks smashing in his uniform – well – except for that blue beret. That makes him look drippy.'

Molly giggled. 'He loves that uniform, and he can't wait until he joins the proper RAF,' she said, 'and don't you go telling him he looks daft in his beret.'

'I already have,' Lily scoffed.

* * *

Kitty couldn't help feeling rather annoyed that Molly had decided to marry so soon. Yet, she reminded herself, she had been younger than Molly when she married Tom. *And look how that turned out.* She was aggravated and, if she was honest, a bit jealous because Molly was going to live with Bridie after she and Mickey were married.

'That's because none of us want our chickens to fly the coop,' May Walker said, leaning on the garden wall to talk with Kitty, who was on her way to the shops. 'When our Ronnie went off to live in Toxteth where his wife comes from, I felt as though I'd lost my right arm.' She gave sad a little smile. 'Still, I'm lucky I have our Joey and Rose living next door. I used to have nightmares worrying she'd persuade him to go and live with her dad in Bucking-hamshire, but she seems quite content to stay here, and I don't know what I'd have done if they'd gone and taken our little James away. I love that child to bits.' Her eyes misted. 'Losing a child's the worst thing that can happen to a mother. When our Sammy was killed in the last war, I thought I'd never hold my head up again.' She scowled. 'And now it looks as if they're starting another one. Our Steven'll be in the thick of it if they do, what with him being in the navy, and our Joey and Ronnie could be called up again. Hitler has a lot to answer for.'

Kitty shuddered. Patrick would have to fight too. Thank God Robert was too young. 'Aye, it's lookin' awful grim. Every time I listen to the news, I wish I hadn't bothered.' She forced a smile. 'But remember what Chamberlain said: *Peace in our time*, an' I've a wedding to look forward to, so I'll try to keep me spirits up for the next three months.'

'Beginning of September, isn't it? She'll make a beautiful bride will your Molly, and her and Mickey make a lovely couple,' May said.

'Aye, they're well matched,' said Kitty, 'but standing here gossiping'll not fetch the shopping so I'll be on me way. Ta-ra, May.'

'Ta-ra, love, keep smiling.'

* * *

'No, Mickey, I'm not listening,' Molly protested, her eyes blazing and her voice harsh. 'I don't care how beautiful the countryside is, and how successful your Donal and Liam's business is. I'm not going, and that's a fact.'

'You could always give it a try,' Mickey pleaded. 'If you don't like it, we can always come back.' He raked his fingers through his black curls, exasperated.

'I'll tell you what, Mickey. Forget about the wedding and you beggar off back to Sligo with your precious mammy and daddy' – the latter said in a tone dripping with sarcasm – 'and I'll get on with living the rest of my life...' she stormed out of Bridie's front room, yelling, 'in Liverpool.'

Kitty was crossing from her parlour into the kitchen when

Molly barged into the hallway. 'I'm just about to make cocoa, do you want some?' her mother asked.

'No, I don't. I'm going to bed,' Molly snapped, stamping along the hallway and up the stairs.

Kitty's eyebrows shot up. What had brought that on? Shrugging, she went into the kitchen and was pouring milk into a pan when she heard a sharp rap on the back door.

'I'll get it,' John shouted from the parlour. Seconds later, he called out, 'It's Mickey. He wants to see Molly.'

Oh, oh, it was just as Kitty suspected. They'd had a tiff. Lowering the gas under the pan, she went into the hallway. 'I'll go and tell her,' she said, giving John a lopsided grin then making her way upstairs. She tapped on Molly's bedroom door, opened it and popped her head through the gap. 'Mickey's here, he wants to talk to ye.'

'Tell him to go away. I don't want to talk to him,' Molly snapped.

'Ye should never sleep on a quarrel,' Kitty said softly.

'I'll do exactly as I please,' Molly fired back. 'I don't want to see him.'

'Well, if that's how ye feel...'

Mickey looked downcast when she delivered the message. He slouched off into the darkness without a word of explanation.

'They'll sort themselves out,' John said, 'best not interfere.' He went back into the parlour and Kitty went to make the cocoa.

Upstairs in bed, Molly seethed with anger. How dare Mickey presume that she'd want to live in Sligo just because that's what his parents expected him to do? How was it that he hadn't had the decency to discuss it with her, just like they discussed everything, even things as trivial as what colour they'd paint their bedroom, or what they'd call their children when they came along? It had always been that way, talking things through until they reached an agreement. But he'd told her of his plans as if it was a foregone conclusion that she'd agree with them.

Well, he's sadly mistaken, she told herself, tossing and turning in temper. *Whither thou goest, I go*, she thought bitterly, *but I'm no Ruth, I'm Molly Conlon, and I have a mind of my own and deserve to be treated with consideration and asked for my opinion on such an important matter.* Her heart aching – she still loved Mickey – she fell into a restless sleep.

A week passed by, the July weather warm and sunny. Molly made no mention of the argument to Kitty. She got up each morning to work on the early shift in the hospital then stayed in the city until late, saying she'd been out with the other nurses, something she'd rarely done since she and Mickey had become engaged. He called at Kitty's each evening after work, dejected when John or Kitty told him Molly wasn't in.

'Ye're givin' our Mickey an awful lot of grief,' Big Mick said one evening when she passed him in the lane.

'A wife should go where her husband goes,' Bridie had tartly told Molly when, out of Kitty's hearing, she had called with the takings from the café.

'Ye can't avoid him forever,' Kitty said one morning at the end of the second week. 'Ye'll have to sort something out. It's less than six weeks to the wedding, and it's either on or off. To my mind, Mickey wants it to be on, so ye'd better let him know one way or the other.' She gave Molly a searching look. 'I still don't know what all this fuss is about. Bridie's being very cagey, in fact she's been acting proper strange just lately, an' I don't know whether I'm coming' or goin'.'

Molly burst into tears. Pushing her porridge bowl away, she cried, 'Oh, Mam, it's all her fault. She's to blame for all this.'

Kitty eyes popped. 'Why, what has she done?'

Molly gulped back her tears. 'I'm not supposed to tell you until she tells you herself,' she spluttered, 'but her and Big Mick are going back to Ireland after the wedding and they've persuaded Mickey to go with them, and he expects me to go,' she clicked her fingers, 'just like that.'

Kitty's jaw dropped. She had known for some time that Bridie missed her sons, and that she was disenchanted with living in Weaver Street, but she had thought it was nothing more than talk. A cold hand clutched her heart. What if Molly changed her mind and went too? She'd miss her just as much as Bridie missed her family.

Kitty sat down at the table and took Molly's hands in her own.

'Ye love Mickey, don't ye?'

Molly nodded, tears dripping from her long dark lashes.

'Here's what I think,' her mother said gently. 'Stop hiding from him, go and talk to him, talk it through properly an' put an end to your misery. It pains me to see ye so unhappy' – she squeezed Molly's hands and grinned – 'ye haven't had a smile for the cat these past weeks, and Mickey's no better. If I have to answer the door to him once more and watch him trudge off with his heart on his sleeve, me own will break. Now, get ye off to your work, an' tonight go an' make up with him. Whatever ye decide, I'll be here for ye. Your happiness is my happiness.'

Molly gave a watery smile. 'Thanks, Mam.'

She got to her feet, and wiping her face with her hands, she then put on her nurse's cape and went to catch the tram into the city.

Mavis was at the tram stop and when the tram arrived, they sat together.

'How are things with you, Molly?' Kitty had told her about Molly and Mickey's falling out. To her surprise, Molly answered with a question of her own.

'Did you and Jack never think of getting married?'

Mavis blinked and pursed her lips.

'I can't say that we did,' she said thoughtfully. 'We're happy as we are. Jack likes his own space, and I like mine.'

Molly's cheeks reddened. She'd been impertinent.

Mavis read her mind and was quick to say, 'Not that I recommend it for other people. If you love someone truly and deeply, then marriage is the perfect solution.' She patted Molly's hand. 'As for my friendship with Jack, I'm a great believer in if it's not broken, don't fix it, so we'll carry on just as we have for the last fifteen years.' She smiled. 'Like I say, we're content with what we've got.'

'And you make a lovely couple,' Molly replied, her voice thick with emotion. 'Never change, stay just as you are.'

Mavis could almost smell Molly's unhappiness and desperately wanted to ease her pain.

'Marriage is a very big undertaking, but to share your life with someone you love, no matter where that life might be, is one of God's greatest gifts.'

Molly thought about her life without Mickey. It would be unbearable.

'I always find that talking helps in every situation, whether its sharing one's joys – or problems,' Mavis continued, 'and if I'm not sure about something, I always talk it over with Jack. Nine times out of ten, we reach a happy solution.'

By the time the tram reached the city and Molly and Mavis went their separate ways, Molly had made up her mind to talk to Mickey that evening.

On a building site not too far away from the hospital where Molly worked, Mickey O'Malley was stirring cement, his thoughts as heavy as the stuff he was mixing. He ached for Molly in every fibre of his tired arms and throbbing head. He'd let the news in Donal's letter go to his head, and spoken without thinking. Word that Sligo's main town had embarked on a major housebuilding scheme, and that his brothers' team of men had work and good wages for years to come, had influenced him into believing that's where he should be: that and his mother's persuasive tongue. It had left him torn between making a fortune like Donal and Liam or marrying Molly.

In his heart, he knew which one he most wanted, but the idea of having both had seemed too good an opportunity to pass over. He should have talked it over with Molly before making his announcement, they were a team, and he loved her more than life itself. Somehow he had to get her to listen to him. They'd wasted enough time, and he wouldn't let another day go by.

* * *

The riverbank was wearing the last of its summer best, rosebay willow herb and ragged robin a showy backdrop for clusters of white meadow sweet. Glistening water flowed serenely down-stream on its journey to the sea, its smooth surface broken now and then by skimming birds or dabbling ducks: a perfect place for lovers to walk.

Mickey had called on Molly at eight o'clock that evening and she had agreed to see him. She'd almost smiled when she saw how smart he looked, his black curls neatly combed and his sparkling white shirt without a wrinkle. He'd dressed for the occasion, but then so had she. Smoothing the skirt of her pretty blue frock, she stepped out of the house and they walked in silence, both of them lost for words as they made their way down the lane then up Weaver Street to the towpath. A gentle evening breeze caressed Molly's glossy hair, blowing it delightfully about her shoulders and tugging fragile black tendrils to her cheeks. Mickey thought she had never looked more beautiful.

They strolled along the towpath, drinking in the beauty of

their surroundings and passing remarks when they caught the sight of a magnificent kingfisher then a water vole sliding out of its lair. When they came to the café – closed at this time in the evening – Mickey went and sat on a bench on the veranda. Molly sat down beside him. The back of her hand brushed against his, and he automatically entwined her fingers with his. He skewed his head to look into her face, his own wearing a serious expression.

'God knows I've missed you, Molly. You'll never know how much,' he said, his voice breaking into a sob.

'I do know,' she said, her voice barely above a whisper.

'I'm sorry, Molly,' he said, 'so very sorry.'

Molly's heart lurched. Sorry for not talking things through with her, or sorry because he was calling off the wedding and going to Sligo without her?

'I've been a fool,' he said. 'I couldn't go anywhere without you. I love you more than anything, so please forgive me and say you'll still marry me.'

Molly heard the anguish in his voice and felt the tremor in his hand. She tightened her grip, the pressure of her fingers letting him know that she felt the same. 'And I've been pathetic,' she said, 'refusing to see you when all along I knew I couldn't live without you.'

'Oh, Molly,' he groaned, releasing her hand, drawing her into his arms and kissing her with all the pent-up passion that had troubled him for so long. A thousand butterflies took flight in her stomach and then surrounded her heart. Then, in between kisses, they finally talked.

'It isn't that I find the idea of living in Sligo absolutely awful,' she said, 'it's just that I'd like to start married life here where we know everyone, not be a new wife in a strange place – and yes, I was angry because you and your mam seemed to have decided what we should do.'

'Not any more,' Mickey said stoutly. 'From now on, we make our own plans, nobody else, and we won't do anything unless we both agree on it.' Their faces an inch apart, their eyes locked, Molly felt the intensity of what he was saying. She nodded solemnly and they sealed the promise with a kiss.

By now, dusk had faded into night and one by one stars studded an indigo sky. Other than the babble of the river and the occasional shuffling of small, wild creatures, all else was stillness. Molly and Mickey sat with their arms wrapped round each other, perfectly content to let the balmy breeze blow away their misunderstandings. The rift had been healed and their joy knew no bounds.

* * *

'Bloody daughters! Who'd have 'em?' moaned Maggie.

'Think yourself lucky you've only got one,' Kitty said, laughing. 'You could be like that Dionne woman in Canada. Remember her, she had five all at one go an' she had nine kids already.'

'Poor bugger!' Maggie groaned and lit another cigarette. 'Still, I'm glad your Molly's sorted things out. I only wish our Lily 'ud do the same. She's still gadding off to the Grafton every weekend looking for Mr Right. I told her it's not the sort of place she'd find a man like my Stan.' She gave a beatific smile.

Just then, the door opened, and almost apologetically Beth entered Kitty's kitchen. Of late, she had absented herself from the regular chats Kitty and Maggie, and Mavis and Rose, shared. She had always been the quiet one, her confidence never having quite recovered from her father's cruel tongue. Now, she looked tentatively at Kitty then flinched as Maggie sneered, 'Well for some,' after Beth had asked Kitty if she and Blair could take Robert with them to Scarborough.

'He'll be company for Stuart,' she said, avoiding meeting Maggie's eye. 'They can sail on the boating lake in Peasholm Park and swim in the pool at North Bay. Do say Robert can come.'

'Aye, well, I can't see why not. He'd love to, and I'm sure John won't object,' Kitty said, grinning as she added, 'Mind you, our Robert only just learned to swim, so don't let him drown in the lake. His dad would object to that.'

Beth looked mildly shocked. 'Oh, Kitty, you know I'll guard him as closely as I will Stuart.'

'Aye, like a bloody prisoner,' Maggie muttered, and Kitty talked over her by saying loudly, 'I was joking, love. You just make sure he does as he's told.'

Appeased, and not wanting Kitty to think she was going to let the boys run wild, Beth warmed to her theme. 'They can explore the castle to learn some history and visit the museum, it's very educational, you know.'

'Yeah, an' if they get lost in the castle or die of boredom in the museum, you an' Blair can sit drinking tea in the Italian Gardens,' Maggie scoffed.

Beth flushed, and trying to hide her irritation, she mumbled, 'It's much more fun if you have someone your own age to do things with, and if the landlady in the boarding house is amenable, she might keep an eye on them one evening so that Blair and I can go to the theatre.' She looked at Kitty for her approval.

'The thee-ater,' Maggie drawled. 'Oh, aren't we posh.' Beth's shoulders rose two inches and two bright spots lit her cheeks as she glared at Maggie.

'That's fine by me,' Kitty cut in before a full-blown row could start. 'I'll mention it to John when he comes home. When are you going?'

'On Saturday,' said Beth, and refusing the offer of tea, she left, still stinging from Maggie's taunts.

'This summer's shaped up nicely,' Kitty said as she switched on the kettle. 'Our Molly's wedding's back on, Patrick's thrilled to be going to Cranford, an' now our Robert's off to Scarborough.'

'It's well they can bloody afford it,' Maggie grumbled. 'I can't even afford the tram fare to New Brighton.'

'Oh, for God's sake, Maggie! Stop carping.' Kitty's patience running out, she slammed two mugs on the table. 'And don't be so hard on Beth. You were downright rude. It's good of her to offer.' She filled the mugs with tea, shoving one ungraciously across the table to Maggie and doing the same with the sugar bowl. 'Drink that an' see if it won't sweeten you up 'cos you're proper bloody sour today.'

Maggie flushed. 'I know, and I don't know why. I've got my Stan and things couldn't be lovelier, but I've grown that used to moaning and being bitter, I can't help meself.' She gave Kitty an imploring look. 'I'm sorry for being nasty to Beth but she allus manages to make me feel inferior, an' you allus take her side.' Then, shrugging off her contriteness and adopting her usual brash manner, she said, 'But you have to admit she's obsessed with that bloody child. Education this and education that, and mind your manners, Stuart. She's making the poor little soul into a right sissy.'

Kitty held her tongue and raised her eyes to the ceiling.

* * *

'Well, what did Kitty have to say?' Blair asked as Beth entered her own kitchen.

'She's all for it, and she's going to ask John tonight. I don't think he'll object.'

'That's good,' Blair said, his smile widening. 'If Stuart has company, it'll give us some time to ourselves.' He took off his glasses and polished them carefully then went and put his arms round his highly strung wife. 'What's wrong?' he asked, feeling the tension in her body. 'I thought you'd be pleased.'

'It's Maggie. She's so spiteful and sneering, she really makes me cross,' Beth said against his shoulder. 'She mocks me at every turn.'

Blair stepped back and looked into Beth's tearful eyes. Her constant anxiety and sensitivity worried him, and he considered that her obsessive devotion to their son's upbringing bordered on the unhealthy. He wondered how long it would take before she recovered from the damage her father had inflicted. He hoped the holiday would relax her, and was about to say some comforting words when the door opened and Rose came in. Blasted neighbours, he thought, plastering a smile on his face and greeting Rose. There were times when he found the close-knit community in Weaver Street too close.

'I'm bringing back your copy of *Cold Comfort Farm*,' said Rose, handing the book to Beth. 'It's a brilliant story. It reminded me a bit of myself.'

'I'm glad you enjoyed it,' Beth said, feeling somewhat reassured that at least she had a friend and neighbour who shared her interests, unlike Maggie Stubbs. They discussed the book for a while then, still rattled by her encounter with Maggie, she reiterated what she had told Blair.

Rose was sympathetic. 'You mustn't let Maggie annoy you. It's just her rough and ready way. She's all heart when it comes to being a good friend. She did wonders for my confidence' – Rose patted her blonde tresses – 'and not just in the way I do my hair. She taught me that it's no bad thing to grow a tougher shell and just get on with things you can't change, and both her and Kitty, and darling Mavis, are all so easy in their own skins and sure of themselves that I can't help thinking they've all contributed to the way I now see myself.' She giggled at what she'd just said then added, 'Don't let your differences come between you.'

Beth smiled wanly. 'I know, I should be used to her by now. Blair's never done telling me I'm far too sensitive for my own good.' She gave a careless shrug.

'That's the spirit,' Rose said brightly. 'Now, I must be off. I've left Joey minding James. Goodness knows what they'll get up to.'

She walked down the lane, surprised to see Gerda Muller standing in her garden shaking her fist at Gladys Midwood, the woman who had recently come to live in number one where the recluse, Cissie Stokes, had lived. A big frowsy woman in her forties, she was standing in the lane, hands on hips and a belligerent look on her face. 'Bugger off back to Germany. We don't want any bloody Nazis here,' Rose heard her shout.

'It is not right,' Gerda retaliated. 'We are not Nazis.'

Oh dear, thought Rose, *the war hasn't started, if it ever does, and already the Midwood woman's making it on her own doorstep.* She hurried to the Mullers' gate and up the path.

Gerda was quivering with frustration. 'We are not Nazis,' she repeated, letting Rose take her arm and lead her indoors. 'Is that not so?' she said, looking to Gottfried for affirmation.

He nodded grimly. 'They abuse me also. We do not want trouble with our neighbours so I tell Gerda to ignore them, but she does not listen.'

'She shouldn't have to put up with that, neither of you should. I'll get Joey to have a word with that family.' Rose was saddened to see them so downcast.

Gerda harrumphed, and turning to Rose, she said, 'Thank you for your assistance.' She went to the sink and began rattling dishes.

* * *

The next morning, on their way back from church, Rose mentioned the incident to Kitty and Mavis, and later to Maggie when she joined them in Mavis's house for a chat and a cup of tea. 'It's not the sort of thing we want in Weaver Street,' Mavis said primly, 'times are hard enough without having neighbours at loggerheads.'

'Right enough,' said Kitty, 'we all get on grand an' we want to keep it that way.' She screwed up her face thoughtfully. 'Maybe it 'ud be easier to sort out Gerda's problem if we'd been a bit more welcoming. I've been that busy I've barely spoken to Gladys Midwood.'

'I should have invited her in for a cup of tea,' Mavis said regretfully.

'Our Lily's friendly with that lad of hers, Frankie,' Maggie said, having nothing else useful to contribute.

They continued to discuss the problem and by the time the friends left Mavis's house to go and make their Sunday dinners, they had devised a plan. Two hours later, Gladys opened her back door to find a delegation standing on her steps. She stared suspiciously at the five women. 'What do you want?' she said.

'We've come to say hello,' Mavis said brightly. 'We should have done it sooner but we've been busy. We want to welcome you to Weaver Street. I'm Mavis Robson from number fifteen, and this is Kitty Sykes from the new house and Maggie Stubbs from number nine. You've already met Rose and Gerda.'

Gladys looked nonplussed. Before she could gather her wits, Kitty launched into an explanation of how everyone looked out for everyone else in Weaver Street. 'We always stick together. That way, nobody's left feeling that they have to deal with their problems on their own,' she concluded.

'I heard you and Gerda have fallen out,' Maggie said, looking

Gladys directly in the eye. 'She's upset about that.' Gladys squirmed.

'I am,' said Gerda. 'I do not dislike you, but I dislike the names you call me.'

'And Mrs Muller's not a Nazi. She's completely the opposite. That's why she left her home in Germany to come here,' Rose said. 'Like all of us, she wants a quiet life and to be friends with her neighbours.'

Outnumbered and dumbfounded, Gladys bit her bottom lip as she looked into the women's faces. Each wore a smile, only one slightly threatening.

'We're all going back to mine for a cup of tea, why don't you join us?' said Kitty.

By, but they're a rum lot, thought Gladys, and deciding she'd rather have these women for friends than enemies, she said, 'All right, I will.'

They trooped up the lane to Kitty's.

'I'm sorry if we got off on the wrong foot,' Gladys said to Gerda.

'I am sorry also,' Gerda replied, 'and now I am happy that we can be friends.'

Kitty gave Mavis a cheeky wink as she led the way to her own back door.

* * *

A light drizzle spattered the leaves and grasses along the riverbank and trickled down the café windows. It was the first wet day for almost a month and as Kitty walked on the towpath to the café, she prayed for Molly's wedding day to be dry and sunny.

'It looks set in for the afternoon,' she said as she entered the café and walked to the counter, where Bridie was arranging buns on a cakestand.

'Aye, not much doing today,' said Bridie, nodding at the two customers sitting at a table by the window.

Things had been strained between them since Molly's refusal to go to Sligo, and although they had never been close friends, it saddened Kitty.

'I'll miss ye when ye go,' she said.

'Aye, I imagine ye will, but ye're sure to find somebody to give ye a hand.' Bridie's eyes didn't meet Kitty's as she placed the last bun on the stand.

Kitty's brow creased. This wasn't the response she had expected.

'I didn't mean that, Bridie. I will miss ye, for the friend ye are.'

Bridie's cheeks reddened. She mumbled something and went to wash her hands at the sink, her back stiff.

'Let's have no hard feelings,' Kitty pleaded. 'I know ye're disappointed that Mickey's not going with ye, but it's his choice.'

Still with her back to Kitty, Bridie muttered something that Kitty thought was 'Is it?' She gave an irritated shrug.

'When will ye go?' she asked.

'After the wedding, we'll travel back with Donal and Liam. It'll be handy them helpin' us with all the luggage.' Donal was to be Mickey's best man, and Liam an usher. Her sons were arriving the day before the wedding and returning to Ireland two days later.

'So soon.'

Bridie grimaced. 'Aye, they'll not want to be long away from Sligo, an' to tell the truth, I wish I'd never left.'

'I thought ye were happy here,' Kitty said, her tone showing her surprise.

'I'm happy when *all* me sons are close by me,' Bridie replied pointedly.

Seeing that Bridie had no intention of forgiving Molly for

keeping Mickey in Liverpool, Kitty admitted defeat and began taking note of what supplies were needed for the weekend.

'Will ye be renting out the house again?' Bridie asked.

'In a manner of speaking,' Kitty told her curtly. 'Molly and Mickey will move in when they come back from their honeymoon.' She couldn't resist a smug smile.

'Ye're lettin' our Mickey have the house?' This time, it was Bridie's turn to sound surprised. 'That's awful good of ye,' she said, her voice softening as she guessed correctly that her son would most likely be getting it at a favourable rent – or for free. 'When did ye decide that?'

'Just last night, I'm surprised Mickey didn't mention it. There's no point in them looking for anywhere else,' said Kitty as four cyclists parked their bikes and bustled into the café.

'Aye, well, it'll keep your Molly close by ye.' Bridie busily addressed the new customers, and gathering up her notebook and umbrella, Kitty left her to it.

Molly was delirious with happiness at the prospect of starting married life in number eleven without having to share it with his parents, and Mickey was relieved to know that he wouldn't have to find somewhere else for them to live.

'Ye can have it rent-free for the time being till ye get on your feet,' Kitty had told them. 'After that, we'll come to some arrange-ment 'cos ye'll have to learn to manage your finances. Any alter-ations or decorating ye want to do ye'll pay for yourselves. Nothing in life comes free – except for love an' respect – an' even the latter has to be earned. So make sure ye work at it.'

Now, as Molly sat in what would soon no longer be Bridie's kitchen, she couldn't resist thinking about all the changes she'd make. She'd get rid of the drab brown that Mick had painted on the cupboards, and all those holy pictures would have to go; most likely Bridie would take them with her to Sligo.

'What are you dreaming about?' Mickey asked as they waited for his mother to put the tea on the table – they usually had Saturday tea if Molly wasn't working a shift at the hospital; Kitty had said that this was a good way for Molly to get to know what living with her soon-to-be mother-in-law was like. But now it didn't matter because Bridie wouldn't be there much longer.

'I was thinking that by this time next Saturday, I'll be Mrs Molly O'Malley,' she lied, thinking it would be rude to comment on the horrible brown cupboards. 'Molly O'Malley,' she giggled, 'it sounds like a character in a nursery rhyme. Molly O'Malley went dilly-dally down the alley,' she trilled.

'I'll have ye know it's a well-respected name in Sligo,' Bridie said tartly, placing the teapot on the table with a thud.

'Oh, I'm sure it is,' said Molly, her cheeks pink, 'and I'll be proud to be called it.' She was glad she wouldn't have to share the house with Bridie.

* * *

Saturday, 2 September 1939 dawned bright and clear. Kitty was the first out of bed, and down in the kitchen she began preparing a special breakfast: today was a big day. Her daughter was getting married.

The sound of heavy footsteps on the stairs announced that John was making his way down. He went straight into the parlour. Moments later, she heard the voice of an announcer on the wireless, his precise English pronunciation harsh in the quiet house. She glanced at the clock. It was a few minutes after eight. She'd not call Molly and the boys until the food was ready to put on the table, she thought, slipping rashers of bacon into hot fat then stirring the porridge. Let them lie on. It would be a long day.

John entered the kitchen. 'German troops have attacked the

Polish border, and the Luftwaffe's dive-bombing airfields and ships.' He shook his head despairingly.

Kitty heaved a huge sigh. 'When the Poles declared a state of emergency yesterday, I knew it could only get worse.' Angered, she slopped porridge into five bowls carelessly.

'Well, now they've declared a state of war and we'll all be dragged into it.' Sounding bitter, John slumped into a chair at the table, resting his head in his hands. Kitty turned smartly round from the stove, her eyes flashing.

'I'm not going to think about it. Today's Molly's wedding day and we are going to celebrate it with love and happiness. We'll deal with what happens afterwards when the time comes, so no more mention of wars and fightin'! Right, John?' She clattered dishes on the table then, going to the foot of the stairs, she shouted cheerily, 'Rise and shine, sleepy heads, breakfast's on the table.'

'You look like a queen, Molly,' cried Robert, his mouth hanging open as he sauntered into the dining room some two hours after breakfast and saw his sister teetering precariously on the high heels of her white leather shoes. He gazed up at the dress's high-necked bodice decorated with seed pearls then ran his eyes down the length of the close-fitting sheath that swathed Molly's slender figure.

'Thanks, Robert.' Molly glowed under her brother's praise.

Kitty smiled fondly at her younger son.

'Does my hair look all right, Mam?' Molly's voice wobbled as she patted the shiny black curls on the crown of her head.

'It looks perfect, up like that. It shows off your neck, an' those little tendrils hanging loose stop it lookin' severe.' Her eyes misted as she took Molly's hand and led her from the dining room into the hallway. Today her only daughter and firstborn child would fly the nest, and whilst she was happy for her, she couldn't help feeling rather old and bereft.

'I'll go and chivvy John up,' she said briskly to hide her emotions.

Molly stayed in the hallway, gazing out at the garden. *Thank goodness the weather's fine and dry*, she thought, as the sun broke through a bank of clouds. *In just over an hour from now, I'll be a married woman and before the day ends, I'll be on my honeymoon, sharing a bed in a boarding house in Blackpool with Mickey.* Her tummy fluttered and she felt hot as she wondered if she would know what to do once they were in bed together. Would Mickey know what to do? She gave an impish smile, certain that they would.

When Kitty and John joined her, John looking smart in his good grey suit, Molly wrapped her arms round both of them. 'Thanks for everything, Mam and Dad,' she said, her eyes misting. She knew she was lucky to have such a wonderful mother and the kindest stepfather. They hugged her back, and a lump planted itself in Kitty's throat and she noisily swallowed unshed tears.

'I'll call the boys,' she croaked and in answer to her shout, Patrick and Robert clattered downstairs, both spruced up and looking their best. 'Time to go to the church, lads. Your dad and Molly will come on later.'

The sweet solemnity of the nuptial mass was soothing after the hustle and bustle of the preparation that had led up to it. Then, the wedding march resounding up into the church's vaulted ceiling, Molly walked down the aisle on Mickey's arm. Kitty dabbed her eyes. Her little girl was a married woman, but to Kitty, Molly would always be her little girl.

The congregation trooped out into the bright September sunshine, smiling and congratulating the young couple, posing for photographs and laughing and joking before they piled into the cars taking them to the Adelphi Hotel. If, during the celebrations that followed, their thoughts strayed to the awful news of impending war, nobody let it be known and by the time Molly and Mickey left to catch the train to take them to Blackpool, the mood was buoyant.

'You've lost your daughter, but I've still got mine, worse luck,' Maggie said tipsily as they made their way back to Weaver Street in John's car.

'I'll never lose our Molly,' Kitty answered tearfully, looking at the back of Patrick's tawny head as he sat up front next to his step-father. A gut-wrenching pain curdled her inside as she wondered what the war would mean for him. It made her feel cold, old and weary. Ireland had declared its neutrality, and she wished with all her heart that Britain would do the same. The thought of sending her beautiful son to fight in some foreign land was beyond bearing.

That night Kitty barely slept. The house felt empty without Molly in it, and how long would it be before Patrick was called away?

* * *

The next morning, in a comfortable lodging house in Blackpool, Molly lay back on the pillows, starry-eyed and overwhelmed. This was what it felt like to love and be loved.

She sat up, and propping her elbow on the pillow, she gazed down at her husband. Dark lashes fanned his tanned cheeks and his lips were curved in a dreamy smile. Molly leaned over and kissed him. Mickey opened his eyes, their dark blue glinting with pleasure.

'Pardon me for waking you, but I need your attention.'

Mickey gave it willingly.

They were late for breakfast. The wisp-thin landlady gave them a stern look as they entered the little dining room. The only other occupants were an elderly couple at one table and a single man at another. The elderly woman gave Molly and Mickey a sad smile and shook her head then whispered something to her husband.

'She must know we're honeymooners, and she either thinks we're too young or that marriage isn't all it's cracked up to be,' Molly whispered to Mickey who chuckled and whispered back, 'She most likely can't remember how great it is.'

When the landlady brought over a pot of tea, toast and two plates, one rasher of bacon and a fried egg on each of them, she dismally announced, 'Britain's given Germany a deadline of eleven o'clock. If it doesn't withdraw its troops from Poland, we'll go to war.' And with that, she plodded back into the kitchen.

Molly and Mickey stared wide-eyed at one another, and Molly understood the real meaning behind the woman's sad smile and the despairing shake of her head: she was old enough to remember the last war. The news wasn't entirely unexpected, but the landlady's lugubrious pronouncement took the joy out of the morning. Mickey glanced at the clock. It was twenty-five minutes past nine. He reached for Molly's hand. 'There's a bit to go yet. We'll just have to wait and see.'

She nodded hopefully, but she'd suddenly lost her appetite.

Determined not to let it spoil their day, they walked the promenade to the Pleasure Beach then back again to Blackpool Tower, where they stared up at its mighty iron girders. 'It's ten past eleven,' Mickey said, pointing to a huge clock on the wall above a jewellers' shop doorway.

'Let's not think about it,' said Molly, tugging Mickey's hand, but no sooner had she spoken than the shop door flew open and an irate elderly man burst onto the crowded pavement, waving his arms and shouting. Molly and Mickey and other passers-by gave him their attention.

'We're going to war against Germany. Chamberlain's just announced it on the wireless,' he shouted. This was met by a hullabaloo of protests, moans and groans from those who heard him, and Mickey threw his arms round Molly.

'The Germans didn't meet the deadline then,' he said brokenly.

She clung to him, trembling. 'What do we do now, Mickey?' she sobbed.

'We pretend we never heard him,' Mickey said stoutly, and silently cursed the shopkeeper's untimely intervention. 'I'll be damned if I let Adolf Hitler spoil our honeymoon.'

'Me an' all,' said Molly, sobbing and giggling at one and the same time. 'We'll make today and tomorrow as special as our wedding day and look back and remember them as the best three days of our lives.'

In Weaver Street, shortly before six o'clock, the friends had gathered in Kitty's parlour to listen to the wireless: King George VI was about to address the nation. Kitty was sitting on the couch between Maggie and Beth, Blair standing behind with a protective hand on Beth's shoulder. Mavis and Jack were in the armchairs by the fireplace, and Lily was perched on a footstool. Bill and Joey Walker leaned in the doorway and May and Rose sat on chairs brought in from the kitchen. John and Patrick stood either side of the large walnut wireless, ready to adjust the volume. Up above, gentle thuds and muffled laughter let them know that Robert and Stuart were having fun, and as the adults below made quiet conversation, Kitty felt as if she could reach out and touch the tension in the room.

Big Ben chimed the hour. Everyone fell silent. John turned up the volume and the strains of the National Anthem flooded the room. With ears pricked, the good friends listened to the king's hesitant words.

'For the second time in the lives of most of us, we are at war.'

Holding their breaths and nodding, they heard him talk of

dark days ahead and that they had to do what was right, and that with God's help, they would prevail.

Rose turned to look fearfully at Joey. Beth burst into tears. Maggie snorted and lit a cigarette. Lily rolled her eyes.

'Oh, dear me, what are we going to do?' Mavis cried.

'The same as we always do,' Kitty said firmly. 'We'll stick together and do the best we can. We've done it before and we can do again.' She smiled lovingly at John, then Patrick, then into the faces of her friends. 'None of us would get by without each other, and that's the truth of it. We've all pulled together over the years an' we'll keep on doing just that, 'cos that's what life's all about.'

ACKNOWLEDGMENTS

Dear Readers,

Welcome back to Weaver Street and the chance to catch up with Kitty, Maggie, Beth and Mavis as they struggle to keep their families safe in the Hungry 1930s. This is my second book in the 'Weaver Street' stories, the first being *Welcome to Weaver Street*, and by now these four strong women are like old friends to me, and I hope they are to you. In *Hard Times in Weaver Street* you'll meet a new, intriguing character, Rose, whose life becomes entwined with these good, hard-working women and changes hers for the better. And all this done through friendship and love. I really enjoy writing about ordinary people in extraordinary times for they are the backbone of society and their fortitude and kindness is what makes the world a better place. As always, I'll look forward to hearing what you all think of my stories and I hope you enjoy reading them with the same pleasure that it gives me when I'm writing them.

Of course, a book doesn't just happen because it has been written. The inspiration for the plot might belong to the author but behind the scenes there is an army of dedicated agents, publishers, editors and marketers who make the book as good as it can be. Therefore, I'd like to give a massive thank you to my agent, Judith Murdoch, for her constant support and wise advice. I wouldn't be where I am without her. I am also deeply grateful to the wonderful team at Boldwood for their unstinting support and attention to detail. They are blessed with great minds and sharp eyes.

In particular, I must show my appreciation for Sarah Ritherdon, Boldwood's publishing director, for her friendly, good-humoured and brilliant advice; she's a pleasure to work with. Grateful thanks are also due to the wonderful marketing team, Claire Fenby, Nia Beynon and Marcela Torres: isn't the book cover terrific? Thanks also to Sue Lamprell and Sandra Ferguson for proof-reading: hawk-eyed Sandra doesn't miss a thing. Thanks also to Amanda Ridout for heading up this wonderful team. You all make my ideas a reality.

A novel written about a particular time in history always requires research and I found the following especially helpful so thanks to them: *Time of Our Lives* by Michael Oke, The National Archive, Historic UK and 'Social Conditions 1930' Blacksacademy.net

Thanks also to the book bloggers, reviewers and most of all my readers.

I've dedicated this book to my dear friend Kay Jones who sadly passed away in January 2023. A friend for almost fifty years, she was always interested in my writing and as the dedication states 'we talked and talked' and out of that came some of the ideas I've used in my books. She will be missed.

Finally, thanks to my family without whom none of this would be possible. Their love and support keep me going.

MORE FROM CHRISSIE WALSH

We hope you enjoyed reading *Hard Times on Weaver Street*. If you did, please leave a review.

If you'd like to gift a copy, this book is also available as an ebook, large print, hardback, digital audio download and audiobook CD.

Sign up to Chrissie Walsh's mailing list for news, competitions and updates on future books.

https://bit.ly/ChrissieWalshNewsletter

Welcome to Weaver Street, the first instalment in this series, is available now...

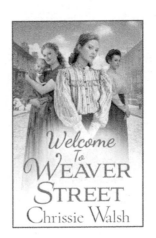

Welcome
To
WEAVER
STREET
Chrissie Walsh

ABOUT THE AUTHOR

Chrissie Walsh was born and raised in West Yorkshire and is a retired schoolteacher with a passion for history. She has written several successful sagas documenting feisty women in challenging times.

Follow Chrissie on social media:

 twitter.com/walshchrissie

 facebook.com/100063501278251

Boldwood

Boldwood Books is an award-winning fiction publishing company seeking out the best stories from around the world.

Find out more at www.boldwoodbooks.com

Join our reader community for brilliant books, competitions and offers!

Follow us
@BoldwoodBooks
@BookandTonic

Sign up to our weekly deals newsletter

https://bit.ly/BoldwoodBNewsletter

Printed in Great Britain
by Amazon

26171822R00195